"Soldats de la Légion,
De la Légion Étrangère,
N'ayant pas de nation,
La France est votre Mère." . . .

THE

COLLECTED

SHORT

STORIES

Volume 1

Fiction Titles by P. C. Wren

Dew and Mildew. 1912
Father Gregory. 1913
The Snake and Sword. 1914.
Driftwood Spars. 1916
The Wages of Virtue. 1916
The Young Stagers. 1917
Stepsons of France. 1917
Cupid in Africa. 1920
Beau Geste. 1924
Beau Sabreur. 1926
Beau Ideal. 1928
Good Gestes. 1929
Soldiers of Misfortune. 1929
The Mammon of Righteousness. 1930 (U.S. title: Mammon)
Mysterious Waye. 1930
Sowing Glory. 1931
Valiant Dust. 1932
Flawed Blades. 1933
Action and Passion. 1933
Port o' Missing Men. 1934
Beggars' Horses. 1934 (U.S. title: The Dark Woman)
Sinbad the Soldier. 1935
Explosion. 1935
Spanish Maine. 1935 (U.S. title: The Desert Heritage)
Bubble Reputation. 1936 (U.S. title: The Cortenay Treasure)
Fort in the Jungle. 1936
The Man of a Ghost. 1937 (U.S. title: The Spur of Pride)
Worth Wile. 1937 (U.S. title: To the Hilt)
Cardboard Castle. 1938
Rough Shooting. 1938
Paper Prison. 1939 (U.S. Title: The Man the Devil Didn't Want)
The Disappearance of General Jason. 1940
Two Feet From Heaven. 1940
The Uniform of Glory. 1941
Odd—But Even So. 1941

The

Collected

Short Stories

of

Percival Christopher Wren

Volume 1

Edited

by

John L. Espley

Riner Publishing Company
Riner Virginia
2012

ISBN-13:
978-0-9850326-0-9

Contents

PREFACE vii

INTRODUCTION ix

TEN LITTLE LEGIONARIES 1

À LA NINON DE L'ENCLOS 20

AN OFFICER AND—A LIAR 25

THE DEAD HAND 38

THE GIFT..51

THE DESERTER 58

FIVE MINUTES 70

"HERE ARE LADIES" 78

THE MacSNORRT 86

"BELZÉBUTH"..92

THE QUEST 104

"VENGEANCE IS MINE . . ." 118

SERMONS IN STONES 123

MOONSHINE 133

THE COWARD OF THE LEGION.......................................138

THE SAXON AND THE GAEL AND THINGS...................147

ANCIENT BRITONS AND MODERN 151

TOSH AND FUNNY-DOG 159

BOBBALL..165

CONCERNING WILLIAM HENRY WINTERBOTHAM.....169

THE STUART QUEEN 175

THE VIRTUOUS TIGER...179

BOBBALL AGAIN, AND A STUDY IN CONTRASTS 187

GRAPE-SHOT 195

DRUMMERS AND RUMMERS 200

THE RAFTERS 207

THE VEGETARIAN MUGGER OF SONI 211

THE MODERN DESDEMONA 218

"QUIS SEPARABIT?"..229

THE ROYAL AND ANCIENT GAME AT KARABAD........236

AT OXFORD: INNOCENT ERNEST AND ARTFUL EINTZ
....247

MAHDEV RAO 258

THE MERRY LIARS..273

THE DOUBLE SADDLE..284

PREFACE

The Collected Short Stories of Percival Christopher Wren (hereafter *The Collected Short Stories*) began as a desire on my part to make the short stories and articles written by P. C. Wren more available to the reading public. His novel, *Beau Geste*, is usually recognized by most of the book dealers I have met over the years, but his other works are not so easily remembered. In my opinion, his short stories are some of his best work and worthy of greater recognition.

I have been collecting P. C. Wren for almost fifty years now, and have been working on a comprehensive bibliography for almost as long. Hopefully, the bibliography will be published later this year (2012), which is the 100th anniversary of Wren's first published work of fiction, *Dew and Mildew*.

The text of the 116 short stories published in the seven Wren collections, *Stepsons of France*, *The Young Stagers*, *Good Gestes*, *Flawed Blades*, *Port o' Missing Men*, *Rough Shooting*, and *Odd—But Even So* were easily obtained from copies in my own collection. For that collection, I certainly need to thank the hundreds of used book dealers I have purchased items from, but I need to thank by name, Steven Temple, David Mason, Walt Barrie and, especially, the late Denis McDonnell for the advice and help they have provided over the years.

For helping me obtain the text of the remaining items in *The Collected Short Stories*, I need to acknowledge the assistance and guidance of the "chums" of the Fictionmags listserv and specifically Mike Ashley. My friend, Lane Rasmussen, was able to obtain a copy of the article, "Wonderful Egypt", through the Inter-Library Loan department of our local university. My friend, Robert Maxwell, from Brigham Young University went beyond the "call of duty" when over one weekend he was able to find (after a search in the stacks for a potentially lost item) a copy of the rare periodical *Prediction*, in which the article "I Saw a Vision" appeared. The book dealer, Bevis Clarke, of Clearwater Books, is owed a great deal of thanks for making the manuscript available of the unpublished short story "Broken Glass".

Mr. John Venmore and Mr. Philip Fairweather, both descendants of the late Mr. Richard Alan Graham-Smith, Wren's stepson, and the executor of Wren's estate, have both been very helpful in providing information about Wren. Based on information provided by Mr. Venmore and Mr. Fairweather attempts have been made to contact their relative, Elizabeth Jane Ellen, the person last known to own the works of P. C. Wren. It is presumed that Ms. Ellen is deceased, but I have been unable to verify that. It has been over seventy years since the death of P. C. Wren (November 21, 1941), and it is assumed that his works have passed into the public domain.

I also need to acknowledge the help and guidance of the members of my family: my daughter and son-in-law, Dawn and Andrew; my son and daughter-in-law, Jared and Claudia; and my long-suffering wife, Cathy. Thank you.

In conclusion, I need to thank Percival Christopher Wren for the many years of great enjoyment that his stories have provided. I know that Wren is not a literary or critical success, but, at least for me, he is one of the great storytellers of the early twentieth century.

John L. Espley
Riner, Virginia
July 4, 2012

INTRODUCTION

Percival Christopher Wren is best known as a novelist, publishing twenty-eight novels from 1912 to 1941, the most famous of which being *Beau Geste* (1924). Wren also published seven short story collections: *Stepsons of France* (1917), *The Young Stagers* (1917), *Good Gestes* (1929), *Flawed Blades* (1933), *Port o' Missing Men* (1934), *Rough Shooting* (1938), and *Odd—But Even So* (1941). These short story collections contained a total of 116 stories. There were also two omnibus collections published, *Stories of the Foreign Legion* (1947) and *Dead Men's Boots* (1949), containing stories taken from *Stepsons of France*, *Good Gestes*, *Flawed Blades*, and *Port o' Missing Men*.

Wren was a man of mystery in that the more popular biographical statements about him seemed to be more fiction than fact. A typical biography has him born in Devon in 1885, educated at Oxford, and having a career of world traveler, hunter, journalist, tramp, British cavalry trooper, legionary in the French Foreign Legion, assistant director of education in Bombay, and a Justice of the Peace. Most of the above biography, however, has not been verified. Wren was born Percy Wren November 1, 1875 in Deptford, a district of South London on the banks of the Thames. He did attend Oxford University, graduating in 1898 with a 3rd class honours in History leading to a Bachelor of Arts degree. He attained his "M.A." in 1901. In those days, a person acquired a "M.A." after a certain number of years (three in Wren's case) and purchasing it.

After leaving Oxford he was a teacher at various commercial schools until 1903 when he and his family left England for India. He married Alice Lucie Shovelier in December 1899 with whom he had a daughter, Estelle Lenore Wren, born in February 1901. From 1903 to approximately 1919 Wren was employed as an educator by the Indian Educational Service (I.E.S.). During that time he published a number of educational textbooks, some of which are still in use in Indian schools today. It was at this time that he started using the name Percival C. and Percival

Christopher on the textbooks. From 1905 to 1915, he also served in the Volunteer Corps (Sind and Poona) in India (see the novel *Driftwood Spars*), and was appointed a Captain in the Indian Army Reserve of Officers, the 101st Grenadiers of the Indian Infantry, in November 1914. He probably saw action in the East African campaign of World War I (see the novel *Cupid in Africa*), and resigned from the Indian Army Reserve of Officers in November 1915.

Wren's first novel, *Dew and Mildew*, was published by Longmans, Green in 1912. His first novel of the French Foreign Legion, *The Wages of Virtue*, was published by John Murray in 1916 (written in 1913). One of the many questions about Wren, is whether he actually did serve in the French Foreign Legion. Given the chronology of his documented biography it is hard to see where he had time to actually serve in the Legion. Wren himself always maintained that he had served, and his stepson, Richard Alan Graham-Smith, who died in 2006, "strongly maintained that Wren had indeed served in the French Foreign Legion and was always quick to refute those who said otherwise."[1]

The Collected Short Stories is an attempt to bring Wren's shorter fiction back into print. Twenty-six of the 116 stories published in the seven collections have been identified as being first published in the newspapers and fiction magazines of the early twentieth century. Many of the other stories were probably published in the newspapers and fiction magazines but information about these appearances is limited since the indexing of the fiction in the newspapers and magazines of the early twentieth century is incomplete. A bibliographical history (as known as of 2012) is included in each introductory commentary to each story.

The order that the stories are presented is primarily chronological, but there are some discrepancies in order to keep some stories that were presented within a frame together. The original spelling, punctuation, and grammar have been preserved as found in the latest editions/printings of the stories during Wren's lifetime (1875-1941). The footnotes within the individual

---

[1] http://en.wikipedia.org/wiki/P._C._Wren

stories are also found in the original source material.

In addition to the 116 stories published in Wren's short story collections there are some additional items. "At Oxford: Innocent Ernest and Artful Eintz" is a short story originally published in 1919 in an obscure fiction magazine. "The Romantic Regiment" and "Twenty-Four Hours in the Foreign Legion" are "factual" articles originally published in magazines. "Wonderful Egypt" is an article (more a photographic essay) originally published in *The Strand Magazine*. The article "I Saw a Vision!" originally appeared in a rare psychic magazine, *Prediction*. There is also an interesting article found in an Australian newspaper, "Meaning of Dreams", where Wren relates a couple of dreams he had experienced. Finally there is "Broken Glass", an unpublished short story.

Volume One

Volume one of *The Collected Short Stories* contains all of the stories included in *The Young Stagers* and *Stepsons of France*. Volume one also includes "Double Saddle" (from *Flawed Blades*), and the first book appearance of "At Oxford: Innocent Ernest and Artful Eintz". The thirty-four stories originally appeared from 1917 to 1929.

The stories from *Young Stagers* are a sequel to Wren's first fiction work, *Dew and Mildew* (1912). The stories are more juvenile in nature than Wren's other fiction in that they are primarily from the viewpoint of two children: Boodle and Ficcie (sister and brother). Their parents have set up a "Sporting, Dramatic, Literary, and Social Club" for them, and a number of the stories are about the children playing in the club. As Wren wrote in the foreword to *Young Stagers* (first edition):

> Eavesdroppers are supposed to be a base and despicable race—but I must confess to having "dropped" an enormous number of "eaves" in the Junior Curlton Club of Karabad.
>
> It was my deceitful practice to occupy the next room to the big club-room at every possible opportunity, to set the communicating-door ajar, and to listen.

> To listen to what is surely one of the sweetest,
> most innocent, most natural, and most instructive
> of all languages—the unrestrained un-
> selfconscious chatter of happy children.

The children are most likely based on Wren's own children: his daughter Estelle Lenore and his son, Percival Rupert Christopher.

The stories from *Stepsons of France* are a sequel to Wren's first novel of the French Foreign Legion, *The Wages of Virtue*. The stories feature some of the characters from that novel, plus other characters included in future short stories and novels.

Of the stories from *Stepsons of France*, particular favorites of the editor, include "Ten Little Legionaries" and "Belzébuth" and the introductions of the recurring characters, La Cigale and McSnorrt. The story "Bobball Again, and Study in Contrasts", from *The Young Stagers* is interesting because of the humor in the account of the "district-visiting" of the vicar's wife.

TEN LITTLE LEGIONARIES

"Ten Little Legionaries", the longest story in volume one, was the first story in Stepsons of France *(1917). It is the story of ten legionaries who desert from an outpost in the North African desert. Some of the characters mentioned in passing are from other Wren stories and novels (John Bull, Bucking Bronco, Tant-de-Soif, and others). A recurring theme, seen most prominently later in* Beau Geste *(1924), is that of the harsh Sergeant that drives the men to desert. The Sergeant in* Beau Geste *is Lejaune, which is the name of one of the deserters in this story. The title "Ten Little Legionaries" is a deviation of a popular song "Ten Little Niggers" (original title "Ten Little Indians") that was originally written in 1868. The original title,* Ten Little Niggers, *of Agatha Christie's 1939 novel* And Then There Were None, *is now probably the most well-known instance of the unfortunate phrasing. As far as is currently known, the first publication of "Ten Little Legionaries" was in December of 1917 in the first edition of* Stepsons of France. *The story has been reprinted in the Murray omnibus collection* Stories of the Foreign Legion *(1947) and the abridged Macrae-Smith collection (1948) of the same title.*

At the Depôt at Sidi bel-Abbès, Sergeant-Major Suicide-Maker was a devil, but at a little frontier outpost in the desert, he was *the* devil, the increase in his degree being commensurate with the increase in his opportunities. When the Seventh Company of the First Battalion of the First Regiment of the Foreign Legion of France, stationed at Aïnargoula in the Sahara, learned that Lieutenant Roberte was in hospital with a broken leg, it realized that, Captain d'Armentières being absent with the Mule Company, chasing Touareg to the south, it would be commanded for a space by Sergeant-Major Suicide-Maker—in other words by The Devil.

Not only would it be commanded by him, it would be harried, harassed, hounded, bullied, brow-beaten, and be-devilled; it would be unable to call its soul its own and loth so to call its body.

On realizing the ugly truth, the Seventh Company gasped

unanimously and then swore diversely in all the languages of Europe and a few of those of Asia and Africa. It realized that it was about to learn, as the Bucking Bronco remarked to his friend John Bull (once Sir Montague Merline, of the Queen's African Rifles), that it had been wrong in guessing it was already on the ground-floor of hell. Or, if it had been there heretofore, it was now about to have a taste of the cellars.

Sergeant-Major Suicide-Maker had lived well up to his reputation, even under the revisional jurisdiction and faintly restraining curb of Captain d'Armentières and then of Lieutenant Roberte.

Each of these was a strong man and a just, and though anything in the world but mild and indulgent, would not permit really unbridled vicious tyranny such as the Sergeant-Major's unsupervised, unhampered sway would be. Under their command, he would always be limited to the surreptitious abuse of his very considerable legitimate powers. With no one above him, the mind shrank from contemplating the life of a Legionary in Aïnargoula, and from conceiving this worthy as absolute monarch and arbitrary autocrat.

The number of men undergoing *cellule* punishment would be limited only by standing room in the cells—each a miniature Black Hole of Calcutta with embellishments. The time spent in drilling at the *pas gymnastique*[2] and, worse, standing at "attention" in the hottest corner of the red-hot barrack-yard would be only limited by the physical capacity of the Legionaries to run and to stand at "attention." Never would there be "*Rompez*"[3] until some one had been carried to hospital, suffering from heat-stroke or collapse. The alternatives to the maddening agony of life would be suicide, desertion (and death from thirst or at the hands of the Arabs), or revolt and the Penal Battalions—the one thing on earth worse than Legion life in a desert station, under a half-mad bully whose monomania was driving men to suicide. *Le Cafard*, the desert madness of the Legion, was rampant and chronic. Ten legionaries under the leadership of a Frenchman calling himself Blondin, and who spoke perfect English and

---

[2] The "double" march.

[3] Dismiss.

German, had formed a secret society and hatched a plot. They were going to "remove" Sergeant-Major Suicide-Maker and "go on pump," as the legionary calls deserting.

Blondin (a pretty, black-eyed, black-moustached Provençal, who looked like a blue-jowled porcelain doll) was an educated man, brilliantly clever, and of considerable personality and force of character. Also he was a finished and heartless scoundrel. His nine adherents were Ramon Diego, a grizzled Spaniard, a man of tremendous physical strength and weak mind; Fritz Bauer, a Swiss, also much stronger of muscle than of brain; a curious Franco-Berber half-caste called Jean Kebir, who spoke perfect Arabic and knew the Koran by heart (*Kebir* is Arabic for "lion," and a lion Jean Kebir was, and Blondin had been very glad indeed to win him over, as he would be an invaluable interpreter and adviser in the journey Blondin meant to take); Jacques Lejaune, a domineering, violent ruffian, a former merchant-captain, who could steer by the stars and use a compass; Fritz Schlantz, a wonderful marksman; Karl Anderssen, who had won the *médaille* for bravery; Mohamed the Turk—just plain Mohamed (*very* plain); Georges Grondin, the musician, who was a fine cook; and finally the big Moorish negro, Hassan Moghrabi, who understood camels and horses.

The Society had been larger, but Franz Joseph Meyr the Austrian had killed Dimitropoulos the Greek, had deserted alone, and been filleted by the Touareg. Also Alexandre Bac, late of Montmartre, had hanged himself, and La Cigale had gone too hopelessly mad.

It had been for a grief unto Monsieur Blondin that he could by no means persuade old Jean Boule to join. On being sworn to secrecy and "approached" on the subject, ce bon Jean had replied that he did not desire to quit the Legion (*Bon sang de Dieu!*), and, moreover, that if he went "on pump," his friends les Légionnaires Rupert, 'Erbiggin, and le Bouckaing Bronceau would go too—and he did not wish to drag them into so perilous a venture as an attempt to reach the Moroccan coast across the desert from Aïnargoula. Moreover, if he came to know anything of the plot to kill the Sergeant-Major he would certainly warn him, if it were to be a mere stab-in-the-back assassination affair, some dark night. A fair fight is a different thing. If Blondin met the

Sergeant-Major alone, when both had their sword-bayonets—that was a different matter. . . .

Monsieur Blondin sheered off, and decided that the less Jean Boule knew of the matter, the better for the devoted Ten. . . .

> "Ten little Légionnaires
> Going 'on pump,'
> Got away safely
> And gave *les autres* the 'ump,"

sang Monsieur Blondin, who was very fond of airing his really remarkable knowledge of colloquial English, British slang, clichés, rhymes, and *guinguette* songs. Not for nothing had he been a Crédit Lyonnais bank-clerk in London for six years. Being a Provençal, he added a pronounced *galégeade* wit to his *macabre* Legion-humour.

One terrible day the Sergeant-Major excelled himself—but it was not, as it happened, one of the Ten who attempted to "remove" him.

Having drilled the parade of "defaulters" almost to death, he halted the unfortunate wretches with their faces to a red-hot wall and their backs to the smiting sun, and kept them at "attention" until Tou-tou Boil-the-Cat, an evil liver, collapsed and fell. He was allowed to lie. When, with a crash, old Tant-de-Soif went prone upon his face, paying his dues to Alcohol, the Sergeant-Major gave the order to turn about, and then to prepare to fire. When the line stood, with empty rifles to the shoulder, as in the act of firing, he kept it in the arduous strain of this attitude that he might award severe punishment to the owner of the first rifle that began to quiver or sink downward. As he did so, he lashed and goaded his victims mercilessly and skilfully.

At last, the rifle of poor young Jean Brecque began to sway and droop, and the Sergeant-Major concentrated upon the half-fainting lad the virulent stream of his poisonous vituperation. Having dealt with the subject of Jean, he began upon that of Jean's mother, and with such horrible foulness of insult that Jean, whose mother was his saint, sprang forward and swung his rifle up to brain the cowardly brute with the butt. As he bounded forward and sprang at the Sergeant-Major, that officer coolly drew his automatic pistol and shot Jean between the eyes.

Had Blondin acted then, his followers, and the bulk of the parade, would have leapt from their places and clubbed the Sergeant-Major to a jelly. But Monsieur Blondin knew that the Sergeant-Major had seven more bullets in his automatic, also that the first man who moved would get one of them, and suicide formed no part of his programme.

"Not just anyhow and anywhere in the trunk, you will observe, *scélérats*," remarked the Suicide-Maker coolly, turning Jean over with his foot, "but neatly in the centre of the face, just between the eyes. My favourite spot. *Cessez le feu! Attention! Par files de quatre. Pas gymnastique. . . . En avant. . . . Marche!*" . . .

The plan was that the Ten, stark naked—so as to avoid any incriminating stains, rents, or other marks upon their garments—should, bayonet in hand, await the passing of the "Suicide-Maker" along a dark corridor that evening. Having dealt with him quietly, but faithfully, they would dress, break out of the post, and set their faces for Morocco at the *pas gymnastique*.

As for Monsieur Blondin, he was determined that this should be no wretched abortive stroll into the desert, ending in ignominious return and surrender for food and water; in capture by *goums*[4] in search of the 25 franc reward for the return of a dead or alive deserter; nor in torture and death at the hands of the first party of nomad Arabs that should see fit to fall upon them. Blondin had read the *Anabasis* of one Xenophon, and an *Anabasis* to Maroc he intended to achieve on the shoulders, metaphorically speaking, of the faithful nine. Toward the setting sun would he lead them, across the Plain of the Shott, through the country of the Beni Guil, toward the Haut Atlas range, along the southern slopes to the Adrar Ndren, and so to Marakesh and service with the Sultan, or to escape by Mogador, Mazagan, or Dar-el-Beida. No more difficult really than toward Algiers or Oran, and, whereas capture in that direction was certain, safety, once in Morocco, was almost equally sure. For trained European soldiers were worth their weight in silver to the Sultan, and, in his

---

[4] Arab gens d'armes.

service, might amass their weight in gold. A Moorish villa (and a harem) surrounded by fig-orchards, olive-fields, vineyards, palm-groves, and a fragrant garden of pepper-trees, eucalyptus, walnut, almond, oleander, orange and lemon, would suit Monsieur Blondin well. Oh, but yes! And the Ouled-Naël dancing-girls, Circassian slaves, Spanish beauties. . . .

The first part of the plan failed, for *ce vieux sale cochon* of a Jean Boule came along the corridor, struck a match to light his cigarette, saw the crouching, staring, naked Ten, and, being a mad Englishman and an accursed dog's-tail, saved the life of the Sergeant-Major. That the Ten took no vengeance upon Jean Boule was due to their lack of desire for combat with the mighty *Americain*, le Bouckaing Bronceau, and with those tough and determined fighters, les Légionnaires Rupert and 'Erbiggin. All four were masters of *le boxe*, and, if beaten, knew it not. . . .

The Ten went "on pump" with their wrongs unavenged, save that Blondin stole the big automatic-pistol of the Sergeant-Major from its nail on the wall of the orderly-room.

They took their Lebel rifles and bayonets, an accumulated store of bread and biscuits, water, and, each man, such few cartridges as he had been able to steal and secrete when on the rifle-range, or marching with "sharp" ammunition.

Getting away was a matter of very small difficulty; it would be staying away that would be the trouble. One by one, they went over the wall of the fort, and hid in ditches, beneath culverts, or behind cactus-bushes.

At the appointed rendezvous in the *village Négre*, the Ten assembled, fell in, and marched off at the *pas gymnastique*, Blondin at their head. After travelling for some hours, with only a cigarette-space halt in every hour, and ere the stars began to pale, Blondin gave the order "*Campez!*", and the little company sank to the ground, cast off accoutrements and capotes, removed boots, and fell asleep. Before dawn Blondin woke them and made a brief speech. If they obeyed him implicitly and faithfully, he would lead them to safety and prosperity; if any man disobeyed him in the slightest particular, he would shoot him dead. If he were to be their leader, as they wished, he must have the promptest and most willing service and subordination from all. There was a terrible time before them ere they win to the

Promised Land, but there was an infinitely worse one behind them—so let all who hoped to attain safety and wealth look to it that his least word be their law.

And the Ten Bad Men, desperate, unscrupulous, their hand against every man's, knowing no restraint nor law but Expedience, set forth on their all but hopeless venture, trusting ce cher Blondin (who intended to clamber from this Slime-pit of Siddim on their carcases, and had chosen them for their various utilities to his purpose).

At dawn, Blondin leading, caught sight of a fire as he topped a ridge, sank to earth, and was at once imitated by the others.

He issued clear orders quickly, and the band skirmished toward the fire, *en tirailleur*, in a manner that would have been creditable to the Touareg themselves. It was a small Arab *douar*, or encampment, of a few *felidj* (low camel-hair tents), and a camel-enclosure. Blondin's shot, to kill the camel-sentry and bring the Arabs running from their tents, was followed by the steady, independent-firing which disposed of these unfortunates.

His whistle was followed by the charge, which also disposed of the remainder and the wounded, and left the Ten in possession of camels, women, food, weapons, tents, Arab clothing, and money. Fortune was favouring the brave! But the Ten were now Nine, for, as they charged, the old sheikh, sick and weak though he was, fired his long gun into the chest of Karl Anderssen at point-blank range. . . .

An hour later the *djemels* were loaded up with what Blondin decided to take, the women were killed, and the Nine were again en route for Maroc, enhearted beyond words. There is a great difference between marching and riding, between carrying one's kit and being carried oneself, and between having a little dry bread and having a fine stock of goat-flesh, rice, raisins, barley, and dates when one is crossing the desert.

In addition to the *djemels*, the baggage-camels, there were five *mehari* or swift riding-camels, and, on four of these, Monsieur Blondin had mounted the four men he considered most useful to his purposes—to wit, Jean Kebir, the Berber half-caste who spoke perfect Arabic as well as the *sabir* or lingua-franca of Northern Africa, and knew the Koran by heart; Hassan Moghrabi, the Moorish negro, who understood camels and horses;

7

Mohamed the Turk, who also would look very convincing in native dress; and Jacques Lejaune, who could use a compass and steer by the stars, and who was a very brave and determined scoundrel.

When allotting the *mehari* to these four, after choosing the best for himself, Blondin, hand on pistol, had looked for any signs of discontent from Ramon Diego, Fritz Bauer, Fritz Schlantz, or Georges Grondin, and had found none. Also when he ordered that each man should cut the throat of his own woman, and Hassan Moghrabi should dispose of the three superfluous ones, no man demurred. The Bad Men were the less disposed to refuse to commit cold-blooded murder because the stories of the tortures inflicted upon the stragglers and the wounded of the Legion are horrible beyond words—though not more horrible than the authentic photographs of the tortured remains of these carved and jointed victims, that hang, as terrible warnings to deserters, in every *chambrée* of the *casernes* of the Legion. They killed these women at the word of Blondin—but they knew that the women would not have been content with the mere killing of *them*, had they fallen into the hands of this party of Arabs.

As, clad in complete Arab dress, they rode away in high spirits, le bon Monsieur Blondin sang in English, in his droll way—

> "Ten little Légionnaires
> Charging all in line—
> A naughty Arab shot one
> And then—there were *Nine*."

The Nine rode the whole of that day and, at evening, Blondin led them into a wadi or canyon, deep enough for concealment and wide enough for comfort. Here they camped, lit fires, and Georges Grondin made a right savoury stew of kid, rice, raisins, barley, dates, and bread in an Arab *couscouss* pot. The Nine slept the sleep of the just and, in the morning, arose and called ce bon Blondin blessed. With camels, food, cooking-pots, sleeping-rugs, tents, clothing, extra weapons, and much other useful loot, hope sprang strong as well as eternal in their more or less human breasts.

Blondin led them on that day until they had made another fifty miles of westing, and halted at a little oasis where there was a well, a *kuba* (or tomb of some marabout or other holy person), and a small *fondouk* or caravan rest-house. Jean Kebir having reconnoitred and declared the *fondouk* empty, and the place safe, they watered their camels, occupied the *fondouk*, and, after a pleasant evening and a good supper, slept beneath its hospitable and verminous shelter—four of the party being on sentry-go, for two hours each, throughout the night.

At this place, the only human beings they encountered were a horrible disintegrating lump of disease that hardly ranked as a human being at all, and an ancient half-witted person who appeared to combine the duties of verger and custodian of the *kuba* with those of caretaker and host of the *fondouk*. Him, Jean Kebir drove into the former building with horrible threats. Fortunately for himself, the aged party strictly conformed with the orders of Kebir, for Blondin had given the Berber instructions to dispatch him forthwith to the joys of Paradise if he were seen outside the tomb. Next day, as the party jogged wearily along, Blondin heard an exclamation from Jean Kebir and, turning, saw him rein in his *mehara* and stare long and earnestly beneath his hand toward the furthermost sand-hills of the southern horizon. On one of these, Blondin could make out a speck. He raised his hand, and the little cavalcade halted.

"What is it?" he asked of Kebir.

"A Targui scout," was the reply. "We shall be attacked by Touareg—*now* if they are the stronger party, to-night in any case—unless we reach some *ksar*[5] and take refuge. . . . That might be more dangerous than waiting for the Touareg, though."

"How do you know the man is a Targui?" asked Blondin.

"I do not know *how* I know, but I *do* know," was the reply. "Who else would sit all day motionless on a *mehara* on top of a sand-hill but a Targui? The Touareg system is to camp in a likely place and keep their horses fresh while a chain of slaves covers a wide area around them. In bush country they sit up in trees, and in the desert they sit on camels, as that fellow is doing. Directly

---

[5] Fortified village.

9

they spot anything, they rush off and warn their masters, who then gallop to the attack on horseback if they are in overwhelming strength, or wait until night if they are not."

Even as he spoke the watcher disappeared.

"Push on hard," ordered Blondin, and debated as to whether it would be better for the *mehari*-mounted five to desert the *djemel*-mounted four and escape, leaving them to their fate, or to remain, a band of nine determined rifles. Union is strength, and there is safety in numbers—so he decided that the speed of the party should be that of the well-flogged *djemels*.

"Goad them on, *mes enfants*," cried he to Diego, Bauer, Schlantz, and Grondin. "I will never desert you—but you must put your best leg foremost. We are nine, and they may be ninety or nine hundred, these *sacrés chiens* of Touareg." An hour of hard riding, another—with decreasing anxiety, and suddenly Blondin's sharp, clear order:

"*Halte! . . . Formez le carré! . . . Attention pour les feux de salve!*" as, with incredible rapidity, an avalanche of horsemen appeared over a ridge and bore down upon them in a cloud of dust, with wild howls of "*Allah Akbar!*" . . . "*Lah illah il Allah!* " and a rising united chant "*Ul-ul-ul-ul Ullah Akbar.*"

Swiftly the trained legionaries dismounted, knelt their camels in a ring, took cover behind them, and, with loaded rifles, awaited their leader's orders. Coolly Blondin estimated the number of this band of The-Forgotten-of-God, the blue-clad, Veiled Men of the desert. . . . Not more than twenty or thirty. They would never have attacked had not their scout taken the little caravan to be one of traders, some portion of a migrating tribe, or, perchance, a little gang of smugglers, traders of the Ouled-Ougouni or the Ouled-Sidi-Sheikhs, or possibly gun-running Chambaa taking German rifles from Tripoli to Morocco—a rich prey, indeed, if this were so. Each Chambi would fight like Iblis himself though, if Chambaa they were, for such are fiends and devils, betrayers of hospitality, slayers of guests, defilers of salt, spawn of Jehannum, who were the sons and fathers of murderers and liars. Moreover, they would be doubly watchful, suspicious, and resolute if they, French subjects, were smuggling German guns across French territory into Morocco under the very nose of the Bureau Arabe. . . . However, there were but nine of them, in any case, so *Ul-ul-*

ul-ul-ul Ullah Akbar!

"Don't fire till I do—and then at the horses, and don't miss," shouted Blondin.

The avalanche swept down, and lances were lowered, two-handed swords raised, and guns and pistols presented—for the Touareg fire from the saddle at full gallop.

Blondin waited.

Blondin fired. . . . The leading horse and rider crashed to the ground and rolled like shot rabbits. Eight rifles spoke almost simultaneously, and seven more men and horses spun in the dust. At the second volley from the Nine, the Touaregs broke, bent their horses outward from the centre of the line, and fled. All save one, who either could not, or would not, check his maddened horse. Him Blondin shot as his great sword split the skull of Fritz Bauer, whose poor shooting, for which he was notorious, had cost him his life.

"*Cessez le feu,*" cried Blondin, as one or two shots were fired after the retreating Arabs. "They won't come back, so don't waste cartridges. . . . See what hero can catch me a horse."

As he coolly examined the ghastly wound of the dying Fritz Bauer, he observed to the faithful Jean Kebir "*Habet!*" and added—

> "Nine little Légionnaires—
> But one fired late
> When a Touareg cut at him—
> And so there were *Eight*."

"*Eh bien, mon Capitaine?*" inquired Kebir.

"*N'importe, mon enfant!*" smiled Monsieur Blondin, and turned his attention to the property and effects of the dying man. . . .

"We shall hear more of these Forsaken-of-God before long," observed Jean Kebir when the eight were once more upon their way.

They did. Just before sunset, as they were silhouetted against the fiery sky in crossing a sand-hill ridge, there was a single shot, and Georges Grondin, the cook, grunted, swayed, observed "*Je suis bien touché,*" and fell from his camel.

Gazing round, Blondin saw no signs of the enemy. The plain was empty of life—but there might be hundreds of foemen behind the occasional aloes, palmettos, and Barbary cacti; crouching in the *driss*, or the thickets of lentisks and arbutus and thuyas. Decidedly a place to get out of. If a party of Touareg had ambushed them there, they might empty every saddle without showing a Targui nose. . . .

A ragged volley was fired from the right flank.

"Ride for your lives," he shouted, and set an excellent example to the other seven.

"What of Grondin?" asked Kebir, bringing his *mehara* alongside that of Blondin.

"Let the dead bury their dead," was the reply. (Evidently the fool had not realized that the *raison d'être* of this expedition was to get one, Jean Blondin, safe to Maroc!)

An hour or so later, in a kind of little natural fortress of stones, boulders, and rocks, they encamped for the night, a sharp watch being kept. But while Monsieur Blondin slept, Jean Kebir, who was attached to Georges Grondin, partly on account of his music and partly on account of his cookery, crept out, an hour or so before dawn, and stole back along the track, in the direction from which they had come.

He found his friend at dawn, still alive; but as he had been neatly disembowelled and the abdominal cavity filled with salt and sand and certain other things, he did not attempt to move him. He embraced his cher Georges, bade him farewell, shot him, and returned to the little camp.

As the cavalcade proceeded on its way, Monsieur Blondin, stimulated by the brilliance and coolness of the glorious morning, and by high hopes of escape, burst into song.

> "Eight little Légionnaires
> Riding from 'ell to 'eaven,
> A wicked Targui shot one—
> And then there were *Seven*,"

improvised he. . . .

Various reasons, shortness of food and water being the most urgent, made it desirable that they should reach and enter a small *ksar* that day.

Towards evening, the Seven beheld what was either an oasis or a mirage—a veritable eye-feast in any case, after hours of burning desolate desert, the home only of the hornéd viper, the lizard, and the scorpion.

It proved to be a small palm-forest, with wells, irrigating-ditches, cultivation, pigeons, and inhabitants. Cultivators were hoeing, blindfolded asses were wheeling round and round *noria* wells, veiled women with red *babooshes* on their feet bore brightly coloured water-vases on their heads. Whitewashed houses came into view, and the cupola of an adobe-walled *kuba*.

Jean Kebir was sent on to reconnoitre and prospect, and to use his judgment as to whether his six companions—good men and true, under a pious vow of silence—might safely enter the oasis, and encamp.

While they awaited his return, naked children came running towards them clamouring for gifts. They found the riders dumb, but eloquent of gesture—and the gestures discouraging.

Some women brought clothes and commenced to wash them in an irrigation stream, on some flat stones by a bridge of palm trunks. The six sat motionless on their camels.

A jet-black Haratin boy brought a huge basket of Barbary figs and offered it—as a gift that should bring a reward. At a sign from Blondin, Mohamed the Turk took it and threw the boy a *mitkal*.

"Salaam," said he.

"*Ya, Sidi, Salaam aleikoum*," answered the boy, with a flash of perfect teeth.

Blondin glared at Mohamed. Could not the son of a camel remember that the party was dumb—pious men under a vow of silence? It was their only chance of avoiding discovery and exposure as accursed Roumis[6] when they were near the habitations of men.

A burst of music from tom-tom, derbukha, and raita broke the heavy silence, and then a solo on the raita, the "Voice of the Devil," the instrument of the provocative wicked note. Some one was getting born, married, or buried, apparently.

---

[6] Europeans.

Fritz Schlantz, staring open-mouthed at cyclamens, anemones, asphodels, irises, lilies, and crocuses between a little cemetery and a stream, was, for the moment, back in his Tyrolese village. He shivered. . . .

Jean Kebir returned. He recommended camping on the far side of the village at a spot he had selected. There were strangers, heavily armed with yataghans, lances, horse-pistols, flissas, and *moukalas* in the *fondouk*. In addition to the flint-lock *moukalas* there were several repeating rifles. They were all clad in *burnous* and *chechia*, and appeared to be half-trader, half-brigand Arabs of the Tableland, perhaps Ouled-Ougouni or possibly Aït-Jellal. Anyhow, the best thing to do with them was to give them a wide berth.

The Seven passed through the oasis and, camping on the other side, fed full upon the proceeds of Kebir's foraging and shopping.

That night, Fritz Schlantz was seized with acute internal pains, and was soon obviously and desperately ill.

"Cholera!" said Monsieur Blondin on being awakened by the sufferer's cries and groans. "Saddle up and leave him."

Within the hour the little caravan had departed, Jacques Lejaune steering by the stars. To keep up the spirits of his followers Monsieur Blondin sang aloud.

First he sang—

> "Des marches d'Afrique
> J'en ai pleine le dos.
> On y va trop vite.
> On n'y boit que de l'eau.
> Des lauriers, des victoires,
> De ce songe illusoire
> Que l'on nomme 'la gloire,'
> J'en ai plein le dos,"

and then *Derrière l'Hôtel-Dieu*, and *Père Dupanloup en chemin de fer*. In a fine tenor voice, and with great feeling, he next rendered *L'Amour m'a rendu fou*, and then, to a tune of his own composition, sang in English—

"Seven little Légionnaires
Eating nice green figs,
A greedy German ate too much—
And then there were *Six*."

Day after day, and week after week, the legionaries pushed on, sometimes starving, often thirsty, frequently hunted, sometimes living like the proverbial *coq en pâte*, or, as Blondin said, "Wee peegs in clover," after ambushing and looting a caravan.

Between Amang and Illigh lie the bones of Jacques Lejaune, who was shot by Blondin. As they passed out of the dark and gloomy shade of a great cedar forest, there was a sudden roar, and a lioness flung herself from a rock upon Lejaune's camel. Lejaune was leading as the sun had set. Blondin, who was behind him, fired quickly, and the bullet struck him in the spine and passed out through his shattered breast-bone. He had been getting "difficult" and too fond of giving himself airs on the strength of his navigating ability, and, moreover, Monsieur Blondin had learnt to steer by the stars, having located the polar star by means of the Great Bear. Jean Kebir shot the lioness through the head.

It was a sad "accident," but Blondin had evidently recovered his spirits by morning, as he was singing again.

He sang—

"Six little Légionnaires
Still all live,
But one grew *indiscipliné*—
And then there were *Five*." . . .

Distinctly of a *galégeade* wit and a *macabre* humour was Monsieur Blondin, and even as his eye roamed over the scrubby hill-sides and he thought fondly of the *mussugues*, the cistus-scrub hillocks of his dear Provence, he calculated the total sum of money now divided among the said Five, and reflected that division, where money is concerned, is deplorable. Also, as he gazed upon the tracts of thorn that recalled the *argeras* of Hyères, he decided that, all things considered, it would be as well for him to reach Marakesh alone. He understood the principle of rarity-value, and knew that either one of two newcomers would not fetch a quarter of the price of a single newcomer to a war-harassed Sultan whose crying need was European drill-sergeants and centurions.

Jean Blondin would rise to be a second Kaid McLeod, and would amass vast wealth to boot. . . .

At Aït-Ashsba, bad luck overtook Ramon Diego. At the *fondouk* he smote a burly negro of Sokoto who jostled him. The negro, one of a band of departing wayfarers, was a master of the art of *rabah*, the native version of *la savate*, and landed Ramon a most terrible kick beneath the breast-bone. As he lay gasping and groaning for breath, the negro whipped out his razor-edged yataghan and bent over the prostrate man. Holding aloof, Blondin saw the negro spit on the back of Ramon Diego's neck, and with his finger draw a line thereon. Stepping swiftly back, the gigantic black then smote with all his strength, and the head of Ramon Diego rolled through the doorway and down the stony slope leading from the *fondouk*. As the negro mounted his swift Filali camel, Blondin investigated the contents of a leather bag which Ramon always wore at the girdle, beneath his *haik*. On being told of the mishap, Jean Kebir was all for pursuit and vengeance. This, Blondin vetoed sternly. There were now only four of them, and henceforth they must walk delicately and be *miskeen*, modest, humble men. Only four now!

> "Five little Légionnaires,
> Each man worth a score;
> But a big nigger 'it one—
> And then there were *Four*,"

sang Monsieur Blondin.

But what a four! Jean Kebir, the genuine local article, more or less; Hassan Moghrabi, near his native heath and well in the picture; Mohamed the Turk, a genuine Mussulman, able to enter any mosque or *kuba* and display his orthodoxy; and himself, a pious man hooded to the eyes, under a vow of silence.

In due course, the Four reached the Adrar highlands, and tasted of the hospitality of this grim spot, with its brigands' *agadirs* or castles of stone. A band swooping down upon them from an *agadir* (obviously of Phœnician origin), pursued them so closely and successfully, that Mohamed, the worst mounted, bringing up the rear, was also brought to earth by a lance-thrust through his back, and ended his career hanging by the flesh of his thigh from a huge hook which protruded from the wall above the door of the *agadir*.

Though greatly incensed at the loss of the Turk's camel and cash, Monsieur Blondin was soon able to sing again.

> "Four little Légionnaires
> Out upon the spree,
> The Adrar robbers caught one—
> And soon there were *Three*," . . .

he chanted merrily.

As the Three watched some hideous Aïssa dervishes dancing on glowing charcoal, skewering their limbs and cheeks and tongues, eating fire, and otherwise demonstrating their virtue one night, near Bouzen, a *djemel*, thrusting forth his head and twisting his snaky neck, neatly removed the right knee-cap of Hassan Moghrabi, and he was of no further use to Monsieur Blondin. He was left behind, and died in a ditch some three days later, of loss of blood, starvation, gangrene, and grief.

Clearly Jean Blondin was reserved for great things. Here were the Ten reduced to Two, and of those two he was one—and intended to be the only one when he was safe in Maroc. Singing blithely, he declared that—

> "Three little Légionnaires
> Nearly travelled through,
> When a hungry camel ate one—
> And now there are but *Two*." . . .

On through the beautiful Adrar, past its forests of arbutus, lentisk, thuya, figs, pines, and palmettos to its belt of olive groves, walnut, and almond; on toward Djebel Tagharat, the Lord of the Peaks, the Two-Headed. On through the Jibali country, called the "Country of the Gun" by the Arabs, as it produces little else for visitors, toward the Bled-el-Maghzen, the "Government's Territory," experiencing many and strange adventures and hair-breadth escapes. And, all the way, Jean Kebir served his colleague and leader well, and often saved him by his ready wit, knowledge of the country and the *sabir*, and his good advice.

And in time they reached the gorge of Bab el Jebel, and rode over a carpet of pimpernels, larkspur, gladioli, hyacinths, crocuses, wasp-orchids, asphodels, cyclamens, irises and musk-balsams; and Blondin realized that it was time for Jean Kebir to die, if he were to ride to Marakesh alone and to inherit the whole of what remained of the money looted in the fifteen-hundred-mile journey, that was now within fifteen hours of its end. . . .

He felt quite sad as he shot the sleeping Jean Kebir that night, but by morning was able to sing—

> "Two little Légionnaires
> Travelling with the sun,
> Two was one too many—
> So now there is but *One*,"

and remarked to his camel, "'*Finis coronat opus,*' mon gars." . . .

Even as he caught sight, upon the horizon, of the sea of palms in which Marakesh is bathed, he was aware of a rush of yelling, gun-firing, white-clad lunatics bearing down upon him. . . . A Moorish *harka*! Was this a *lab-el-baroda*, a powder-play game—or what? They couldn't be shooting at him. . . . What was that Kebir had said? . . . "The Moors are the natural enemies of the Arabs. We must soon get Moorish garb or hide"—when . . . a bullet struck his camel and it sprawled lumberingly to earth. Others threw up spouts of dust. Blondin sprang to his feet and shouted. Curse the fools for thinking him an Arab! *Oh, for the faithful Jean Kebir to shout to them in the* sabir *lingua franca!* . . . A bullet struck him in the chest. Another in the shoulder. He fell.

As the Moors gathered round to slice him in strips with flissa, yataghan and sword, they found that their prey was apparently expending his last breath in prayers and pæans to Allah. He gasped:

"One little Légionnaire,
To provide *le bon Dieu* fun,
Was killed because he killed his friend—
And now there is *None*." . . .

There was.

Decidedly of a *galégeade* wit and a *macabre* humour to the very last—ce bon Jean Blondin.

"Que voulez-vous? C'est la Légion!" . . .

À LA NINON DE L'ENCLOS

"À La Ninon de L'Enclos" is a story related by one of the more persistent characters in Wren's Foreign Legion fiction: La Cigale, the "Grasshopper." The story is in one of Wren's more popular formats: a group of legionnaires are together and one of them relates a story. In this instance the tale is one of incest and its consequences. The original woman in the story, Ninon de l'Enclos, is a historical person who lived in seventeenth century Paris. The person La Cigale talks about was a woman who lived in Hanoi and was a "les filles de joie" for the soldiers of the Legion. As far as is currently known, the first publication of "À La Ninon de L'Enclos" was in December of 1917 in the first edition of Stepsons of France. *The story has been reprinted in the Murray omnibus collection* Stories of the Foreign Legion *(1947) and the abridged Macrae-Smith collection (1948) of the same title.*

It was one of La Cigale's good days, and the poor "Grasshopper" was comparatively sane. He was one of the most remarkable men in the French Foreign Legion in that he was a perfect soldier, though a perfect lunatic for about thirty days in the month. When not a Grasshopper (or a Japanese lady, a Zulu, an Esquimaux dog or a Chinese mandarin) he was a cultured gentleman of rare perception, understanding, and sympathy. He had been an officer in the Belgian Corps of Guides, and military attaché at various courts. . . .

From a neighbouring group talking to Madame la Cantinière, in the canteen, came the words, clearly heard, *"Ah! Oui! Oui! Dans la Rue des Tournelles."* . . .

"Now, why should the words 'Rue des Tournelles' bring me a distinct vision of the Café Marsouins in Hanoï by the banks of the Red River in Tonkin?" asked the Grasshopper a minute later, in English.

"Can't tell you, Cigale; there is no such *rue* in Hanoï," replied Jean Boule.

"No, *mon ancien*," agreed the Grasshopper, "but there was Fifi Fifinette's place. Aha! I have it!"

"Then give us a bit of it, Cocky," put in 'Erb (le Légionnaire

'Erbiggin—one, Herbert Higgins from Hoxton).

"Yep—down by the factory, near Madame Ti-Ka's joint, it were," observed the Bucking Bronco.

"Aha! I have it. I remember me why the words 'Rue des Tournelles' reminded me all suddenly of the Café Marsouins in Hanoï," continued the Grasshopper. "It was there that I heard from Old Dubeque the truth of the story of Ninon Dürlonnklau, who was Fifi Fifinette's predecessor. She was a reincarnation of Ninon de l'Enclos, and of course Ninon dwelt in the Rue des Tournelles in Old Paris a few odd centuries back."

"Did they call the gal Neenong de Longclothes because she wore tights, Ciggy?" inquired 'Erb.

"Put me wise to Neenong's little stunts before I hit it for the downy,"[7] requested the Bucking Bronco.

"Ninon de l'Enclos was a lady of the loveliest and frailest," said the Grasshopper. "Oh! but of a charm. *Ravissante!* She was, in her time, the well-beloved of Richelieu, Captain St. Etienne, the Marquis de Sevigné, Condé, Moissins, the Duc de Navailles, Fontennelle, Des Yveteaux, the Marquis de Villarceaux, St. Evrémonde, and the Abbé Chaulieu. On her eightieth birthday she had a devout and impassioned lover. On her eighty-fifth birthday the good Abbé wrote to her, 'Cupid has retreated into the little wrinkles round your undimmed eyes.'". . .

"*Some* girl," opined the Bucking Bronco.

"And she lived in the Rue des Tournelles, and so the mention of that street called the Café Marsouins of Hanoï in Tonkin to my mind (for there did I hear the truth of the fate of Ninon Dürlonnklau, the predecessor of Fifi Fifinette whom some of us here knew). . . .

"And the chevalier de Villars, the son of Ninon de l'Enclos, was her lover also, not knowing that Ninon was his mother, nor she that de Villars was her son—until too late. Outside her door a necromancer prophesied the death of de Villars to his face. An hour later Ninon knew by a birth-mark that de Villars was her son, and cried aloud, 'You are my son!' So he fulfilled the prophecy of the necromancer. He drove his dagger through his throat—just where this birth-mark was. What you call *mole*, eh?

---

[7] Go to bed.

... Shame and horror? No ... Love. They who loved Ninon de l'Enclos loved. Her arms or those of death. No other place for a lover of Ninon. You Anglo-Saxons could never understand. ...

"And in Hanoï lived her reincarnation, Ninon Dürlonnklau, supposed to be the daughter of one Dürlonnklau, a German of the Legion, and of a perfect flower of a Lao woman. And, mind you, *mes amis*, there is nothing in the human form more lovely than a beautiful Lao girl from Upper Mekong.

"And this Ninon! Beautiful? Ah, my friends—there are no words. Like yourselves, I seek not the bowers of lovers—but I have the great love of beauty, and I have seen Ninon Dürlonnklau. Would I might have seen Ninon de l'Enclos that I might judge if she were one half so lovely and so fascinating. And when I first beheld the Dürlonnklau she was no *jeune fille*. . .

.

"She had been the well-beloved of governors, generals, and officials and officers—and there had been catastrophes, scandals, suicides . . . the usual *affaires*—before she became the hostess of legionaries, marsouins,[8] sailors. . . .

"She had herself not wholly escaped the tragedy and grief that followed in her train, for at the age of seventeen she had a son, and that son was kidnapped when at the age that a babe takes the strongest grip upon a mother's heart and love and life. . . . And after a madness of grief and a long illness, she plunged the more recklessly into the pursuit of that pleasure and joy that must ever evade the children of pleasure, *les filles de joie*."

'Erb yawned cavernously.

"Got a gasper, Farver?" he inquired of John Bull.

The old soldier produced a small packet of vile black Algerian cigarettes from his *képi*, without speaking.

"Quit it, Dub!" snapped the deeply interested Bucking Bronco. "*Pro*duce silence, and then some, or beat it."[9]

"Awright, Bucko," mocked the unabashed 'Erb, imitating the American's nasal drawl and borrowing from his vocabulary. "You ain't got no call ter git het up none, thataway. Don't yew git locoed an rip-snort—'cos I guess I don' stand fer it, any."

---

[8] Colonial infantry.

[9] Go away.

"Stop it, 'Erb," said John Bull, and 'Erb stopped it. There would be trouble between these two one hot day. . . .

"The Legion appropriated her to itself at last," continued the Grasshopper, "and picketed her house. Marsouins, sailors, *pékins*[10] —all ceased to visit her. It was more than their lives were worth, and there were pitched battles when whole *escouades* of *ces autres* tried to get in, before it was clearly understood that Ninon belonged to the Legion. And this was meat and drink to Ninon. She loved to be La Reine de la Légion Étrangère. This was not Algiers, mark you, and she had been born and bred in Hanoï. She had not that false perspective that leads the women of the West to prefer those of other Corps to the sons of La Légion. And there were one or two moneyed men hiding in our ranks just then. She loved one for a time and then another for a time, and frequently the previous one would act rashly. Some took their last exercise in the Red River. An unpleasant stream in which to drown.

"Then came out, in a new draft, young Villa, supposed to be of Spanish extraction—but he knew no Spanish. I think he was the handsomest young devil I have ever seen. He had coarse black hair that is not of Europe, wild yellow eyes, and a curious, almost gold complexion. He was a strange boy, and of a temperament decidedly, and he loved flowers as some women do—especially ylang-ylang, jasmine, magnolia, and those of sweet and sickly perfume. He said they stirred his blood, and his prenatal memories. . . .

"And one night old Dubeque took him to see La Belle Dürlonnklau.

"As he told it to me I could see all that happened, for old Dubeque had the gift of speech, imagination, and the instinct of the drama. . . . Old Dubeque—the drunken, depraved scholar and *gentilhomme*.

"Outside her door a begging soothsayer whined to tell their fortunes. It was the Annamite New Year, the Thêt, when the native *must* get money somehow for his sacred jollifications. This fellow stood making the humble *lai* or prolonged salaam, and at once awoke the interest of young Villa, who tossed him a piastre.

---

[10] Civilians.

"Old Dubeque swears that, as he grabbed it, this *diseur de bonne aventure*, a scoundrel of the Delta, said, 'Missieu French he die to-night,' or words to that effect in pigeon-French, and Villa rewarded the Job-like Annamite with a kick. . . . They went in. . . .

"As they entered the big room where were the Mekong girls and Madame Dürlonnklau, the boy suddenly stopped, started, stared, and stood with open mouth gazing at La Belle Ninon. He had eyes for no one else. She rose from her couch and came towards him, her face lit up and exalted. She led him to her couch and they talked. Love at first sight! Love had come to that so-experienced woman; to that wild *farouche* boy. Later they disappeared into an inner room. . . .

"Old Dubeque called for a bottle of wine, and drank with some of the girls.

"He does not know how much later it was that the murmur of voices in Madame's room ceased with a shriek of '*Mon fils*,' a horrid, terrific scream, and the sound of a fall.

"Old Dubeque was not so drunk but what this sobered him. He entered the room.

"Young Villa had fulfilled the prophecy of the necromancer. He had driven his bayonet through his throat—just where a large birthmark was. What you call *mole*, eh? It was exposed when his shirt-collar was undone. . . . Ninon Dürlonnklau lived long, may be still alive—anyhow, I know she lived long—in a *maison de santé*. Yes—a reincarnation. . . .

"That is of what the words *la Rue de Tournelles* reminded me."

"'Streuth!" remarked le Legionnaire 'Erbiggin, and scratched his cropped head.

AN OFFICER AND—A LIAR

*"An Officer and—a Liar" is the story of a Legion officer and his wife.
The wife is, as the first line states, "inclined to the occult, to
spiritualism, and to dabbling in the latest thing psychic and
metaphysical." They have a small boy and since the officer is stationed
in Indo-China (Vietnam), the boy is sent home to France. The boy dies
in a tragic fire and the mother (and father) are devastated. The officer
has to help his wife in her grief by pretending to be in communication
with their dead son via a psychic writing device: a planchette. What
makes this story noteworthy is the parallel in Wren's own life. He and
his first wife, Alice, sent their daughter, Estelle, home to England (from
India) and received word in 1910 that Estelle had died from pertussis
(whooping cough). Wren was probably writing from his heart about
how the characters in this story felt about the death of their beloved
child. "An Officer and—a Liar" was first published in* Stepsons of
France *(1917) and has been reprinted in four different subsequent
collections:* Stories of the Foreign Legion *(Vallancey, 1945),* Tales of
the Foreign Legion *(Vallancey, 1946),* Stories of the Foreign Legion
(Murray, 1947), and Stories of the Foreign Legion *(Macrae-Smith,
1948).*

Little Madame Gallais was always a trifle inclined to the
occult, to spiritualism, and to dabbling in the latest thing psychic
and metaphysical. At home, in Marseilles, she was a prominent
member and bright particular star of a *Cercle* which was, in
effect, a Psychical Research Society. She complained that one of
the drawbacks of accompanying her husband on Colonial service
was isolation from these so interesting pursuits and people.

Successful and flourishing occultism needs an atmosphere,
and it is difficult for a solitary crier in the wilderness to create
one. However, Madame Gallais did her best. She could, and
would, talk to you of your subliminal self, your subconscious
ego, your true psyche, your astral body, and of planes. On planes
she was quite at home. She would ask gay and sportive *sous-
lieutenants*, fresh from the boulevards of Paris, as to whether they
were mediumistic, or able to achieve clairvoyant trances. It is to

be recorded that, at no dance, picnic, garden-party, "fiv' o'clock," or dinner did she encounter a French officer who confessed to being mediumistic or able to achieve clairvoyant trances.

Nor was big, fat Adjudant-Major Gallais any better than the other officers of the Legion and the *Infanterie de la Marine* and the *Tirailleurs Tonkinois* who formed the circle of Madame's acquaintance in Eastern exile. No—on the contrary, he distinctly inclined to the materialistic, and preferred red wines to blue-stockings—(not blue silk stockings, *bien entendu*). For mediums and ghost-seers he had an explosive and jeering laugh. For vegetarians he had a contempt and pity that no words could express.

A teetotaller he regarded as he did a dancing dervish.

He had no use for ascetics and self-deniers, holding them mad or impious.

No, it could not be said that Madame's husband was mediumistic or able to achieve clairvoyant trances, nor that he was a tower of strength and a present help to her in her efforts to create the atmosphere which she so desired.

When implored to gaze with her into the crystal, he declared that he saw things that brought the blush of modesty to the cheek of Madame.

When begged to take a hand at "planchette" writing, he caused the innocent instrument to write a naughty *guinguette* rhyme, and to sign it Eugénie Yvette Gallais.

When besought to witness the wonders of some fortuneteller, seer, astrologer or *yogi*, he put him to flight with fearful grimaces and gesticulations.

And this was a great grief unto Madame, for she loved astrologers and fortune-tellers in spite of all, or rather of nothing. And yet *malgré* the fat Adjudant-Major's cynicism and hardy scepticism, the very curious and undeniable fact remained, that Madame had the power to influence his dreams. She could, that is to say, make him dream of her, and could appear to him in his dreams and give him messages. The Adjudant-Major admitted as much, and thus there is no question as to the fact. (Indeed, when Madame died in Marseilles many years later, he announced the fact to us in Algeria, more than forty-eight hours before he received confirmation of what he knew to be the truth of his dream.)

Two people less alike than the gallant Adjudant-Major and his wife you could not find. Perhaps that is why they loved each other so devotedly.

"I wonder if my boy will be mediumistic," murmured little Madame Gallais, as she hung fondly over the cot in which reposed little Edouard André. "Oh, to be able to hold communion with him when we are parted and I am in the spirit-world."

"Give the little *moutard* plenty of good meat," said the big man. "We want *le petit Gingembre* to be a heavyweight—a born and bred cuirassier." . . .

"*Mon ange*, do you see any reason why twin souls, united in the bonds of purest love and closest relationship, should not be able to communicate quite freely when far apart?" Madame Gallais would reply.

"Save postage, in effect?" grinned the Adjudant-Major.

"I mean by medium of rappings, 'planchette,' dreams—if not by actual appearance and communication in spirit guise?"

"Spirit guys?" queried the stronger and thicker vessel.

"Yes, my soul, spirit guise."

"Oh, ah, yes. . . . Better not let me catch the young devil in spirit guise, or I'll teach him to stick to good wine and carry it like a gentleman. . . . He must learn his limit. . . . How soon do you think we could put him into neat little riding-breeches? . . . Cavalry for him. . . . Not but what the Legion is the finest regiment in the world. . . . Still Cuirassiers for him."

"My Own! Let the poor sweet angel finish with his first petticoats before we talk of riding-breeches. . . . And how, pray, would the riding-breeches accord with his so-beautiful long curls. They would not, *mon ange, n'est ce pas?*" . . .

"No—but surely the curls can be cut off in a very few moments, can't they?" argued the Major, with the conscious superiority of the logical sex.

But she, of the sex that needs no logic, only smiled and replied that she would project herself into her son's dreams every night of his life.

And in the fulness of time, Edouard André having arrived at boy's estate, the curse of the Colonial came upon little Madame

Gallais, and she had to take her son home to France and leave him there with her heart and her health and her happiness. She, in her misery, could conceive of only one fate more terrible—separation from her large, dull husband, whom she adored for his strength, placidity, courage, adequacy, and, above all, because he adored her. Separation from him would be death, and she preferred the half-death of separation from *le petit Gingembre*.

She wrote daily to him on her return to Indo-China—printing the words large and clear for his easier perusal and, at the end of each weekly budget, she added a postscript asking him whether he dreamed of mother often. She also wrote to her own mother by every mail, each letter containing new and fresh suggestions for his mental, moral, and physical welfare, in spite of the fact that the urchin already received the entire devotion, care, and love of the little household at Marseilles.

Their unceasing, ungrudging devotion, care and love, however, did not prevent a gentle little breeze from springing up one summer evening, from bulging the bedroom window-curtain across the lighted gas-jet, and from acting as the first cause of poor little Edouard André being burnt to death in his bed, before a soul was aware that the tall, narrow house was on fire.

Big Adjudant-Major Gallais was in a terrible quandary and knew not what to do. He had but little imagination, but he had a mighty love for his wife—and she was going stark, staring mad before his haggard eyes. . . . And, if she died, he was going to take ship from Saigon and just disappear overboard one dark night, quietly and decently, like a gentleman, with neither mess, fuss, nor post-mortem *enquête*.

But there was just a ghost of a chance, a shadow of a hope—this "planchette" notion that had come to him suddenly in the dreadful sleepless night of watching. . . . It could not make things worse—and it might bring relief, the relief of tears. If she could weep she could sleep. If she could sleep she could live, perhaps—and the Major swallowed hard, coughed fiercely, and scrubbed his bristly head violently with both big hands.

It would be a lying fraud and swindle; but what of that if it might save her life and reason—and he was prepared to forge a cheque, cheat at cards, or rob a blind Chinese beggar of his last *sabuk*, to give her a minute's comfort, rest, and peace. . . . For clearly she must weep or die, sleep or die, unless she were to lose her reason—and while she was in an asylum he could not take that quiet dive overboard so that they could all be together again in the keeping and peace of *le bon Dieu*. . . . Rather death than madness, a thousand times. . . . But if she died and he took steps to follow her—was there not some talk about suicides finding no place in Heaven?

Peste! What absurdity! For surely *le bon Père* had as much sense of fair-play and mercy as a battered old soldier-man of La Légion? But it had not come to that yet. The Legion does not surrender—and the Adjudant-Major of the First Battalion of The Regiment had still a *ruse de guerre* to try against the enemy. He would do his best with this "planchette" swindle, and play it for what it was worth. While there is life there is hope, and he had been in many a tight place before, and fought his way out.

To think of Edouard André Lucien Gallais playing with "planchette"! She had often begged him to join hands with her on its ebony board, and to endeavour to "get into communication" with the spirits of the departed—but he had always acted the *farceur*.

"Ask the sacred thing to tip us the next Grand Prix winner," he had said, or "But, yes—I would question the kind spirits as to the address of the pretty girl I saw at the station yesterday," and then he would cause the innocent machine to say things most unspiritual. Well—now he would see what sort of lying cheat he could make of himself. To lie is not gentlemanly—but to save life and reason is. If to lie is to blacken the soul—let the soul of Adjudant-Major Gallais be black as the blackest *ibn Eblis*, if thereby an hour's peace might descend upon the tortured soul of his wife. The good Lord God would understand a gentleman— being one Himself.

And the Major, large, heavy, and slow-witted, entered his wife's darkened room, and crept toward the bed whereon she lay, dry-eyed, talking aloud and monotonously.

". . . To play such a trick on me! May Heaven reward those who play tricks. Of course, it is a hoax—but why does not mother cable back that there never was any fire at all, and that she knows nothing about the telegram? . . . How could *le petit Gingembre* be dead, when there he is, in the photo, smiling at me

29

so prettily, and looking so strong and well? What a fool I am! Anyone can play tricks on me. People *do*. . . . I shall tell my husband. He would never play a trick on me, nor allow such a thing. . . . A trick! A hoax! . . . Of course, one can judge nothing from the handwriting of a telegram. Anybody could forge one. A letter would be so difficult to forge. . . . The sender of that wicked cable said to himself, 'Madame Gallais cannot pretend that the message does not come from her mother on grounds of the handwriting being different from that of her mother—because the writing is never that of the sender, but that of the telegraph-clerk. She will be deceived and think that her mother has really sent it.' . . . How unspeakably cruel and wicked! No, a letter could not be forged, and that is why there is no letter. Let them wait until my husband can get at them. *Mon petit Gingembre!* And it is his birthday in a month. . . . What shall I get for him? I cannot make up my mind. One cannot get just what one wants out here, and if one sends the money for something to be bought at Home, it is not the same thing—it does not seem to the child as though his parents sent it at all. How lucky I am to have mother to leave him to. She simply worships him, and he couldn't have a happier time, nor better treatment, if I were there myself. No—that's just it—the happier a child is the less it needs you, and you wouldn't have it unhappy so that it *did* want you. How the darling will . . ." and then again rose the awful wailing cry as consciousness of the terrible truth, the cruel loss, the horrible fate, and the sensation of utter impotence of the bereaved, surged over the wearied, failing brain. She must cry or die.

The Major sat beside her and gently patted her, in his dull yearning to help, to relieve the dreadful agony, to do something.

A gust of rebellious rage shook him, and he longed to fight and to kill. Why was he smitten thus, and why was there no tangible opponent at whom he could rush, and whom he could hew and hack and slay? He rose to his feet, with clenched fists uplifted and purpling face.

"Be calm," he said, and took a hold upon himself.

Useless to attempt to fight Fate or the Devil or whatever it was that struck you from behind like this, stabbed you in the back, turned life to dust and ashes. . . . He must grin and bear it like a man. Like a man—and what of the woman?

"He's happy now, *petit*, our *petit Gingembre*," said the poor wretch.

"He's just a jolly little angel, having a fête-day of a time. He's not weeping and unhappy. Not he, *peaudezébie!*"

"Burning!" screamed the woman. "My baby is burning! My *petit Gingembre* is burning, and no one will help him. . . . My baby is burning and Heaven looks on! Oh, mother!—Annette!—Marie!—Grégoire! rush up to the bedroom! . . . Quick—he is burning! The curtain is on fire. The blind has caught. . . . The dressing-table is alight. . . . The blind has fallen on the bed. His pillow is smouldering. He is suffocating. The bed is on fire . . ." and scream followed heartrending scream.

The stricken husband seized the woman's hands and kissed them.

"No, *petit*, he never woke. He never felt anything. He just passed away to *le bon Dieu* in his sleep, without pain or fright, or anything. He just died in his sleep. There is no pain at all about that sort of suffocation, you know," he said.

"Oh, if I could but think so!" moaned the woman. "If I could only for a moment think so! . . . Burning to death and screaming for mother. . . . Edouard! Shoot me—shoot me! Or let me . . ."

"See, Beloved of my Soul," urged her husband, gently shaking her. "I do solemnly swear that I know he was not hurt in the least. He never woke. I happen to know it. I am not saying it to comfort you. I *know* it."

"How could you know, Edouard? . . . Oh, my little baby, my little son! Oh, wake me from this awful *cauchemar*, Edouard. Say I am dreaming and am going to wake."

"The little chap's gone, darling, but he went easy, and he's well out of this cursed world, anyhow. He'll never have suffering and unhappiness. . . . And he had such a happy little life." . . .

Then, for the first time in his career, the Major waxed eloquent, and, for the first time in his life, lied fluently and artistically. "I wonder if you'll believe me if I tell you how I *know* he wasn't hurt," he continued. "It's the truth, you know. I wouldn't lie to you, would I?"

"No, you wouldn't deceive me, and you haven't the wit if you would," replied his wife.

"No, dearest, that's just it. I wouldn't and couldn't, as you say. Well, look here, last night the little chap appeared to me. *Le petit Gingembre* himself! Faith of a gentleman, he did. . . . I may have been asleep, but he appeared to me as plain as you are now. . . . As pretty, I mean," he corrected with a heavy, anxious laugh and pat, peering into the drawn and disfigured face to see if his words reached the distraught mind, "and he said, 'Father, I want to speak to mother, and she cannot hear because she cries out and screams and sobs. It makes me so wretched that I cannot bear it.'"

The man moistened parched lips with a leathery tongue.

"And he said, 'Tell her I was not hurt a little bit—not even touched by the flames. I just slept on, and knew nothing. . . . And I couldn't be happy, even in Heaven, while she grieves so.'"

The woman turned to him.

"Edouard, you are lying to me—and I am grateful to you. It is as terrible for you as for me," and she beat her forehead with clenched fists.

"Eugénie!" cried her husband. "Do you call me a liar! *Me?* Did I not give you my word of honour?"

"Aren't you lying, Edouard? *Aren't* you? . . . Don't deceive me, Edouard André Gallais!" and she seized his wrist in a grip that hurt him.

"I take my solemn oath I am not lying," lied the Major. "Heaven smite me if I am. I swear I am speaking the absolute truth. *Nom de nom de Dieu!* Would I lie to you?"

He must convince her while she had the sanity to understand him. . . . "I believe you, Edouard. You are not deceiving me. Oh, thank God! I humbly thank the good merciful Father. And it was—it was—a real and actual communication, Edouard—and vouchsafed to you, the scoffer at spirit communication."

"Yes, but that's not all, my Eugénie. The little chap said, 'I cannot come to mother while she cries out and moans. Tell her to talk with me by "planchette," you joining with her.' He did," lied the Major.

"Oh! Oh! Edouard! Quick! Where is it? . . . Oh, my baby!" cried Madame Gallais, rising and rushing to a cabinet from which she produced a heart-shaped ebony board some ten inches long and six broad, having at the wide end two legs, an inch or so in length terminating in two swivelled ivory wheels, and, at the other end, a pencil of the same length as the legs.

Seating herself at her writing-table, she placed the instrument on a large sheet of paper, while her husband brought a chair to her side.

Both placed their hands lightly on the broad part of the board and awaited results.

The pencil did not stir.

Minute after minute passed.

The Adjudant-Major was a cunning man of war, and he was using all his cunning now.

The woman uttered a faint moan as the tenth minute ebbed away.

"Patience, Sweetheart," said he. "It's worth a fair trial and a little patience, isn't it?"

"Patience!" was the scornful reply. "I'll sit here till I die—or I'll hear from my boy. . . . You *didn't* lie to me, Edouard?"

The pencil stirred—stirred, moved, and stopped.

The woman groaned.

The pencil stirred again. Then it moved—moved and wrote rapidly, improving in pace and execution as the Major gained practice in pushing it without giving the slightest impression of using "undue influence."

His wife firmly and fanatically believed that the spirit of her child was actually present and utilizing, through their brains, the muscles of their arms, to convey to the paper the message it could neither speak nor write itself.

Presently the pencil ceased to move, and, after another period of patient waiting, the stricken mother took the paper from beneath the instrument and read the "message" of the queer, wavering writing, feeble, unpunctuated, and fantastic, but quite legible, although conjoined.

"My Dearest Maman," it ran. "Why do you grieve so for me and make me so unhappy? How can I be joyous when you are sad? Let me be happy by being happy yourself. I cannot come to you while you mourn. Be glad, and let me be glad and then you must be more happy still, because I am happy. I never felt any pain at all. I just awoke to find myself here, where all would be joy for me, except for your grief. I have left a world of pain, to wait a little while for you where we shall be together in perfect happiness for ever. Let me be happy, dearest Maman, by being resigned, and then happy, yourself. When you are at peace I can come to you always in your dreams, and we can talk together. Give me happiness at once, darling Mother. Please do. Your *Petit Gingembre*". . . which was not a bad effort for an unimaginative and dull-witted man.

He had his instant reward, for on finishing the reading of the "message," Madame Gallais threw her arms round his neck and burst into tears—the life-giving, reason-saving, blessed relief of tears.

An hour later she slept, for the first time in five days, holding her husband's big hand as he sat by her bed.

When she stirred and relinquished it, the next morning, the Major arose and went out.

"What a sacred liar I am!" quoth he. "Garçon, bring me an *apéritif*."

It is notorious what a tangled web we weave when first we practise to deceive. And Major Gallais practised hard. Two and three and four times daily did he manufacture "messages" from the dead child, and strive, with his heart in his mouth, to make the successful cheat last until the first wild bitterness of his wife's grief had worn off.

His hair went grey in the course of a month.

The mental strain of invention, the agony of rasping his own cruel wound by this mockery—for he had loved *le petit Gingembre* as much as the child's mother had done—and the constant terror lest some unconvincing expression or some unguarded pressure on the "planchette" should betray him, were more exhausting and wearing than two campaigns against the "pirates" of Yen Thé.

But still he had his reward, for his wife's sane grief, heavy though it was and cruel, was a very different thing from the mad abandonment and wild insanity of those dreadful days before he had his great idea.

Many and frequent still were the dreadful throes of weeping and rebellions against Fate—but "planchette" could always bring distraction and comfort to the tortured mind, and the soothing belief in real presence and a genuine communion.

But there was no anodyne for the man's bitter grief, and the "planchette" became a hideous nightmare to him. Even his work was no salvation to him, for though the *Adjudant-Major* is a regimental staff officer, corresponding somewhat to our Adjutant—(the "Adjutant" is a non-com. in the French army)— and a very busy man, Gallais found that his routine duties were performed mechanically, and by one side of his brain as it were, while, undimmed, in the fore-front of his mind, blazed the baleful glare of a vast "planchette," in the flames of which his little son roasted and shrieked.

And still the daily tale of "messages" must be invented, and daily grew a greater and more distressing burden and terror.

How much longer could he go on, day after day, and several times a day, producing fresh communications, conversations, messages, ideas? How much longer could he go on inventing plausible and satisfactory answers to the questions that his wife put to the "spirit" communicant? How could Adjutant-Major Gallais of La Légion Étrangère describe Heaven and the environment, conditions, habits, conduct and conversations of the inhabitants of the Beyond? How much longer would he be able to use the jargon of his wife's books on Occultism and Spiritualism, study them as he might, without rousing her suspicions? The swindle could not have lasted a day had she not been only too anxious to believe, and only too ready to be deceived.

What would be the end of it all? What would his wife do if she found out that he had cheated her? Would she ever forgive him?   Would she leave him?   Would the shock of the disappointment kill her? Would she ever believe him again?

What *could* the end of it be?

He must stick it out—for life, if need be—and he was not an imaginative man.

What would be the end?

The end was—that she felt she must go home to France and see her boy's grave, tend it, pray by it, and give such comfort as she could to her poor mother, almost as much to be pitied as herself.

Gallais encouraged the idea. The change would be good for her, and he would be able to join her in a few months. Also this terrible "planchette" strain would cease for him, and he might recover his sleep and appetite. . . .

"To think that we shall be parted, this time to-morrow, my dearest Edouard," wept Madame Gallais, as they sat side by side in their bed-sitting-room, in the *Hôtel de la République* at Saigon. "I on the sea and you on your way back alone. If everything were not arranged, I would not go. Let us have a last 'planchette' with our son, and get to bed. We are having *petit déjeuner* at five, you know."

The Major racked his brain for something to write, as Madame went to her dressing-case for the little instrument (to the Major, an instrument of torture)—racked his brain for something he had not said before, and racked in vain. He grew hotter and hotter and broke into a profuse perspiration as she seated herself beside him. *Nom de nom de Dieu de Dieu de sort!* What could he write? Why had his brain ceased to operate?

Nombril de Belzébuth! Could he not make up one more lie after carrying on for weeks—weeks during which his waking hours—riding, drilling, marching along the muddy causeways between the rice-fields, working in his office, inspecting, eating, and drinking—had been devoted to hatching "messages," conversations, communications and lies, till he had lost health, weight, sleep, and appetite. . . .

No. . . . He could not write a single word, for his mind was absolutely blank.

Minutes passed.

Sweating, cursing, and praying, the unfortunate man sat in an agony of misery, and could not write a single word.

Would not *le bon Dieu* help him? Just this one last time? . . .

Minutes passed.

Not to have saved his life, not to have saved the life of his wife, not to have brought back *le petit Gingembre*, could the poor tortured wretch have written a single word. . . . What would his wife do when she discovered the cheat—for if no words came during the next minute or two he knew he must spring to his feet, make full confession, and throw himself upon his wife's mercy.

That or go mad.

What would she do? . . . Leave him for ever? . . . Spit upon him and call him "Liar," "Cheat," and "Heartless, cruel villain"?

Would the dreadful reaction and shock kill her?—deprive her of reason?

Suddenly he perceived that, with hands which were acres in extent, he was endeavouring to move a "planchette" the size of Indo-China—a "planchette" that was red-hot and of which the fire burnt into his brain. Its smoke and fumes were choking him; its fierce white light was blinding him; the thing was killing him.

By the time, several weeks later, that little Madame Gallais had nursed her husband back to sanity and consciousness, the first bitterness of grief was past and she herself could play the comforter.

"Oh, my Edouard," she wept upon his shoulder when first the brain-fever left him and he knew her, "we have lost our little Gingembre—but you have me, and, oh, my brave hero-husband, I have you. I shall weep no more." . . .

"Planchette" stands on Madame's desk—but she does not use it.

THE DEAD HAND

"The Dead Hand" is again one of those stories in which a group of people are sitting around telling stories. In this case it is a group of French army officers. One of them, d'Amienville, is a young, brash, highly opinionated Chasseurs lieutenant. The other main character is the older, grizzled, Foreign Legion veteran, Captain d'Armentières who relates the story. A remark is made about a psychic experience to which d'Amienville expresses disbelief. Captain d'Armentières counters with his story of being choked by a "dead hand". "The Dead Hand" was originally published in Stepsons of France *(1917), and reprinted in the magazine* The Thriller *(no. 296, October 6, 1934), an anthology titled* Mystery, *edited by A. K. Barton (1937),* Stories of the Foreign Legion *(Vallancey, 1945),* Tales of the Foreign Legion *(Vallancey, 1946), and* Dead Men's Boots *(1949).*

Chubby, cherubic, and cheerful, with the pure wholesome blood of his native Provence yet glowing in his cheeks, Extreme Youth was the only trouble really—and there are many worse diseases—of Lieutenant Archambaut Thibaut d'Amienville of the Chasseurs d'Afrique, of the glorious XIXth Army Corps of La République Française.

As he sat back from the table, fingering his glass, he looked exceedingly handsome, dashing, and romantic in his beautiful pale-blue uniform. But he had not found his level, and he was making some bad breaks. It does not always conduce to modesty and diffidence in a young man that his papa is a very prominent and powerful politician, and his mother a leader of Paris Society. As the deft native waiters, arrayed in spotless white, moved the table-cloth and set forth fresh glasses, ash-trays, shapely bottles and cigarette-boxes on the shining mahogany that reflected the electric lights like a mirror, he rushed in once again. There was no squashing him.

One has heard of people being young enough to know better—young enough, that is, to have high ideals, generosity, and purity of motive—but Lieutenant Archambaut Thibaut d'Amienville was young enough to know best. He was so young, so wise, and so well informed that he was known as *Général* and not *Lieutenant* d'Amienville among his intimates. And he was at the moment giving generously and freely to his seniors of the stores of his wisdom and knowledge.

Captain Gautier d'Armentières, of the First Battalion of La Légion Étrangère, scarred and war-worn hero of Tonquin, Dahomey, and Madagascar, beloved as few officers are beloved by the wild and desperate men he led, fine soldier and fine gentleman, remarked to the officer on his left—a gorgeous Major of Spahis, resplendent in scarlet cloak (huddled in which he shivered with fever), *ceinturon*, and full baggy trousers:

"So you are going to have another try for a lion?" But the Major had no time to reply for "Général" d'Amienville had caught the ultimate word. (He had promised his mamma a select consignment of lion-skins of his own procuring when he left for the wilds of Algiers and the Soudan, and she had helped in the purchase of the battery of sporting weapons that he had bought at the gun-shop in the Rue de la Paix, guiding his taste to the choice of "pretty ones with nice water-marking on the barrels," and dainty ornament in the way of engraving, chasing, damascening and mounting.)

"Lion?" said he quickly. "What you want for lion, d'Armentières, is impact, concussion, force—er—weight, a-ah-stunning blow. . . . It is absolutely useless, you know, for you to go and drill him through and through with neat little holes of which he is unaware, and which trouble him not at all. . . . None of your Mausers or Lebels, you know. . . ."

Eight pairs of eyes regarded the young gentleman without enthusiasm or affection; nay, with positive coldness.

The strong and clever face of one of the party, a Captain of Zouaves, looked somewhat Machiavellian, as, with a cold smile, he encouragingly murmured "Yes?"

Colonel Leon Lebrun, famous chief of Tirailleurs and old enough to have been the young gentleman's grandfather, assumed a Paul-at-the-feet-of-Gamaliel air, and with humility also said "Yes?"

"Yes," continued d'Amienville, "never take one of these small-bore toys, no matter what the muzzle-velocity. Get something with a good fat bore and a good fistful of cordite.

Then you know where you are and what you are doing. . . . I'd as soon go with my automatic pistol as with a small-bore. . . . And never go on foot—especially in those reedy places. And never touch a *tablier*—what the English call a *machan* when they put them up for tiger in their Indian colonies. . . . No good. . . . Suicide in fact. . . . What you want to do is to have a platform—like a sentry's *vue*—strongly lashed in the branches of a convenient high tree, near the 'kill,' put a mattress on it, and make yourself comfortable."

"And if, in effect, there be no tree?" respectfully inquired Médecin-Major Parme, twirling his huge moustache without revealing the expression on his thin lips.

"Oh-er-well, then, of course, you might—er—well, perhaps dig a pit and fence yourself round. You might, in fact, have a sort of cage. . . . Just as good for keeping wild beasts out as for keeping them in."

"Excellent!" murmured the Colonel. "Now *I* should never have thought of going lion-hunting in a cage. But original! Original! Of a cleverness! . . . How many lions have you shot?"

The flush of embarrassment deepened that of youth and juiciness in the plump cheek of the young officer.

"Oh-er-well, I have never actually *shot* any, you know," he replied, in some confusion, but still with a suggestion of having done something very similar—of having ridden them down with a hog-spear, or caught them on a rod and line.

"*Haven't* you?" asked Captain d'Armentières in apparent surprise. From the discomfort of his confession the youth quickly recovered with the attempted *tu quoque*—

"Have you?"

"Yes," admitted the Captain, hesitatingly.

"*Oh?*—and when did *you* shoot one, pray?" inquired d'Amienville, with a sceptical note, sufficiently impertinent to be irritating.

The Captain's uniform of dark blue and red was a very modest affair beside that of the young Chasseur—and, *nom de Dieu!* who was he to attempt a sneer at the son of Madame d'Amienville—not to mention of Monsieur d'Amienville, politician of international fame and importance ?

The young officer raised his absinthe to the light, crossed a leg, admired a neat boot, and glanced a trifle disdainfully at the grizzled, unfashionable old *barbare* of whom the elegant salons of Paris had never heard. (A mere St. Maizent man snubbing an alumnus of St. Cyr!)

"My last, about this time last year," was the reply.

"Your *last*? And how many, pray, have you shot?" asked d'Amienville languidly.

"*Eighty-three*," replied the officer of the Legion, fixing a bleak and piercing grey eye upon the youth.

Wry smiles wreathed the faces of the audience, and the "Général" changed the subject forthwith. As the fresh and verdant one was their fellow-guest (of d'Armentières), the others forbore to laugh aloud.

Drawing a bow at a venture, the Lieutenant had a shot at the horse, he having just purchased his very first pony.

"Excellent riding country, this," he observed patronizingly to his neighbour, a hard-bitten saturnine officer, hawk-eyed, hawk-nosed, and leathern-cheeked. "I shall do a lot of it. . . . Very keen on riding and awfully fond of horses. I love the *chasse au renard*. . . . Ah! Horses! I know something about them too. . . . A thing, most useful—to understand horses. It is not given to all. . . . Incredible lot to learn though. . . . A difficult subject. . . . Difficult. . . ."

"Very," acquiesced the neighbour, finding himself the more immediate recipient of the information.

"But yes—very. Any time you may be thinking of buying, let me know, and I shall be charmed to place my knowledge and experience at your disposal. Charmed. Yes, I will look the beast over. . . . Always best to take advice when buying a horse. Terrible rogues these Arabs. You are certain to be swindled if you rely on your own judgment. Cunning fellows these native *piqueurs*. Hide any defect from inexperienced eyes—bad hoofs, sand-crack, ring-bone, splint, wind-galls, *souffle*, sight, teeth, age, vice—anything. Charmed to give you my opinion at any time. . . . Try him for you too. . . ."

"Most extremely amiable of you, I'm sure. *Most* kind. A thousand thanks. I realize I have a terrible lot to learn about horses yet," replied the favoured one.

"Yes, they take a lot of knowing," replied the "Général," and, as the man rose, bade farewell to his host, saluted the company, and departed to catch the ten-fifteen to Oran, that young but knowing gentleman observed generously:

"An agreeable fellow that—a most amiable person. Who is he?"

"Vétérinaire-Colonel Blois!" replied d'Armentières. "Probably the cleverest veterinary-surgeon in the army. . . . You may know his standard work . . .' But Lieutenant d'Amienville again changed the subject hastily, and then scolded a servant for not bringing him what he had not ordered. Thereafter he was silent for nearly five minutes.

Some one mentioned Adjudant-Major Gallais and his curious end. (He dreamed that he saw his wife murdered by burglars in their little flat at Marseilles, was distraught until news came that such a tragedy had actually happened at the very time of the dream, and at once shot himself.)

"A very remarkable case of coincidence, to say the least of it," observed Captain d'Armentières. "Personally I should be inclined to call it something more."

But Lieutenant d'Amienville was a modern of the moderns, an agnostic, a sceptic.

"All bosh and rubbish," quoth he. "*Sottise*. . . . There is no such thing as this occultism, spiritualism, telepathy, and twaddle. To the devil with supraliminal, transliminal, subliminal, astral, and supernatural. There *is* no supernatural. . . ."

"So?" murmured a dapper little man in scarlet breeches and a black tunic which had the five-*galon*ed sleeve of a Colonel.

"All nonsense," continued the young gentleman. "All this that one hears about mysterious and inexplicable occurrences is always second-hand. Second-hand and third person. . . . Third person singular—very singular. Ha! Ha! . . . Yes, all rot and rubbish. Now, has anyone of *us* here ever had an experience of the supernatural sort? Not one, I'll be bound. Not one. . . . But we all know somebody who has. It's always the way. . . ."

"Well," remarked Captain d'Armentières, "I was once throttled by a Dead Hand—if you would call that an experience."

"I was speaking seriously," replied the Lieutenant loftily.

"So was I," answered the Captain coldly.

"What do you mean?" queried the youth, fearing the, to him,

worst thing on earth—ridicule.

"Precisely what I say," was the quiet reply. "I was once seized by the throat, and all but killed, by a Dead Hand, in the middle of the night as I lay in bed. . . . I give you my word of honour—and I request—and advise—you not to cast any doubt on my statement."

The pointed jaw of Lieutenant d'Amienville dropped, and he stared round-eyed and open-mouthed at the officer of the Legion, apparently sane and obviously sober, who could say such things seriously. . . . Could it be a case of this *cafard* of which he had heard so much? No—*le cafard* is practically confined to the rank and file—and this man was, moreover, as cool as a cucumber and as normal as the night. He glanced round the table at his fellow-guests. They looked expectant and interested. This *vieux moustache* was evidently a man of standing and consideration among them.

"Tell us the story, *mon gars*," said the Major of Spahis, pouring cognac into his coffee.

"Do," added the Captain of Zouaves.

"Let's go out into the garden and have it," proposed the Colonel of Tirailleurs Algériens, half rising. "May we, d'Armentières?"

"Yes—I must hear this," acquiesced the young Lieutenant with an air of open-mindedness, but reserved judgment.

"Come on, by all means," answered d'Armentières. "I should have thought of it before, Colonel"; and the party rose and strolled across the veranda out into the garden of the *Cercle Militaire*.

Legionnaire Jean Boule, or John Bull, standing at the gate leading into the high-road, and awaiting his officer as patiently as a good orderly should, thought the scene extraordinarily stage-like and theatrical, albeit he had seen it many times before.

The brilliant moonlight on the tall and beautiful plane-trees, the cypress and the myrtle, the orange, magnolia, wistaria, bougainvillea, the ivy-draped building of the *Cercle* with its hundreds of lights, the gorgeous scarlet of the Spahi, the pale blue of the Chasseur, the yellow and blue of the Tirailleur, the scarlet and black of the Legionary, and the other gay uniforms made up a picture as unreal as beautiful.

Gazing upon it, he thought of days when he, too, sat in such groups in such club-gardens, when Life went very well. In the distance, the famous band of the Legion was playing Gounod's *Serenade*—probably in the Public Gardens outside the Porte de Tlemçen. . . .

"*En avant, mon choux*," said the Médecin-Major, as the party settled into wicker chairs, and the bare-footed, silent servants ministered to its needs with cigarettes, cheroots, and weird liqueurs.

"And forthwith," added the Colonel, puffing a vast cloud as he lay back and gazed sentimentally at the moon.

"Well—as you like, gentlemen—but it was nothing. Just a queer little experience. It won't interest you much, I'm afraid," said d'Armentières.

Then Lieutenant d'Amienville commenced a dissertation upon auto-suggestion, illusion, and self-deception, but the remainder of Captain d'Armentières' guests intimated clearly to their host that they wanted his story, and wanted it at once.

"Have it for what it is worth, then," said that officer. "But I request Lieutenant d'Amienville clearly to understand that what I am about to tell you is *the absolute truth*—the plain and simple tale of what actually occurred to me personally. Moreover, should he, while believing in the honesty of my belief, doubt the trustworthiness of my observations and conclusions, I may mention that my *ordonnance* will be found waiting near the gate—and may be called and questioned. For he was concerned in the matter, and not only saw the marks upon my throat, but actually touched the Dead Hand which all but choked the life out of me."

The voice of the "Général" was stilled within him, but his face was very eloquent indeed.

"It happened in Haiphong," continued the quiet, cultured voice of the weary-looking man, "when the Legion sent big drafts out to Tonkin in '83. I was commanding a detachment then, with the rank of Lieutenant. We had disembarked at the mouth of the Red River into two old three-decker river-gunboats, and I had had an infernally busy day—what with the debarkation from the ship and then again at Haiphong, after the six-hour journey up the river. On top of all I had high fever.

"Now, before getting into bed that night, I turned out the lamp that hung on a nail on the wall, and then lay down, finished my cigarette, and turned out the tiny hand-lamp which I had brought in from the bathroom and placed on the little *petit-déjeuner* table beside my bed, noting, as I did so, that the matches were beside it. I always lock my door at night and sleep without a light, but with the means of getting a light easily accessible. Funny things are apt to occur at night in some parts of the shiny East. . . . I expect they've got electric light in Haiphong by now. . . . Well, in two minutes I was sound asleep—sleeping the sleep of the just and enjoying the reward of my good conscience, virtuous life, and hard work. . . ."

"*Va t'en, blagueur*," murmured Colonel Lebrun with a smile.

"An hour or two later, I awoke suddenly—awoke to the knowledge that I was being murdered, was dying, and, in effect, very nearly dead. Some one had me by the throat and was choking my life out with as deadly and scientific a grip as ever fastened upon a man's neck. . . . The human mind is curiously constituted, and, even in that moment, I tried to remember the name of a book about the garotters of India, the 'Thugs'—a book I had read many years before, when studying English—written by a Colonel of the Army of India. . . . 'Chinese garotters,' thinks I to myself, and realized that I was in for it, for I could no more yell for assistance than I could fly. There was my orderly sleeping on a rug in a little ante-chamber a few feet from me, and I could not call to him. I must face my fate alone and live or die without help from outside. I was terrified." . . .

One or two of his audience glanced at the medals and decorations on the speaker's breast (they included the *Croix de Guerre* and the *Médaille Militaire*) and smiled.

"I should have felt for his eyes and blinded him!" announced Lieutenant d'Amienville.

. . . "Simultaneously with the awakening to the knowledge that I was being throttled by some silent, motionless, invisible assailant, came my attempt to strike him, of course—to spring up, and to grapple with him; but, simultaneously again with the attempt, came the knowledge that my right arm was absolutely useless beneath his weight, and that I was pinned to the pillow, like a butterfly to a cork, by the weight and power of the hand that had me in its grip. Finding my right immovable, I naturally struck out with my left and hit again and again with all my strength—to find that I struck *nothing*—until, being at my last gasp, I grabbed at the hand that was choking me and strove to tear it from my throat.

"Even at that terrible moment I was startled at the extraordinary coldness of the hand I grasped. It was as deadly cold as it was horribly strong, and as brain reeled and senses failed, I seemed to visualize a terrible marble statue endowed with life and superhuman strength, leaning its cruel weight upon the frozen hand that clutched my throat. And I could not seize or even touch any part of this horrible assailant but the Hand. . . . And I tell you the thing was dead—dead and cold. . . . I was dying—throttled by a Dead Hand, and that is the simple truth." . . .

None of the party moved or spoke—not even d'Amienville. That, and the fact that scarcely a cigar or cigarette remained alight, were remarkable tributes to d'Armentières' dramatic and convincing way of speech. And those of the party who knew him well, also knew him to be incapable of telling a lie, when he had given his word that what he said was the truth.

. . . "Well, I have never believed in taking things lying down, so I tried once again to get up, and, putting all my heart and soul and strength into a mighty heave, I strove to throw my assailant off before I lost consciousness completely. . . . In vain. . . .

"All this takes time in the telling, but it must have taken mighty little time in the doing, for I was almost dead from suffocation when I first awoke.

"As I strained and tore at the hand, I struggled to rise. My body writhed, but my right arm budged not a fraction of an inch, and the grip on my throat perceptibly tightened, though I thought the limit had surely been reached. . . . I must get one breath, or ears and eyes and brain must burst. . . . Surely I was black in the face and my eyeballs were on my cheekbones? . . . I lived a lifetime in a second. . . . So this was the end and the finish of Gautier d'Armentières, was it? Here were to end all dreams of military glory and distinction, all visions of fine, quick death in action against the foes of La France? . . . A dog's death! To be slowly suffocated in my bed—choked to death by a cold Dead

Hand, a Hand without a tangible body. . . .

"As my frame was convulsed and my senses finally reeled in unconsciousness or death, I made my last wild attempt, and probably put forth such a violent concentration of coordinated effort as never before in my life—and, with a gasp and sob of thankfulness, I flung my assailant off!

"And, as he fell, he stabbed me in the arm.

"Yes—with the last vestige of my strength I flung it off, and the crash of falling lamp and table was the sweetest sound I ever heard, and the pain of the stab in my arm was absolutely welcome. . . . For I don't mind confessing that I prefer human, or rather *real*, antagonists when I have to fight—and when lamp and table smashed to the ground under its weight, and I felt myself knifed, I knew that this cold, dead hand belonged to something actual and tangible—something alive, something human. . . .

"But I have never touched anything that seemed more dead and cold, for all that.

"Well, my assailant was hardly on the ground before I was there too, for, although my right arm was absolutely useless from the stab, I meant to have him somehow. I hate being choked at night when I am getting my due and necessary sleep, and I wanted him badly. I was really annoyed about it all. ...

"But he wasn't there, and, as I sprang to my feet and struck and grabbed and clutched, I clutched and grabbed and struck—precisely nothing!

"My terror returned tenfold. Was the Thing supernatural after all? I had fallen practically on top of it and actually holding it—and it *was not*. . . . But—nonsense! The most violent and virulent Oriental djinn, spirit, ghost, devil, afrit, *esprit malin*, or demon, does not stab one, even if it throttles—as some of them are said to do. . . .

"I crouched still and silent with restrained breathing, hoping to hear other breathing or some movement.

"Perfect silence and stillness!

"I burst into a cold perspiration—as I imagined the thing to be behind me, and about to seize my neck again in its frozen, vice-like grip.

"I whirled around with extended arms, and then, rising to my feet, struck out in every direction, dealing *coups de savate* when my arms tired. And then again I crouched and listened and waited—with my hands at my throat.

"Perfect silence and stillness!

"And, do you know, my friends, it positively never occurred to me to cry out for help! . . . I suppose my faculties were all so engrossed in this strange struggle that no corner of my brain was free to think, '*One shout and Jean Boule will burst in your door, sword-bayonet in hand.*'" . . .

"More likely you wanted to see it out all by your little self, *mon ancien*," smiled Colonel Lebrun.

"But no, I assure you. I never thought to shout for help. . . . And then, as I put a hand to the floor, I touched the matches that had fallen with the table. And I thanked *le bon Dieu*. . . . With trembling fingers I struck a light—wondering what would be revealed to my staring eyes, and whether the light would be the signal for my death-blow. Should I get it in the back—or across the neck? Was it a common Chinese 'pirate'? I hoped so, . . . but they do not have dead hands and intangible bodies. . . .

"The match flared. . . .

"The room was empty. .. .

"Absolutely empty. And, look you, my friends, the door was still locked on the inside; there was no fireplace and chimney, and not so much as a cat could have escaped by the window without knocking down the articles which stood on the inner ledge of it—some little brass ornaments, a crude vase, and one or two framed photographs or pictures. I went cold all over. What had throttled me? What had stabbed me? Where was the cold Dead Hand which I had grasped? . . .

"I lit the wall-lamp.

"There lay the table, overturned in the struggle. There lay the little lamp which I had carried in from the neighbouring bathroom. Its glass chimney was shattered and oil was running from its brass reservoir. And there, in my right arm, was the great, gaping stab.

"Going to the mirror, I saw at a glance that there were marks of fingers on my throat. . . . *And I knew that nothing bigger than a rat could have left the room!*

"I felt that I had had enough of mystery in solitude, and remembered my orderly. I was weak and faint from the awful struggle, and a little sick from the stab. . . . Also, my friends, I was frightened. . . . A murderous foe who can throttle and stab does not lock the door on the inside as he leaves the room, look you, and neither does he climb through a small window in silence without disturbing bric-à-brac upon the sill. . . .

"I unlocked the door, and shouted to my Jean Boule. He replied on the instant, and came running.

"He must have thought me mad when he heard my tale—until I directed his attention to the stab in my arm and the finger-marks on my neck. . . .

"He stared at the débris on the floor, at the undisturbed ornaments on the window-ledge, at the door, and finally at the marks on my person.

"'Why does not Monsieur le Capitaine bleed?' said he suddenly. 'Has he used anything to stop the hæmorrhage so successfully?' and he took my arm in his hands.

"Sure enough—no drop of blood had flowed from the deep stab in my forearm.

"'Why, the arm is dead,' cried Jean Boule, as he felt it. 'What have you been doing to it, mon Capitaine? . . . Excuse me' . . . and he placed a thumb on each side of the stab, opened it, and peered. Then he laughed in his quiet gentlemanly way, and glanced at the smashed lamp.

"'I thought so,' he said. 'Glass. No circulation. The hand dead,' and he laughed again.

"'What do you mean, Légionnaire?' I asked, nettled by his amusement.

"'Why—Monsieur le Capitaine has had a great and terrible fight *with himself*—and won. He went to sleep on his right side with his right arm raised and bent over his neck—and the arm also went to sleep as the circulation ceased, owing to the position—and Monsieur le Capitaine got hold of his throat and choked himself. Then he had nightmare, *cauchemar*, turned on his back, and woke up choking, and it was some time before he could budge the cold, stiff arm. . . . When he did, he flung it straight on to the lamp, broke the thing, and cut himself to the bone.' . . .

"And so it was! . . .

"But I contend that *I have been throttled by a Dead Hand,*

d'Amienville. . . ."

Lieutenant d'Amienville made a strange noise in his throat and then rose and escaped from the circle of mocking eyes.

It was felt that Captain d'Armentières had not only moved an immovable arm, but had, as the droll English say, "pulled" an unpullable leg.

THE GIFT

"The Gift" is another story related by Captain d'Armentières in response to comments from the young, brash, opinionated Chasseurs lieutenant, d'Amienville. The topic was gratitude and ingratitude, with d'Armentières telling the story of the most important gift he had ever received: a sausage. John Bull, one of the main characters in Wren's first novel of the Foreign Legion (and a recurring character in many short stories) is the person who bestows the gift. One of the more interesting aspects of this story is Wren's descriptions of being on active duty in Tonkin. I am sure that any veteran of the US-Vietnam War will recognize and sympathize with the descriptions. "The Gift" has appeared in Stepsons of France *(1917) and was reprinted in* Dead Men's Boots *(1949).*

It was Guest Night at the Spahis' mess.

"What *I* complain of is the utter absence of gratitude among natives," said "Général" Archambaut Thibaut d'Amienville of the Chasseurs d'Afrique of the XIXth Army Corps of La République Française. "It is highly significant that there is no word for 'Thank you' in the vernacular, isn't it? . . . If you do a native a good turn, he either wonders what you want of him, or else casts about in his mind for the reason why you want to propitiate him. If you had cause to punish one of your Spahis and did not do it, he would think you were afraid to. Kindness is in their eyes pure weakness. If you forgo vengeance, it *must* be because you think the offender may avenge that vengeance. No, gratitude doesn't flourish under a tropical sun." . . . Lieutenant d'Amienville was very young and therefore very cynical.

"Is it a plant of very hardy growth under a temperate one?" inquired Captain Gautier d'Armentières of the First Battalion of the Legion. "I seem to have heard complaints, and I fancy that poets from the days of Homer to those of this morning have had something to say about it."

"Quite so," agreed Médecin-Major Parme; "but pass me the matches, and I will promise a brief pang of gratitude. . . . Quite so. . . . If a fellow does you a really good turn, he is strongly

51

inclined to like you for evermore, and you are equally strongly disposed to regard him as a nuisance, and his mouldy face as a reminder of the time when you had to *faire la lessive*[11] or were in some fearful scrape. . . . I could name a certain absinthe-sodden old Colonel who absolutely loathes me for having saved him, body and soul, some years ago when he had been betting (and, of course, losing, as all people who bet do) and had then gone to Monte Carlo to put everything right at the gaming-tables! What made it worse was the fact that the departed francs were rather the property of Madame la République than of the Colonel. And Madame prefers to do her own gambling. His position, one Sunday night, was that Monday morning must find him with gold in his pocket or lead in his brain. I found the gold, as I had been at school with him, and had stayed with his people a lot . . . but I am sure he merely remembers a very shady passage in his career every time he sees me, and loathes me in consequence. He paid the debt off long ago, too."

"I believe you are right," agreed Colonel Lebrun. "One uses the expression '*debt* of gratitude,' and nobody really likes being in debt. . . . The gratitude is rarely paid though. I suppose it is because the creditor of gratitude occupies the higher ground, and one resents being on the lower."

"I certainly once lost a friend by doing him a kindness," put in Adjudant-Major Berthon of the Legion, who was also dining at the Spahis' mess. "This was a loan case, too, and a slight coolness ending in a sharp frost followed immediately upon it. . . . And it wasn't my fault the coolness arose, I am sure."

"Of course the benefactor always likes the beneficiary better than the beneficiary likes the benefactor," said the cynical "Général" d'Amienville, "and the kind action always dwells longer in the mind of the doer than in that of the receiver. Far longer. Always."

"Not always," observed Captain d'Armentières. "Only yesterday . . ."

"*Always*," contradicted d'Amienville.

"I was about to say," continued d'Armentières, "that, only yesterday, I reminded a man of a good turn he did me years ago,

---

[11] See up everything.

and he had clean forgotten it. . . . And it was a deed I could not forget if I lived to be a hundred years old."

"I simply don't believe a man could give you half of his kingdom, or save your valuable life or honour, and forget all about it," replied the "Général."

"I did not say he gave me a half of his kingdom or saved my valuable life or honour," was the quiet answer. "I said he did me a good turn and had absolutely forgotten the incident though I have not, and never shall. I feel the deepest gratitude towards him and always will. I should be very glad of an opportunity of proving the fact." . . .

"A very noble sentiment," sneered the young gentleman.

"No," said d'Armentières patiently. "I am not concerned to exhibit my high morality, fine nature, and noble sentiments, but am stating an example in opposition to your theory; a fact of memory—the respective memories of benefactor and beneficiary. He had forgotten doing the kindness, while I had remembered receiving it."

"What was the nature of the action, if one might inquire?" put in Médecin-Major Parme.

"Yes, what did he do, *mon salop*?" added Colonel Lebrun. "Surrender the beauteous damsel whom you both loved, with the hiccuping cry, 'Take her. She is thine,' and thenceforth hide a breaking heart beneath a writhing brow or a wrinkling tunic or something?"

"Did he leap into the raging flood, or only place his huge fortune at your disposal? What was the noble deed?" asked Adjudant-Major Berthon.

"It was a gift," replied d'Armentières, smiling. "A free, unsolicited, unexpected, magnificent gift."

"And he had *forgotten* it?" asked d'Amienville, with cold incredulity.

"Absolutely. But I never shall," said d'Armentières.

"And pray, what was this magnificent gift?" sneered d'Amienville. "A priceless horse, a mistress, an estate, a connoisseur's collection, an invaluable secret, your freedom—or what? What wonderful thing did he present to you and forget?"

"A sausage," was the grave answer.

The Spahis roared with laughter at their unpopular brother-officer. He was their guest, but they could not forbear to laugh. A very little goes a long way in the matter of wit in a bored mess, exiled from Home and the larger interests of life.

The "Général" coloured hotly, and remarked that some people were doubtless devilish funny—in season and out of season.

"I assure you it is my misfortune and not my fault if I am funny," was the grave statement of the Legionary. "I have been the recipient of other kindnesses, but not one of them has made such a mark on the tablets of my memory as that sausage."

"They do make marks, I know," observed Médecin-Major Parme. "My wife threw one at me once, just as I was going out to call on the Commander-in-Chief-in-Algeria. He noticed the mark before I did."

"Tell us the touching tale," put in Colonel Lebrun. "Were you on a raft in mid-ocean with one sausage between you and death, and did he say, 'Thy belly is greater than mine,' or 'Your bird,' or something?"

"Surely he'd remember that," observed the sapient d'Amienville.

"No. 'Twas thus," said d'Armentières. "You Spahis don't, for your sins, get sent to Indo-China. We do. And it can be more truly damnable along the Red River than in any desert station in the Sahara. You *have* got the sun, though you grumble at it, and too much heat is always better and less depressing than too little, to my way of thinking. What did Dante know of Hell when he had never been in a place consisting wholly of muddy water and watery mud—with nothing else for hundreds of square miles—except fever, starvation, dysentery, and the acutest craving for suicide? Yes. A low black sky of wet cotton wool, a vast river of black, muddy water, and its banks vast expanses of black watery mud. Nothing else to see—but much to feel. I was a young soldier then—a private of the Legion in my first year. . . ."

Captain d'Armentières paused. No one moved or spoke. It was not easy to "get him going"—but it was worth a lot of trouble, for d'Armentières was a man of very great experience, very great courage, and very great ability. Soldier, philosopher, reformer, hero, thinker, and something of a saint.

"Yes—you can go for weeks along the Red River of Tonkin, in an old stinking sampan, drenched, chilled to the bone, shivering, until you envy the Annamese boatmen in their straw hut in the stern—and see nothing but clouds, water, and mud, save when the unceasing rain is too heavy for you to see anything at all. If God is very good, you *may* perhaps see a castor-oil plant sailing along in the water to tell that there are other human beings somewhere in the terrible world of mud, water, fog, clouds, and rain—Annamese peasants who have sown castor-oil plants in the mud, apparently for the pleasure of seeing that accursed river change its course in order to engulf them.

"I remember wondering why I, why any single one of my Company, consented to live another day. . . . You Spahis and Chasseurs, Zouaves and Tirailleurs Algériens, Turcos and others of the XIXth Army Corps talk of your desert hardships—thirst, *cafard*, Arabs, heat, *ennui*. . . . Pah! I have tried both, and I'd serve a year in the Sahara rather than a week in the Annam jungles in the rains. I remember asking the man to whom I have been referring, my benefactor, an Englishman calling himself John Bull, or Jean Boule, why *he*, for example, went on living.

"'I don't know,' he replied. 'Partly hope of better things, I suppose. Partly a feeling that suicide is cowardice, and partly the strongest instinct of the human mind—that of self-preservation.'

"And yet, he was obviously a very unhappy man—as any refined person of breeding and education must be, in the ranks of the Legion. I pondered this until, night falling, the boatmen steered for the shore and anchored our junk. The happy souls then shut themselves in their straw hut and caroused on *shum-shum*, the poor man's absinthe in China—an awful rice-spirit— while we huddled, foodless, sodden, and frozen in that ceaseless rain, fog, and bitter wind. . . . Who would not drink himself insensible and unconscious when there was nothing of which to be sensible and conscious but misery of the acutest? . . . It always interests me to hear the comfortably-placed rail against the drunkenness of the poor and wretched. . . . What would not the smuggest bourgeois Bonpère not have given, had he been with us that night, to drown his shuddering soul in the vilest form of alcohol, and escape that bitter fog, fever, hunger, sickness, and awful ache; the mosquitoes, stench, pain, and homeless, lonely misery. . . . When the 'Black Flags' came, with the full moon, I was glad. I would have consented to fall into their hands alive rather than not die—and they could have taught the Holy Inquisition a whole language and literature of torture of which the Inquisition only knew the alphabet. . . . Yes. I knew I had malarial fever, and I feared I had yellow fever. I knew I had dysentery, and I feared I had cholera. I knew I had an appalling cold and cough, and I feared I had consumption. I can now smile at myself as I was then—but I can also make allowances, for I was a starving, fever-wrecked child of seventeen—nearly dead with dysentery. . . . The bullets of the Black Flags were striking all around us, and it was a case of attacking them for our own safety. They were so close and had the range so well that I suspected our boatmen. I remember old Ivan Plevinski suddenly grunted hideously, heaved himself to his feet, removed his *képi*, and bowed toward the bank. '*Merci, messieurs*,' he gasped, '*Milles remerciments. Je vous remercie. Slava Bogu,*[12]' and died. I envied old Ivan Plevinski, and, judging by his way of life, decided that it would not be from cold that he would suffer in the Hereafter. . . .

"Meanwhile, John Bull, by right of his superior ability, experience, personality, and force, had taken command, and the sampan was being poled and hauled ashore. I tried to take a hand at heaving-in the anchor-rope, but fell on it from sheer weakness and was kicked clear of it. As the junk grounded in the mud, the Legionaries sprang over the side, led by John Bull, and struggled through the mud toward the swamp-jungle whence the bullets came. I staggered as far as I could, and then fell and began slowly to sink in the black clayey mud. No—I was not afraid, only very glad to die. And half delirious, watched the fight in the moonlight. I remember being bitterly disappointed that I could not distinguish the features of a man who, on his half-engulfed arms and knees, was vomiting blood just in front of me. I did so want to know who had 'got it,' for he also would accompany me and Ivan Plevinski to the Judgment Seat. I wondered what St. Peter would say if the fellow vomited blood on the doorstep of the Gates of Heaven. Then I became unconscious, delirious. . . . The junk following ours—in which was Lieutenant Egrier, as he then was—came ashore, took the 'pirates' in flank, and drove

---

[12] Glory to God.

them off. . . .

"All this leading up to the Sausage of Contention" (with a little bow and smile in the direction of Lieutenant d'Amienville, fingering his wine-glass and endeavouring to maintain a cynical smile). . . . "You know Egrier's bluff, jolly way. 'What would you like, Jean Boule—recommendation for the *Croix de Guerre* or one of my tinned sausages,' he cried, as he approached Jean, who was pulling me out of the mud. I had broken into a perspiration, and was my own man again by then, and desperately anxious to live. (What was wrong with a world that held 'recommendations,' the *Croix de Guerre*, the *Médaille Militaire*, promotion, a career of glory fighting for La Belle France?)

"'A sausage, mon Lieutenant,' replied Jean Boule, laying me on a bed he had made of mangrove twigs, straw from the boat, and his *capote*.

"'Wise philosopher,' laughed Egrier. 'You shall have two— one for distinguished conduct in the field and one for wisdom.'

"He was as good as his word. Before our sampans resumed their way to Phu-lang-Thuong, he gave Jean two sausages from the tin he opened. As I live, that gaunt, starving man cooked them both, gave one to me, and made the rest of our boat-load cast lots for the other.

"I met him recently. He is still *Soldat deuxième classe*, for he has consistently refused promotion. When I shook him by the hand, he remembered me, but he had absolutely and completely forgotten the episode of the sausage.

"I have not—and I regard his gift to me that day on the Red River in Tonkin as one of the noblest ever given. . . . He is my orderly now. . . . Have you ever starved, d'Amienville? . . . No?"
. . .

THE DESERTER

"The Deserter" is the story of a recently married couple who, on a voyage to Australia, stop in Marseilles and go ashore for a few hours. The husband is identified as a deserter from the Legion and is arrested by a former Sergeant (now a Lieutenant) of the Legion. Captain d'Armentières appears as a minor character in this story. "The Deserter" first appeared in Stepsons of France *(1917) and was reprinted at least three times in the Sunday newspapers of 1927: most likely in the magazine section (possibly the supplement,* This Week Magazine*). The known newspapers are the* Oakland Tribune *(May 22, 1927), the* Los Angeles Times *(June 5, 1927), and the Ohio* Mansfield News *(November 27, 1927). The story was also reprinted in the magazine* The Thriller *(no. 305, December 8, 1934), and in* Stories of the Foreign Legion *(Murray, 1947).*

As she stood on the deck beside her lover-husband and gazed upon the thrillingly beautiful panorama of Marseilles, there was assuredly no happier woman in the world. As he looked at the rapt face and wide-opened glorious eyes of the lovely girl beside him there can scarcely have been a man as happy.

They had been married in England a week earlier, were on their way to his vast house and vaster estate in Australia, and had come round by sea, instead of suffering the miseries of the "special" across France (which saves a week to leave-expired returning Anglo-Indians).

Happy! Her happiness was almost a pain. As a child she had childishly adored him; and now he had returned from his wanderings, after a decade of varied, strenuous life—to adore her. Life was too impossibly, hopelessly wonderful and beautiful. . . . He, who had been everywhere, done everything, been everything—soldier, sailor, rancher, planter, prospector, hunter, explorer—had come Home for a visit, and laid his heart at the feet of a country mouse. Happy! His happiness frightened him. After more than ten years of the roughest of roughing it, he had "made good" (exceeding good), and on top of good fortune incredible, had, to his wondering bewilderment, won the love of the sweetest, noblest, fairest, and most utterly lovable and desirable woman in the world. She whom he had left a child had grown into his absolute ideal of Woman, and had been by some miracle reserved for him.

And which would now know the greater joy in their travels— he in showing her the fair places of the earth and telling her of personal experiences therein, or she in being shown them by this adored hero who had come to make her life a blessed dream of joy? Not that the fair places of the earth were necessary to their happiness. They could have spent a happy day in London on a wet Sunday, or at the end of Southend pier on a Bank Holiday, or in a prison-cell for that matter—for the mind of each to the other a kingdom was.

"Would you like to go ashore? . . . 'Madame, will you walk and talk with me,' in the *Cannebière*?" he asked.

"Of *course*, we must go ashore, Beloved Snail," was the reply. "I have no idea what the *Cannebière* is—but," and she hugged his arm and whispered, "you can always 'give me the keys of Heaven,' and walk and talk with me There." (He was "Beloved Snail" when he was a Bad Man and late for meals; "Bill" when he was virtuous or forgiven.)

The ship being tied up, and a notice having guaranteed that she would on no account untie before midnight, this foolish couple, who utterly loved each other, walked down the gangway, passed the old lady who sells balloons and the old gentleman who sells deck-chairs, the young lady who sells glorious violets and the young gentleman who sells un-glorious "field"-glasses; through the echoing customs-shed and out to where, beside a railway-line, specimens of the genus *cocher* lie in wait for those who would drive to the boulevards and in hope for those who know not that four francs is ample fare.

To the sights of Marseilles he took her, enjoying her enjoyment as he had enjoyed few things in his life, and then in the *Cannebière* dismissed the fiacre.

"In Rome you must roam like the Romans," he observed. "In Marseilles you must sit on little chairs in front of a café and see the World and his Wife (or Belle Amie) go by."

"Fancy sitting outside a public-house in Regent Street or the Strand and watching Londoners go by!" said the girl. "Isn't it extraordinary what a difference in habits and customs one finds by travelling a few miles? Think of English officers sitting, in uniform, on the pavement, like those are, and drinking in public," . . . and she pointed to a group of French officers so engaged. "Do let's go and sit near them," she added. "I have never seen soldiers dressed in pale blue and silver, and all the colours of the rainbow. . . . Aren't they pretty—dears!" . . .

"Their uniforms look quaint to the insular eye, madam, I admit," he replied, as he led the way to an unoccupied table near the brilliant group, "but they are not toy soldiers by any means. They all belong to regiments of the African Army Corps, the Nineteenth, and there isn't a finer one on earth."

"Darling, you know *everything*," smiled his wife. "Fancy knowing a thing like that now! I wonder how many other Englishmen know anything about this African Army and that it is the Ninety-Ninth. Now how do you know?"

It was his turn to smile, and he did so somewhat wryly.

"What will you have?" he asked, as an aproned *garçon* hovered around. "Coffee or *sirop* or—how would you like to be devil-of-a-fellow and taste a sip of absinthe? . . . You'll hate it."

"No, thank you, Bill-man. Is the syrup golden-syrup or syrup-of-squills or what? No, I'll have some coffee and see if it is."

"Is what?"

"Coffee." . . .

Meanwhile an elderly, grizzled officer, with a somewhat brutal face, was staring hard and rudely at the unconscious couple. He wore a dark blue tunic with red-tabbed and gold-braided collar and cuffs, scarlet overalls, and a blue and red *képi*. So prolonged was his unshifting gaze, so fierce his frown, and so obvious his interest, that his companions noticed the fact.

"Is the old hog smitten with *la belle Anglaise*, I wonder, or what?" murmured a handsome youth in the beautiful pale blue uniform of the Chasseurs d'Afrique to an even more gorgeous officer of Spahis.

"I have never known Legros take the faintest interest in women," replied the other. "There will be a beastly *fracas* if the husband glances this way. He'll promise Legros to *ponch ees 'ead* if he thinks he's being rude—as he is."

Certainly the elderly and truculent-looking officer *was* being rude, for not only was he staring with a hard, concentrated glare, but he was leaning as far forward as he could, the better to do it. Anyone—man, woman, or child—being conscious of this deliberate, searching gaze, must resent it. It was that of a gendarme, examining the face of a criminal and endeavouring to "place" him and recollect the details of his last encounter with him, or of a *juge d'instruction* examining a criminal in that manner which does not find favour in England.

"It is as good as sitting in the stalls of a theatre, sitting here and seeing all these varied types go by, isn't it, Bill?" observed the girl. "Oh, *do* look at *that*—that boy in brown velvet and a forked beard!"

"We are sitting in the Stalls of the Theatre of Life, my child," was the sententious reply, but in reality they were sitting nearer to the Pit.

The brutal-looking officer scratched the back of his neck slowly up and down with the forefinger of his left hand, a sure sign that he was wrestling with an elusive reminiscence. For a moment he took his eyes from the face of the Englishman and looked sideways at the pavement, cudgelling his brains, ransacking the cells of his memory. With a muttered oath at failure to recapture some piece of long-stored information, he put his hand into the inside pocket of his tunic and produced a tiny flat case. From this he took a pair of pince-nez and adjusted them upon the bridge of his broad, short nose. From the slowness and clumsiness of his movements it was evident that he had only just taken to glasses, or else wore them very seldom.

The latter was the case, as Lieutenant Legros considered spectacles of any kind a most unmilitary and *pékinesque* adjunct to uniform.

A quiet, gentlemanly-looking officer, a Captain, wearing a similar uniform to that of Legros, observed the action.

"Evidently something interests our friend beyond ordinary," he remarked, and followed the look that the elderly Lieutenant again fixed upon the Englishman, whom the Captain now noticed for the first time.

Sitting with his back to the road, and almost facing Legros, he got a better view of the Englishman's features than did that deeply interested officer, who, without reply, continued his searching scrutiny. Evidently a person of great powers of concentration. As his glance fell upon the young couple, the Captain started slightly and then looked away.

"Who's for a stroll?" he remarked, half rising. But his suggestion was not adopted, for glasses were charged, cigarettes alight, the shade of the café and awning very agreeable, and the sunshine hot without.

"Have an *apéritif* first, *mon ami,* and be restful," said a Zouave officer, and tinkled the little table-bell loudly.

The Englishman half-consciously turned toward the sound, and looked away again without noticing the baleful, steady glare fixed upon him through the glasses of the Lieutenant.

"*Dame!*" grunted that officer, and smote his brow in an agony of exasperation at the failure of his memory. . . . Curse it! Was he getting old? He had the fellow's name and the circumstances of his case on the tip of his tongue, so to speak—at the tips of his fingers, as it were—and he could not say the word he was bursting to say; could not lay his twitching mental fingers on the details. . . . He *knew*. . . . He was right. . . . He would have it in a minute. . . .

A paper-boy passed the long front of the café and shouted some wholly unintelligible word as he gazed over the serried ranks of chairs and loungers.

"What does he say, Bill?" asked the girl. "It sounds like *Barin*. How ill the poor lad looks! Fancy having to sell papers for a living when you are starving and horribly ill, as he obviously is," and as her hand stole to her charitable purse, she gratefully thought of the utter security, peace, comfort, and health of *her* life—now that Bill had linked it to his. . . . What was the phrase? . . . Yes—she had "hitched her wagon to a star"; her poor little homely wagon to the glorious and brilliant star of her Bill's career. . . . The inquisitorial Lieutenant used the paper-boy for the purposes of his tactics. Rising, he made his way between the chairs and the groups of *apéritif*-drinking citizens, to where the boy stood, bought a paper, and returned by a route which brought him full face-to-face with the Englishman. Recognition was instantaneous and mutual. The brutal countenance of the elderly Lieutenant was not improved by a sardonic smile and look of mean and petty triumph as he thrust an outstretched index-finger in the Englishman's face and harshly grunted.

"Henri Rrrobinson!" and then laughed a sneering, hideous cackle.

Staring in utter bewilderment from the French officer to her husband, the girl saw with horror that his jaw had dropped, his mouth and eyes were gaping wide, and he had gone as white as a sheet.

"Sergeant Legros!" he whispered.

"Lieutenant Legros," grunted the other.

What had happened? What in the name of the Merciful Father was this? Was she dreaming? Her husband looked deathly. He seemed paralysed with fright.

The Lieutenant half turned, and shouted to a couple of sombre and mysterious-looking gens d'armes who had been standing for some time on the little "island" under the big lamp-post in the middle of the road. As they approached, the Englishman rose to his feet.

"Listen, darling!" he hissed. "Get out of this quick—to the ship. Take a *fiacre* and say '*P. and O. bateau.*' I'll join you all right. They have . . ."

The Lieutenant put a heavy hand on his shoulder and swung him round.

"Arrest this man," said he to the gens d'armes, "and take him to Fort St. Jean. He is a deserter, one Henri Rrrobinson, from the First Battalion of the Foreign Legion. Deserted from Sidi-bel-Abbès eight years ago. But *I* knew the dog. Aha!"

The group of officers whom Legros had just left, joined the gathering crowd.

"Poor devil!" said Captain d'Armentières. He too had recognized the *soi-disant* Henry Robinson. . . . "Poor girl!" he added. "Poor little soul!" She looked like *une nouvelle mariée* too. Of course Legros had only done his duty—curse him. Curse him a thousand times for a blackguardly, brutal ruffian. The girl was going to faint. . . . Her wedding-ring looked brand-new. "If this is his wedding night, he'll spend it in the *salle de police* of Fort St. Jean," he reflected. "If he is on his honeymoon, he'll spend it in the *cellules* until the General Court-Martial at Oran gives him a few years *rabiau* with the Zephyrs. If he survives that, which is improbable, he will finish his five years of Legion service. No—she won't see much of him during the next decade. . . . Poor little soul!"

The gens d'armes duly arrested the deserter. He caught the eye of the Captain.

"Captain d'Armentières," said he, "you are a French gentleman. This lady is my wife. We have been married a week. I beg of you to see her safe on board the P. and O. steamer *Maloja*, which we have just left, for an hour's visit here."

"I will do so," said d'Armentières.

A fat and kindly Frenchman, who understood English, translated for the benefit of the crowd. It became intensely sympathetic—at least with the girl. The French, for some reason, imagine their Foreign Legion to be composed of Germans, and the French do not love Germans. . . . And then, having commended his wife to d'Armentières (whom he had liked and admired in the past when he had played the fool's prank of joining the Legion "for a lark"), he thought rapidly and clearly. . .
.

If they once got him inside Fort St. Jean (the clearing-house for drafts and details going to, and coming from, Algeria— recruits, convalescents, leave-expired, all sorts; Legionaries, Zouaves, Turcos, Spahis, Tirailleurs) he was done. In a short time he would be a convict, in military-convict dress, enduring the living-death of existence in the Zephyrs, the terrible Disciplinary Battalion, compared with whose lot that of the British long-sentence convict at Dartmoor, Portland, or Wormwood Scrubbs is a bed of roses in the lap of luxury. After that—back to the Legion *if* he were alive to finish his five years, of which there were four unexpired. And his wife—stranded, without money, in Marseilles, unless d'Armentières got her to the ship. And what would she do then—at the end of the voyage? . . . God help them! . . . A few minutes ago—happiness unspeakable, safety, security, peace, all life before them. Now— in a few minutes he would be in gaol and his adored, adoring wife a deserted, friendless stranger in a strange land. . . . Would they *allow* d'Armentières to take her to the ship? Would they want her to give evidence—put her in some kind of prison until the Court-Martial sat? Suppose d'Armentières had not been there, and she had been left to the tender mercies of Legros—or utterly deserted, fainting on a café chair. . . .

Well, things couldn't be much worse (or *could* they) if he "resisted the police," assaulted the duly-appointed officers of the law in the execution of their duty, and made a break for liberty. No, things couldn't be worse. Neither he nor she would survive the next ten years. And there was a *chance*, or the ghost of a shadow of a chance. The deck of the *Maloja* was English soil, and they could not lay a finger on him there. If only she were safe on board, he'd make the attempt. There *was* a chance—and he had always taken the sporting chance, all his life. . . . And this vile cur of a Legros! He had many a score to pay off to Sergeant Legros—the prize bully of the XIXth Army Corps. Now *this*! If he could only have his hands at the throat of Legros. As these thoughts flashed through his brain, "May I say farewell to my wife and see her into a *fiacre* with you, Captain d'Armentières?" he asked. He appeared to be as cool as he was pale. The Captain was the senior officer present.

"Yes," he said. "I will drive her as quickly as possible to the ship," and willing hands helped the fainting girl into the *fiacre*. . . . Was she dying? As she lost her hold and sank into the bottomless depths of unconsciousness she was finally aware that her husband winked at her violently. That wink, in a face which was a pallid, tragic mask, was the most dreadful and heartrending thing she had ever seen. Anyhow, it meant some kind of reassurance which he could not put into words without disclosing some plan to his captors. She fainted completely, in the act of wondering whether this was merely that he was putting a good face on it and pretending for her benefit, or whether he really had a plan. Anyhow, she was to go to the ship—and, in any case, she was dying of a broken heart. . . .

As he watched his wife driven rapidly away, the Englishman formulated his plans.

He would delay as long as he could in order that his wife might be on board the ship before he reached it, if ever he did.

He would go quietly and willingly—but as slowly as possible—while the road to Fort St. Jean was the road to the ship. He would then break away from his pursuers and run for it. He would show them what an old Oxford miler and International

Rugger forward could do in the way of running and dodging, and, perchance, what sort of a fight an amateur champion heavy-weight could put up.

But strategy first, strength and skill afterwards, for he was playing a terrible game, with his wife's happiness at stake, not to mention his own liberty. With a groan, he artistically smote his knees together and sank to the ground. That would gain a little time anyhow, and they'd hardly carry him to Fort St. Jean, nor waste a cab-fare on the carcase of a Legionary.

He wasn't quite certain as to the nearest way from the Cannebière to Fort St. Jean, but he remembered that it was down by the waterfront. Yes, he could again see its quaint old tower, like a lighthouse, and its drawbridged moat, as he closed his eyes. Part of the way to it would be the way to the P. and O. wharf at Mole C, or whatever it was, anyhow. Would they take him by tram? That might complicate matters. If they were going to do that, should he make his break for liberty at once, or on the journey, or at the end of it? It would be comparatively easy to make a dash before or after the tram-ride, but they'd surely never let him escape them from a crowded tram. Would they handcuff him? If so, that would settle it. He'd fight and run the moment handcuffs were produced. You can't run in handcuffs, although you think you can. Would they shoot? It would be Hell to be winged in sight of the ship. Was the P. and O. wharf British soil, as well as the ship?

Almost certainly not.

Lieutenant Legros kicked him in the ribs.

"Get up, *tricheur*," he shouted. He was in his element, and fairly gloated over his victim, who only groaned and collapsed the more.

To those of the crowd who realized that he was an Englishman, he was an object of pity; to those who concluded that, being a Legionary, he was a German, he was merely an object of interest.

The officers who had been sitting with Legros departed in some disgust, and the crowd changed, eddied, and thinned. . . . Only a sick man being attended to by a couple of gens d'armes!

These latter grew a little impatient. The sooner they could dispose of this fine fellow the better, but they certainly weren't going to march to Fort St. Jean at the request of a Lieutenant of Legionaries. Let the army do its own dirty work. They'd run him in all right to the nearest lock-up, and he could be handed over to the military authorities, to be dealt with, whenever they liked to fetch him. To the devil with all Légionnaires, be they deserters or Lieutenants! "He had better be taken to the police-station on a stretcher, mon Lieutenant," suggested one of them. "It would appear that he has fainted."

"Stretcher!" roared Legros, and spat. "Pah! That is not how we deal with swine of Légionnaires who sham sick. Stretcher! Drag him face downward by one toe at the tail of a dust-cart more likely!"

Oho! Police-station, was it? Not Fort St. Jean immediately. And where might the nearest police-station be, wondered the prostrate Englishman. He must not let them get him there. The boat would sail at midnight, whether he were on board or not—and once the cell door closed on him it would not open till the morning.

Perhaps he had better take his leave at once. Unless they went in the direction of the docks for some part of the way it would be a cruelly punishing run. . . . Just as bad for them though, and he'd back himself against any of these beefy old birds for a four-mile race. . . .

His wife must be half-way there by now—more, if d'Armentières urged the *cocher*, as he would.

Was it likely that d'Armentières would collect a guard of gens d'armes, dock police, soldiers, or customs officials at the wharf gate or the ship's gangway, and lie in wait to see if he tried to get on board? No—d'Armentières was not that sort.

(He was not, and when, later, Lieutenant Legros was reduced to the rank of sergeant for what was practically the brutal murder of a Legionary, Captain d'Armentières thought of this incident and rejoiced.)

And if he did—let them stop him if they could. He'd break through the scrum of them all right. Lay some of them out too.

What was Legros saying? Urging the gens d'armes to boot him up and lug him off by the scruff of his neck, eh?

He groaned again, sat up with difficulty, shakily and painfully rose to his feet, then smote Legros a smashing blow between the eyes, butted the gendarme who stood on his right, and with a dodge, a jump, and a wriggle was away and running like a hare.

To the end of his life he never forgot that race for life, and for more than life. Scores of times he lived through it again in terrible nightmares and suffered a thousand times more than he did on the actual run itself. For then he was quite cool, steady, and unafraid. He imagined himself to be running with the ball at Blackheath or Richmond, threading his way through the hostile fifteen, dodging, leaping, handing-off. But there were one or two differences. In Rugger you may not drive your clenched fist with all your might into the face of any man who springs at you. . . . Nor do you run for miles over cobbles. . . .

It was really surprisingly easy. Once he had got clear and put a few yards between himself and the uninjured gendarme, it was even betting that he'd win—provided his wind held and he didn't get the stitch, and that he did not slip and fall on the cursed stones. For the folk behind he cared nothing, and with such in front as grasped the situation in time to do something, he could deal. Some he dodged, some he handed-off as at Rugger, and some he hit. These last were slower to rise than those he handed-off, or caused to fall by dodging them, as they sprang at him.

When he turned a sharp corner he was so well ahead of the original pursuers that he was merely a man running, and that is not in itself an indictable offence. Certainly people stopped and stared at the sight of an obvious foreigner running at top speed, but he might have a boat to catch, he might be pursuing a train of thought or his lost youth and innocence. *Que voulez-vous?* Besides, he might be English, and therefore mad.

And then the blue-faced, panting gendarme would round the corner at the head of such *gamins*, loafers, police agents, and other citizens as saw fit to run on a hot afternoon. Whereupon people in this sector of street would look after the runaway and some run after him as well. So the pursuing crowd continually changed, as some left it and others joined it, until there remained of the old original firm scarcely any but the distressed and labouring gendarme—who, at last, himself gave up, reeled to the wall, and whooping and gasping for breath, prepared to meet his Maker.

Before the poor man had decided that this event was not yet, the Englishman had dashed round another corner and actually leapt on to an electric tram in full flight toward the *quais*!

Ciel! How mad were these English! Fancy a man running like that now, just to catch a tram. No, he would *not* go inside; he preferred to stand on the platform, and stand there he would.

He did, and anon, the tram having stopped at his polite request to the conductor, he strolled on to the P. and O. wharf and marched up the gangway of the good ship *Maloja*.

A steward informed him that his wife were ill, 'aving been brought aboard by a French gent and took to 'er cabing. She were still lying down. . . .

She was, at that moment, very ill indeed, mentally and physically.

But not for long, when his arms had assured her that they were not those of a vision and a ghost. . . .

If you ever travel Home with them, you'll find they don't go ashore at Marseilles. No, they don't like the place—prefer to stay on board, even through the coaling.

FIVE MINUTES

"Five Minutes" is the story of a dying legionnaire who tells the story of his great, unrequited, love. The "black flags" mentioned in this story, and others set in Vietnam, are a reference to an actual group of irregular soldiers that fought against the French during the 1870's and 1880's. "Five Minutes" was first published in Stepsons of France *(1917). The story has been reprinted in the Murray omnibus collection* Stories of the Foreign Legion *(1947) and the abridged Macrae-Smith collection (1948) of the same title.*

Le Légionnaire Jacques Bonhomme (as he called himself) was dying, and Sergeant Baudré, in charge of the convoy of wounded, proceeding from the nasty, messy fighting at Hu-Thuong to the base hospital at Phulang-Thuong, kindly permitted a brief halt that he might die in peace.

The good Sergeant Baudré could not accord more than an hour to the Legionary for his dying arrangements, because he had been instructed by his captain to get back as quickly as possible, and Phulang-Thuong lies only twenty-four miles south of Hu-Thuong.

Sergeant Baudré had other reasons also. For one, he was apprehensive of attack by some wandering band of De Nam's "pirates," and the outlaw brigands who served Monsieur De Nam, mandarin of the deposed Emperor of Annam, Ham-Nghi, were men whose courage and skill in fighting were only excelled by their ingenuity and pitilessness in torturing such of their enemies as fell into their hands. No, Sergeant Baudré had seen the remains of some of the prisoners of these "Black Flags," and he shuddered yet whenever he thought of them.

And what could he do, strung out over a mile, with a weak escort of Tirailleurs Tonkinois to provide his point, cover-point, and main body with the wounded, and an *escouade* of Legionaries for his rearguard? The sooner he got to Phulang-Thuong, the better. Returning, unhampered by the wounded, he could take care of himself, and any band of "Black Flags" who chose to attack him could do so. They should have a taste of the fighting qualities of Sergeant Baudré and his Legionaries. As it was—Sergeant Baudré shrugged his shoulders and bade Legionary Jacques Bonhomme die and be done with it.

"I thank you, Sergeant," murmured the dying man. "May I speak with le Légionnaire Jean Boule, if he is with the squad?"

The Sergeant grunted. He ran his eye along the halted column. Would those Tirailleurs Tonkinois stand, if there were a sudden rush of howling devils from the dense jungle on either side of the track? And why should they be allowed to take their women about with them everywhere, so that these should carry their kit and accoutrements for them? Nobody carried Sergeant Baudré's hundredweight of kit when he marched. Why should these Annamese be pampered thus? Should he send the squad of Legionaries to the head of the column when they advanced again? It would be just his luck if the column was attacked in front while the Legionaries were in the rear, or *vice versâ*.

Sergeant Baudré strolled toward the rear. He would get the opinion of "Jean Boule" in the course of a little apparently aimless conversation. He had been an officer before he joined the Legion, and these English knew all there is to know about guerilla fighting. . . .

From his remarks and replies it was clear to the good Sergeant that the Englishman considered that any attack would certainly come from the rear.

"Without doubt," agreed Sergeant Baudré. "That is why I keep the *escouade* as rearguard."

"By the way," he added, "Légionnaire Bonhomme wishes to say '*Au 'voir*' to you. He is off in a few minutes. Go and tell him to hurry up. We march again as soon as we have fed. He is the first stretcher in front of the Tirailleurs' women."

Legionnaire John Bull hurried to the spot. He knew that poor Jacques Bonhomme's number was up. It was a marvel how he had hung on, horribly wounded as he was—shot, speared, and staked, all at once, and all in the abdomen. He had been friendly with Jacques—an educated man and once a gentleman.

A glance showed him that he was too late. The man was delirious and semi-conscious. If he had any message or commission, it would never be put into words now.

The Englishman sat on the ground beside the stretcher and took the hand of the poor wretch. Possibly some sense of sympathy, company, friendship, or support might penetrate to, and comfort, the stricken soul.

After a while the over-bright eyes turned toward him.

"Any message, Jacques, *mon ami*?" he whispered, stroking the hand he held.

But Jacques Bonhomme talked on in the monotonous way of the fever-smitten, though with a strange consecutiveness. John Bull listened carefully, in the hope that some name, rank, office, or address might be mentioned and give a clue to relatives or the undelivered message or last commission.

. . ."Only five minutes in each year! Morel tells me there are five hundred and twenty-five thousand and six hundred minutes in each year, and I believe him implicitly, for he is the finest mathematical professor the Sorbonne ever had. I believe him implicitly. He is no Classic, but he has good points and can do wonderful things with figures. Wonderful feats! He knows all about things like the Metric System, Decimals, and Vulgar Fractions and similar things of which one hears but never encounters. He can not only add up columns of francs and centimes, such as are found in the bills which tradesmen are fond of writing, even when they have received payment, but he can deal with things like pounds, shillings, and pence; dollars and cents; yen and sabuks; or rupees, annas, and pice, not only with marvellous accuracy, but with incredible rapidity. This makes him an invaluable travelling companion for a Classic who knows none of these things—apart from the fact that he can also find out the times of trains and steamers from railway and shipping guides. It is wonderful to see him seize a book, scan it for a moment, and then say unhesitatingly that a train will leave the Gare de Lyon at a certain hour on a certain day, that it will just catch a ship at Marseilles on the next day, and that this ship will just catch another at Aden, so many days later, and that this one will land you in Japan at a certain hour on a certain day. And yet he is not a bit proud of these things—no prouder than I am of my little metrical translation of the Satires and Odes of Horace into Greek. And he thinks I travel with him for the sake of his delightful company! A man who cannot utter a hackneyed Latin quotation without some horrible false quantity. Poor Morel! . . .

"And this piece of information as to the number of minutes in a year is one of the most useful calculations he ever did on my behalf, except the one he did in answer to my query as to how many waking minutes there are—how many minutes in what one might call an active or waking year. That is to say, counting only the minutes when one is not asleep. He tells me there are three hundred and seventy-two thousand and three hundred waking minutes in the year for a man who averages seven hours sleep a day, or rather night—for he never sleeps in the day. How he knows I cannot tell, but I believe him absolutely, for he is as truthful as he is clever. So now I know that if I subtract five from this last appalling total I can tell how many minutes of the year I spend in thinking of the other five. After arriving at an aggravating variety of results, I again sought the good Morel's help, and he assures me that, subtracting five from the last total with which he furnished me, I have three hundred and seventy-two thousand and two hundred and ninety-five minutes.

"Thus I can now tell you clearly, that I spend three hundred and seventy-two thousand and two hundred and ninety-five minutes of the year in thinking of the other five—the five I spend with *Her*. . . .

"That is my point—do you understand?

"But although these magnificent figures give me much gratification, they cannot be taken as what Morel calls 'final,' for though during the majority of those minutes I am thinking of the other five consciously, I am only thinking of them subconsciously during the remainder, when I am lecturing, writing Greek hexameters, or reconstructing Greece and Rome for bored students who care for none of these things so long as they pass their absurd examinations—for we have not the spirit of study any more in France, but only the letter, thanks to those same examinations that prohibit thought, research, reading and culture absolutely. Moreover, the figures are also what Morel calls 'vitiated,' by the fact that a vast number of my sleeping moments are also given to dreaming of those five, and dreaming, as any philosopher will tell you, is far better and finer than thinking. Morel stoutly denies this—but that one would expect from so uneducated and uncultured a man. What I want to know is whether you think I might balance the waking moments when I can only think of her subconsciously against the sleeping moments when I am actually dreaming of her, and consider that the total of three hundred and seventy-two thousand and two hundred and ninety-five is approximately correct? The matter is of the first importance to me. I hate figures, as a rule, for they give me a headache, but in this one instance I want them correct. As I am so often told that I must be more scientific, accurate, and exact, I have tried to express myself mathematically and can do no better. To me it seems that I might just as well have said, 'I spend all the year in thinking of five minutes of it'—but I suppose some queer child of the new generation of Frenchmen would at once point out that I spend nearly a third of my time in sleeping, and much of it in working. . . . My head is in a dreadful whirl and muddle about it though. . . .

"Every year she goes to the tiny Breton village of Poldac for one week. I suppose she feels that she must have one week's rest and communion with her own soul if she is to live. On the first day of every July she goes, and her train stops at Pennebecque for five minutes. As you have guessed, I go to Pennebecque every year for that five minutes. It is the longest stop that the train makes. . . . And the setting of the scene is so wonderful, it is worthy to frame such a picture. I would not see her in the dust and noise and bustle of the Gare de l'Ouest, or at any ugly little wayside station. Yes, I go to Pennebecque to see her for five minutes every year. The only other train that passes through that tiny place does so at night. So I arrive over-night and sit on a seat and wait, almost too happy and exalted to breathe. . . .

"I have sat on that seat, for the last night of June, for seven years. And I have striven not to pray that the Marquis might die. And yet would not he be better dead—the poor, lolling-tongued, squint-eyed, half-witted Marquis? Think of that marvel of beauty, grace, goodness, and wit, the Marquise de Montheureux, making herself the nurse, the attendant, the keeper, of a lunatic!

"Yes, but for that one week in the year she is never out of his sight, night or day. If she but turns her back he weeps and sobs aloud. She tends that great, slobbering, dribbling lout, that mindless, soulless clod—no more sentient nor responsive than a hippopotamus—as the most devoted of young mothers tends and nurses her firstborn. . . .

"For one week in the year she lives her own life, and for five minutes in the year I see her. For six months I do nothing but look forward to that five minutes, and for six months again I do nothing but look back upon it.

"The first time, she did not see me, or did not recognize me as the man whom she had seen at the neighbouring château of the de Grandcourts—where I was tutor to the young Comte.

"The second time I ventured to bow, having debated the matter for a year, and she bowed and smiled, with the remark that only the other day, the Comtesse de Grandcourt was speaking of me and my good influence over the headstrong and rather wild boy who had been in my charge.

"The next year she spoke to me and commented on the curious coincidence of my being there again. She is of the real and true *noblesse*, you see, and has the kind, gentle, and unassuming manner of the genuine aristocrat. *Noblesse oblige*. She was as sweetly, graciously kind to the village curé, to her own servants, or to me as she was to de Grandcourt himself. She was a noble, and her nobility was made patent by her nobleness. It is your bourgeois 'noble' whose nobility has to be advertised by gilt and plush and display and rudeness to 'inferiors.'

"The fourth year she did not remark on the 'coincidence' of my presence at the station. She understood. And she accepted the bunch of roses I took. Oh, the sleepless nights I passed in the agony of that struggle to decide whether to take the roses!

"The year she did not come was rather terrible. I did not know what an eternity could be covered by two years. The bellowing calf of a Marquis was 'ill,' forsooth, and she never left his bedside. . . . Curse him! Had he not even the sense and understanding to see what he was making of her life, and to die like a man?

"*Bon Dieu!* Surely *to die* is easy—it is living that is so hard. But no—Monsieur le Marquis de Montheureux could not die. He must go on living, even though he could not wash his own face nor feed himself. . . .

"The sixth year she gave me so beautiful and kind and understanding a smile! She knew that I lived but for that five minutes. How I sang through the next twelve months! She knew. She understood. She smiled at me. Why should I not love her? It did neither her nor anyone else any harm, and it made my life—well—glorious, and gave it all the fineness and fulness that it possessed.

"For I simply did everything as though she were watching me, and as though account were to be rendered to her instead of to God. Was this an offence against *Le Bon Dieu*? . . .

"Sin? I dare to think for myself in religious matters. And I say that what is absolutely good must be of God—and if it isn't, I can't help it. And I lived as though she were watching me.

"The seventh year she gave me her hand. Had my heart been other than strong I should have died. . . . For twelve months I pondered the possibility of daring to put my lips to it, should she give me her hand again. Whenever she encountered de Grandcourt, he used to bow in the ancient grand manner, sweeping the ground with his hat, as though it were a great *mousquetaire* headdress, and as she swept him a mock curtsey in return he could kiss her hand. Why should not I? No de Grandcourt could honour her more nor love her as much. . . .

"That eighth year, I, poor fool, had determined that, if she again gave me her hand, I would kiss it. What Emperor then could have the pride and glory of the man who had kissed the hand of the Marquise de Montheureux? Would I, Cæsar Maximilien Raoul de Baillieul, then change with any king on earth?

"The day came, and I sat in the usual place, awaiting her, and picturing her. She would wear, this year, a silken dust-cloak of a lavender tint, and her glorious hair would be uncovered. One hand would be bare, the other gloved in a shade of lavender. I felt certain of these details.

"The train came at last, and yet all too soon. When she had come and gone there would be twelve months to live through, before I might see her again.

"I went to the window of the nearest first-class carriage.

"There she sat alone, and, as I approached, the beautiful slow smile, to me the loveliest thing on earth, warmed her glorious face.

"She was arrayed in lavender-coloured silk, her head was bare and so was her hand. She extended it towards me. With heart beating as though I had just run a race, I stepped to the window—*and she was not*. The carriage was empty, and as I clung to the handle, a little faint, her maid, dressed in deep mourning, came to a neighbouring window and looked out. . . .

"Madame la Marquise had died of typhoid which had broken out in Montheureux village. She would stay and work among her stricken people. The Marquis had died within twenty-four hours. No, not of the disease. Of grief. He had grasped that she was dead, and that he would never see her again. The maid was on her way to Poldec to arrange about Madame's cottage and property there.

"It appears that I fell there as one dead and lay ill for weeks.

"But no, I must not commit suicide or I might not enter the Heaven where she is . . . the Heaven that our Wise Men decided does not exist, when they turned God out of France. . . . But I must crucify myself in some way or go mad. Physical pain and strife and stress alone can save me.

"I shall enlist in the Foreign Legion. Perhaps I shall earn an honourable death against the enemies of France.

"Oh, Rose of the World. Rosemonde, Rosemonde, Rosemonde—"

"Finished?" quoth Sergeant Baudré, approaching. "Dump him in that rice-mud. He'll be more useful dead than he ever was alive." . . .

"HERE ARE LADIES"

"Here Are Ladies" is a story from the Second Franco-Dahomey War (1892-1894), in which John Bull and the Bucking Bronco are attacked by the Dahomey Amazon warriors. "Here Are Ladies" first appeared in the first edition of Stepsons of France *(1917). The story has been reprinted in the Murray omnibus collection* Stories of the Foreign Legion *(1947) and the abridged Macrae-Smith collection (1948) of the same title.*

A sluggish, oily river with mangrove-swamp banks; a terrible September day with an atmosphere of superheated, poisonous steam; and the two French gunboats, *Corail* and *Opale*, carrying a detachment of the French Foreign Legion, part of an expeditionary force entrusted with the task of teaching manners, and an enhanced respect for Madame la République, to Behanzin, King of Dahomey.

The Legionaries standing, squatting, and lying on the painfully hot iron decks, were drenched in perspiration. The light flannel active-service kits, served out to them at Porto Novo, clung wetly to their bodies. From under the big ugly pith helmets of dirty white, dirty white faces showed cadaverous and wan. For a month they had forced their way through the West African jungle, sometimes achieving as much as a mile an hour through the sucking mud of a swamp; sometimes thrusting their stifling, choking way through elephant grass eight to ten feet in height; and again fighting through dense tangled bush with chopper, *coupe-coupe*, and axe. They had travelled "light," with only rifle and bayonet and one hundred and fifty rounds of ammunition, but even this lightness had been too heavy for some. The more coffee and quinine for the rest! To give variety to the sufferings of fatigue, fever, hunger, thirst, and dysentery, the Dahomeyans frequently attacked in the numerical superiority of a hundred to one. No mean opponents either, with their up-to-date American rifles and batteries of Krupp guns for long range work, and their spears and machetes for the charge.

As usual, the Legion was marking its trail with the generous distribution of the graves of its sons.

And now the VIIth Company had left swamp and jungle for the floating ovens *Corail* and *Opale*. Terrific heat, but no sunshine; the "landscape" minatory, terrible; life, the acme and essence of discomfort and misery. Even the Senegalese boatmen seemed affected and depressed.

"Say, John! Is this-yer penny-steamboat trip fer the saloobrity of our healths?" asked the Bucking Bronco, in a husky voice, of his neighbour le Legionnaire Jean Boule or John Bull. The old soldier wiped the sweat from his face with his sleeve.

"I overheard Commandant Faraux telling Colonel Dodds that there is a ford up here somewhere, and that it must be found and seized," he answered wearily. "I expect we're looking for it now."

"Well, I ain't got it. Search me!" said the American. "I allow Ole Man Farrow's got another think comin' if he . . ."—a ragged crash of musketry from the bank a hundred yards distant, and the ironwork of the *Opale* rang again under a hail of bullets.

In ten seconds the Legionaries were lining the sandbagged bulwarks with loaded rifles at the "ready."

"Oh, the fools—the silly bunch o' boobs!" murmured the Bucking Bronco. "I allow thet's torn it! The pie-faced pikers hev sure wafted the bloom off the little secret."

"Yes," agreed John Bull, "you'd have thought even Behanzin's generals would have had the sense to lie low and not announce themselves until we'd got our column fairly tied up in the middle of the ford." . . .

The roar of Hotchkiss guns and Lebel rifles from the two boats drowned his further remarks, as well as the irregular crashings of the bursts of Dahomeyan musketry. . . .

The debarkation of the VIIth Company was unhindered, the ford seized, and the safe passage of the Expeditionary Force guaranteed, the Dahomeyans having retired.

"Waal!" remarked the Bucking Bronco to his friend as half the VIIth Company moved off next morning, as Advance Guard. "Strike me peculiar ef thet ain't the softest cinch I seen ever. Guess Ole Man Behanzin ain't been to no West Point Academy. They say his best men is women—an' I kin believe it!"

"Amazons," remarked Jean Boule. "I pray we don't come across any. Fancy shooting at women."

"You smile your kind, fatherly smile at 'em, John, an' I allow they'll come an' eat outer yer hand. . . . Are they really fightin'-*gals*, with roof-garden hats an' shirt-waists, and mittens on their pasterns? . . . Gee-whiz! Guess I'll take a few prisoners an' walk with a proud tail!"

"They're women, all right," was the reply, "and I believe they are as dangerous as dervishes—apart from any question of one's not shooting to kill when they charge. . . . If all I've heard about them is true, chivalry is apt to be a trifle costly."

"Waal, John, as Légionnaires, we ain't habituated to luxury any, and can't afford nawthen costly. Ef any black gal lays fer me with an axe—it's a smackin' fer hers."

"Yes—but what are we going to do if an Amazon regiment opens an accurate and steady fire on us with Winchester repeaters and then charges with the bayonet?"

"Burn the trail for Dixie," grinned the American. "I guess we'd hit the high places some, an' roll our tails for Home. *Gee*-whillikins! Charged by gals!"

"That's all very well," grumbled the Englishman, "but the Legion doesn't run, either from men or from women. If an Amazon regiment charges us, we've *got* to fight. . . . It would be ghastly."

Even as he spoke the deadly silent forest suddenly gave birth to thousands of black shadows, all moving swiftly and noiselessly, and from all directions, upon the tiny column of the Advance Guard.

With one accord, at some signal, they halted, rested the butts of their rifles on their thighs, fired, and then, howling like devils, charged with great *élan*, led by a number of tall, muscular women, handsome and finely made.

"*Gals!*" gasped the American, as the column instinctively halted, faced outwards in two ranks, and poured magazine fire into the dense masses of the charging savages.

"*Look* at her!" he cried, and pointed to a young woman, who, bare to the waist, and wearing a fez cap, a short blue cotton kilt, and a leather belt and cartridge-cases, came bounding straight toward him. In her right hand she brandished a thick-backed, heavy chopping-sword like a *coupe-coupe* or machete, and in her left carried a bright new repeating-carbine. Nothing could have been more dashing, courageous, and inspiring than the leading of this Fury, as she rushed straight for the levelled rifles of the Legionaries, waving her men on and yelling mingled words of encouragement, threat, and taunt at them as she strove to bring them to the consummation of the charge.

Her efforts were in vain, however. The Dahomeyan male warrior is not of very heroic stuff, and does his best fighting in a surprised camp, a broken square, or against a scattered line. His *métier* is the ambush, the rush at dawn, the hacking and hewing hundred-to-one fight in dense jungle where the foe cannot form or charge, the tree-top sniping, the trampling flat of a worn-out enemy by sheer weight of numbers.

Before the steady fire of an unbroken line he generally wilts away, and vanishes shadow-like into the impenetrable depths of his native jungle, to try another surprise, another ambush, another dawn-rush of ten thousand men, at the next opportunity.

As usual, beneath the accurate fire that mowed them down in swathes, the Dahomeyans broke and fled, slowly followed by their Amazon leaders, who shrilly cursed, and fiercely struck at, the retiring faint-hearts.

Just as the "cease-fire" whistle blew, the woman who had been charging at the Bucking Bronco and John Bull (and who had stood screaming at her followers as they halted, faltered, and broke) threw up her arms and fell.

"That weren't *me*," quoth the Bucking Bronco, "an' I hope it was a dod-gasted accident. She was some gal, that gal. Let's have a look at her if we ain't agoin' to charge nor nawthen."

The officer commanding the Advance Guard was certainly not going to charge. He was only too thankful to have beaten off the sudden and well-executed attack. How marvellously the brutes had materialized from the apparently uninhabited forest, still silent and gloomy as the tomb. But what *fools*! That force alone, properly handled, and attacking while the column was in the middle of the wide deep ford, might have told a very different story.

"Bugler," called he, "blow the 'alarm' and the 'regimental-call' till your veins crack and your lungs burst. . . . No—turn toward the river, *sot*, I want the main body to hear. . . . Sergeant-Major, send two of the strongest running back with this." . . .

They were the last words he spoke. The Amazons themselves were charging this time—a whole regiment—and no regiment in this world ever charged with greater dash, courage, violence, and determination. Firing as they came, and utterly disregarding the steady magazine-fire of the Legionaries, they swept down upon them like an avalanche—like cavalry—and burst upon the little line, through it, and over it, like a hailstorm across a wheatfield.

Rushing at Captain Roux, one fired her Spencer carbine into his chest, while another drove a spear into his abdomen. As he fell, a third stooped and deliberately hacked off his head with her chopping-knife. There was no question of "sparing women" as these furies, each as big and strong and well-armed as any Legionary, hacked, hewed, and thrust, or, kneeling a few yards from their victims, gave them the contents of the magazines of their carbines. . . .

While parrying the fierce thrusts of one stalwart virago, John Bull, struck on the head from behind by two assailants at once, fell to the ground, even as his eye had subconsciously taken in and registered upon his brain a picture of his mighty friend swinging his rifle round and round his head by the muzzle, the butt describing a circle within which he stood unhurt as to his body, though apparently shocked in mind, to judge from his roar of "Scat! ye shameless jumpin' Jezebels!"

Without thought of defending himself, the bugler continuously blew the "alarm" and the "regimental call" (in the hope that it might carry back to the main body, which apparently had delayed longer at the ford than had been expected) until he went down with a bullet through his leg and another in his shoulder, two of seven fired at him from a score paces distance by a young Amazon. A minute later, the man rose to his knees and blew with almost undiminished strength, until the same young woman riddled his chest, at point-blank range, with another magazineful.

Recovering consciousness, John Bull saw a gigantic Amazon make a dive at the knees of the Bucking Bronco, ducking beneath the whirling rifle-butt. A moment later he was down, but, instead of being hacked to pieces, was borne away, kicking and cursing, by a dozen powerful women.

Knowing what that meant, he would rather have seen his friend killed before his eyes. . . . As another wave of faintness swept over him, he heard the distant strains of "Tiens! Voilà du boudin"—the March of the Legion, and knew that the buglers of the column were sending the encouraging notes ahead of their straining bodies, as the remainder of the force hurried to the rescue. Poor Bugler Langout's message had carried on the heavy air, which seems to blanket the sound of rifle fire while transmitting that of a whistle, bugle, or war-drum to a surprising distance.

Heavy fire from the debouching troops saved the few survivors of the Advance Guard—but it was not until the whole column had fought a tough action in company squares, that the Amazons and the rallied and reinforced Dahomeyans acknowledged defeat, for that day at any rate, and disappeared shadow-like into the jungle as suddenly as they had come.

John Bull and the assistant-surgeon decided that the butt-end of a carbine had struck the former on the head, and that almost simultaneously a chopping-sword had struck the butt of the carbine while it was in contact with his skull, inasmuch as his head bore no cut, there were splinters of wood in his hair, and a carbine with a hacked stock lay beside him when he was picked up and examined. He had nearly been handed over to the burial-party instead of to the carriers, and, when he realized that the Bucking Bronco had been carried off, he almost wished that this had actually happened. Most horrible stories of the fate of prisoners of the Dahomeyans were current throughout the expeditionary force, though no proofs of their truth had yet materialized.

When a list of the killed, wounded, and missing was made out, it was found that the Sergeant-Major had disappeared also, and one of the survivors remembered seeing him borne off in a surging crowd of Amazons, "like a band of big black ants carrying off an injured wasp," as he graphically described it.

That night John Bull, old Tant de Soif, the Grasshopper, Jan Minnaerts, Black Gaspard, Achille Martel, and one or two more of the *escouade* to which the Bucking Bronco belonged, volunteered to go out as a scouring-party to reconnoitre for the enemy, and, incidentally, to try to discover some traces of their missing comrade and the *sous-officier*.

"Let Jean Boule be in charge," said Lieutenant Roberte, commanding the remnants of the VIIth Company, *vice* Captain Roux, killed in action, "he has some sense, and can use the stars. If you fall into the hands of the enemy, I shall punish you severely—give you all a taste of the *crapaudine* perhaps. *Bonne chance, mes enfants.*" . . .

*   *   *   *   *

"We must turn back, *mon ami*," said Martel to John Bull at last.

"But yes," agreed old Tant de Soif, "it is useless to throw good meat after bad. . . . They have died their deaths by now—or are being taken to the sacred city of Kana for sacrifice."

"I smell smoke," suddenly said the Grasshopper, wrinkling his delicate nostrils. "*Nom de Dieu!*" he added, "*and* burning flesh."

It soon became more than evident that he was right. Either they were approaching the spot where flesh was being burnt, or a faint breeze had sprung up and wafted the foul smell in their direction.

Treading like Dahomeyans themselves, they turned from the jungle track they had discovered, along another that lay plain in the moonlight across a little open glade, and seemed to lead in the direction of the smell. Thousands of bare feet must recently have made the path—the feet of men hurrying along in single file. . . .

*   *   *   *   *

Although scarcely recognizable as a human being, the Sergeant-Major, a huge stalwart Alsatian, was still alive.

Steel and fire had been used with remarkable skill, that so much could have been done and the spark of life still kept in the unspeakably tortured, defiled, and mangled body. A score of Amazons were at work upon him.

The Bucking Bronco, stark naked, but apparently uninjured, was bound to a young palm. Either he was merely awaiting his turn and incidentally suffering the ghastly ordeal of seeing the tortures of the Sergeant-Major and enduring the agonies of anticipation, or else he was being reserved as an acceptable offering to King Behanzin and a candidate for the wicker torture-baskets of the sacrificial slaughter-house of Kana.

"A volley when I shout," whispered John Bull, "then a yell and the bayonet."

A few seconds later he was killing women, driving his bayonet into their bodies until the curved hilt struck with a thud. The thuds gave him infinite pleasure—and then he was violently sick. Surprised by the sudden volley, ignorant of the strength of their assailants, and only partly armed, the Amazons broke and scattered into the jungle. While John Bull, with shaking hands, prized at the Bucking Bronco's bonds with his sword-bayonet, old Tant de Soif put a merciful bullet into the brain of the Sergeant-Major and then busied himself about collecting the dismembered fragments of that unfortunate.

"For all the world like picking up an old woman's packages when she has slipped up on a banana-skin," quoth he. He was a quaint old gentleman, a *vieux moustache* who had seen many queer things in his forty years of assorted service in the Line, the Infanterie de la Marine, and the Legion.

"We daren't stay to bury him," said Martel; "they'll rally and return in a minute."

As the little party retreated at the *pas gymnastique*, the Bucking Bronco remarked to his friend, panting ahead of him, "Say, John! I allow I'm a what-is-it henceforth—an'-a-dern-sight-more. You know—a Miss-Hog-you-beast."

"A *what*?"

"A Miss-Hog-you-beast."

"Yes! What some people call a misogynist. I don't blame you!"

THE MacSNORRT

In "The MacSnorrt" Wren introduces a character that features in a large number of later stories. MacSnorrt, spelled McSnorrt in the later stories, is a former ship's engineer, who in this story is in a drunken (his normal) state thinking a native soldier is a woman! John Bull is the other legionnaire who helps rescue MacSnorrt. "The MacSnorrt" was first published in Stepsons of France *(1917) and reprinted in* Stories of the Foreign Legion *(Murray, 1947).*

The MacSnorrt was on the downward path, and had been for many years. Physically, mentally, and morally he was deteriorating; and as for the other aspects—social, financial, and worldly—he had been Chief Engineer on a Cunarder, and he was now the blackest of the black sheep of the VIIIth Company of the First Battalion of the Legion. From sitting at meals with the passengers in the First Saloon of a great liner, he had come to sitting with assorted blackguards over their tin *gamelles* of *soupe*; from drawing hundreds per annum, he had come to drawing a half-penny per day; his brain was failing from lack of use and excess of absinthe and mixed alcoholic filth, his superb health and strength were undermined, and he was becoming a Bad Man.

The history of his fall is told in one short word—Drink; and drink had turned a fine, useful, and honourable man into a degraded ruffian. The man who had thought of fame, wealth, inventions, patents, knighthood—now thought of the successful shikarring of the next drink, or the stealing of the wherewithal to get it. Whether this poor soul were married and the father of a family, I never knew, and did not care to ask, but it is quite probable that he was. Such men usually are. Let us hope he was not. Sober, he was a truculent, morose, and savage ruffian— ashamed of his ashamedness, hating himself and everybody else, dangerous and vile; a bad soldier till the fighting began, and then worth two. Drunk, he was exceedingly amusing, and one caught glimpses of the kindly, witty, and genial original.

*　　　*　　　*　　　*　　　*

The best of soldiers, be he *Maréchal* or *Soldat deuxième classe*, as was the MacSnorrt, may be overcome by a combination and alliance of foes, any one of whom he could defeat alone.

As the MacSnorrt endeavoured to make clear to Captain d'Armentières next day, it was merely the conjunction against him of a good dinner, Haiphong, the stupeedity of the Annamese male in wearing a chignon and a petticoat like a wumman, *shum-shum*, sunstroke, and his own beautiful but ardent disposition, that had been his undoing. With any one of these he could have coped; by their unholy alliance he had been—he freely admitted it—completely defeated.

Captain d'Armentières heard him with courtesy, and awarded him eight days' *salle de police* and the *peloton de chasse* with sympathy.

He had known of similar fortuitous concatenations of adverse circumstance before in connection with le Légionnaire MacSnorrt.

It was the Captain's *ordonnance*, one Jean Boule, who had, luckily for that reveller, discovered the MacSnorrt and encompassed his capture by a strong picket.

Passing a pagoda one night, he had heard, uplifted in monologue, a rich voice whose accents, or accent, he had heard before, that of the MacSnorrt, the Bad Man of the VIIIth Company, recently arrived in a draft from Sidi-bel-Abbes to reinforce the VIIth after certain painful dealings with the Pavillons Noirs, the "pirates" of the Yen Thé.

. Mingled with, but far from subduing the vinous voice and hiccups of the MacSnorrt, were the angry murmurings, quick whispers, and the lisping and clicking voices of a native Annamese and Chinese crowd.

Was the fool interfering with those so-tender "religious susceptibilities," and intruding upon priests and their flock in search of moral consolation and fortification? He had no business in there at all.

Following the wall and rounding a corner, Jean Boule came to a gate. Pushing it open gently, he looked in.

Reclining majestically upon the ground, his back against the wall, was the MacSnorrt. In his vast left paw was a bottle of *shum-shum*, the deadly, maddening spirit distilled from rice. Clasped by his mighty right arm to his colossal bosom, the MacSnorrt held—a *doi* or Sergeant of Tirailleurs Tonkinois![13]

The little man, his lacquered hat, with its red bonnet-strings on one side, his chignon in grave disarray, looked even more like a devil than was his normal wont, as he struggled violently to escape from his degrading and undignified situation.

It was clear that, if the Annamese could get at his bayonet, there would be a vacancy at the head of the clan of MacSnorrt and at the tail of the VIIIth Company of the Legion.

"Lie ye still, lassie," adjured the gigantic Legionary, as his captive struggled again vainly, for the great right arm was not only round his waist, but round both his arms, and he could only pick at the handle of his bayonet with ineffectual finger-tips.

"Lie ye still, ye wee prood besom, or I'll e'en tak' ane o' the ither lasses to ma boosom," threatened the MacSnorrt, but softened the apparent harshness of the threat by a warm lingering kiss upon the yellow cheek of the murderously savage soldier.

He then applied the *shum-shum* bottle to his lips, poured a libation of the crude and poisonous spirit, and then frankly explained to his captive that he had not selected "her" from among the other "sonsie lassies" by reason of any superior beauty, but simply because he liked her saucy fancy-dress—quite like a *vivaandière*, and he had always had a tender spot in his hearrt o' hearrts for a *vivaandière*.

The enraged and half-demented Sergeant screamed to the little crowd of priests, loafers, coolies and Haiphong citizens to knife the foreign devil, or, taking his bayonet, to drive it in under his ear. . . . The crowd allowed "I dare not" to wait upon "I would"—for the moment.

"Aye! . . . Oo-aye! It's not Jock MacSnorrt that could reseest the blaandishments o' onny little deevil o' a *vivaandière*," confessed the aged roué. . . . "It was for the sake o' the *vivaandières* I joined the French airrmy, ye'll ken—when I was an innocent slip o' a laddie. . . . Romaantic! . . .

"Aye—an' they're mostly fat auld runts wi' twa chins," he

---

[13] Known as *Les Jeunes Filles* to the Legion, by reason of their long hair.

added, with a sudden fall to pessimism and confession of disillusionment.

"'Tis the ruin o' the British Airrmy, ye'll ken," he confided to the ugly crowd that gradually closed in around him, "that they hae no *vivaandières* to comfort the puir laddies. . . . Hae the Gorrdons onny *vivaandières*, I'll ask ye? The Seaforrths? The Caamerons? The Heelan' Light Infantry? The Royal Scots? . . . They hanna. It a' comes o' such matters being in the han's o' the Southrons—the drunken an' lasceevious deils. Look at the Navy. . . . Is there a ship o' them a'—fra' battleship to river gunboat—that has a *vivaandière*, I'm speirin' ye, lassie? There isna. . . . An' theenk o' the graan' worrk they could do for the puir wounded—instead o' they bluidy-minded, sick-bay orrderly deevils!

"Losh, maan! Contemplate it!

"Eh, Wooman in oor 'oors o' ease
A settin' lightly on oor knees. . . .

"Lie still, ye haverin', snoot-cockin' besom—an' I'll tell ye a' aboot the horrors o' a naval engagement—an' I seen hunnerds. I'll tell ye a' aboot the warrst o' the lot—when I lossed ma guid right arrm. Then conseeder what a deeference ane bonnie *vivaandière* lassie might ha' made . . ." A violent struggle from the insanely incensed and ferocious *doi*.

"*Wull* ye bide quiet, ma bonnie wean? Or shall I send ye awa' oot into the cauld warrld to airrn yere ain leevin'? Ye're awfu' sma' for sic a fate, ye'll ken, ma bairnie! An' this is no Sauchiehall Street, I'm telling ye. . . . Did ye see the wee-bit gunboats we came in, the morrn? Well, imaagine ane o' they ten times increased and multiplied, an', in fact, made a hantle bigger. I sairved in ane o' yon, but I shall not disclose in what capaacity—save an' except that it was honourable to me on the ane side an' to her Majesty on the ither. . . . *Wull* ye bide quiet like a respeckitable *tai-tai* or I'll hae ye awa'. . . .

"Eh! maan, a naval engagement's graand. Watter everywheer! On board, I mean. Everywheer. Gaallons o' it." . . .

"May a cat tread on your heart!" hissed the struggling *doi*. "May dragons tear you! May the bellies of mudfish be your grave! May you be cast on a Mountain of Knives." . . .

"What did ye say, lassie? *Why* do they want watter on booarrd? *To hide the awfu' things that fall aboot!* Eyes, arrms, legs, noses, ears, toes, fingers—ye wouldna hae them lying there plain for the eye o' man to see? No! Gaallons o' watter. . . ."

"Bide ye quiet, *kuniang*, or ye won't be a *kuniang* much longer, I'm thinkin'. Aye! Dozens o' gaallons o' watter. Everywheer. Hoses playin' a' aboot the plaace. Pumps squirrtin' it. Inches o' it on the decks. An' *blood*! Ma certie! Lassie—ye'd never believe. Hunnerds o' gaallons o' watter, an' as the shells burrst a' aroond—what falls into the watter in a pairrfect hail?" . .
.

"Devils draw your entrails!" panted the writhing *doi*.

"Eh? Bullets, d'ye say? That's wheer ye're wrang, lassie. Na! Na!—Eyes, arrms, legs, noses, ears, toes, fingers! Ye'd scarcely credit it. An' thousands o' gaallons o' watter! Juist to hide the awfu' sichts and sounds. . . . There'll be a gun-team working their gun in watter. Thousan's o' gaallons o' watter. Feet deep. An' a maan wull stoop to fish up a shell for the gun—an' what'll he bring up belike?"

"Be the graves of your ancestors torn open by pariah dogs and their bones devoured!" cursed the Sergeant, getting one arm free at last.

"Bring up a shell, d'ye say, ma wean? More likely an eye or an arrm or a leg, or a nose or an ear or a toe or a finger frae beneath that fearfu' flood. . . . Oo-aye! Meelions o' gaallons o' water! Feet deep. An' the bed o' that awfu' sea, a wrack o' spare-parts o' the human forrm divine! Meelions o' gaallons o' watter. Yarrds deep on the decks. They always hae it the like o' that in a naval engagement. Aye—I seen hunnerds . . ." and the *doi* had got at his bayonet at last. Then the *bonze* struck heavy blows upon the big bell hanging near in its bamboo-frame support, and the crowd closed in. If the *doi* struck, they would hack and tear this foreign devil to pieces.

With a *weeeep* of steel on steel the bayonet cleared the scabbard and the *doi* struck at his captor's throat as John Bull sprang forward. But the sound of the drawing of the bayonet had an extraordinary effect on the MacSnorrt—and it was with the weapon held only in his left hand that the *doi* struck—and missed. Seizing him by the throat with both huge hands the

Légionnaire scrambled to his feet and used him as a battering-ram in his headlong roaring drive at the closing knife-drawing crowd.

With a yell of "Ye doomed dirrty Jael!" he wrenched the bayonet from the little Annamese and flung him headlong as the crowd gave back.

John Bull sprang to his side, and the two in a whirling, punching, struggling plunge fought their way to the gate, burst through it—and were promptly arrested by the picket, opportunely passing.

With these new enemies the MacSnorrt did further battle, until a tap on the head from a Gras rifle in the skilful hands of Sergeant Legros brought him to that state in which he was perhaps best—unconsciousness.

"BELZÉBUTH"

"Belzébuth" is the story of the wife of a French officer trying to raise enough money so her family can go home to France for a holiday. Belzébuth is the horse she is training and hopes to sell after she rides him in a race. "Belzébuth" first appeared in Stepsons of France *(1917) and was reprinted in* Stories of the Foreign Legion *(Murray, 1947).*

We were heavy sportsmen (*à l'Anglaise*) at Bellevue at that time. Not only did we lay out a race-course, but we imported hounds and performed the *Chasse au renard*. We got up point-to-point races and paper-chases. There were actually Ladies' races, and some folk went so far as to talk about pig-sticking.

"Of course, Madame Merlonorot will ride when she comes out to Algeria?" asked Madame Paës.

"*Dieu!* Rather!" replied Colonel Merlonorot of the Zouaves. "I am on the look-out for a good thing for her now. She wants all the equine perfections embodied in one Arab pony. Won't keep a string. . . . Too much bother. . . . Must have won a good race or two, must have been hunted by a lady, must hack quietly in both saddles, must trap, and be trusted to take no exception to camels, Arab music, whirling dervishes, or fireworks. Also he must make the promenade in the governess-cart upon occasion! What?"

"It's a far cry from the race-course to the governess-cart, isn't it?" inquired Madame Paës.

"Yes. But she'll expect me to produce all that in the next month—and not to spend more than about three thousand francs! . . . Let's know if you hear of anything that might meet most of the requirements—and available within the month, will you, dear Madame? Must be a racer, though—and that limits the field when you're looking for a hack. . . . She's great on Ladies' Point-to-Points, Hunt-races, *Chasse au renard*, and everything you can do on a horse. She would play *le polo* and would pursue the pig with a spear if I would consent!"

"I will remember, Colonel—and I have an idea. . . . Three

thousand francs for a pony that meets all the specifications?"

"About that, and a thousand thanks. Must be young, thoroughbred, and something to look at—and be vetted sound all over, of course." . . .

Three thousand francs! It would mean Home this year instead of next. Paris in Spring! It would mean avoiding the awful prostrating heat of *la canicule* for the babies—neither of them robust, both of them showing the signs of French babyhood kept too long in Africa's forcing-house. It might mean life to one or both of them, especially with the usual cholera, smallpox, typhoid, and dysentery epidemics about, as they grew weaker. And Guillaume needed his long-overdue leave badly. He was overworked, run down, ill, and his temper—never very good— was getting unbearable. Fancy having leave and being too poor to take it! What a shame it was that the condition of the majority of married junior officers of the XIXth Army Corps should be one of cruel grinding poverty, pitiful shifts to keep up appearances, and a weary, heart-breaking struggle to make ends meet. Well, one must "drag the lengthening chain" and, having once clasped it on, must take the consequences. One can't start life afresh in France at thirty odd—and, well, one can always hope, or nearly always. And one might win a prize in the Lottery. (Think of it! One's chief hope for a brighter future, a chance of winning a prize in the Lottery!) . . . Three thousand francs!

But young Belzébuth had never run a race in his life and never taken part in the *Chasse au renard* nor the pursuit of the spear-threatened pig, unless, perhaps, when he had had an English master in Maroc. Still, he was a real picture, was rising seven, sound as a bell, quiet as a mouse, and undoubtedly thoroughbred.

He hacked in both saddles and was a fast and steady trapper—and took the babies for an airing daily. Certainly he had a turn of speed—and there was simply no tiring him.

He would take Guillaume (a very bad and nervous rider) for a ride in the morning, and in the trap to the barracks after breakfast. He would bring him home to lunch, and then take the babies for their drive in the evening.

Sometimes he would finish up the day by taking the trap to a distant villa when a dinner-party was toward. And when Guillaume was away on manœuvres or marches, Madame Paës, horse-woman born and bred, got her only riding.

Three thousand francs! And Guillaume had bought him for two hundred francs when Lieutenant d'Amienville—who ought not to be allowed to keep a pig or a pariah dog, much less a horse—went away. Starved, neglected, and dying for want of work, Belzébuth had looked a bad bargain at 200 fcs. A man ought not to go unprosecuted who buys a horse and uses a motor-car, leaving the horse to the mercy of a rascally *homard* who feeds it on offal and never takes it out of the stall. Her heart had ached when she had seen the staring coat, blear eye, and overgrown hoofs of the walking skeleton that Lieutenant d'Amienville swore had cost him, raw, a couple of thousand francs. She could have hung her sun-hat on him in a dozen places. But she knew a good horse when she saw one. Had not her father run his own horses at Longchamps and Auteuil before he went bankrupt?

And, under her care, Belzébuth had soon changed into a picture of bright, sleek, healthy happiness, and had served them exceedingly well.

Could she make him worth three thousand francs before Guillaume returned from manœuvres, sell him to Colonel Merlonorot (her father's old comrade), and put the money into Guillaume's hand, saying, "Book the passages for Marseilles to-morrow, *mon ange*."

Could she? For, the utmost screwing and scraping, the most optimistic view of the saleable value of the few goods and chattels, the estimating the cheapest and nastiest journey to Paris—left a gaping chasm of a good thousand francs between hope and realization of a holiday in La Ville Lumière. No, nothing could bridge it—unless Belzébuth would fetch three thousand francs instead of the three or four hundred they had expected. Five hundred was the highest Guillaume had ever dreamed of—and that was after a cheery dinner at some Mess and a little champagne.

Even five hundred would be a profit of a hundred and fifty per cent. she believed.

Yes—four hundred would be cent. per cent., and five would

be half as much again.

What would three thousand be on two hundred? Fifteen per cent.? No, of course not. Fifteen hundred per cent.? It sounded impossible.

And of course it was impossible.

Still—she would add five pounds of *avoine* daily to Belzébuth's *blé* and *son*, and start training him while Guillaume was away. She would join the club of the *Chasse au renard* at once, and she would enter for the Ladies' Race in the Desert Point-to-Point, which would be run just three weeks hence at Bellevue.

But what a terrible plunge! A hundred francs to the *cercle*, and Heaven alone knew what oats were fetching. Or perhaps she could hunt three or four times only, and pay a small donation or something? And she could certainly, avoid getting the Beaune that Médecin-Major Parme had ordered her to take, since she had had malarial fever, and use the money for oats. But what a speculation! It is an ill-wind that blows no good at all—the fever had reduced her weight, and she could ride at about seven stone now.

But what would Guillaume say of the wasted money—if she failed? Well, it wouldn't be all waste, for Belzébuth's value would go up, in any case, if she hunted him well and he got a place in the Point-to-Point.

The proverbs say that where there is a will there is a way, and that Heaven helps those that help themselves.

She would simply *live* to sell Belzébuth to dear rich old Colonel Merlonorot for three thousand francs, as a racer, hunter, hack in both saddles, bright trapper, and confidential nursery-pony! For the next month she would give mind, soul, and body to winning the Desert Point-to-Point. . . .

*   *   *   *   *

Belzébuth was taken for a long quiet ride next morning, and for another in the evening, and his mistress personally superintended his feed and toilet.

Next day he was introduced to a new and glorious place where the going was beautiful and you went straight ahead between railings, with plenty of room and no obstacles.

He took his furlong burst on the race-course at a good pace, and improved daily at two, three, and four furlongs.

Madame Paës' notions of training were original, but based on the sound principle, "Train for what you have to do by repeatedly doing it—and work up gradually to the first doing."

After a week Belzébuth was doing his mile on the racecourse and doing it uncommon well (as one or two observers noted). Also he went down the lane of jumps cleverly and willingly, beautifully schooled.

One morning, Colonel Merlonorot noticed Madame Paës at the meet, on a very likely-looking bay Arab—good in the legs, well ribbed up, high in the withers, and with a blood look about him. ("He liked the look of that beast. *Nom d'un pipe*, he did!")

Madame Paës had not hunted since she had scrambled about with the North Devons in Angleterre—a long-legged, long-haired Diana of fourteen (at a Devonshire school) on a fat pony.

She was now a tiny, slim, pale, big-eyed Diana of twenty-four—and as good as a jockey.

But she looked as though she had been too long in Exile (which was exactly the case), and fitter for a deck-chair on a homeward-bound liner than for a saddle in the hunting-field. . . .

When would they get off? How would Belzébuth behave? Would he belie his nursery mildness and go *fou* when it was a case of full cry and all away? Would the unwonted oats and the rousing on the race-course and over the jumps react unfavourably now for the weak-backed, weary rider? He was certain to be *méchant*, and might buck or bolt. Would trembling hands and aching arms be unable to hold him? How her back ached, too! . . . Dear old Belzébuth, be good! It's for the babies and Guillaume. . . . God knew she'd sooner be in bed than in the midst of this gay throng of strong and happy men and women, well-content, well-clad, well-fed. . . .

Well-fed! A melancholy fact. Madame Paës, wife of a French commissioned officer, was not well fed. A woman of the unselfish sort does not buy costly tonic-foods, dainties, and wines, and eat the money that is sorely needed for other things. For plain food she had no appetite. To people who have been brought up in a château atmosphere, an income—which to *ci-*

devant dwellers in Montmartre or the bourgeois suburbs is wealth—may be degrading poverty.

The Paës had expenses which it was due to their honour and proper pride to have—and which are not due to the honour and proper pride of the bourgeoisie. . . . And these expenses and the health of Guillaume and the babies came before food and clothes for Madame Paës, in Madame Paës' opinion.

*   *   *   *   *

A note of music from the clump of jungle that had swallowed up the hounds. A crash of the grand wild music. A line! Hounds are off and the first "run" is on.

Belzébuth commenced by a series of bounds, the outcome of a high and joyous heart, good feeding, and good condition. He felt a touch of the curb, arched his back in protest and went along at a smart canter, a vision of dainty horse-flesh.

The jackal got into a vineyard, was put out again, and had to make for open country.

It was fine going, and Madame Paës let Belzébuth go. He went—and in five minutes the first rider behind the Master was Madame Paës, and she was holding Belzébuth in, or he would have passed the Master's big Syrian-Barb who was doing his possible under Colonel de Longueville's fifteen stone.

When the end came, Madame Paës was in at the death, lengths ahead of the second arrival, and minutes ahead of the field. Belzébuth had hardly turned a hair, and the Master presented the rider with the brush and a compliment. Madame Paës took her pony home, the while the field jogged on to the next likely cactus covert.

In another week Belzébuth was doing two kilometres on the race-course, morning and evening.

At the next meet, a very long run (twenty-two kilometres, the Master said) was finished by a field of four arriving thus: the Master and Madame Paës together; Captain Dutoit of the Spahis, seconds later; fourth man, Major Bruil of the Chasseurs d'Afrique, minutes later. Rest nowhere—and strung out for miles. Belzébuth had been held, while the other horses had been spurred.

Belzébuth hunted twice more, and the hunt-correspondent of the "Depêche Algérienne" singled him out for high praise.

Madame Paës dropped race-course practice and hunting, and let him do exercise walks in the compound on one day, and a point-to-point run on another.

Riding out alone to some scrubby, sandy jungle, she would endeavour to estimate a two-kilometre distance, note a clump of palms, a tree, a hut, a hillock, and other natural landmarks, and then ride from one to the other at Belzébuth's best speed.

Once she had a narrow escape of settling the question of Belzébuth's value, and all other values, finally. Emerging at a furious gallop from a cactus-strewn area, in which pace could only be maintained and disaster avoided by skilful "bending," she came upon a beautiful smooth patch with a gentle rise ending in—a *wadi* or gully, thirty feet deep and fifty wide. She realized the fact in time to bring Belzébuth round in a curve that missed the precipice by inches.

On the Wednesday before the Saturday on which the race would be run, Madame Paës took Belzébuth out for his last training gallop. In the middle of it she put him at a *terrasse*, a "bund," or low earthen embankment, round what had once been a cultivated field.

The three-foot banks Belzébuth preferred to clear. The four-foot variety he liked to treat as on-and-offs—alighting on the two-foot top and leaving it like a bird.

This particular bank was a delusion and a snare.

Though fair-seeming to the eye on Madame Paës' side of it, on the other it was eroded, crumbling, beetling.

Belzébuth landed beautifully on the top—and horse and rider went down in a cloud of dust and an avalanche of clods and stones.

The horse turned a complete somersault across the woman.

But the flood that had caused the erosion had made some amends by scooping a channel at the base of the undermined bank, and instead of breaking every bone in Madame Paës' body and crushing her chest, Belzébuth's weight forced her into this channel and rested on its sides.

He arose and stood steady as a troop-horse.

His mistress lay still and white.

Soon she stirred, sat up—and straightened her tricorne hat. Then, too shaken to stand, sick and faint, giddy and stunned, not knowing whether she was seriously injured, she crawled to Belzébuth and examined his knees.

"*Oh! Thank God!*" she whispered, on finding that, instead of being broken as she had expected, they were unmarked.

What did her own injuries matter so long as Belzébuth's knees were right?

A blemish there—and two hundred francs was his price.

An hour later, Madame Paës, looking like death on a bay horse, rode into the compound of her villa and went straight to bed.

Next day she could not move.

On the Friday she was better, but unable to get up.

On Saturday she would leave her bed and, if necessary, be carried downstairs, driven to the starting-point, and lifted on to Belzébuth.

Who could ride him for her at seven stone—and ride him as she would? Nobody.

All Bellevue was *en route* for the scene of the famous Bellevue Point-to-Point races, consisting of team-races for horses, another for ponies, a handicap, and an open race for quadrupeds of any size and bipeds of any weight.

Then came the Ladies' Point-to-Point, over two and a half kilometres of fairly good course and a few jumps.

The ordinary course was a stiff one, and so arranged that a really bold and resolute rider could shorten the distance on the average man by taking *wadis*, and the other "places" that discretion would ride round.

The Ladies' Course included nothing that gave the stout heart and strong seat a marked advantage. So much the worse for Madame Paës, who was out, not so much to win a race and glory, as to win health and happiness, possibly life itself, for her children and husband.

A large crowd, on horseback for the most part, surrounded the tents (where the officers of the *Chasseurs d'Afrique* were "At Home"), the starting-point, and neighbouring winning-post.

Madame Paës lay in a long chair, with closed eyes—while the men's four races were run—limp, relaxed, and weary to death.

Oh, for a cushion to put under her weak and aching back!—and oh, for a *petit verre* of *eau de vie* to give her heart and strength! But her idolized Guillaume (a prig of the first water and petty domestic tyrant) did not "approve" of alcohol for ladies. There were so many things of which Guillaume did not "approve" for other people, though he appeared to approve of most things for Guillaume.

At last! The bell for the Ladies' Point-to-Point, the most popular and famous race in the Colony.

Madame Paës mounted Belzébuth and walked him to the starting-point.

Nine competitors.

Colonel Lebrun's wife on the pride of the Chasseurs (but a heavy, bumping, mouth-sawing rider who would spoil any horse's chance).

Madame Maxin on a characterless, unreliable racer.

Little Angélique Dandin, on her brother's one and only pony.

Madame Malherbe, cool, quiet, neat, and businesslike, on a light and dainty black mare with slender legs but powerful quarters.

Major Parme's wife on the best horse that her money could buy—but a woman who thought far more of hat, habit, and figure than of seat and hands.

Madame Deville, riding (astride) her husband's charger and intending to win if spur and quirt would do it.

Colonel de Longueville's wife, a fine horsewoman, handsome, smart, and clever, on the pick of her husband's racing-stable. And a couple of quidnuncs.

A bad field to beat.

Betting was on Madame Maxin if her horse "behaved." If he didn't, Madame de Longueville must win in a common canter.

Strangers liked the look of Madame Malherbe, but local wisdom knew her mare couldn't live with the two other.

General Blanc, starter, drew the attention of the ladies to a pair of red flags half a kilometre away, a pair of blue ones to the right of these and half a kilometre from them, another pair of red to the right of the "field," and a pair of white, at present behind their backs and some three furlongs distant.

"You must pass between the red flags, then between the blue, then the red, and lastly between the white, and finish here," said he. "There is nothing serious in the way of ditch or wall. Pick your own route—and any competitor not passing between the flags is, of course, disqualified."

A silly question from Madame Lebrun—politely answered.

All ready? . . . The flag falls.

Madame Paës thanked Heaven they were away at last.

A hundred yards from the starting-point is a brushwood jump which must be taken—or a large patch of dense cactus-jungle skirted to the left or right.

Should she try and take it first of all?

She hated jumping in company. Yes. A flick told Belzébuth he might stretch himself for a bit, and he cleared the jump ten lengths ahead of the next horse.

"*Nom de Dieu!* It's an 'outsider's year,'" said General Blanc. "Bar accidents, that's the winner. Who is she?"

Madame Lebrun's horse—with a round dozen stone hanging on his mouth—refused; the lady and the animal parted company, and the subsequent proceedings interested them no more.

Madame Parme elected to skirt the jungle, and was out of the race from that moment.

A quidnunc took alarm at the pace and pulled with all her strength.

The virtueless and evil-reputed racer drew level with Belzébuth, Madame Maxin spurring, and Madame de Longueville passed both.

Madame Paës was holding Belzébuth in from the moment he had cleared the first jump.

Madame Deville began flogging, like a jockey, in the first quarter-mile of the race, and passed Madame de Longueville with a spurt. Shortly after she took fifth place and kept it. . . .

Between the first flags passed Madame de Longueville with the wicked racer at her girth and Belzébuth at her tail, Madame Malherbe a dozen lengths behind, and Madame Deville thirty.

Angélique Dandin came later in the day, having lost her way. Neither quidnunc continued her wild career to this point. . . .

Gradually the distance between the leading three and the following two lengthened—and, for a kilometre, Madame Paës, Madame de Longueville, and Madame Maxin ran neck and neck.

Suddenly the bad-charactered racer took a line of his own, missed the next flags by a few metres, and bolted into the desert. At the second flags, Madame de Longueville led, Belzébuth consenting—or rather, being made, to consent; Madame Malherbe, creeping up, passed the flags three lengths behind, and Angélique Dandin, catching Madame Deville, led her through, a score lengths in rear. . . .

Madame Paës was filled with hope.

Should she let Belzébuth out yet? No, not till the last flags—if she could live so long—if her heart would beat instead of stabbing—if her brain would not reel so—if the blue mist would clear from her eyes.

(Those who had climbed to points of vantage shouted that Madame de Longueville would win in a walk—had led from the start—was going strong—except for that dark horse which seemed to manage to hang on. . . .)

A fairish jump ahead—should she pass Madame de Longueville? No, let her take it first, and let Belzébuth save himself for the three-furlong run home.

At the last flags Madame de Longueville led by twenty lengths, Madame Paës second, Madame Malherbe third, Angélique Dandin a neck behind, and Madame Deville, still flogging, a safe fifth.

And then Madame Paës gave Belzébuth a sharp flick, raised her bridle hand, and called to him.

The roar of applause and welcome to Madame de Longueville died down with curious suddenness as Belzébuth sprang forward, passed Madame de Longueville's lathered grey Arab as though he were standing, forged rapidly and steadily ahead, and, finishing in a quiet canter, won the race by a good furlong. Madame Paës reeled in the saddle and fell heavily into the arms of Colonel Merlonorot, who came forward to help her to dismount.

"Splendid! Splendid!" said he. "*Mon Dieu!* If I hadn't just bought my wife a horse, I'd ask if that pony of yours is for sale. You should run him at Longchamps!"

. . . "*If I hadn't just bought my wife a horse*". . . what was he saying? "*If I hadn't just bought my wife a horse*, I'd ask if that pony of yours is for sale." . . .

Then it was all for nothing—and money wasted!

Madame Paës fainted quietly and privately in a comfortable chair at the back of the empty reception-tent of the Spahis.

Colonel Merlonorot drove her home in his uncomfortable high dogcart—(quite *à l'Anglaise*).

Just time to change and rest before Guillaume arrived. . . .

He burst into her room, looking fagged, white, and weary—and his greeting, after five weeks' absence, was—

"What on earth have you been doing with my horse? It's as lame as a tree, and the *valet* has got its near fore in a bucket of hot water. . . . It's a shame, I say. . . . The only horse I have got, and you can't take a little care of it! What am I to do to-morrow? I suppose it doesn't trouble *you* that I must cycle to barracks in the sun? . . . *Peste!* . . . *Nom d'un Nom!* . . ." and much more.

Poor Guillaume! He was so overworked and ill—but she wept bitterly, and, lying awake all night, wished she were dead. But a note was handed in at breakfast, next morning, from Colonel de Longueville, which ran:

"DEAR MADAME,
"I should like to offer my very hearty congratulations on your, and your pony's performance yesterday, and to ask whether your husband would take 4,000 fcs. for him.
"I gave that for the pony that Belzébuth left standing yesterday—so it's not a very brilliant offer. I should train him for bigger things.
"With my most distinguished regards and compliments,
"HENRI DE LONGUEVILLE,
"Colonel."

Madame Paës, being very weak and tired, wept again.

THE QUEST

"The Quest" is story of a legionnaire who has served his five years enlistment with the Foreign Legion. He is quite ill, and the description of how he feels and how he struggles to survive is quite interesting in that Wren himself seems to have been quite ill throughout most of his later life. The quest of the story is a reverse to the stereotypical Foreign Legion story: a man joins the Legion because of his thwarted love. In this case, the story is about such a man, but it is concerned with how he copes after he has served in the Legion. "The Quest" first appeared in Stepsons of France *(1917), and was reprinted at least four times in the newspapers of 1927. The known newspapers are the* Winnipeg Free Press *(April 23, 1927),* Oakland Tribune *(May 1, 1927), the* Los Angeles Times *(May 29, 1927), and the Ohio* Mansfield News *(May 29, 1927). The story was also reprinted in* Tales of the Foreign Legion *(The Master-Thriller Series, #1, July 1933),* The Thriller *(v. 13, no. 344, 1935),* Stories of the Foreign Legion *(Vallancey, 1945),* Tales of the Foreign Legion *(Vallancey, 1946), and* Stories of the Foreign Legion *(Murray, 1947).*

Ex-No. 32867, *Soldat première classe*, shuffled out of the main gate of the barracks of the First Battalion of La Legion Étrangère at Sidi-bel-Abbès for the last time, and without a farewell glance at that hideous yellow building. He had once been Geoffry Brabazon-Howard, Esquire, of St. James's Street and the United Service Club, but no one would have thought it of the stooping, decrepit creature in the ill-fitting blue suit of ready-made (and very badly made) mufti, the tam-o'-shanter cap and blue scarf, from the *fourrier-sergent's* store. He looked more like a Basque bear-leader whose bear has been impounded, or an Italian organ-grinder who has had to pawn his organ—save that the rather vacant eye in the leathern face was grey and the hair, beneath the *beret*, of a Northern fairness. A careful observer (such as a mother or wife, had he had one to observe him) would have noticed that his hands shook like those of an old man, that his eyes were heavy and blood-shot, as though from sleeplessness, and that his legs did not appear to be completely under control. A casual passer-by might have supposed him to be slightly drunk, or recovering from a drunken bout.

He had that day received his discharge from the Legion, his bonus as holder of the *médaille* and *croix,* his papers and travelling-warrant to any place in France, the blessing of his Captain, and the cheery assurance of Médecin-Major Parme that he was suffering from cerebro-spinal sclerosis, and would gradually but surely develop into a paralysed lunatic.

Certainly he felt very ill. He was in no great pain, and he regretted the fact. He would far rather have felt the acutest pain than the strange sensation that there was a semi-opaque veil between himself and his fellow-men, that he lived quite alone and unapproachable in a curious cloud, and that, although he slept but little, he lived in a dream. He was also much distressed by the feeling that his hands were as large and thick as boxing-gloves, that his feet had soles of thick felt, and that he had *fourmis* (pins-and-needles) in his legs. He would gladly have exchanged the terrible feeling of weakness (and imminent collapse) in the small of his back for any kind of pain. And, above all things, he wanted *rest.* Not sleep! Heaven forbid. Sleep was the portal of a Hell unnameable and unimaginable, and the worst of it was that insomnia led to the very same place, and one lived on the horns of a dilemma. If one did things to keep oneself awake, they either lost their efficacy and one slept (and fell into Hell) or one got insomnia (and crawled there with racking, bursting head and eyes that burnt the brain).

Rest! That was it. Well—he had done his five years in the Legion and got his discharge. Why shouldn't he rest? He would rest forthwith, before he set out upon his Quest, the last undertaking of his life.

He sat down on the *pavé* in the shade of the Spahis' barracks and leant against the wall. In five seconds he was asleep.

Later, two gens d'armes passed. One turned back and kicked him. "Get out of this," said he tersely.

Ex-No. 32867 of the Premiere Legion Étrangère staggered to his feet with what speed he might.

"I *beg* your pardon," said he in English. "I am afraid . . ." and then he realized who and what and where he was.

Mechanically he walked back to barracks and made to enter

105

the great main gate. The sentry stopped him, and the Sergeant of the Guard came up.

"By no means, verminous *pékin*,"[14] quoth Sergeant Legros. "Is this a doss-house for every dirty tramp of a broken-down *pékin* that chooses to enter and defile it?" and he ordered the sentry to fling the thing out. "But that a French bayonet must not be used as a stable-fork, I would . . ." he began again, but *Ex*-No. 32867 perceived that this was not the place of Rest, and shuffled away again.

Sergeant Legros spat after him. If there was one thing he hated more than a Legionary, it was a time-expired man, a vile dog who had survived his treatment and escaped his clutches. . . .

Ex-No. 32867 passed along the barrack wall, his eyes staring vaguely ahead. If he might not sit on the ground and could not get back to his *chambrée* and cot, where could he go for rest? He could not set forth upon his Quest until he had rested. His back was too near the breaking-point, his knees too weak, his feet too uncertain. There were seats in the gardens by the Porte de Tlemçen, if he could get so far. But in the Place Sadi Carnot he suddenly found that he had sat down. Well—he would. . . . He fell asleep at once. . . .

The gendarme seemed very suspicious, but that is only natural in a gendarme. Yes—the papers were apparently in order, but he would do well to remember that the gendarme had his eye upon him. He could go, this time—so, *Marche!*—and sit down no more for a siesta in the middle of the road. . . .

Where was it he had been going for a rest? . . . A bright idea—*Carmelita's!* She would let him rest, and, if not too busy, would see that he did not fall asleep and go to Hell. . . .

"Bon jour, mon ami!" cried Carmelita, as he entered the little Café de la Légion. "Che cosa posse offrirve? Seet daown. What you drink?"

Ex-No. 32867 raised his *beret*, bowed, smiled, and fell asleep across a table. Carmelita raised puzzled brows. Drunk at this time of day? She pulled him backward on to the wooden bench, untied his scarf, and, going to her room behind the bar, returned with an old cushion which she thrust beneath his head. He at

---

[14] Pékin = civilian.

once sat up, thanked her politely, and walked out of the café.

"Eh! Madonna! These English," shrugged Carmelita, and resumed her work. If one stopped to notice the eccentricities of every half-witted Légionnaire, one might spend one's life at it. . . .

Ex-No. 32867 strolled slowly along to the railway-station, showed his papers to the Sergeant of the Guard on duty there, sat him down, and went to sleep. Five minutes later he arose, approached the ticket-office, tried hard for a minute to penetrate the half-opaque veil that hung between him and his fellow-men, and then sat down beneath the *guichet* and went to sleep. . . .

The station-master was doing his best to make it clear that he hated filth, dust, dead leaves, stray pariah dogs, discharged Legionaries, and similar kinds of offal to remain unswept from the clean floor of his station.

The awakened man peered hard through the half-opaque veil that hung between him and the great man, made a mighty effort of concentration, and then said quite distinctly:

"I want a third single to Oran. I am starting on my Quest, after waiting five years."

"Then wait another five hours, Mr. Discharged Legionary," said the functionary, "and come again at 9.20 for your third single to Oran—if you are not too drunk. Meanwhile, you cannot sleep here, unless it is in the permanent-way with your ugly neck across a rail."

The time-expired considered this.

"No, I go on a Quest," said he, and the station-master, with a gesture of a spatulate thumb in the direction of the door, indicated that the sooner the son of a camel commenced it the better for all concerned.

He was an unsympathetic person—but then he was held responsible when unconsidered trifles of Government property were stolen from the station precincts. And it is well known that a Legionary will steal the wall-paper from your wall while your back is turned, cut it up small, and try to sell it back to you as postage-stamps as soon as darkness sets in.

Ex-No. 32867 got to his feet once more, marched mechanically to barracks, was somewhat roughly handled by the guard at the order of Sergeant Legros, and, having staunched the bleeding from his nose, split lip, and cut cheek with the lining of his *beret*, made his way to the Café de la Légion. Entering, he bowed to Carmelita with a dignified flourish of his pulpy *beret*, fell at full length on the floor, and went to sleep.

"Queer, how differently drink takes different people," mused Carmelita, as she again applied the cushion to supporting the battered head—and yet she had hitherto known this Guillaume Iyoné or Dhyoni (or William Jones!) of the IIIrd Company as a soldier of the soberest and quietest. Quite like old Jean Boule of the VIIth. Doubtless he had been "wetting his discharge papers." Apparently he had done it to the point of drowning them.

At *l'heure verte, l'heure de l'absinthe*, the café began to fill, and for a time the sleeper was undisturbed by the *va et vient* of Carmelita's customers. . . .

"'Ullo, Cocky!" remarked le Légionnaire 'Erbiggin ("'Erb"), entering with his compatriots Rupert and John Bull, followed by the Grasshopper and the Bucking Bronco. "Gorn to yer pore 'ed, 'as it? Come *hup*—an' 'ave s'more," and he sought to rouse the sleeper.

"Strike me strange ef it 'ent thet *com*-patriot o' yourn, John," said the Bucking Bronco. "Willie the Jones, o' the IIIrd Company. . . . Guess he's got a hard cider jag. Didn't know he ever fell off the water-cart any."

"William Jones" sat up.

"Really, I *beg* your pardon," he said. "I thought I . . ." and then peered through the heavy blanketing veil that was daily thickening between him and his fellow-men.

"He's no more drunk than I am," said John Bull. . . . "I suppose he's just discharged. I thought he was in hospital. . . . Looks as though he ought to be, anyhow."

"I have rested, and I must begin my Quest," said "William Jones," *Ex*-No. 32867. "I have a glorious Quest to undertake, and I have little time. I . . ."

"Yus. *Ingk*quest's abaht your mark, Cocky," observed 'Erb. "Crowner's ingkquest."

"Help me up," added the sick man. "I must begin my Quest."

"*De sot homme, sot songe*," murmured La Cigale, shaking his head mournfully. "I too have Quests, but they tangle and jangle in my brain—and folk say I am mad or drunk. . . . Some will say you are mad, *mon ami*, and some will say you are drunk."

"Are you going to England?" asked John Bull, as he helped the man to his feet.

"England? . . . England? . . . Oh, yes, I am going to England. Where *should* I go? She lives in England," was the reply.

"Have you friends?"

"She is my Friend. Of Friendship she is the Soul and the Essence."

"*Chacun aime comme il est*," remarked the Grasshopper. "This is a gentleman," and added, "*Il n'y a guère de femme assez habile pour connaître tout le mal qu'elle fait*."

"I allow we oughter take him daown town to the railway deepôt and see him on the cars," put in the Bucking Bronco. "Ef we don't tote him thar an' tell him good-bye, it's the looney-house for his. He'll set down in the bazaar and go as *maboul*[15] as a *kief*[16] smoker." . . .

"I was going to say we'd better see him off," agreed John Bull. "If he gets to England, he'll have more chance than as a discharged Legionary in Algiers—or France either. Wish we could get an address from him. We could tie a label on him."

But they could not, and after the Bucking Bronco had procured him food from Carmelita's "pie-foundry," as he termed her modest *table d'hôte*, they took him to the station and, under the cold eye of the Sergeant of the Guard at the platform gate, saw him off. . . .

As one in a dream, as one seeing through a glass darkly and beholding men as trees walking, *Ex*-No. 32867, William Jones, *alias* Geoffry Brabazon-Howard, Esquire, made his way to London. There is a providence that watches over children and drunken men, and *Ex*-No. 32867 was as a compound of both. He knew he was exceeding ill and quite abnormal in some directions, such as never being *quite* certain as to whether he was really doing and experiencing things, or was dreaming; but what he did not realize was that, concurrently with severe insomnia, he was liable at any moment to fall suddenly asleep for a few minutes, wherever he might be, and whatever he might be doing. He was

---

[15] Mad.

[16] Hemp.

aware that he had brief periods of "abstraction," but was quite unaware that they were periods of profound slumber. Unfortunately they only endured for a few seconds or a few minutes, and, though serving to place him in endless dangerous, ridiculous, and awkward situations, did not amount to anything approaching a "living-wage" of sleep—rarely to more than an hour in the twenty-four and generally to much less.

At times he was, for a few hours perhaps, entirely normal, to all appearances; and could talk, behave, and transact business in such a way that no casual observer would be aware of anything unusual in the man. He himself, however, when at his best, was still aware of the isolating-medium in which he moved and lived and had his being; the slowly thickening cloud, the imponderating veil, that shut him in, and cut him off, with increasing certainty and speed.

What would happen when he could no longer pierce and penetrate this fog, or wall, of cloudy glass; this vast extinguisher of sombre web, and could hold no communication with the outer world?

Was he becoming an idiot before becoming a paralytic, and thus having the gross presumption to reverse the order of things foretold by Médecin-Major Parme?

On arrival at Charing Cross, he had strolled idly through the streets of London, slept on a bench in Leicester Square; had thought he was in the public gardens outside the Porte de Tlemçen at Sidi-bel-Abbès, and hoped that the Legion's famous band would come and play its sad music in that sad place; and, being "moved on," had wandered away, dazed and bewildered, going on and on until he reached Hammersmith. Here he found his way into one of those Poor Man's Hotels, a Rowton House— vaguely under the impression that it was some kind of barrack.

Here he had a glorious time of Rest, broken only by the occasional misfortune of having a night's sleep, or rather a nightmare in the unnameable Hell to keep out of which he exerted all his failing faculties. And at the Hammersmith Rowton House he became an object of the intensest interest to such of his fellow-inhabitants of that abode of semi-starvation and hopeless misery as were not too deeply engulfed in their own struggle with despair and death to notice anything at all.

For "William Jones" began to blossom forth into a "toff," a perfect dook, until it was the generally accepted theory that he was a swell-mobsman just out of gaol, and now working the West End in the correct garb of that locality.

Little by little the man had replaced his old clothes by new, his *beret* by a correct hat, his scarf by the usual neck-wear of an English gentleman, his *fourrier-sergent's* suit of mufti by a Conduit Street creation, his rough boots by the most modish of cloth-topped kid; and generally metamorphosed William Jones, late of the Foreign Legion, into Geoffry Brabazon-Howard, Esq., late of St. James's Street and the United Service Club.

In one of his hours of mental clarity and vigour, he had called at his bank and drawn the sum of ninety pounds, left at current-account there when he disappeared into the Legion; and in another such hour (and in his new clothes) had called at his Club, seen the secretary, and arranged for the revival of his lapsed membership.

It had taken both the bank-manager and the secretary some time to recognize him, but they had done so eventually, and had been shocked to think of what the man must have been through to have changed as he had, and to look as he did.

He *had* been through a good deal. In addition to the very real hardships of campaigning in the Sahara as a private of the Legion, he had had black-water fever and dysentery, had been wounded in the abdomen by an Arab lance, carried away by the Arabs while unconscious from loss of blood from this wound, and kept until he should recover consciousness and be eligible for torture. (It is pointless to torture a practically dead person.) The badness of his wound had saved his life, for by the time he had sufficiently recovered to be interesting to his captors, they were attacked and routed, and "William Jones" had been restored to the bosom of his company only slightly tortured after all. The shock to an enfeebled man, who was also suffering from a hideous wound, had been considerable, however.

Thereafter, enteric had done little to improve his health, and his resultant slowness and stupidity had earned him the special attention of Sergeant-Major Suicide-Maker and Sergeant Legros.

So there is little wonder that his banker and club-secretary were shocked at the change in him, and wondered how many days or weeks he had to live.

And to the secretary, who saw him almost daily, it was clear that the poor chap was sometimes queer in the head too—and no wonder, looking as awfully ill as he did.

For example, one day he would walk into the Club, sit down on the Hall-Porter's stool, and go to sleep immediately!

Another day he would do the same thing on the stairs, or even the front steps.

If he sat down in a smoking-room arm-chair and fell asleep, as is a member's just and proper right, he would spring up if anyone approached, say, "I really *beg* your pardon. I am afraid I . . ." and walk straight out of the Club.

What would the worthy secretary have thought had he known that Geoffry Brabazon-Howard, Esquire (once of the Black Lancers), walked daily to the Club from the Hammersmith Rowton House in the morning and back to that same retreat in the evening; and that such food as he ate, was eaten in his cubicle there, or at a coffee-stall? At a Rowton House one has the "use of the fire" in the basement for one's cooking purposes, but Geoffry was a most indifferent cook, and it is difficult to purchase really cookable provisions on a sum of fourpence a day. For this was the amount that he had decided upon as the irreducible minimum to be expended on food if he were to keep up the strength required for the daily journey to the West End and back. After paying for his clothes and setting aside his club fees, he would have enough to live on at this rate, until the London season and through it, if he were very, very careful. He would have to renew some of his clothing, perhaps, later on—boots, linen, ties—and there were always incidental and unavoidable expenses. However, with great care and a little luck, he could last to the end of the season and pursue his Quest. And this great absorbing Quest, which had made him expend his all in fine clothing, club membership, and the appearance of being a "person of quality" and a gentleman of means and leisure?

Merely to come face to face with, to meet on terms of equality, to have just one encounter and conversation with—a woman.

Before he died he must see, and speak to, Peggy once again— to Lady Margaret Hillier—because of whom he had vanished into the French Foreign Legion, and of whom he had thought daily and nightly ever since.

He had had a thin time, he was near the end of his tether, life held nothing for him, and he had no desire to prolong it—but before he lay down for the last time he *would* see Peggy again, hear her voice, feast his eyes on her beautiful face, and his ears on the sound of her words and laughter, yea, feast his very soul upon the banquet that it had dreamed of—and then he would have no further use for clubs, fine clothes, a penny chair in the Park, nor anything else.

The ass was quite mad, you perceive. . . .

Now one *can* live on fourpence a day, and for a very long time too. If one starts in robust health and strength, one can maintain an appearance of health and the power to work for a quite surprising period. But if one is really very ill, on the verge of a nervous collapse, and badly in need of a rest-cure with special diet, tonic, and drugs—fourpence a day is not enough.

They give you a surprisingly filling meal at certain coffee-shops and cocoa-houses (like Pearce-and-Plenty or Lockhart's) for fourpence, but one meatless meal per diem is not enough. It is, on the whole, better to have two pennyworth at dawn and two pennyworth at sunset, and a good drink of water at midday. Better still is it, if you are really experienced in the laying-out of money, to have a pennyworth at dawn, two pennyworth at midday and a pennyworth at sunset. (You can go to bed with a full stomach by supping on a quart of water.)

But Geoffry had not complete liberty in the matter. One cannot go for a twopenny midday meal in a silk hat, faultless morning coat buttoned over the white waistcoat of a blameless laundress, and in patent cloth-topped boots. Geoffry was, by force of circumstances, debarred this thrice-a-day system of feeding, and was constrained to breakfast (in rags) at an early coffee-stall and to dine at the same, in the same decrepit clothing, late at night. After breakfast he would return to his cubicle, dress for the Club, and creep forth, still in the early hours of the morning. (One attracts attention if, in the broad light of naked day, one issues from a Rowton House in the correct garb of Pall Mall and Piccadilly.) At night he would undress, carefully fold his immaculate clothes, don his rags, and sally forth to dine on twopence. The coffee-stall keeper regarded him as a broken-down torf and eke a balmy, but coffee-stall keepers are a race blasé of freaks, social, moral, and mental.

Between these meals Geoffry Brabazon-Howard pursued his Quest. He went to his Club and listened eagerly for "society" gossip, and read "society" papers (of the kind that inform the public when Lady Diana Blathers dines at the Fritz, and photographs her inhaling the breath of an abortive animal, apparently a bye-product of the dog-industry; announces the glad tidings that Mrs. Bobbie Snobbie has returned to Town; or that the Earl of Spunge was seen scratching his head in Bond Street yesterday). Having sought in vain for news of Lady Margaret Hillier, he slowly paraded the fashionable shopping thoroughfares, and then, utterly weary, turned into the Park, selected an eligible site for seeing the pedestrians, carriage-exercisers, and riders, and sat for hours watching and waiting, hoping against hope—as he thought. In point of fact he spent a great portion of this time in dropping asleep and being awakened by nearly falling off the chair. He was sometimes tempted to expend this chair-penny in food, but restrained the base cravings of his lower nature. He pictured himself arrayed in the correctest of dress, nonchalantly seated on a Park chair, gaily observing the gyrations of the giddy throng of fashionable human ephemeræ—suddenly seeing Peggy, and rising, accosting her with graceful badinage, airy flippancy, and casual interest. Peggy would laugh and talk amusingly and lightly, he would beg her to come and lunch with him at the Club, or take tea if such were the hour; he would feast his eyes and ears and soul as he had promised himself—and *then*?—then he would lay down his arms and cease to fight this relentless Foe—sickness, disease, and death—that besieged him day and night, and sought to prevent his walk to the Club, sought to thwart the pursuit of his Quest. Having seen Peggy again, heard her laugh and speak, looked into her hopelessly perfect and wonderful eyes, he would surrender the fortress he no longer wished to hold, and would permit the Enemy to enter—trusting that *le bon Dieu, Le Bon Général*, would see to it that, for a broken old soldier, death was annihilation, peace, and rest. . . .

Daily he grew thinner, as a sick man living on fourpence a

day must, and frequently he would finger the sovereign that always lay in his waistcoat pocket—ready for the day when Peggy should lunch at the Club with him. It is not wholly easy to keep a sovereign intact while you slowly starve and every fibre of your being craves for tobacco, for brandy, for food—as you smell choice Havanas in the Club smoking-room, see fat, healthy men drinking their whiskies and brandies, and when you are violently smitten by rich savours of food as you pass the door of the dining-room.

The fragrance of coffee and eggs-and-bacon! The glimpse of noble barons of beef on the sideboard! The sight of tea-and-toast at four in the afternoon when you have had nothing since four in the morning! But the sovereign remained intact. With that he and Peggy could have an excellent lunch—without wine—and Peggy never touched wine. . . .

*　　*　　*　　*　　*

He started to his feet.

"I really *beg* your pardon! I am afraid I . . ." A stranger had awakened him as he slept in a smoking-room arm-chair. . . . He did not recollect how he came to do such a thing when he should have been in the Park. . . . *What* was the man saying—"Ill?"

"I was afraid you were ill. To tell the truth, I jolly well thought you were dead for the moment. Let me drive you to my doctor's. Splendid chap. Just going that way. . . . No—don't run away."

"Most awfully kind," replied Geoffry, peering through the veil, "but I'm *quite* all right. Just a bit tired, you know. I am going to have a real Rest soon. . . . At present I have a Quest."

The poor devil looked absolutely *starved*, thought Colonel Doddington. Positively ghastly.

"Come and have some lunch with me," he said, "and let me tell you about this doctor of mine, anyhow."

Geoffry flushed—though it was remarkable that there was sufficient blood in so meagre a body and feeble a heart for the purpose.

Lunch! A four-course lunch in a beautiful room—silver, crystal, fine napery, good service—perhaps wine, certainly alcohol of some sort, and real coffee. . . .

It was a cruel temptation. But he put it from him. After all, one was a gentleman, and a gentleman does not accept hospitality which he cannot return, from a stranger.

"Awfully sorry—but I *must* go," he replied. "I'm feeding out." He was—late that night, on twopence.

He fled, and outside mopped his brow. It *had* been a terrible temptation and ordeal. For two pins he would go back and have a brandy-and-soda at the cost of two days' food. No, he dared not risk collapse—and two days' complete starvation would probably mean collapse. Collapse meant expense too, and money was time to him. The expenditure of more than fourpence a day would shorten the time of his Quest. A day lost, was a chance lost. She might pass through London at that very time, if he lay ill in the Hammersmith Rowton House.

That night he had to take a 'bus home or lie down in the street. Next day, dressing took so long and his walk to the Club was so painful and slow, that he had to omit the Bond Street, Regent Street, and Piccadilly walk, and go straight to the Park.

There he had shocking luck. A zealous but clumsy policeman rendered him First Aid to the Fainting with such violence that he spoilt the collar and shirt-front that should have lasted another two days. Why could not the worthy fool have left him to come out of his faint alone? He went *into* it alone, all right. And there was an accursed, gaping crowd. Nor could he give the policeman two pennies, and so gave him nothing—which was very distressing. A most unlucky day!

Well—the days of his Quest were numbered, and the number was lessened.

Next day he found the Enemy very powerful and the tottering fortress closely beset. He would be hard put to it to walk to the Club—but come!—an old Legionary who had done his fifty kilometres a day under a hundredweight kit, over loose sand, with the thermometer at 120° in the shade; and who had lived on a handful of rice-flour and a mouthful of selenitic water in the Sahara—surely *he* was not going to shirk a stroll from Hammersmith Broadway to Pall Mall and round the Town to the Park?

He had got as far as Devonshire House, when a lady, who

was driving from the Berkeley Hotel, where she had been lunching, to the Coburg Hotel, where she was to have tea with friends who were taking her on to Ranelagh, suddenly saw him and thought she saw a ghost. As her carriage crawled through the crush into Berkeley Street it brought her within a yard of him.

She turned very pale and lay back on the cushions. Immediately she sat upright again, and then leaned towards him. It *could* not be! Not this poor wreck, this shattered ruin—her splendid *Geoff*—the Geoff who had seemed to love her, five years ago, and had suddenly dropped her, and so been the cause of her marrying in haste and repenting in even greater haste, to the day of her widowhood.

"*Geoff!*" she said.

He raised his hat with a trembling hand and his face was transfigured. . . . Was he dying on his feet, wondered the woman.

"Get in, Geoff," she said, and the footman half-turned and then jumped down.

Geoffry Brabazon-Howard, with a great and almost final effort, stepped into the victoria.

"Will you come to lunch with me at . . ." he began, and then burst into tears.

Later, it was the woman who wept, tears of joy and thankfulness, after the agonizing suspense when the great specialist staked his reputation on his plain verdict that the man was not organically diseased. He was in a parlous state, no doubt, practically dying of starvation and nervous exhaustion—but nursing could save him.

Nursing did—the nursing of Lady Peggy Brabazon-Howard. . . .

"VENGEANCE IS MINE . . ."

"Vengeance is Mine . . ." is the story that a dying legionnaire tells about how he was trained to kill his father. During the Franco-German War of 1870 the legionnaire's mother was raped, and her husband murdered, by a German officer. The mother then raised her son to avenge her tortures and her husband's murder. One of Wren's recurring themes in his fiction is the terrible effect that an overbearing parent can have on someone's life (see especially the novel, Mammon, *and the short story, "The Brave Coward", in volume 4 in* The Collected Short Stories). *"Vengeance is Mine . . ." first appeared in* Stepsons of France *(1917) and was reprinted in* Dead Men's Boots *(1949).*

As Jean Rien expressed it, he was *bien touché*; as le Légionnaire 'Erbiggin put it, he had got it in the neck; as the Bucking Bronco "allowed," his monica was up; as Jean Boule saw, he was dying.

One cannot blame him, since an Arab lance had pinned him to the ground and an Arab *flissa* had nearly severed his arm from his shoulder.

Jean Rien evidently blamed himself however, and for many things—chief among them a little matter of parricide, it seemed to Jean Boule, as he bent over him in his endeavour to comfort and to soothe.

"In much pain, *mon ami*?" the old soldier asked, as he moistened the dying man's lips and forehead.

"Little of body, but in great pain of mind. . . . I would confess to you, Père Boule. . . . I would ease my soul. . . . I would ask if you think I am a murderer. . . . I have not blamed myself until now that I am dying. . . . Now I am afraid. . . . Look you, Père Jean Boule, I was brought up by my mother (*le bon Dieu* rest and bless her soul) with one purpose in life, with one end to fulfil, with one deed to do. Nothing earlier can I remember than her making me repeat after her the words of a promise and an oath. Night after night, as I went to bed, morning after morning, as I arose, I said my prayers at her knee, and followed them by this promise and this oath which she had taught me. Never did we sit down to a meal, never did we rise from one, without this formula. From my very birth I was dedicated, and my life was devoted and avowed, to the fulfilment of this promise, the keeping of this oath. . . . Hear it. . . . *'I, Jean-Without-A-Name, son of Marie Duval and Ober-Leutnant von Schlofen of the Hundred and Thirty-ninth Pomeranian Regiment, do most solemnly swear, that from my seventeenth birthday I will devote the whole of my mind and will, my strength and skill, my time and my money, to finding the man who in 1870 was Ober-Leutnant von Schlofen and who is my father, the torturer of my mother and the murderer of my mother's beloved husband, Jacques Duval. I do most solemnly swear that, having found him, I will call him "Father," I will torture him, as he tortured my mother, and I will kill him even as he killed him who should have been my father, so help me God and the Blessed Virgin. Amen. . . ."*

"Yes, my. friend, morning, noon, and night I repeated this after my mother, and at the conclusion of each repetition this poor soul, who loved and hated me, and whose heart was buried in the pit in which lay Jacques Duval and many more, would kiss me on the brow, and say, 'Thou art the instrument of God's vengeance.' For sixteen years she did this, and on my seventeenth birthday gave me a knife that had belonged to Jacques Duval, together with her savings of seventeen years. The knife had killed poor Jacques, and the money was to help in his avenging by means of the knife. . . . Mad? Yes, mad as ever a human being was, poor soul. . . . But think of what she saw and suffered. . . . Married a week before war broke out, her husband torn from her arms to march away to fight, perhaps to be maimed and mangled, perhaps to die. . . . Months of solitude. . . . Rumours. . . . Hopes. . . . Soul-sickening fears. . . . Can you not see her in their little house—where they were to have been so happy—waiting, hoping, fearing? And then, one dark night, a heavy tramp of soldiers, screams, red-reflections lighting up the clean little room in which she slept, and then—blows on her door, harsh guttural shouts, and the crash of the burst-in door. . . .

"For a fortnight the Herr Ober-Leutnant van Schlofen, in command of the detachment that had occupied the little village, made her house his headquarters, and as, from the first moment, she had defended herself tooth and nail, Marie Duval spent that time, bound hand and foot, and locked in her little room. At first, when she was untied, that she might eat and drink, she refused, but when pain, horror, grief, and every other anguished feeling had merged into a very madness of passion for revenge, she ate and drank, that she might have strength to slay. . . .

"And the night that her teeth met in the Herr Ober-Leutnant's throat, her Jacques came back wounded, and they caught him and brought him to this foul and filthy von Schlofen swine of Germany. . . .

"On learning they were husband and wife, von Schlofen confronted them in their bonds—she, half-dead with shame, exhaustion, and misery; he half-dead with wounds and the brutality of his captors. Then, while two of his vile bloodhounds held the woman, four others flung the man face downward over the kitchen table, placed a pail beneath his head, and von Schlofen cut his throat from ear to ear with that same knife. . . .

"Thereafter they flogged Marie Duval with the Herr Ober-Leutnant's switch that she might learn obedience and gratitude, and that he might find her tamer. . . .

"Mad? Oh yes, quite more than a little mad, this poor Marie Duval. . . . And when I was born, she dedicated me, as I say, her instrument of vengeance, so that on my seventeenth birthday I took train for Strasburg and the beginning of my quest. I had no great difficulty in tracking down this von Schlofen, who had become Colonel of the Hundred and Thirty-ninth Pomeranian Regiment, and then retired to his large estates in Silesia.

"When not hunting the boar and the deer there, he spent most of his time in an ancient, gloomy house in Thorn. And in Thorn I took up my abode and worked at my trade of carpenter. . . .

"I shall never forget my first sight of the man who was my father and my quarry; the man who gave me birth and whom I had been brought up, by the loving mother who hated me, to kill with the knife that had killed the man who should have been my father. My heart beat so fast that I feared I should faint or suffocate and die with my life's purpose unaccomplished. I gripped the haft of the knife beneath my blouse, the haft of the knife whose blade this barbarous German brute had driven into the throat of Jacques Duval, and which I was to drive into his own fat neck as I had been taught and trained to do. . . . Oh yes, taught and trained. Did I tell you how Madame ma mère daily practised my hand at knife-strokes? Never a pig was killed within miles of our village but I must be taken to see the doing of it, while I was a child, and to do it myself when old enough.

"No opportunity was I allowed to lose of driving my knife to the hilt in any dead animal, into anything in which a knife could be driven.

"I can hear her thin and bitter voice at this moment, see the wild glare in her eye as she gloated beside me while I stuck some neighbour's pig and the blood gushed warm into the blood-tub.

"'*Ohé*,' she would cry. '*Gobbets of flesh and gouts of gore!* So shalt thou bleed the foulest pig in all that Prussian sty, thine own father, thou accursed little devil. God and the Blessed Virgin reward and bless thee, my angel.'. . .

"*Oui, mon vieux*, a strange upbringing for a child, *hein*?

"And when I first beheld him, my father, the foulest pig in all that Prussian sty, I looked at the spot beneath his ear where I should strike and bleed him as he bled Jacques Duval—ere I cut his throat from ear to ear, as he cut the throat of Jacques Duval. . . ."

Jean Rien closed his eyes and fell silent.

"Well, 'e might 'a finished 'is tile afore 'e 'opped it," remarked le Légionnaire 'Erbiggin, with apparent callousness, belied by his sympathetic, unhappy countenance. "So fur as I could onnerstan' 'im, 'e wos agoin' ter do 'is pore ol' farver in. . . . 'Ere, give 'im a suck o' this *bapédi*," he added, as he produced a small medicine bottle half-full of the fiery fig-spirit.

"No," replied John Bull; "only increase the bleeding, if he is not dead. All the better if he has fainted."

Jean Rien opened his eyes.

"I can scarcely see you, Père Jean Boule," he murmured. "It is as dark as it was in that room where he lay when at last I had him at my mercy. . . . Yes, at length, after months of weary waiting for my opportunity, months of practice at the burglars' trade, months of scheming and study of the big house where the Pettenkoferstrasse joins the Baseler Alee, he lay before me on his bed, the moon shining on his white face. The hour for which I had been in training for two-and-twenty years had struck. I crept

121

from the window, by which I had entered, to the door, and turned the key, praying that the noise might not awake him. It did not.

"I crept back to the bedside, raised my knife on high, shouted '*My Father*,' thrust his big head over to one side and, as I had done a thousand times in the course of my training, drove the knife home to the very hilt—and even as, in the one motion, my left hand turned his head and my right hand stabbed, I knew that I had struck a stark, rigid corpse! . . . He was dead and cold! . . . I laughed aloud. . . ."

Jean Rien laughed aloud and died.

SERMONS IN STONES

In "Sermons in Stones", John Bull attempts to divert the Bucking Bronco and 'Erb from fighting by telling two stories: one about when he was captured by Arabs and another one about when he was in India. The Indian story is about a holy man and how the he preached a sermon with stones. "Sermons in Stones" *was first published in* Stepsons of France *(1917), and reprinted in* Tales of the Foreign Legion *(second series, The Master-Thriller series, #5, June 1934) and* Dead Men's Boots *(1949).*

It was a truly terrible night, and, to add to his own troubles and sufferings, John Bull had a great and growing anxiety as to the state of his beloved comrade, the Bucking Bronco. For that gentleman was undoubtedly working up for a "go" of *le cafard*, the desert madness of the Legion that so often ends in suicide, murder, or some military "crime," the punishment for which may be death, or the worse-than-death of the Zephyrs.

So awful was the heat of the barrack-room, and so charged was the atmosphere with electricity and human passion and misery, that even 'Erb had succumbed and, in a fit of rage, akin to sheer madness, had dashed his beloved mouth-organ upon the ground and stamped it shapeless, his face contorted with demoniac rage. Thereafter, he set himself to tease and enrage the big American whose mind was as much slower, as his soul and body were greater, than those of the little Cockney.

As he leant across Reginald Rupert's bed to reach his sack of cleaning-rags, John Bull whispered to that legionary, "The Bronco'll run amuck to-night if we don't watch it. He has already said he's going 'on pump' and also that he's going to 'lean agin the Sergeant-Major till he moults'! If 'Erb 'gits his goat,' he'll kill him, and then shoot himself."

"Spin a yarn, Bull," advised Rupert. . . . "If 'Erb gets impossible, I'll knock him out and we'll put him to bed. I'm with you, Old Thing."

Before the old soldier could reply, a loud crash caused him to spring round. The Bucking Bronco had flung his rifle against the whitewashed wall.

"The Devil admire me if ever I clean that gosh-dinged, dog-gasted gas-pipe again," he growled, and added, "Yep! An' if any yaller-dog hobo of a *Caporal* gits fresh with me, I'll wipe his derned dial with it!"

"*You* know Seven Dials, Buck?" queried 'Erb innocently.

"Yep," was the reply.

"Then stuff four of 'em up yer shirt. Yah!" jeered 'Erb.

"You ain't offended, matey, are yer?" he added, in a tone of contrite concern.

"Nope," said the American, staring hard.

"Then stuff up the remainin' three!" yelped his tormentor, and laughed insultingly.

The huge American rose to his feet menacingly, but as Rupert stepped between him and 'Erb, he sat down again.

"Wot I complains of is that all the Seven Dials rolled inter one wouldn't make anything as ugly as *your* dial," he grumbled. "Why don' youse take it to a dime-show mooseum? It's like them faces them Chinese guys paints on their shields to terrify their enner-mies. Why should you be allowed to bring it into this shack an' spile my slumbers? It makes me tired, an' I feel it's my painful dooty to change it some. . . ."

"'Streuth!" shrilled 'Erb. "'Ark at 'im! An' 'im on'y alive becos 'e ain't never see 'isself in a lookin'-glass! 'Ere, fetch a mirror, somebody, and let 'im commit sooicide wiv a single squint in it—if it don't break afore 'e can realize the orful troof. . . ."

"Shut up, 'Erb," interrupted John Bull. "You fellows must help me, I want to talk. If I don't, I shall get *cafard*—and do something that'll put me in the Sergeant-Major's hands. I'm going to spin a yarn. . . . What's the most remarkable thing you've ever seen, 'Erb?"

"The Buckin' Bronco's silly faice, Farver," replied that gentleman.

The Bucking Bronco rose and began removing his shirt as if for battle.

'Erb reached for his bayonet.

Precisely how most *cafard* tragedies begin.

Rupert passed him a rag.

"It does want a bit of a polish," he said.

"That's right, Buck, you'll be cooler without that," remarked John Bull, and added:

"Look here, I'm going to clean your rifle to-night—and you can do mine to-morrow night."

"Please yerself, Johnnie," was the reply, "I'm done with chores in this outfit. I'm going to strip stark, and then I'm agoin' to march to Sidi-bel-Abbes—soon as I twisted ole Suicide-Maker's head 'round three times and catch who you can.' His body remains at attention facin' front while his head goes round—see? . . . Guess I'm *locoed* to-night. Any-haow, I'm gwine to strip naked and go 'on pump' and see Carmelita." (Carmelita was six hundred miles to the north.)

"Well, put a turban on yer 'ead, fer modesty's saike, if you're a callin' on lidies," sneered 'Erb.

"What's the most remarkable thing *you've* ever seen, Bull?" asked Rupert, taking his cue. "That night when it was a case of pearls or impalement must have been about your most exciting time, what?"

"You never tole us nothin' abaht that, Farver. Wot was it?" inquired 'Erb, rising to the fly.

"Oh—rather a queer night I once spent," replied John Bull, "but it wasn't the queerest experience I ever had."

"Well, wot was the rummiest start you ever seen, then?" pursued 'Erb.

"Oh, just some stones—and what they did," was the reply.

"Git busy at 'em both, Johnnie, the pearls an' the other stones," said the Bucking Bronco, and added, "It looks like hell, you cleanin' my gun. Push it here."

Only too glad to see his friend employed, the old Legionary handed the rifle and rag to him and gave him a cigarette.

"There isn't much to the pearl yarn," he said. "It was before you joined, Buck. We were doing some unpeaceful penetration down south, and I was laid out in an Arab charge. They rode right through us, and I got a kick on the head that put me to sleep for hours. When I sat up, the Arabs were looting the dead and killing the wounded—who hadn't already killed themselves. I suppose I was the only one not too badly wounded to be of any use for affording sport under torture. Anyhow I was the only man marched off to the *douar*—a very large one indeed, being that of the Sheikh Abou Moustapha ben Isa Bahr-el-Mandeb, the great Arab guerilla leader—and by the time I got there, I was as glad to see the place as if it had been my home. A *mehari* camel goes at a good pace—and I wasn't on its back."

"Dragged?" queried 'Erb.

"Well, I ran as long as I could, of course, but the sand was very loose and fine. When we stopped, and everybody who wanted a whack at me had finished, I was tied to a palm-tree, and a negro gentleman with a long gun, a sword, three daggers and a flint-lock pistol was set to see I didn't get into mischief. In the evening a gang of them came and untied me and led me into the *douar* of low black tents. I thought I was 'for it' then, and could not keep my mind off the barrack-room photos of mutilated Legionaries. They took me to Sheikh Abou, however, where he sat on a carpet in front of his tent, drinking coffee and smoking cigarettes like a Christian. He was a fine-looking old bird, and spoke very fair French.

"'Bon soir, chien,' says he.

"'Bon soir, chat,' says I.

"'Pourquoi "*chat*"?' says he.

"'Parce que,' says I.

"I also explained that the French dog hunts the Arab cat, but he scored with a quiet smile and the remark that it rather looked as though the alleged cat was going to hunt the dog of an Unbeliever. My attempt at driving him into a rage and earning a swift death failed altogether. He was too big a man really, too balanced, too scholarly, too philosophic, for petty rages and quick stabs.

"'Are you unwounded, dog?' he asked.

"'By the weapons of soldiers,' I replied. 'Only bruised by the *matracks* of brave Arab gentlemen who strike manacled prisoners of war.'

"'What do the Franzawi do to Arab prisoners?' he returned.

"'They don't bind them and beat them,' I said.

"'What do they do to Arab women?' was his next question.

"'What did they do to your daughter?' I asked in turn. I knew that she had been sent straight to him, with a courteous letter, as soon as our general knew who she was.

"'True,' owned the Sheikh. 'See here, dog. My son, the bravest and handsomest man who ever sat a horse, was shot in cold blood by you Franzawi. My daughter was treated as a princess—which she is—and sent safely back to me. At dawn to-morrow, I shall either avenge the death of my son or else reward the kindness to my daughter.'

"He then gave orders to some of the gang, and they cut down a young palm that grew in front of his tent, leaving a stump a couple of feet high. This they trimmed with axes and knives to a point like that of a spear.

"While they were doing this, he went into his tent and came out again with a tiny bag of soft leather. Out of this he tipped some very decent pearls on to the carpet in front of him.

"'See these pearls,' said he. 'In the morning you shall have them as well as a camel and a guide to take you to your camp, *if* I find that gratitude for my daughter's safety is stronger than the desire to avenge my son's murder. Should this not be the case, however, you will be impaled upon that stump like a date on a dagger, and with your face to the sun—after your eyelids have been removed. Go and ponder Life, Death, Kismet, the Goodness of Allah—and the relative values of Pearls and Impalement. After all—wealth is a snare and a delusion whilst Death may be annihilation and peace—even for a dog of a *giaour*.'

"'Which do you think it will be—pearls or death, Sheikh?' I asked.

"'*Mektoub rebib! Inshallah!*[17] . . . I positively do not know. *Barca!*[18] replied the old gentleman—and I was taken back to my tree and given a gourd of water and a few dates.

"I had a merry night, I assure you! I wasn't to die then, however, for, towards dawn, the negro fell asleep, and as they had left me unbound, after giving me the food and water, I grabbed his bag of dates and grain, and did the record long-distance run of my life, most of it over that stony outcrop that takes no footprints. I put in the day in a cave, ran all the next

---

[17] It is written! As God wills!

[18] Enough.

night, and next day reached Safraïna—an outpost of ours."

"'Streuth!" murmured 'Erb, "an' *that* wasn't your rummiest go, Farver? You seen some queer things, you 'ave, since you bin a Legendary!"

"No, the most truly extraordinary thing that ever happened to me took place before I joined the Legion. It was in India."

"What about them stones, John?" queried the Bucking Bronco, wiping his streaming brow with the rag that he had just used for cleaning his rifle.

"That's what I'm going to tell you about," was the reply.

"I was a youngster then, and I had got leave from my ship to go and see my brother who was commanding—who was—er— up country. We were lying in Bombay harbour and going into dock for some repairs or other. It took me a couple of days to get to where my brother was stationed—up in some very hilly country. As my train dropped down a steep incline into the place where I was to get out, I noticed that a branch line ran off to the left and climbed the side of a very steep rock and there ended abruptly. I asked my brother what this was, and he told me that sometimes a truck or two would break away at the end of a climbing train and come rushing down the incline, which was many miles in length. As it approached the station it could be switched off on to this steeply rising branch line and expend its momentum in running up it, instead of dashing into the first train it met on the main line. And thereby hung a quaint and interesting tale. Some months before my visit, a naked Holy Man had rolled up, with his hair plastered with mud and tow, his body smeared all over with ashes, and his soul too lofty and enlightened to let his gross body do a job of work of any sort. He staked out a claim under this great rock near the line, planted himself in the middle of the patch and hand-patted dirt that was to be his home, and there squatted all day long, with his begging-bowl and an ugly-looking steel spike. The neighbouring villagers fed him of course, and, like wise men, propitiated him in every way and gave him anything he wanted—for, judging by his filthiness, nakedness, and laziness, he must be a very holy man indeed, must have acquired great merit, and be very potent to upset the apple-cart of anyone who thwarted him. Also he worked divers miracles, and caused a brazen image of Kali to arise from the earth at his feet. This he put in a circle of red-painted stones—and straightway there was a sacred shrine and the foundations of a great place of pilgrimage and the site of a holy temple.

"But when June drew near, the villagers warned the Holy Man that the rains would break soon and he'd get uncommon damp when it rained. The holy one replied that he would build him a hut perchance.

"The villagers smiled, and said it rained three inches a day for months on end in those parts, when the monsoon broke. 'My hut shall be of stone,' said His Holiness.

"The villagers laughed outright. Where was there stone enough to make a grindstone, let alone a house, in those grassy jungle parts?

"'Stone for my house shall fall at my feet from heaven,' said the holy one. Whereat the villagers stared in round-eyed wonder. His Holiness was going it! Wasn't he biting off a bit more than he could chew? This was a plain issue and no blooming oracle-mongering about it. Either stone would fall or it would not—and the probabilities were strongly in favour of the *not*. Still he had done some good hefty miracles, some of which might not have been bunkum. *'Nous verrons!'* said the headman, in his own vernacular.

"And, a week before the rains broke, a truck or two laden with cut stone broke away from a train, careered gaily down the long incline, were duly switched off on to the safety-siding, and, being unusually heavy and swift, ran clean over the end and shot a truck-load or two of dressed stone at the feet of the Holy Man!

"'*Voila!*' (or the equivalent thereof) said he to the villagers, and smiled patronizingly. You bet they turned to and built His Holiness as eligible a family residence as Holy Man could desire, and with the remainder of the stones they built him a nice stone platform to squat on in the sun, and think his great thoughts.

"I know this is all true, because my brother was told of His Holiness's daring prophecy long before the stones were safely delivered. When I heard the story from him, of course I must needs ride over and have a look at this local lion.

"I arrived at a moment of domestic crisis apparently, for from the hut of this celibate saint came the screams of a woman and

129

the sounds of a real handsome hiding. Being young and foolish, I concluded that the lowing lady was getting the handsome hiding and that I had better take a hand. I barged in and found I was right. His reverence dropped the stick and picked up his spear-headed staff, but I gave him a soother on the point of the chin and cleared out, preceded by the lady, who sprinted like a hare.

"I rode off rather pleased with my silly young self, and half an hour later was crossing a perfectly level stretch of grass, when suddenly, just as I bent to dismount to tighten my girth, a great stone missed my head by a hair's-breadth and struck the ground with a mighty nasty thud. The fraction of a second earlier, it would have got me. I stared at it in amazement, and looked all round. There wasn't another stone for miles, nor, except for a clump of feathery bamboos, a tree, nor a building, a wall, a hollow, nor a fold in the ground where anyone could be hiding. Absolutely nothing but level grass and a clump of bamboos that could not conceal a small monkey—much less a man.

"I was too astounded to move for a minute or two. Then I rode round and round in widening circles, quartering the ground until I had established, beyond all doubt, the fact that whoever threw the stone had thrown it at least four hundred yards—and the man never lived who could have thrown it forty.

"I went back and examined it—and realized, with no added comfort, that it was a stone from my holy friend's house or platform! I remounted my horse—who was trembling and sweating as though he could see a tiger—and started to ride back. If *that* was his game! . . . And as I bent my head to light the cigarette I badly needed, another stone grazed my *topi*. Like the first, it hit the turf with a thud that was sickening to hear. Then I was frightened, I admit, as well as enraged. Again I circled round, this time galloping hard in a frenzy of anger and fear. If either of those stones had hit me, I should have been killed—and there wasn't a sign of a human being nor of a place where one could have hidden! And a blight seemed to have come over the day, chilling my very soul, and making me feel as though I were a child in a nightmare.

"I *knew* there would be another, and that the third one would not miss me. I shall never forget the feeling of utter helplessness, wrath, and terror that possessed me. What could I do? There *was* nothing to do, and at any moment the blow might fall— literally a bolt from the blue. And then I pulled myself together, thought of my fellow midshipmen, and imagined the eyes of the whole of my ship's company to be upon me.

"Tactics for ever! Dismounting and unbuckling the girth, I took off my saddle and, holding the end of the girth in my hand, pulled the big heavy saddle up and put it on my head and neck. Retaining it there with one hand, I set spurs to my horse, and rode hell-for-leather.

"And that's all I know about it—until I came to my senses and found myself lying in bed in my brother's bungalow!

"They told me the horse had come home riderless and unsaddled—and they at once concluded I had come a cropper, as I had remarked, on starting, that it was 'so long since I had seen a horse that I hardly knew the stem from the stern, nor how to sit amidships and hold the rudder lines.'

"My brother had ridden out and found me lying unconscious.

"'You must have taken a frightful toss,' he said, 'but how the deuce did you come to get the saddle smashed? How did it come to be off the horse? It looked as though some one had hit it with a huge sledge-hammer.'

"'Or a stone,' said I.

"'Yes,' said he. 'Why a stone?'

"I told him exactly what had happened, and he laughed.

"'Falling on your head has made you dream dreams and see visions,' said he. He did *not* laugh a fortnight later when he and I went over the ground and found the three stones—in that stoneless place. When we went on, to call on the Holy Man, we learned that the gentleman had gone for a walk—to Benares, a thousand miles away." . . .

"Strike me pecooliar!" murmured the Bucking Bronco. "That tale made outer whole cloth, John?"

"It's every word of it true," was the reply.

"Well, you go to bed, Sonny; yore pore brain's about biled, I allow," counselled the American; and, exchanging a glance with Rupert, the old Legionary allowed himself to be helped on to his cot and soothed.

"We'll fan pore ole Farver wiv a noospaper till he goes ter sleep," said 'Erb, getting an old *Echo d'Oran* from his shelf.

"He's fair off 'is ole napper to-night."

And when the eyes of Jean Boule closed, apparently in slumber, the others silently sought their respective red-hot beds.

MOONSHINE

"Moonshine" is a 'La Cigale' story. La Cigale is one of Wren's more prominent recurring characters in his Foreign Legion stories. In this particular tale, La Cigale tells John Bull and his compatriots about how he was in love with Diane and how he achieved his revenge on her murderer, Delacroix. A different version of Diane and Delacroix is presented in a later La Cigale story, "Moon-set" (see volume three of The Collected Short Stories). *"Moonshine" first appeared in* Stepsons of France *(1917), and was reprinted in the* Los Angeles Times *(June 17, 1927), and in the* Murray *(1947) and Macrae-Smith (1948) editions of* Stories of the Foreign Legion.

La Cigale, the Mad "Grasshopper" of the VIIth Company, was solemnly dancing by the light of the moon. He was a fine soldier and a hopeless lunatic, and had once been a Belgian Officer (Corps of Guides, the most aristocratic in the Belgian Army) and military attaché at various Embassies. No one knew his story, not even le Légionnaire Jean Boule, whom he loved and who, through great suffering, had attained great understanding and sympathy.[19]

This same gentleman, accompanied by the Bucking Bronco, Reginald Rupert, and 'Erb, was even now looking for him, knowing that he was always worse at the period of full moon and apt to do strange things.

They found him—solemnly dancing by the light of the moon—on a patch of green turf by the palms of the oasis.

"Doin' a bloomin' fandango on the light fantastic toe—all on 'is little own!" observed 'Erb.

"Funny how the moon affects madmen," said Rupert.

"Yes," agreed John Bull. "Ancient idea too. *Luna* the moon, *luna*tic. Evidently some connection."

"Shall we butt in an' put the kibosh on it?" asked the Bucking Bronco.

"No," replied John Bull. "Let's settle down and have a

---

[19] Vide "The Wages of Virtue." John Murray.

smoke. We'll see him to bed when he's tired of dancing. If he wearies himself out there'll be more chance of some sleep for us. . .. We can't leave him to himself to-night."

"Nope," agreed the Bucking Bronco. "Remember the night he went *loco* once and for all? When the grasshopper jumped into his soupe."

"Yes; but it wasn't the locust in his *gamelle* that was really the last straw. He'd have had permanent *cafard* from that day, anyhow. . . . Look!—he's stopped." . . .

The Grasshopper, hearing voices, had ceased his posturing, bowing, and dancing. Crouching low, he progressed toward the shadow of the palms by long leaps.

"Hullo, *mon ami*!" cried John Bull; "come and have a smoke."

"*She* always danced like that to the Chaste Huntress of the skies when she showed mortals her full face," said La Cigale, as he flung himself down by his friend.

"'Oo did?" queried 'Erb.

"Diane de Valheureux," was the reply. "That is why Delacroix killed her. That Delacroix of the artillery."

"I could onnerstand 'im killin' 'er if she *sung*, but I don' see wot 'e wanted to kill her for fer dancin'," observed 'Erb. "Too bloomin' pertickler, *I* calls it."

"He was jealous," replied La Cigale, as he pressed his thin hands over his forehead and smouldering eyes.

"Diane was born at the full of the moon out in the beautiful garden of her father's château. It was her mother's whim—a woman of fire and moonbeams and wild fancies and poesies herself: Pan's own daughter.

"And from the day she could walk, Diane must go out and dance in the light of the full moon.

"I loved Diane. Also did Delacroix. He was mad for love of her. I was sane for love of her, since my love showed me all Beauty and Harmony and the utter worthlessness of the baubles that men strive for.

"She loved me—I think. If she did not, certainly she loved no one else. I understood, you see. And, on one evening, given by God, she let me dance with her in the forest while Diana smiled full-face from Heaven.

"And her parents gave her to Delacroix, who had great possessions and a soul that values great possessions at their untrue value. The soul of a pedlar—the base suspicious mind of a ferret.

"After she was married—and broken-hearted—she still had one joy. She could still dance with the fairies in a glade of the forest at full moon. She *could*, do I say? She could not do otherwise when Diana and Pan and the Old Gods called—this night-born elf of night, moonlight, and the open sky and earth. And, returning from her midnight dance with the fairies, by the light of the Harvest Moon, she found that the husband whom she had left snoring, sat glowering—awaiting her—his mind a seething cesspool of foul suspicions.

"He killed her—of course. Such things as Fairy Dianes *are* killed by such other things as Hog Delacroix. And my heart broke. As your fine poet says, I think:

'There came a mist and a blinding rain,
    And life was never the same again.'

Never. Nor had I the satisfaction of dealing with Delacroix. The brave soul fled and disappeared."

"You'll cop 'im yet, Ciggy," interrupted 'Erb. "Cheer up, Ole Cock. We'll all lay fer 'im, an' do 'im in proper, one o' these dark nights."

"I have settled accounts with him, now, I thank you," continued La Cigale. "I suddenly came face to face with him on board the troopship *L'Orient* at Oran. It was when the Legion sent drafts to Tonkin, to fight the Black Flags.

"I was on sentry, and looking up, as a man came along the gangway, beheld the evil face of Delacroix!

"By the time I had recovered my wits, and realized that it was he in the flesh, and not his ghost, he had passed on and was swallowed up by the part of the ship devoted to officers.

"I saw no more of him until it was again my turn for sentry duty. By this time we were at Port Said, and as desertion was easy here—since a man had but to dive overboard and swim a few yards or even rush down a gangway when we were coaling—all sentries were given ball-cartridge and strict orders to shoot any soldier attempting to leap overboard or make a burst for the coal-wharf and British soil. (Once ashore, he must not be touched, or there would be trouble with England—and he might, with impunity, stand on the quay and deride us.)

"It was not likely that any of the French regulars would desert—artillery, line, or *marsouins*—but there would have been but few of the Legion who would not have made the promenade ashore but for these precautions.

"And as I stood there—my loaded Lebel in my hands—who should approach the head of the gangway over which I stood sentry, but this Delacroix, this thing whose foul hands—the very hands there before my eyes—had choked the life out of my Diane!

"Should I blow out his vile brains, or should I give myself the joy unspeakable of plunging my bayonet into his carcase?

"Neither. Too brief a joy for me—too brief an agony for him.

"As he passed, I held my hand with an effort that made me pale.

"The third time I saw him was in the Indian Ocean as we headed south for our next stopping-place, Singapore.

"He was leaning on the rail of the officers' promenade-deck, smoking a cigar after his comfortable lunch. The deck was empty. I ran lightly up the companion from our troop-deck, polluted the promenade-deck with my presence, sprang at him, seized him from behind, flung him overboard, and sprang after him with a cry of '*Diane*'!

"I must watch him drown; I must shout that name in his ear as he died. I must be with him at the last, and my hands must be at the throat of the foul dog. Not mine to fling him overboard and be clapped in irons while they threw him life-belts, and then lowered boats!

"Swimming with powerful strokes to where he had struck the water, I waited till he came up, and then seized him by the throat and strove to choke the life out of him as he had done to Diane. He struck at me wildly, and I thrust his head again beneath the water. But, yes! with a shout of 'Diane!' I dragged him below and swam downward as deeply as I could go. With bursting lungs I swam upward again and gloated upon his purpling face, and then—down, down, down, down, once more. . . .

"When they dragged me into the boat, I was senseless and he was dead. I had swum with him for nearly an hour.

"When I recovered on board the ship, I was the hero of the hour—the man who had sprung into the sea, without stopping to divest himself of so much as his boots, to save an Officer. . . .

"What am I saying? . . . I am sleepy. . . . Bon soir, mes amis," and the Grasshopper rose and retired toward the tents.

"*Some* story!" remarked the Bucking Bronco, as the four followed. "Wouldn't thet jar you! Sure it's the mos' interestin' an' wonderfullest yarn I heerd him tell yet. Ain't it, John?"

"M—m . . . yes. . . . It is the more interesting and wonderful," was the reply of John Bull, as he thoughtfully flicked the ash from the end of his cigarette, "by reason of the fact that I happen to know—that the Grasshopper cannot swim a stroke."

THE COWARD OF THE LEGION

"The Coward of the Legion" is the story of a man, who after an act of heroism, confesses to John Bull that he is a "branded" coward, since he failed to participate in an attempted double suicide. John Bull suggests a way that the branding can be erased. "The Coward of the Legion" was the last story in the first edition (1917) of Stepsons of France. *It has been reprinted eight times: in* The Thriller Magazine *(no. 353, 1935),* Tales of Valour *(The Master-Thriller Series, no. 12, 1936),* Stories of the Foreign Legion *(Vallancey, 1945),* Tales of the Foreign Legion *(Vallancey, 1946), the Murray (1947) and Macrae-Smith (1948) editions of* Stories of the Foreign Legion, *and the Hamlyn (1985) and Mallard Press (1990) editions of* The Best War Stories.

Jean Jacques Dubonnet had distinguished himself that day, and he lay on his bed that night and cried. His companion, old Jean Boule, in that little hut of sticks and banana-leaves, had just been congratulating him on the fact that he had almost certainly won himself the *croix de guerre* or the *médaille militaire* for his distinguished bravery. And he had burst into tears, his body shaken with great rending sobs.

John Bull was not only a gentleman; he was a person of understanding and sympathy, and he had suffered enough, and seen enough of suffering, to feel neither surprise, disgust, nor contempt.

"God! Oh, God! I am a coward. I am a branded coward!" blubbered the big man on the creaking bed of boughs and boxes.

Was this fever, reaction, drink, *le cafard*, or what?

Certainly Dubonnet had played the man, and shown great physical courage that day against the Sakalaves, the brave Malagasy savages who have given Madame la République a good deal of trouble and annoyance, and filled many a shallow grave with the unconsidered carcases of *Marsouins*[20] and Légionnaires in the red soil of Madagascar. As the decimated Company had slowly fallen back from the ambush in the dense plantations of

---

[20] Colonial Infantry (Infanterie de la Marine).

the lovely Boueni palms, Lieutenant Roberte had fallen, shot through the body by a plucky Sakalave who had deliberately rested his prehistoric musket on his thigh and discharged it at a dozen yards range, himself under heavy fire.   With insulting howls of "*Taim-poory, taim-poory*," half a dozen of the enemy had sprung at the fallen man, when Dubonnet, rushing from cover, had shot two in quick succession, bayoneted two others, kicked violently in the face a fifth, who stooped over the Lieutenant with a *coupe-coupe*, and then, swinging his Lebel by the butt, had put up so good a fight that he had driven the savages back and had then partly dragged and partly carried his officer with him, to where the Company could rally, re-form, and make their stand to await reinforcements.   Undeniably Dubonnet had risked his life to save that of his officer, and had fought with very great courage and determination or he could never have reached the rallying-place with an unconscious man, when so many of his comrades could not reach it at all.

Yet there he lay, weeping like a child, and calling upon his Maker to ease his guilty bosom of the burden it had borne so long—the knowledge that he was a "branded" coward.

It was terribly, cruelly hot in the tiny hut, and, to John Bull, who arose from his camp-bed of packing-case boards, it seemed even hotter outside, as he went to fetch the hollow bamboo water-"bottle" which hung from the tree under which the hut was built. Was it possible that the Madagascan moon gave out heat-rays of its own, or reflected those of the sun as it did the rays of light? It really seemed hotter in the moonlight than out of it. . . . Carrying the bamboo water-receptacle, a cylinder as tall as himself—really a pipe with one end sealed with gum, wax, or clay, when a joint of the stem does not serve the purpose—the Englishman passed in through the doorless doorway and delivered an ultimatum.

"Whatever may be the trouble, *mon ami*, weeping will not help it. Enough! . . . Sit up and tell me all about it, or I'll wash you off that bed like the insect you're pretending to be. . . . Now then—a drink or a drenching?"

"Give me a drink for the love of God!" said Dubonnet, sitting up. "Absinthe, rum, cognac—anything," and he clutched at the breast of his canvas shirt as though he feared it might open and expose his breast.

"Yes. Good cold water," replied John Bull.

"Cold water!" mocked the other between sobs. "Cold Englishman! *Cold water!*" and he bowed his head on his knees and groaned and wept afresh.

The old soldier carefully poured water from the open end of the great pipe into a *gamelle* and offered it to the other, who drank feverishly. "Are you wounded in the chest, there?" he asked.

This *cafard*, the madness that comes upon soldiers who eat out their hearts in the monotony of exile and wear out their stomachs and brains in the absinthe-shop, takes strange forms and reduces its victims to queer plights. How should le Légionnaire Jean Jacques Dubonnet, *Soldat première classe*, recommended for decoration for bravery in the field, be a coward?

"Oh, merciful God—help me to bear it. I am a Coward—a branded Coward!" wailed the huddled figure on the rickety, groaning bed.

"See here, comrade," said John Bull, overcoming a certain slight, but perceptible, repugnance, and placing an arm across the bowed and quivering shoulders, "I am no talker, as you are aware. If it would give you any relief to tell me all about it—rest assured that no word of it will ever be repeated by me. It may ease you. I may be able to help or comfort. Many Légionnaires, some on their death-beds, have felt the better for telling me of their troubles. . . . But do not think I want to pry." . . .

Swiftly the wretched man turned, flung his arms about the Englishman's neck, and kissed him.

John Bull forbore to shudder. (Heavens! How different is the excellent French *poilu* from the British Tommy!) But if he could bring peace and the healing, soothing sense of confession, if not of anything approaching absolution, to this tortured soul, the night would have been well spent—better spent than in sleep, though he was very, very tired.

"I *will* tell you, *mon ami*, and will pray to you then to give me comfort or a bullet in the temple. A little accident as you clean your rifle! *I* cannot do it. I *dare* not do it—and no bullet will touch me in battle—as you have seen to-day. I live to die, and am too big a coward to take my life. . . . I am a branded coward. . . . See! See!" and he tore open the breast of his shirt. At once he closed it again, and hugged himself.

"No, no! I will tell you first," he cried.

The madness of *le cafard*, no doubt. The man had only recently been drafted to the VIIth Company from the depôt, and had appeared a morose, surly, and unattractive person, friendless and undesirous of friends. Accident had made him the stable-companion of the Englishman in this little damp fever-stricken hell in the reeking corner of the Betsimisarake district, in which the remains of the Company were pinned. . . .

The deplorable and deploring Dubonnet thrust his grimy fists into his eyes and across the end of his amorphous nose, as, with a sniff which militated against the romantic effect of the declaration, he said, "I swear I loved her. I loved her madly. It was my unfortunate and uncontrollable love that caused the trouble in the first place. . . . But it was her fault too, mind you! Why couldn't she have *told* me she had a husband, away at Lyons, finishing his military service—a husband whom she had not seen for six months, and whom she would not see for another six? . . . Too late the fool confessed it—a month before he was coming, and a couple of months before something else was coming! And he famous, as I learned too late, for having all the jealous hate of Hell in his heart, if she so much as looked at another man. He, a porter of the Halles, notorious for his quarrelsomeness and for his fearful strength and savage temper. She hated him nearly as much as she feared him—and me, me she loved to distraction. And I her. . . . Believe me, she was the loveliest flower-seller in Paris—with a foot and ankle, an eye, a figure, ravishing, I tell you . . . and he would break her neck when he saw how she was and stab me to the heart. *She* would never have told him it was I she loved, but those others would— for dozens knew that she was my *amie*, and many in my gang did not love me. I am not of those whom men love—but women, ah!—and there were jealous ones in our *ruelle* who would have gone far to see her beauty spoiled and my throat cut. . . . It was all her fault, I say! Did she not deceive me in hiding the fact that she had a husband? She deceived us all. But when this *scélérat* should turn up from Lyons, and find her at her pitch or in the flower-market, would any of them have held their tongues? . . . Can you not see it? . . . The crowd at the door, the screams as he entered and dragged her out into the gutter by the hair, his foot on her throat . . . and, afterwards—his knife at my breast. . . . Would any of the gang have stood by me? No, they would have licked their chops and goaded him on . . . and, oh God, I am a *coward*. . . . I can fight when my blood is up and I have to struggle for my life. . . . I can fight as one of a regiment, a company, a crowd, all fighting side by side, each defending the other by fighting the common foe. . . . I can take my part in a mélée and I can do deeds then that I do not know I have done till afterwards. . . . I can fight when the tiger in me is aroused and has smelt blood— but I am a *coward* if I am alone. I, alone, dare not fight one man alone. . . . Were I being tracked alone through the jungle here by but one of the six men I attacked to-day, my knees would knock together and my legs would refuse to bear me up. I should flee if they would carry me, flee shrieking, but they would not bear me a hundred metres. They would collapse, and I should lie shuddering with closed eyes, awaiting the blow. I can hunt— with the pack—but I cannot be hunted. No. When our band waylaid the greasy bourgeois as he lurched homeward from his restaurant in the Place Pigalle or his Montmartre cabaret, I was as good an *apache* as any in the gang, and struck my blow with the best; but if it was a case of a row with the *agents de police*, and we were being individually shadowed, my heart turned to water, and I lay in bed for days. In a fair fight between about equal numbers of anarchists and *apaches* on the one hand, and *messieurs les agents* on the other, if it came upon us suddenly as they raided our rookery, I could play a brave man's part in the rush for the street; but I cannot be the hunted one—I cannot fight alone with none on either side of me. Oh God, I am a coward," and the wretch again buried his face in his knees and wept and sobbed afresh.

A common, cowardly gutter-hooligan apparently; an *apache*, a Paris street-wolf, and, like all wolves, braver in the pack than when alone; but in John Bull's gaze there was more of pity than anything. Suppose he, John Bull, had been born in a foul corner of some filthy cellar beneath a Paris slum? Would he have been so different? Was the *man* to blame, or the Fate that gave him the ancestry and environment that had made him precisely what he was?

"You will be called out before the battalion and decorated with the cross or the *médaille, mon ami,* for your heroism to-day. Put the past behind, and let your life re-date from the day the Colonel pins the decoration on your breast. Begin afresh. You will carry about with you always the visible sign and recognition that you are a hero—there on your breast, I say." . . .

With a shriek of "*What do I bear on my breast now?*" the ex-*apache* tore open his shirt and exposed two strips of strong linen sticking-plaster, each some ten inches long and two inches wide, that lay stuck horizontally across his broad chest.

What was this? Had he two ghastly gashes beneath the plaster? Had all that he had been saying been merely the delirium of a badly-wounded man? Seizing their ends, the *apache* tore them violently from his skin, and, by the light of the little lamp, John Bull saw, deeply branded, and most skilfully tattooed in the ineradicable burns, the following words (in French):

J. J. DUBONNET
LIAR AND COWARD

The Englishman recoiled in horror, and the other thought it was in contempt.

"Where are your fine phrases *now?*" he snarled, with concentrated bitterness. "'*You will carry about with you always the visible sign and recognition that you are a hero,*'" he mocked. "I do indeed! . . . Oh God, take it from me. Let me sleep and wake to find it gone, and I will become a monk and wear out my life in prayer," . . . and he threw himself face-downward on the bed and tore the covering of his straw pillow with his teeth.

"See, *mon ami*," said John Bull, "the *médaille* will be above that. It will be superimposed. It will bury that beneath it. Let it bury it for ever. That is of the past—the *médaille* is of to-day and the glorious future. That is man's revenge—the cruel punishment and vengeance of an injured brute. The *médaille* is man's reward—the glad recognition of those who admire courage." . . .

"It is not the husband's work," growled Dubonnet. "He never caught me. My own gang did that—my comrades—my *friends*! Think of their loathing and contempt, their hatred and disgust, that they could do that to a man and leave him to live. Think of it! ... And I dare not kill myself and meet *her*. I am a coward. I fear Death himself, and I fear her reproachful eyes still more. ... I *am* a coward and I *am* a liar. I broke my faith and word and trust to her—and I feared the death that she welcomed because *I* was by her side to share it. She drank the poison in her glass, threw herself into my arms, and bade me drink mine and come with her to the Beyond, where no brutal, hated husband could drag her from me to his own loathed arms. ... And I did not. I could not. She died in my arms with those great reproachful eyes on mine, and whispered, 'Come with me, my Beloved. I am afraid to go alone.' And when I would not, she cursed me and died. And I let her go alone—I, who had planned our double suicide, our glorious and romantic suicide in each other's arms— that we might not have to part, might not have to face her husband's wrath, might be together for all time, though it were in hell. ... Before she drank, she blessed me. Before she died, she cursed me—and still I could not drink. ... And now I have not the courage to go on living, and I have not the courage to take my life. ... And they are going to brand me as a hero, are they? ... *That* on my coat and *this* beneath it!" and peals of hysterical laughter rang out on the still night.

"Yes—*that* on your coat," said the Englishman. "Does it count for nothing? Let the one balance the other. Put the past behind you and start afresh. ... Can you bear pain? Physical pain, I mean?"

"Is not all my life a pain?—did I not have to bear the pain of being branded with a red-hot iron? What is physical pain compared with what I bear night and day—remorse, self-loathing, the fear of the discovery of *this* by my comrades? How much longer will it be before some prying swine sees these strips and refuses to believe they hide wounds—laughs at my tale of attempted suicide in a fit of *cafard*—*hara-kiri*—self-mutilation with a knife." ...

"Because, if you can face the pain, we can obliterate that. We can remove the record of shame, and you can wear the record of courage and duty without fear of discovery of the ..."

"*What* do you say?" cried Dubonnet, as the words penetrated his anguished and self-centred mind. "*What?* Remove it?

How—in the name of God?"

"Burn it out as it was burnt in," was the cool reply. "I will do it for you if you ask me to. . . . The pain will be ghastly and the mark hideous—but it will *be* a mark and nothing else. Anyone seeing it will merely see that you have been severely burnt—and they'll be about right."

Dubonnet sat up.

"You could and would do that?" he said.

"Yes. I should make a flat piece of iron red-hot and lay it firmly across the writing. It would depend on you whether it were successful or not, and would be a good test of nerve and courage. Have it done—and make up your mind that cowardice and treachery were burnt out with the words. Then start life afresh and win another decoration." . . .

"There are anæsthetics," whimpered Dubonnet. "Chloroform." . . .

"Not for Legionaries in Madagascar," was the reply. "Unless you'd like to go to Médecin-Major Parme with your story and ask him to operate, to oblige a young friend?"

Dubonnet shivered, and then spat. "*Médecin-Major Parme!*" he growled.

"If you like to wait a few weeks or months or years, you may have the opportunity and the money to buy chloroform," continued the Englishman, "or the means for making local injections of cocaine or something; but I suggest you make a kind of sacrament of the business—have the damnable thing burnt out precisely as it was burnt in, and as you clench your teeth on the bullet in manly silence and soldierly stoicism, realize it is *the past* that is being burnt also, and that the good fire is burning out all that makes you hate yourself and hate life. Let it be symbolic."

John Bull knew his man. He had met his type before. Too much imagination; too little ballast; the material for a first-class devil, or a first-class man; swayed and governed by his symbols, shibboleths, and prejudices; the slave and victim of an *idée fixe*. . . . If he could get him to undergo this ordeal, he would emerge from it a new man—a saved man. An anæsthetic would spoil the whole moral effect. If he would face the torture and bear it, he would regard himself as a brave man, just as surely as he now regarded himself as a coward. He would recover his self-respect, and he would be brave because he believed himself to be brave. It would literally be his regeneration and salvation.

"It would hurt no more in the undoing than it did in the doing," he continued.

The poor wretch shuddered.

"She had written a few words of farewell to one or two," he said, "and told how we were going to die together, and when and where. . . . Her mother and some others burst in and found me with her body in my arms and my untasted poison beside me. . . . I went mad. I raved. I denounced myself. A vile woman who had once loved me, jeered at me and bade me drink my share and rid the world of myself. . . . I could not. . . . My own gang bound me on my bed, and one of them brought an old chisel and the half of an iron pipe split lengthways. With the straight edge and the semicircular one, they did their work. I was their prisoner for— ah! *how* long? And then they tattooed the scars—not satisfied with their handiwork as it was. . . . Before her husband found me I had fled to the shelter of the Legion. . . . I told the surgeon at Fort St. Jean that it was done by a rival gang because I had pretended to join them and did not. He gave me a roll of the sticking-plaster and advised me, for my comfort, to hide my '*endossement*' as he brutally called it." . . .

"Well, now get rid of it," interrupted John Bull.

"The flat iron clamp, binding the corners of that packing-case, would be the very thing. You are *not* a coward. You proved that to-day. Prove it more highly to-night, and, when they decorate you, let there be a still more honourable decoration beneath—the scars of a great victory. . . . Come on." . . .

When old Jean Jacques Dubonnet fell, many years later, at Verdun, the Colonel of his battalion, on hearing the news, remarked, "I have lost my bravest soldier."

The marks of a terrible burn on his chest were almost obliterated by German bullets and bayonets.

THE SAXON AND THE GAEL AND THINGS

In "The Saxon and the Gael and Things" the children, Boodle and Ficcie, are playing the characters from Sir Walter Scott's 1810 narrative poem, The Lady of the Lake. *Boodle is the highland chief, Roderick Dhu, and Ficcie is King James V of Scotland, in disguise as Fitz-James. "The Saxon and the Gael and Things" was first published in* The Young Stagers *(1917).*

The Chief in silence strode before and reached the torrent's sounding shore.   The torrent was provided by the bath-room water-tap, and did very well. Too well, Ayah thought, when she returned from her meal and siesta. The Chief strode in silence and little else, as his tartan plaid was a piece of tartan ribbon and his kilt a brief petticoat—brief even for this little girl of eight. Fitz-James in silence strode behind, and then spoilt everything by breaking the silence and becoming a brass band. Association of ideas, no doubt, for when he marched behind the President he was usually a band, procession, Greek Chorus, or a general choral atmosphere.

"Shut up, Fizz-James, you 'normous ass," hissed the Chief, casting a fiery eye over her bare shoulder. "You've only got to strode, like me, till we get to Koil-and-Poggle Ford, and thou must keep thee with thy sword—until I let you do me in."

Fitz-James ceased to play an imaginary bugle and to beat a figmentary drum. He sighed at his unworthiness.

Having circumambulated the bath-room and parts adjacent, the Chief halted, well within the radius of the splashes from the torrent, shook his sword menacingly, raised his shield, scowled horribly, and suddenly thrusting his ferocious face into that of the fascinated Fitz-James, cried :

"And, Stranger, *I* am Brodrick Two!"

Fitz-James over-acted, being but young.   He rendered "surprise and slight consternation," by collapsing upon the ground, fetching a deep groan, and murmuring "Help!

The President remembered that the years of the Vice were not six, and was lenient.

"Pull yourself together, Fizz-James, and play the man this day," continued Roderic Dhu. "Get out of the wet, and buck up, for I have sworn this braid to stain in the best blug that warms thy vein—(where did I put that beastly braid?) D'you hear, Fizz-James? And I shall jolly well cut any vein I like."

"You be careful, Robberic," said Fitz-James, rising and attempting to draw his sword.

"Not at all," was the reply, "and this rock shall fly from its firm base as soon as I. See?"

The rock was the inverted bath, resting upon its handles. The Vice, essaying to lean upon it while he wrestled with his recalcitrant sword, found that it was not based with such firmness as to warrant its use as a simile.

Roderic Dhu looked to earth, and sky, and plain, as things he ne'er might see again.

"Would you mind helping me out with this thword, Robberic?" politely asked Fitz-James. "If I pull, this button will come *right* off, and my drawers will come down." As he was arrayed only in two tight garments this seemed undesirable, particularly in a Stranger.

"I *will*, James Fizz," replied Roderic, "but some people wouldn't. Not for the person by whom they were just going to be done in—and with that very sword. . . . There you are. . . . If you are ready, it's got to ill-fare it then with Brodrick Two when on the ground his Taj he threw, whose studs of brass and tough bull-hide had death so often dashed aside. They are bone studs of Daddy's because he hadn't any studs of brass, and didn't seem to want to lend any gold ones. And the bull's hide is card-board— but it's a Taj all right."

"I thought the Taj was a hotel," observed Fitz-James. "I wemember we went . . ."

"You're too fond of thinking, James Fizz," interrupted Roderic. "What about Blue Murder—no, Red Murdoch—I mean?"

Fitz-James's eye gleamed. He had his cue. "He's staff and stick," he said.

"He's *what*, you ass?" queried Roderic coldly.

"He's stark and stiff," the other corrected, and, striking the attitude shown him by the President at rehearsal, and confirmed by the picture, he declaimed:—

> "The wriggle is already dead
> And I wemember what you said—
> Er—and beneath the whiff
> There lies Red Murdoch stark and stiff."

"Oh, really?" sneered Roderic, "and who stark-and-stiffed him, pray?"

"*I* did," replied Fitz-James. "I did him in proper." (Subaltern language, this.)

"H'm," commented Roderic. "That's awkward—because the side wins that gets first blood. . . ."

"*Was* there any blood?" he added, as an idea struck him, and he saw a loop-hole of escape from the operation of the baleful prophecy.

"Lots," was the depressing answer. "I stained a whole roll of braid in the best of it. All my clo'ves too—*and* his. Norful mess!"

"Well, anyhow, it's beneath the *cliff*, he lies, not 'whiff'. I dare say there *is* a whiff, by now—but that's not what you meant."

The bitterness of death was not past for Roderic, and he spoke bitterly.

As he prepared to fight his last fight and meet his end at the hand of the hated Southron, he protruded his tongue and made a shocking grimace.

"Yah! Fizz-Jimmy, you beastly Sack-Son," quoth he. "Come on! Beware! Thy hand must keep thy head and all the rest of thee for, as I said before, this is Koil-and-Poggle Ford, and Sack-Son, I am a perfect *Gale*! Lay on—and no prodding in the stummick. . . .

Ill-fared it then with Roderic Dhu, as d(h)uly laid down in the poem and shown forth in the picture.

It was a truly Homeric combat, and when Brodrick Two got a nasty crack across the knuckles, he only put his sword in his other hand the while he sucked them. But his eye flashed fire.

"*I'll* be Fizz-James next time," he panted, as he received, but recked not of, a wound. Apparently Fitz-James concluded that the best thing to do, in view of this threatened change of *rôle*, was to make hay while the sun shone, for, as, with a heart-rending groan, Roderic sank to earth and closed his eyes, he dealt him a superfluous and uncalled-for *coup de grâce*. Worse, it partook of the nature of a prohibited "prod in the stummick". Too immersed in the enthralling business of artistic death-throes to protest, Roderic but rolled over on to the illegally assaulted part, and with his head upon his folded arms, continued to render up his spirit with the calm dignity of a Chieftain of Clan Alpine.

Here it was that the Vice displayed that lack of complete sense of the fitness of things, perfect histrionic taste, and absolute reliability which occasionally caused sorrow and chagrin to the President.

Raising his blood-stained weapon aloft in both hands, he flourished it above the prostrate body of the Chieftain, and, then (alas, that this faithful though eaves-dropping chronicler must painfully set it forth), brought it down with a resounding thwack upon the proud Gael's exiguous kilt—even as he murmured, all unsuspecting such baseness:—

"Oh, Golly! I am slain at last!"

But the while he stiffened and grew cold in *rigor mortis*, he opened one eye, glared at the swaggering victor, and hissed, with deadly meaning, "Yes, *I*'ll be Fizz-James next time!"

ANCIENT BRITONS AND MODERN

In "Ancient Britons and Modern" the children are play-acting a version of the Roman invasion of Britain. Boodle takes the part of Queen Boadicea and an invading Roman centurion, and Ficcie is the Queen's loyal follower. In fact, the real Queen Boadicea led a revolt against the already present Romans around A.D. 60 or 61, burning Londonium to the ground. It was in the Victorian age that Boadicea became a popular patriotic figure. "Ancient Britons and Modern" was first published in The Young Stagers *(1917).*

In India, during the monsoon, and at other times, damp clothes are dried by laying them over a vast inverted basket beneath which smoulders a brazier of charcoal.

Ayah was airing clean clothes upon such a basket as the children passed through the big empty landing behind the Club premises—(the Nursery, to wit).

Ayah removed the warm, dry clothes and departed to bestow them in their respective cupboards.

As the eye of the President fell upon the dully glowing charcoal, visible through the large interstices and apertures of the crude basket-work, an idea germinated in her fertile brain.

"I say, Fic," quoth she to the faithful Vice, "how'd you like to play Judgment Day? Or would you rather have the Invasion of Britain, or the Forty Thieves?"

The Invasion he knew, and the Thieves he knew, but what was Judgment Day?

"Will you be a Miserable Sinner, an Ancient Briton, or a Forty Thief?" continued the President.

"What d'you have to do, if you're a Mitherable Thinner?" inquired the Vice.

"Oh, be tried on Judgment Day," was the reply. "If found guilty, you'd go to Hell. That would make a *fine* Hell for Miserable Sinners," and she pointed to the fire-enclosing basket.

"What would *you* be, if I was a Mitherable Thinner?" queried the junior official.

"God," was the prompt reply. "I should sit on a Throne and judge you. . . . I might have to send you to Hell."

"What would I do there?" asked the Vice doubtfully.

"Burn," replied the President sepulchrally.

The Vice preferred to bear a hand in the Invasion of Britain, or in resisting the same.

"I wonder what we could have for woad," pondered the President, on finding that her colleague had rooted objections to sustaining the *rôle* of a Miserable Sinner on Judgment Day.

"Woad is what the Ancient Britons went about in," she said. "Buster told me all about the Invasion of Britain when I showed him the picture. He said they went about in the woad buff and didn't care a blow. Not if it rained. . . . No police and no Grundies, he said."

"But what *is* woad?" asked he of the tenacious and inquiring mind.

"Paint. Blue paint. Something like the blue devils and dragons on Buster's arm. Like tattooing."

The Vice's spirit soared, and he produced an idea, simple as all great notions are.

"Paint me blue with the 'pwussian blue' in your box of water colourths," he said, and capered with glee at the very bare idea.

His leader congratulated him upon his quiet brilliance, bade him disrobe to the irreducible minimum the while she disinterred her paint-box and procured a cup of water.

The Vice was quickly rendered woady, and so were his tight, brief, nether garments, as the paint trickled. He was then stood in the sun and breeze of the verandah to dry.

"Try and dry a *nice* blue," adjured the President, "while I tie the lid of the soap-dish on to a stick for a stone-axe. You'll have to be jolly careful how you chop me with it when I'm the Censurian of the Tenth Legion."

"Might I cut a bit off you?"

"You might break the lid of the soap-dish, silly."

Having provided the Woady One with a stone-axe and a bone-headed spear which had once been a bone-handled umbrella, the President proceeded to set him up in life with even greater opulence. Visions of nothing less than a scythe-axled chariot were floating in her enterprising and inventive mind.

"You know those things in the picture, like milk-carts with grass-scythes on the wheels, don't you?" said she. "They were called *chariots*, and you stood up in them, and drove them about, cutting people's legs off as you went by. It *must* have been lovely. . . . b'lieve I could make one. Only if you fall out you mustn't fall on the scythe—or you'll get into trouble. . . . Your old go-cart and a couple of carving-knives would do."

They toyed with the idea until the Vice became ecstatic, and the President knew the double joy of creation and applause.

It was easier than had been expected, to secure two knives, poke them through the wheels and fasten them with string to the axle. The protruding blades were most realistic, almost too much so when the Vice scratched a woady leg on the point of one, and the President cut her finger. However, there cannot be an Invasion of Britain without the effusion of blood. You couldn't expect it. Besides, a good layer of thickish cloggy woad soon stops the bleeding.

The rocking-horse, Amir, having been harnessed to the chariot and a bear-skin rug thrown over it, no one with the imagination of a flea and the soul of a frog could have failed to perceive in it the very last word in scythe-wheeled chariots. Surely the most ancient of the honourable order of Ancient Britons would have described it as a vastly modish war-curricle, in fact the Ancient British War Office sealed-pattern war-car.

Indeed it so appealed to its delighted inventor that she hung in doubt as to whether she should side with the Ancient ones and be Boadicea of the Iceni, or undo them in the part of the Centurion of the Tenth Legion, until she decided to play both *rôles*, *seriatim*.

"Look here, Hog-and-Magog, which is your Ancient British name, only I shall call you Hog for short, I am going to be Queen Bawdy Seer of the Eye-seen-eye first, and this is *my* chariot, and Amir has got to reckon himself three horses at once, as is usual in war-chariots. I . . ."

"I thought it was *my* chariot," interrupted the disappointed Vice.

"You're always thinking," rebuked his senior colleague. "You better *thtoppit* if we are to get on with things. *Your* chariot! And I suppose you'd like the Queen of the Eye-seen-eye to walk while

153

you *tool* along in a chariot! Well art thou named *Hog*, O Ancient Briton. And aren't you about dry now?"

"Yes. Are you going to be an Ansiatic Briton? Can I paint *you*? I'm a norful good artith, Buthter thaid tho!" said the Vice hopefully.

"No, Ancient British ladies didn't paint," was the chilling answer. "Besides, I am going to be a Queen—not a woady buffer. My name's Bawdy Seer, and you can call me Baw or Bawdy, for short, if you can't remember it all."

"Thanks," returned the Vice, conscious of terrible deficiencies in this direction. He did his best to remember and understand, but realized that his stupidity, ignorance, and inferior histrionic powers often took the gilt off the ginger-bread, when they did not actually take the ginger-bread from under the gilt.

"Now, then, Hog," continued the Queen, "can you *surge*? If so, crowd round my chariot into a fearful, howling, surging mob, and I will make a stirring speech. . . . Mind you are stirred a lot," she added *sotto voce*.

"Friends, Britons, Countrybreds, lend me your ears," were the opening words of the stirring speech.

The fearful, howling mob had heard them before, but howled with no less enthusiasm. It was a part in which the Vice was at home and which he supported well. He loved being an army, procession, crowd, retainers, jury or alarums-and-excursions-without. In a collective part he was free from self-consciousness and *mauvaise honte*. But—

"Stop that filthy row," were the following words as the incensed monarch found her voice all but drowned by the superabundant howling of the mob. "Be a fearful howling mob without so much noise while I am talking. Some of you mobs have no more sense than rabbits. I'm *always* telling you about it. *Pukka poggles!* Howl every time I stop for breath—not *all* the time."

Cowed by the Queen's flashing eye and biting words, the mob fell silent—feeling that life was hard even while awaiting so much as a catch in the breath of the Queen, that it might dutifully let its most mobby howl.

"Friends, Britons, Countrybreds," continued Boadicea, "lend me your ears and" (with a nod to the Vice) "your mouths."

Loud and prolonged howls from the surging mob.

"These snifty Romans are about to invade our private country, and we must arise in our might and—er—puck them in the neck."

Loud and prolonged howls from the surging mob.

"I have got it in for them because they scourged me too—*you* know, gave me an awful hiding. I was licked by the Lictor—lammed like anything."

Loud cheers from the mob.

"That's nothing to cheer about you 'normous Asses. . . . Anyhow, they are about to invade us somewhere about Bournemouth beach, and it is up to all good Ancient Britons to arise in their might and biff them on the napper. . . . (Cheer, you Fat-heads !) . . . I shall lead you in battle and drive this chariot myself. You will see many Romans cut in halves and, if you watch carefully, perhaps Julius Cæsar himself—though perhaps he has got more sense than to get in my way. My faithful armour-bearer, Hog, will have a free ride by my side and pot any Roman seen interfering with the horse—I mean the three horses—as they gallop along. He is Company Marksman—"

Wild yelps from the mob.

—"at very short range."

Soft murmurs from mob.

"Thank you, my friends, thank you," concluded the Queen. "The collection will be in aid of the families of me and the Hog."

The next thing was to discover some reasonably satisfactory Romans.

"I don't thuppothe Widdy and Venus would mind taking part," suggested the Vice.

Widdy was a big white Persian cat, and Venus a bigger white bull-dog.

"No," agreed the Vice, "they wouldn't mind obliging. Rout them out."

Widdy, as usual, was asleep in her basket on the back verandah and Venus was in his kennel. They expressed no objection to sustaining the *rôles* of Romans. Augmented by a bronze Buddha, a large doll, and a set of big skittles, they made a satisfactory army, and, all being arranged, the Vice climbed carefully into the chariot, and the battle began.

It was evident from the speed at which Amir rocked that they were dashing along at a terrible pace.

Knowing that something was expected of them, Widdy and Venus remained *in statu quo ante*, but while Widdy sat up and took an intelligent interest, Venus lay down, grinned fatuously, and wumped the floor with his tail in an idiotic manner.

"*That's* Julius Cæsar—and he's not trying," cried Boadicea, pointing at him.

The hint was sufficient, and the armour-bearer raised his mighty bow, drew it to his shoulder—and caught Venus fairly in the stomach. With a yelp of disgust the stricken Cæsar scrambled to his feet and returned to his kennel. Anybody who wanted him to play Romans some more, could come and fetch him. His demoralization spread, and Widdy followed him, pursued by a grey-goose shaft.

"I think the wily foe have had enough," said Boadicea, several of the skittles having fallen. The bronze Buddha, unperturbed, was captured and bound to the chariot-wheels of the conqueror—and that was *that*. . . .

"Now I'm going to be the Standard-bearer of the Tenth Legion," stated the President, "also the Censurian. And the battle *may* end differently this time. Go and get that brown iron paper-knife from the drawing-room because its copper, and this is the Bronze Age."

The Vice obeyed.

"Make a jolly good Roman short sword," observed the President, examining it in this new light. "You'll have to be nippy with your shield, though—it's got rather an edge."

"I'll watch it," replied the Vice—using another of the unfortunate expressions learnt from Buster and his undesirable subaltern friends.

"What is your name?" he inquired. "I can't call you 'Thtandard-blarer of the Tenth Legium' the whole time, nor yet 'Cen-chew-rium'."

"Call me Reginald or Reggie, then," permitted the President. "No—Samuel would be nicer, I think, 'Samuel the Standard-bearer' or 'Samuel the Censurian' sounds all right."

"Right O, Thammy," acquiesced the Vice, and prepared to do

battle.

"No—you get in the chariot," directed the President, "and I come ashore in a boat. Then I hop out and make a speech to my soldiers who hang back a bit. They're not for it, at first, you know, and . . ."

"Can I take a pot at you while you speech?" interrupted the Vice.

The President considered this.

"It *is* a battle, you know," urged the Vice, "and I didn't ask you to come invading on my sands when I might want to be fishing or paddling or playing with my children or anything."

"Yes—but *I*'ve got to win, you know. It is History, and we can't alter that. . . . Tell you what—you can hit me in the shield while I am making the speech—or knock my helmet off. Yes— make it all the more real. . . ."

An empty drawer provided the Roman galley, and in the prow thereof proudly stood Samuel the Standard-bearer. In his hand he bore the S.P.Q.R. standard of the Tenth. It looked like a curtain-pole and a pinafore—but no matter. Nor matter that his helmet was frankly the paraffin-oil funnel with an ostrich feather stuck down its up-turned nozzle, his shield of card-board, his sword a paper-knife, his cuirass a tea-tray, and his greaves a pair of Daddy's leggings. The play is the thing—and Imagination is life and salvation.

Bravely he leapt into the waves, and turned to his daunted followers as an arrow smote his shield.

"Buck up, you fellows," quoth he, "a little wetting won't hurt you—*nor* spoil your bronze clothes. Come on, you're not salt nor yet sugar. A bath will do some of you good. . . ."

Still they hung back.

"Behold!" he continued, "I take the Standard of the Tenth Legion among the enemy!"

He did, and another arrow took him well in the centre of the cuirass ere the enemy, leaping from the chariot, rushed upon him with spear and axe. Dropping the axe, the enemy seized the standard with a cry of—

"Leggo, Thamuel!—or die!"

Samuel did neither. He rapped the knuckles of the presumptuous hand sharply, and the enemy drew back with a yelp of anguish.

"Hop it!" cried the Centurion, pressing his advantage and prodding the retreating foe with the butt-end of the standard. "Bung off! Barbarium," and the barbarian fled.

Leaping into the deserted chariot the Centurion said "Home" to a supposititious driver and poked out his tongue at the defeated enemy—and that was *that*.

TOSH AND FUNNY-DOG

"Tosh and Funny-Dog" is a story that relies on nonsense poetry; especially limericks and puns. Of interest is the comment that the children loved their mother's poetry. Alice Lucille, Wren's wife when he was in India, was a poet. Examples of her poetry can be found in the first edition of Snake and Sword *(1914). "Tosh and Funny-Dog" first appeared in* The Young Stagers *(1917).*

The difference between Tosh and Funny-Dog is the difference between the humour of *Alice in Wonderland, Through the Looking-Glass*, or *The Hunting of the Snark* and the humour of a halfpenny "comic" paper.

Tosh was dear to the souls of the members of the Junior Curlton, while for Funny-Dog they had a quiet contempt. If you talked proper Tosh you could stay for hours, but if you only talked Funny-Dog they did not mind how soon you went.

Buster was great at Tosh, but of course could not always live at the high level of real proper and genuine Tosh, and sometimes descended perilously near to mere and common Funny-Dog,

It was felt that he had done so, for instance, when at a Literary session of the Club he produced as his contribution:—

> There was once a funny old toff
> Who spent all his time playing golf,
> He drove *on* to the linx
> With a naughty young minx,
> Saw his better ½/T and drove *olf*.

It was received in dead silence.

"There are points about *toff, golf,* and *off,*" he suggested diffidently. "And about *drove on* and *drove off.* You know how you 'drive off' at golf, don't you?"

"We do," said Boodle. "We did it with some pin-fire cartridges."

"And then this—'better ½/T,' is quite a new way of saying he

159

saw his wife—his better-half—over her tea, or, if you like, bending over her tee on the green, you know. . . ."

"If you *say* it's very funny, Buster, no doubt it is," was the reply. . . . "Prob'ly most 'scruciating."

"Oh, no! I don't say *that*," the unhappy youth replied, "but well—it *is* Tosh, I think."

"Well, we won't *say* it's Funny-Dog, anyhow," conceded Boodle, and the matter dropped.

Daddy laughed consumedly at Buster's discomfiture. (He was held to have the right Tosh touch, and Boodle declared that he never lapsed into Funny-Dog, but she may have been partial and biassed in her judgment, for she loved Daddy "mos' tremenjous". Was he not so wise and clever and understanding that he was fit to take part in their games and able to enter into their imaginings and occasions, lawful and unlawful? So great and able a mind had he that he knew the utter unimportance of Grown-up things—like time, money, dignity, and silence, or being late for dinner-parties, must-go-to-office-now, mind-my-hair-and-clothes, not-quite-so-much noise, and mustn't-play-with-that. He was that sensible you would have thought he was a child, but for his size and his grey hair. In fact he was nearly as valuable, brilliant, and child-like as Mummy herself.)

When the Club held its Literary meetings, Daddy was expected to provide either Tosh or a Stirring Tale (plenty of good sound robbers, wolves, Red Indians, and things), but Mummy was always looked to for something that made you feel good, and funny all over, and desirous of seeing and doing beautiful things as well as hearing the beautiful things he was reading or telling or reciting.

What they loved best was some of Mummy's *own* poetry. Even if they could not understand a word of it, it was so satisfying to the, ear, so musical and beautiful—besides being Mummy's very own. That was perhaps the chief element of the pleasure of listening to the sweet and sonorous sounds, the pleasing and satisfying rhythm. There was also the element of pride in the fact that not *all* children have a Mummy who can read them her own poetry. . . .

"Don't try poetry, Buster dear," continued Boodle. "You can't do it like Mummy. Make up a nice Toshy tale if you are going to talk Tosh. . . . I think the best Tosh I know is:

> 'Three Wise Men of Gotham
> Went to sea in a bowl.
> If the bowl had been stronger
> My story had been longer. . .

I love that. It tells you they were Asses without *saying so*, and it tells you they were drowned without *saying so*. . . . I like jokes that don't have all the joke in the words."

"You put your finger on the point, President Sahib," remarked Daddy from the Club arm-chair, "and sum up a whole treatise on humour-by-implication. . . . Most learned President! A Daniel come to judgment."

"Don't *be* a Funny-Dog, Daddy," besought the flattered President.

"We nearly played 'Judgment' the other morning," put in the Vice, who was less bored by Literary meetings than might have been expected. There were always the Fairy Tales, and Daddy's lurid stories, and the better, sorts of Tosh, not to mention the joy of hearing Mummy recite or read, or, best of all, say her own poetry.

"This is the story," quoth Buster, "of two other Wise Men of Gotham famous as *not* having gone to sea in a bowl. They were, in their student days, the Wisest Men in the University of Dantzig, and were very fond of doing so."

"Doing what?" inquired Boodle.

"Dantzig," replied Buster. "I have a cold in by dose. They spent most of their time, even in extreme, old age, in Dantzig."

"But they were Wise Men of *Gotham*," said Boodle.

"Yes, and always dwelt there. They simply loved Dantzig in Gotham."

"*Is* Dantzig in Gotham?" asked Mummy.

"*They* were, Dear Lady, most of the day and all the night."
Mummy smiled.

"*What* were they, Buthter?" inquired the puzzled Vice.

"Dantzig," was the reply. "Dantzig all over the place. Dantzig in Gotham, you know. They Dantzed with each other, mostly."

" That's better Tosh," put in the President kindly. "What was the end of them?"

"Well—one lepped so much in Dantzig that he became a leper. A confirmed professing leper, and it was no good arguing with him."

"And the other Withe Man?" put in the Vice.

"Oh, he bounded in Dantzig, frightfully," was the answer. "Became a perfect bounder. People didn't like it. They were expelled from the Senior Curlton Club of Dantzig, who won't keep lepers and bounders. Not anyhow. Then the two Wise Men took up the cause of Progress. They progressed by leaps and bounds of course. . . ."

"What became of them in the *very* end," pursued the Vice, tenacious ever, as Buster stopped.

"Oh, they sat under the famous Omelette Tree of Gotham and egged each other on, and poached. They also boiled—with indignation."

"Poached what? Boiled what?"

"Eggs. They *scrambled* up the——"

"Funny-Dog!" said the Vice suddenly, and Buster collapsed. (Later the President told the Vice that he had been severe and premature—and in the presence of the President—a little presumptuous. He would have had a perfect right to make any comment had he been in the Chair. Privately the President entirely agreed with the Vice. The story should have stopped short of egg-puns. They *are* so banal, though *banal* is not the word the President used. In fact she used no word at all, but merely felt that egg-puns are distinctly of the Funny-Dog tribe and required a lot of elevating into Tosh.)

"It was distinct Tosh until you fell among eggs, Buster," said Daddy.

"Yes," agreed the President. "Tell us it again without boiling eggs with indignation."

"Tell it like Miss Ha-Ha in the Higher Water," begged the Vice. "You know Minnie Ha-Ha."

And Buster, who had a well-known gift that way, burst into saga of familiar metre:—

"Two Wise Men that were of Gotham,

You have heard ere this of Gotham?
In a bowl went *not* to sea they.
Loved they well their Universi-
Ty of Dantzig and were always
Doing it in season. Out of
Season also did they do it.
If you ask me what they *did* do,
All that I can say is 'Dantzig'.
Dantzig there in famous Gotham,
Dantzig each one with the other.
One he lepped so much in Dantzig
He at last became a leper.
Bounding so high went his brother
That men said he was a Bounder.
Said he was an awful Bounder.
From the Dantzig Club they thrust them,
Búnged thĕm fórth *nĕm ínĕ cóntră*
Dí cĕn té yŏu'll úndĕrstánd mĕ,
Bút thĭs métrĕ spóils thĕ quántĭ
Tiés ŏf thém thĕre Látĭn wórdsĕs. . . ."

"Funny-Dog!" said Mummy suddenly.

And with a cry of "Comfort me, Old Thing!" Buster laid his head in Boodle's lap and wept.

"Try again, darling," said Boodle. . . . "What did they wear?"

"Breeches of Faith and breeches of Promise," was the reply.

"What is those?" asked the Vice.

"Well, when they ordered breeches and got them on tick, they were breeches of Faith, but when the clothes-cook took their measure and never sent the things, they were breeches of Promise," explained Buster.

"Why the cook, and not the tailor?" inquired the President.

"Because the tailor only made tales, of course," was the reply, "while the builder made storeys."

"What else did they wear?" pursued the President—being a Woman.

"Oh—lots of things—sunny smiles . . . an air of mystery . . . rue with a difference . . . worried looks. They lived *in* hope, and they lived *on* sufferance. But they were very just. *Always* just.

163

Just about everything. Just about to work, just about to pay, just about to repent, just about to wash their necks—but they were fond of saying 'Well! I never did'—and they never *did*. . . . Their names? . . . Let's see. There was 'Ugo—who never went himself, and Alfred—who was really 'alfblack. Their children were Percy Vere—who never did so; Og—who hadn't a single H to his name because he didn't want to be a Pig; Edward—so called because his beer always went that way. . . ."

"What did they eat—apart from eggs?" inquired the President.

"Well, they imbibed virtue and assimilated facts. They chewed the cud of bitter reflection and inwardly digested exhortations and were . . ."

"*Fed up*, I should think," interrupted Boodle. "You're off colour to-day, Buster. Sing us something."

And lifting up his voice, Buster sang:—

> "Never beat your Mother, boys, tho' she is old and grey,
> If you do not like her, show it in some other way.
> No—*never* strike your Mother, boys, whatever she may do,
> For, though she's but a woman—she has feelings just like you. . . ."

And was turned out of the Club forthwith.

BOBBALL

Bobball is Robert Hall (Bob 'All), a private in the Army who is a friend of the children. In this story, Bobball tells the children the story of a horse race and his favorite horse, Bill. Wren writes the conversations between Bobball and the children as they probably sounded and with incorrect spellings, so the dialogue is sometimes hard to understand. If the reader has problems understanding the story, reading it aloud will probably help. "Bobball" first appeared in The Young Stagers *(1917).*

As Boodle rode her sturdy little Arab pony down on to the beach that evening, her face lit up with pleasure when she caught sight of the beloved and admired Bobball.

Chacun à son goût. The face of Colonel Jones of the Rutlands never lit up with pleasure when *he* caught sight of Bob 'All, but then he neither loved nor admired Private Robert Hall. He gave him more C.B. than affection.

Bobball was a garrulous, plausible blackguard—but not the Compleat Blackguard, for he loved children. That he had won the devotion of Boodle and her brother, should stand him in good stead when his last Account is being made up. . . .

"Hullo, Bobball dear," quoth the young lady, riding up to where Bobball, seated pensive, pondered the seldomness of beer, the frequency of Sergeants, the condemnability of India, and the ruddiness of things in general.

The Vice, aided by Ayah and Mowlah, toiled through the loose sand and joined the President, the servants retiring to a discreet distance,

Bobball arose, stiffened to attention, and saluted.

"Yore a soight fer sore heyes," quoth he.

"Have you got sore eyes, Bobball?" asked the President. "I *am* sorry. You ought to go to the chemist, and——"

"No, Missy. I'll go to the Canteen an' wash away all sech sorrers, byembye. Better'n the chimist," interrupted Bobball.

"Oh? I didn't know you could get eyewash at the Canteen,"

was the reply.

"Lots of heye-wash in the harmy, Missy," laughed Bobball, patting Jock. "Lemme lift you dahn orfen yore charger, an' you two 'ave a buck wiv' ole Bobball—and then 'e'll go an' get dr—er—get some heye-wash. . . . Nice liddle 'oss that," and he lifted the President to the ground, and signed to Mowlah to come and take the pony.

"*Pukkaro* 'im," quoth he, "an' lead 'im *upar* an' *niche* so as 'e don' get *tundah*. Naow!—don' *baitho* 'ere, *jao upar* an' *niche*, I tell yer, yer silly *poggle*."

"Don't you *love* horses, Bobball?" asked Boodle, as the three seated themselves on the sand. "*I* do."

"I loved one 'oss, Missy," replied Bobball. "I worshipped the graound as it trod on."

"It trod on me toe, once," he added reminiscently.

"Was it *your* horthe, Bobball?" asked the Vice.

"It were not, me lord," was the reply. "Not iggsackly mine. It were a race-'oss, an' it belonged to my Capting. . . . Ah! 'Ow I loved that 'oss! 'E won me a fi'-pun-note 'e did, and I 'ungered not, nor thirsted I, for a munf. . . . I didn't *thirst* any'ow. . . ."

"Tell us all about it," commanded the President, scenting a story.

Bobball removed the cutty clay from the midst of the thicket of his vast red moustache, screwed up his tiny grey eyes till they almost disappeared, wrinkled his sharp, short nose, and, so far as a recumbent person may, struck an attitude.

"*Kissin' Cup's Last Rice,*" he ejaculated, and then in a falsetto, mincing voice continued:—

> "You'd hask of the great rice, Sir,
>   When Kissin' Cup saved our 'Ouse?
>   As I stood in the Grand Stand that day, Sir,
>   I felt like a bloomin' l—no—*mouse!*"

"Wath its name 'Kiththing Cup'?" inquired the Vice.

"It were not," replied Bobball, "that spasim of po'try were what is called a proluminary canter. No—its nyme were Bill, an' a nice Christian sort of nyme too.' *Kissin' Cup!* 'Nough to make an 'oss feel faint. . . .

"'Ow I loved that 'oss, Bill! *And* 'ow Bill loved me! Wotsmore, Bill could unnerstand every word wot I said to 'im— an' when 'e was agoin' to run in a rice as the Capting *wanted* 'im to win, I allus 'ad to go to 'is stall, put my arms around 'is bloomin' neck an' say, 'Bill, I've backed yer *'eavy*! You carries my little all,' like that—all pathetic, wiv' a break in me little voice. An' Bill—'e'd give a 'iccup of onderstanding and let a neigh which meant, 'Dear Master, back your little Bill, an' 'e'll be there or thereabahts.' An' 'e *would* too. . . . Then come the grite day when the Capting 'ad to win a pot o' money or send in 'is pipers, and 'e fair put 'is shirt on Bill, 'e did. . . ."

"Did he tie it round his neck?" inquired the enthralled Boodle, visualizing the strange proceeding. "Was it a sort of—gage of battle, like?"

"It's a manner o' speakin', Missy," explained Bobball. "If yore Papa or Mamma goes racin', an' backs a 'orse 'eavy-like, they says they put their last shirt on 'im—see? On'y a manner o' speakin', o' course. . . . Well, the Capting 'e sends fer me and says, "All, me faithful ole friend,' 'e says, 'go an' do yore best with Bill. Make 'im onnerstand that I'm broke to the world, stony to the wide, onless 'e wins terday. I'm done,' he says, 'an' if Bill fails me now, I shall make a beastly mess in my bedroom wi' my brains to-night.' Seizin' 'im by the 'and, I wrung it till 'e 'owled, an' orf I goes to the stables.

"'Bill,' I says to 'im, 'you carries the Capting's las' shirt termorrer, an' Bill—you carries my little hall as well,' I says."

"Your little *haul*?" inquired Boodle.

"Yes, Missy, my little absoberlutely hall, an' b'lieve me or b'lieve me not—I stood to win a fi'-pun-note!"

"How much is that in rupees?" mused the President.

"I don' rightly know—but gittin' on fer an 'underd, anyhow," was the reply, "an' that little 'oss won it fer me! Saved the Capting's honner—an' pervided me with the biggest ' drunk of a long and 'appy life. . . .

"Ah! Wot a rice that wos! I kin see it naow. . . . The flag fell. The 'osses lep forward. Neck an' neck they ran twice raound the course, an' you could acovered 'em with an 'ankerchief. Then, suddingly, hout shot two 'osses from the ruck, Kissin' Cup—I mean Bill—an' a rakin', hugly roan. Neck an' neck they run fer miles! Nearer an' nearer they droo to the winnin' post, neck an' neck, level as an arrer, an' *then*, a few yards from 'ome, one of them drew six hinches a'ead o' the other. *Which was it?*"

"Bill," breathed both the thrilled, enraptured children, as they hung upon the words of this Ancient Mariner.

"*No!* It were *not!* That rakin', hugly roan 'ad forged a'ead. 'E was good at forgin', I reckon, and there 'e was, winnin' by a short 'ead,—by a bare six hinches. There was Bill, six hinches be'ind, strivin' 'is huttermost, doin' 'is damdest, an' never a hinch could 'e gain! *'Ruined!'* I cries. *'Ruined!* An' the 'omes of me fathers alaid in the dust—not ter mention the 'omes o' the Capting's fathers.' In another second they would sweep past the winnin'-post with that rakin', hugly roan six an' three quarter hinches in front. I was jest about ter close me eyes an' breathe a prayer for 'elp—when be'old, wot did I see? *Bill shoved 'is bloomin' tongue out seven hinches, and won the rice by a quarter hinch!* There's sense for yer!"

*   *   *   *   *   *   *

Slowly returning homeward the children pondered the sagacity of animals and the depth of the incumbency upon mankind to treat them kindly, to love them, to understand and cherish them even as Bobball did.

CONCERNING WILLIAM HENRY WINTERBOTHAM

"Concerning William Henry Winterbotham" is actually two stories related by Buster, the subaltern friend of the family. In the first part, Buster relates to the children's mother a faux pas he makes concerning his Commanding Officer's wife—it is quite humorous. In the second part, Buster tells the children about his grandfather's dog, William Henry Winterbotham, and what happened to the dog when he was old and decrepit. "Concerning William Henry Winterbotham" was first published in The Young Stagers *(1917).*

"You are sad, my Buster," quoth Mummy as that man of war sat somewhat distrait, toying with his tea-spoon. "Second supper disagree with you at the Ball?"

"I am, Lady," was the reply, "for my young life is blighted, and though, apparently, I sit at tea in your delightful and hospitable drawing-room, in reality I sit among the shattered fragments of my wrecked and ruined career. . . . Second supper *never* disagrees with me."

"Who is she?" inquired Mummy forthwith.

"Mrs. Crickford-Crocker," confessed the youth.

"*Buster!* She's nearly old enough to be your mother," said Mummy, and laughed. To appreciate the joke one had to know the General's wife, Mrs. Crickford-Crocker, commonly known as Caledonia—because she was stern and wild. When a new-comer inquired who the local Brigadier was, waggish folk would reply, "Mrs. Crickford-Crocker". Her husband commanded the Brigade, and she commanded her husband. In person Mrs. Crickford-Crocker was imposing, not to say terrifying (unless really annoyed), being very tall, very broad, and very bony. Her cheekbones were, like her thoughts, large and lofty, her hair was scant and sandy, her teeth obtrusive, and her eye bleak and piercing, a perfect gimlet.

The Brigade feared God and Mrs. Crickford-Crocker—save that in some cases it reversed the order of precedence. . . .

"Yes," agreed Buster, "and ferocious enough to be my grandfather. . . . I lived in ghastly terror of my grandfather when I was a child—of him and his black familiar, Woby Tijer."

"Wobitijer?" repeated Mummy, puzzled.

"Yes, Woby Tijer. He haunted my days and made my nights a terror and a nightmare. . . . My grandfather never struck me, never punished me in any way, never even threatened me— except to fix me with his awful eye (an eye like that of Mrs. Crickford-Crocker) and say, 'Do that again—and *Woby Tiger*,' and he'd shake his forefinger at me and I'd wilt in terror, and look round for Woby Tijer. I expected him to spring on my back every time I went upstairs in the dark, and, when I woke from a ghastly dream of him, I used to lie and hold my breath, quaking, while I waited for his cold cold claw to clutch my throat. . . ."

"*Buster!* How dramatic! . . . But what did the old gentleman mean?" asked Mummy.

"I have since realized that the worthy old General was merely saying, 'Do that again—and *woe betide you*.' . . . What? . . . Well, Mrs. Crickford-Crocker has got it in for me, and I feel like I did when Woby Tijer was on my track."

"Tell me *all* about it, my child."

"Well, 'twas thus, dear Lady. I *knew* something would happen to me when you and Burgoyne would not come to the beastly Ball. Fancy Dress Balls ought to be held every Saturday night. Well, I rolled up, quite pleased with myself in my black velvet, as Hamlet, and who should I see before my astonished eyes but Mother Crickford-Crocker *not* in Fancy Dress, as I thought,—and she the very one who says that any man who goes to a Fancy Dress Ball in ordinary dress is a lazy hound, and any woman who does so is an unoriginal slut. Her own sweet words, I assure you. . . . Well, I was so flabbergasted at seeing her there in her usual dowdy, shabby style, only a bit worse than usual, that, like the silly Ass I am, I blurted out:—

"'Hullo, Mrs. Crickford-Crocker, why aren't you in Fancy Dress?'

"She just gave me one fearful glare, lasting about five minutes, and then snorted:—

"'Insolent *puppy*,' and marched off! And now I may as well chuck the Army, I s'pose."

"But what annoyed her so?" asked Mummy.

"Why—I asked the same thing of Lady Peggy Hillyer and she *shrieked* with laughter. When she could speak she mocked my simple '*Why aren't you in Fancy Dress,*' and then squealed 'The woman has come as "*My Grandmother*"'! I thought she'd have a fit. . . . How was *I* to know the old thing was got up as her own grandmother? I thought the spring-side boots and cameo brooch and mittens and things were merely a slight accentuation of her usual up-to-date Paquin-cum-Worth style."

"My poor Buster—you *have* done it this time," agreed Mummy, when she had finished laughing. "The stupid woman must have thought it was a carefully studied insult!"

"Yes. She did. Shall I go and explain?" asked the ingenuous subaltern.

"Do," was the reply. "Go and tell her that it was a very natural mistake. Say she *always* looks so like her own grandmother that the error was natural and inevitable."

Buster groaned.

"I must go and play with the kids till I feel better," he said at last, and sighed wearily, as he rose to go upstairs to the Club.

*　　*　　*　　*　　*　　*　　*

"Venus is getting fat and lazy," remarked Boodle to Buster as they rested after winning the Derby—Boodle in the *rôle* of the King's Jockey and Buster in that of Favourite—the Vice and Amir representing the Also Ran fraternity. "He simply *wouldn't* take part in that Derby, and he understood perfectly well what he had to do. He doesn't try. He grins when you show him his part, and when the time comes for him to do it, he just grins again and lies down and wumps his tail—and looks awfully pleased with himself."

"He's gettin' on, y'know, President Sahib," was the reply. "He isn't the lad he was. I don't know when his birthday comes round—but he's gettin' a bit long in the tooth."

"How old do dogs live to be?" inquired the King's Jockey, peering from under Daddy's cap, which represented the correct silk confection of the royal colours.

"Oh—some more, some less, some about as old as you,"

171

replied the Favourite. "We had a big black retriever, when I was a boy, who lived to be a frightful age. His name was William Henry Winterbotham, known as W. H. Freeze-me-tail for short. He simply *wouldn't* die—and he wouldn't be put out of his misery either. Simply hated the idea. My grandfather thought he *ought* to be put out of his misery, but not he,—he preferred to stay in it."

"Tell uth *all* about it—like a thtory, pleathe, Buthter," panted the Vice, who had just been "placed" in the Derby (six times round the Club premises on all fours).

"Well—William Henry Winterbotham had been a grand sporting dog of my Grandfather's for I don't know *how* many years—and Grandfather loved him better than anything on earth, I think. He'd never been out shooting, or for a ride or walk, or drive, never been outside the house in fact, for about twenty years, without old William Henry Winterbotham. Then suddenly the poor old chap crocked up, went deaf, dumb, blind, and silly, and began to lose his teeth, hair, and temper. Grandfather *was* upset. He worried over that dog a sight more than he would have done over me, if *I*'d begun to crock up. He used to get a fresh doctor to him every day—and they all said the same thing—'We can't cure old age.' Fact was, old W. H. W. ought to have died long ago,

"At last Grandfather realized the truth—that nothing could be done for William Henry, and that it would be true kindness to put him out of his misery. Sometimes a doctor would offer to do it. 'Sort of 'Dogs Painlessly Extracted' idea, but Grandfather would get purple at the mere thought of it.

"'Sir!' he would say to the doctor who dared to suggest such a thing. 'This hand has fed that faithful hound for twenty years. This hand has fondled him and cherished him;—and no other hand but this shall—er—help him over his last stile.' That was the sort of way the old boy talked, y'know. . . . Pompous. . . ."

"What'th '*pompouth*'?" inquired the Vice.

"*That* is," replied Buster, evading explanations.

"As a matter of fact, it was a groom's hand that had done the feeding, but that's a detail."

"A dog's tail?" queried the Vice intelligently.

"Sit on your head, Vice," requested the President.

"Anyhow, this is a dog's tale, Mr. Vice," replied Buster, and the end of it is this:—

"At last poor old Grandfather screwed himself to the point of doing the dreadful deed, and he decided that as W. H. Freeze-me-tail had been a sporting-dog all his life, and a fine gun-dog, he ought to die by being shot, and not by being poisoned like a beastly sewer-rat. It preyed on poor Grandfather's nerves so that he lost his sleep and his appetite—until, one dark and stormy night, he crept forth to do the awful deed of blood. He took his old army-revolver, loaded, it in all six chambers, and, with tearful eyes and shaking hand, crept on tip-toe toward the stables where was the kennel of his faithful old friend. . . ."

"Why did he crep' on tip-toe?" inquired the Vice.

"So that he should not wake William Henry Winterbotham if he were asleep," was the reply. "He felt, in the first place, that if the noble hound came out, wagging its tail with pleasure, to lick the hand of its beloved master—that hand would fall in palsied impotence before it could do the awful deed. In the second place—if W. H. W. were asleep, how much better that he should never wake again. How much better that he should pass painlessly away as the merciful bullet crashed into his unconscious brain.

"Nearer and nearer crept Grandfather, and still no sound broke upon the stilly watches of the night. . . ."

"Had it thtopped?" inquired the Vice.

"Had what stopped?"

"His stilly watch?"

"No, my son—it's a manner o' speakin', a figure of speech, like. I mean there was no noise. No rattle of poor Freeze-me-tail's chain. He *was* asleep.

"Averting his face, closing his eyes, holding his breath, my anguished Grandfather thrust the revolver into the kennel, fired six times, and then, sobbing, with bursting heart, he fled from that unhallowed spot. . . .

"But he was a man with a high and stern sense of duty. He would see the thing through properly. He would give poor William H. Winterbotham a proper funeral and attend it himself. So in the morning he arose, dressed himself, and went to take his last look at the dead body of his poor dear old faithful friend in the kennel. As he stooped with a tragic groan to look into it, W. Henry Winterbotham rushed out and bit him. Grandfather had missed him every time. William Henry Winterbotham is alive still. . . ."

THE STUART QUEEN

In "The Stuart Queen", the children act out the execution of Mary, Queen of Scots, with Boodle playing the part of the queen and Ficcie the executioner. "The Stuart Queen" was first published in The Young Stagers *(1917).*

"Bags—I Tablo-Weevongs to-day," quoth the Vice, as he and the President went upstairs to the portion of the Club premises devoted to Literary, Sporting, Dramatic, and Social purposes.

"Right O," acquiesced the President. "Fish out the History Pictures."

The Vice preferred *Tableaux Vivants* to the Legitimate Drama as there was practically nothing to remember; one merely had to pose oneself gracefully in the *rôle* of the represented personage, and either hold one's peace, or "gag" as the spirit moved one.

In acting, as distinct from the *tableau*, there is such a dreadful lot to remember, what with appropriate gestures, prescribed postures, and ordainéd words.

"Let's do the Excruciation of Mary Queen of Thcotth," suggested the Vice, as they turned over the pages of the portfolio of Historical Pictures—a valued property of the Dramatic Society of the Club.

"Nothin' doin'," replied the President tersely, in the manner of Buster.

"Why not?" inquired the Vice. "It's eathy, and it weally only wants two."

"I know what you are, with an *axe*," replied the President, without considering the fundamental truth that only two are really essential to an Execution. "You'd be nearly as good an Executioner as I should be a Queen."

The Vice felt his muscles.

"I could have a card-board akth," he modestly suggested. That would certainly go far to counteract his terrible strength and inflexible sense of duty as an Executioner.

"Good idea!" quoth the President. "Let's get the lid of one of

Mummy's big card-board boxes. I'll soon make an axe. Or, better still, let's nail a small square of card-board to a stick. There's a big photograph without a frame in the drawing-room— it would make a jolly good axe-head—and it's not too stiff. . . ."

The photograph was unobtrusively borrowed, and put to novel uses. A low stool made an excellent block, and a rug did for the scaffold. Orders, squeaked from a back window, evoked Mowlah, who was ordered to bring a handful of hay. Little did he realize that it was for the seemly absorption of the blood of a Queen as it flowed red upon the gallows of Fotheringay Castle.

"It's straw in the picture," observed the President, "but I don't suppose Mary would have kicked up a row if they'd brought hay."

"No," agreed the Vice, "and she wouldn't care if there *were* a meth—afterwards."

"Besides, it wasn't her castle and furniture," added the President. "It was Elizabeth's. She'd make all the mess she could."

The block, axe, and straw-strewn scaffold being ready, the *dramatis personæ* made their personal preparations.

The doomed Queen erected an ill-constructed "bun" of her hair on the top of her head, for the convenience of the Headsman; pinned a large Union Jack skirt-wise around her waist; and made those preparations, as to the upper portion of her person, which usually preceded the washing of her neck. Being a Queen, she placed an inverted brass bowl over the precarious "bun" by way of a crown, but experienced considerable difficulty in preventing this well-known adjunct and symbol of Royalty from tilting forward and obscuring the vision of one eye. Being thus "armed and well prepared," she sank gracefully to the ground, in the attitude depicted, and awaited the Executioner. The Executioner had done himself proud. With burnt cork he had made an excellent simulation of a mask, and had given himself the kind of beard and moustache worn by all the Best Executioners. A condemned soiled-linen bag, inverted, and provided with three holes, gave full play to his arms and head, if not to his legs. On his head he wore, by way of a Black Cap, a. small milk-saucepan. It was certainly black.

The Queen bandaged her eyes—or, to be exact, one eye and a

corner. She did not wholly trust the Executioner perhaps.

"There ought to be mourners about, surely, when a Queen is done in!" she observed. "Here, Venus, you lazy fat thing, come and mourn. You can do *that* much for your living, surely."

Venus came over, smiled foolishly, and licked the Royal nose.

"Stop it, you Ass," said the Queen. "You've got to *mourn*, I tell you, not giggle. Lie down, and look as though you have lost Hope or a bone or something—*go* on. . . ."

Venus wagged his tail and mounted the block. The Headsman's eye gleamed and he raised his axe.

"My faithful follower wishes to die for me," exclaimed the delighted Queen. "He can."

As the Executioner poised himself for the stroke, Venus saw his mistake and vacated-the block.

"He has thought better of it," said the disappointed Queen.

"He's an *Ath*," said the equally disappointed Executioner.

"He's got to mourn, anyhow," announced the doomed Monarch, "or he'll jolly well get something to make him."

Venus turned round twice, lay down near the block, and heaved a long deep sigh.

"*That's* better, my faithful Rissole," commended his mistress. "I knew you could mourn if you tried."

"No—Rithole was murdered," observed the Vice. "I wemember—because I *was* Rithole, and Buster was the band of murderers. He couldn't be here at your funeral when he's had one of his own."

"Quite right," agreed the Queen, and quoted "'the faithful Rissole slain'."

"He can be a Maid of Honour then," she added. "Venus, be a Maid of Honour—and try and look like one. . . . Get him that big doll's-nightdress or something. He doesn't look a bit like a Maid of Honour as he is. . . . And tie that black hair-ribbon on his tail, for mourning. . . . Now, I'm ready," and the Queen stepped on to the scaffold. Turning to the little throng of halberdiers, officers, retainers, ladies and gentlemen in waiting, the Queen made her dignified farewell with the words:—

"My Lords, My Dooks, the Captive cried,

Were I but once more three,
For ten good-nights on yonder hill
To aid my caws and me,
This garment would I scatter wide
To every freeze that flows,
And once more brain a stupid queen,
And all resourceless foes.
Yours sincerely,
Mary Stuart,"

which was as near as she could remember to what she had heard Mummy read.

She then turned to the Headsman, who, one regrets to relate, was spitting on his hands, the better to grip his mighty axe. (He had seen Bobball adopt that method when about to dig him a trench in the sand.) He overdid it altogether, however.

"Dirty dog!" remarked the Queen, *sotto voce.*

"Well—of corthe—if Your Highety *wants* the akth to thlip and give you a fearful wump with the back of it, *I* don't mind," replied the Headsman.

"You'd better *not*," said Mary Stuart truculently, as she knelt and placed her head upon the block, "or I shall shed tears copiously. . . . They'll be your tears."

"Kindly bleed on to that thtraw, your Liege," requested the Executioner.

"I shall bleed just where I please," replied the Queen. "I shall bleed as much as I can too, and I hope it'll squirt all over the place. I hope it'll spoil Queen Elizabeth's carpet and furniture and make a mess on the wall-paper. Perhaps that'll teach her not to be so fast. She's too fond of chopping people's heads off. You can tell her I said so. . . . So there," and the unfortunate Queen laid her head upon the block.

The Headsman struck, and for the next minute the decapitated Queen appeared to be directing a stream of blood (much as a fireman does a stream of water) in an intelligent though truncated effort to make a little go a long way, and also to cover a wide area.

THE VIRTUOUS TIGER

*In this story, Buster tells the children about "The Virtuous Tiger",
which a "wicked" visiting Member of Parliament hunts. One
interesting thing about this story is the relationship to Wren's first
novel,* Dew and Mildew *(1912). One of the major themes in* Dew and
Mildew *is concerned with a visiting Member of Parliament and how
Buster is able to divert him from bothering the children's father and
mother. "The Virtuous Tiger" first appeared in* The Young Stagers
(1917), but might have originally been intended for inclusion in Dew
and Mildew.

What does 'a stitch in time saves nine' mean, Buster?" asked
Boodle, as her guide, philosopher, and friend entered the Club in
search of tea ere bearing his modest part in a Literary session of
the same. "Daddy said it about his saddle."

"Well, the mother of eight once sewed—no, that's a different
story. It's like this," was the reply. "There were once nine
Virtuous Children, like you and the Vice, y'know, and they were
being pursued by an Abominable Policeman. . . ."

"Whaffor?" inquired the Vice.

"Well, it is their nature *to*. It's a Law. Abominable
Policemen do it to fulfil the law of their being—and Virtuous
Children get pursued to fulfil the law of their *not* being—not
being there when the Abominable Policeman arrives, you know.
Do you understand?"

"No," said the Vice.

"Nor do I," replied Buster, "but this will make it as plain as
yourself, Sir. (No offence, of course.) The nine Virtuous
Children, secure in the knowledge of their unimpeachable and
unassailable Virtue, fled with such dispatch that the pursuing and
Abominable Policeman got the Stitch. D'you see? He got the
stitch in Time and it saved the Nine."

"Good Tosh," commended the President.

Buster bowed his thanks of the appreciation of his effort.

"I know a lot about Virtue," he admitted. "It's like Beauty,
you know, 'Beauty is in the eye of the beholder'."

"Don't be *vain*, Buster," adjured the President. "What do *men* want with beautiful eyes? 'Sides, yours are very or'nary."

Buster wept. "Misunderstood!" he wailed. "*Mis*-understood!"

"Who was *she*?" inquired the Vice.

Buster positively yelped in his anguish.

"You wrong me, Gentlemen," he said, with quiet dignity. "Beauty does not exist until it is seen. Same with Virtue. Virtue is in the mind of the appreciator. I trust I make myself clear. I once knew, a Virtuous Tiger."

The yawn which was frankly distending the mouth of the Vice was nipped in the bud, if yawns do bud, or, to express the fact better, was stifled untimely. Tigers are tigers. Man-eaters he knew, and tigresses he knew, but what was this? Did it gambol friskily around the feet of its owner, a small boy; sleep at night beside his bed, guarding him from harm; give him rides upon its back, and sustain many and varied *rôles* in play-acting?

"What ith a wirtuouth tiger?" he inquired.

"A tiger Redolent of Virtue," was the reply. "A *good* tiger. A really nice-minded tiger. A gentlemanly, quiet, steady, reliable tiger. A tiger you could trust with the joint. Quiet to ride or drive. No vice. Ridden by a lady—but no smile on the face of the tiger."

"A darling *pet* tiger," supplemented the President.

"Tell uth *all* about it, pleathe, Buthter," besought the Vice.

"It is a sad tale," said the Subaltern. "It is like 'Gelert,' 'The Arab's Farewell to his Steed,' 'The Falcon of Ser Federigo,' 'Ginevra,' and that sort of thing. Poignant."

"Lucy Gray," murmured the President.

"Precisely. In fact, that was the Virtuous Tiger's name among the Simple Villagers. Exactly.

> 'I met a little cottage loaf,
> Er— . . .'"

"No—that's 'We are Seven,' and it wasn't a cottage loafer. Cottage *girl*," corrected the President.

"Quite so. My mistake. But some *are*, you know. 'Specially in villages like London. Let's see. Lucy Gray. . . . Wasn't it she

who dwelt in beauty side by side, or beside the cottage door—
while by her sported on the green her giddy grandpa Might-have-
been."

"No, Buster, it was *not*. But what about the Virtuous Tiger?
Never mind the other Lucy now."

"Buck up, Buthter, pleathe," adjured the Vice.

"Well, gentlemen, the Virtuous Lucy, a tiger of blameless
life, lived and moved and had his being, or his pitch, in some hills
near a village called Soni, far far away from here, and was greatly
loved and respected by all the Simple Villagers of those parts. It
is said that such people are never grateful, but the Simple
Villagers of Soni were, for I myself saw them at it."

"But why were they grateful to a *tiger*?" asked the President.

"Because he was their Father and Mother and Protector of the
Poor. He killed a black-buck or some other deer, not to mention
the porkish wild pig, every night of his life—and the saving in
young crops was more than you'd believe. I forget exactly *how*
many tons of *jowri* and *bajri* and similar interestin' things one
healthy deer eats in the course of a stilly night—but it would
surprise you. 'Normous quantity. The headman alone reckoned
that Lucy was worth a good Sandown tip to him in February; a
winner in the Sandown Military Meeting in March; and in April
alone, as good as a triple event in the Newmarket Two Thousand
Guineas, the Epsom Spring meeting and the Grand National.
Fact! In May that tiger was worth a win and a place in the
Kempton Jubilee Stakes; and as for June,—why, in June he
wouldn't have parted with that tiger for a dead cert for the Derby,
Oaks, and Ascot. He wouldn't—not he. In July that beast was
worth a Good Thing in the Eclipse Stakes and at Goodwood.
When September came round, Lucy was worth a well-backed
outsider in the St. Leger, while as for October,—in that month the
kind animal was as good as top-hole luck at Gatwick, and a
genuine straight-from-the-stable for the Caesarewitch and the
Cambridgeshire Stakes. Believe me or believe me not. And
during the rest of the year, that headman would sooner have lost
his wife than Lucy Gray. A lot sooner. . . . Same with all the
other villagers. They simply loved the Virtuous Lucy and hoped
he might live for ever. He really was worth thousands of rupees a
year to the Simple Villagers of Soni."

"Didn't he never eat none of them?" inquired the Vice. "Not even the fat little boys?

"Now, my dear Vice," was the slightly pained reply, "what decent tiger *would* eat Simple Villager while he could get venison? Would you yourself? . . . No, he never dreamt of interfering with them in any way. It was a beautiful example of lovely Nature's pretty way of keeping—what is it?—the Balance of Trade or the Survival of the Fattest or something—the Simple Villagers tilled the soil, the soil yielded crops, the crops attracted the deer, and the tiger lived on them. Seems as though the deer were 'Also Rans,' rather, don't it? Anyhow, that was the happy state of affairs in sweet Soni, loveliest village of the plain, when a Traveller came to the Travellers' Bungalow—and nearly spoilt the show. He was one of those wretched beasts who always want to put things right before they're wrong—what's called a Member of Parliament in scientific language. And even among Members of Parliament, he was the limit, the ultimate outside edge. Believe me, he was a Rooter. . . . And for what fell purpose do you suppose he had come to sweet Soni, auburnest village of the Plains? He had come to murder Lucy, the Virtuous Lucy, friend and patron of the sons of Soni. . . .

> 'The Fathers of the City had met within their Hall
> The men whom good King George had charged to
> watch the tower and wall'—

In other words, the village *panchayet* had assembled under the banyan to see about it.

"'Nay, brother,' quoth the *shikari* (whom the Travelling M.P. had brought with him) to the headman of Soni. 'Mad, he is not, but very, very foolish, a babe at the hunting and most wondrous ignorant. There is indeed but one thing to equal his great ignorance, and that is his great admiration for his own knowledge and wisdom. Surely there can be no *shikar* in his own country. . . . But from *me* he will learn much, provided his folly anger not the gods. . . .'

"'But he must not slay our virtuous tiger in the process of learning,' interrupted the headman, and he clucked the cluck of uttermost negation.

"'He will pay well,' said the *shikari*.

"'Will he pay the equivalent of all the damage that pig, nilghai, sambur, black-buck, chinkara and other beasts will do to the growing crops night after night and year after year, throughout all the village cultivation?' answered the headman. 'Will he pay the value of the goats, sheep, cows, buffaloes, children, and women that will be killed if our virtuous tiger's place be taken by some old toothless scoundrel of a man-eater, who will not hunt for himself but will batten upon our flocks and herds and upon us? Not he! . . .'

"And again the headman clucked.

"But the *shikari* was not a villager of Soni and cared nothing for its fate. He was out for fame and fortune, and the man who gets hold of a Travelling M.P. and gains not both, does not deserve either. Many rupees and much honour (among Sahibs) would be his if he guided the feet of so foolish and ignorant an employer to the slaying of a fine tiger. His position was a sad one. It appeared that he must either forego his hopes of gold and honour or find that something most finally fatal had been put in his supper by the hospitable villagers of Soni. He could see no way out of the difficulty, but, being an Indian and a wily *shikari*, he could see one round it. The foolish Wandering Sahib should *see* the Virtuous Tiger and have a run for his money, or rather the *shikari's* money, but shoot it, he should not. In fact, a miracle should be worked, for the foolish Sahib should depart from Soni bearing a tiger's skin, the Virtuous Tiger should remain in Soni wearing a tiger's skin, the good *shikari* would have rupees and honour, and the villagers of Soni much *baksheesh* and their Loving Lucy. Excellent—but what a lot of trouble caused by a little virtue! A hard case. Here was a Sahib desperately anxious to slay a tiger. Here was an admirable *shikari* to whom he had made known his desire—and his preparedness to pay handsomely in the event of success. Here was a tiger to be shot, at any time, by anybody who chose to sit upon a rock over-looking the well-worn tiger-path from the cave, and await him at early morn or dewy eve. What a conjunction!—and to be ruined by Virtue.

"'Something must be done,' he remarked to the headman. 'You would not have him and his rupees depart forthwith.'

"'Anything you please, brother,' was the reply, 'provided no harm cometh to our striped Rajah of the nullah.'

"'I must think. His tiger's skin is worth a hundred rupees to me, over and above pay and commission on *bandobast*,' said the *shikari*.

"'Our Lord, the tiger, is worth a hundred rupees to every soul in this village—and we be many,' was the firm reply.

"'But there is no reason why the Sahib should not *see* our Protector's tracks for a few days and be detained in our midst until he grow weary,' he added thoughtfully.

"'Nor why he should not see the tiger itself, thereafter—when he begins to weary of seeing only its pugs,' suggested the *shikari*.

"'None,' agreed the headman, 'provided he have not his gun with him at the time.'

"'On my head be it,' answered the shikari. . . .

*   *   *   *   *   *   *

"The *shikari* thought for days. So did the headman. So did the *bannia* (whom the *shikari* sought and who picked his brains in five minutes). So did the police *patel*—who was a good man at such little games. So did the good priest, who was a better one. So did the *kulkarni*. So did the schoolmaster, a learned man on nine rupees a month, and no bad hand himself at little games. So did the civil *patel*. So did all the adult male villagers and all the children. For it *was* an interesting and piquant situation—a Virtuous Tiger who must *not* be molested and a Travelling M.P. who *must* molest one or depart unmulct, with buttoned pockets. One thing was certain. Lucy must not bleed. Another thing was equally certain, the Traveller must be bled. . . ."

"When's the tiger hunt going to begin, pleathe, Buthter?" interrupted the Vice.

"Well, my son, to make a short story long—the next time the Simple Villagers of Soni went up to Lucy's cave with sackbut, harp and psaltery, praise and oblations and the carcase of a goat that had otherwise outlived its days of usefulness, as was their wont at the new moon—they didn't. The *shikari* just took the goat up without any *tamasha* whatever, and presently after took the good M.P. for a quiet evening stroll to the very spot where Lucy, full of contentment and goat, sat washing her face beside her cottage door. For the first time in his life the travelling M.P.'s tongue failed him, and he stood as though turned to stone. Then, when Lucy sat up, yawned, hiccoughed, and put her paw up to her mouth as who should say 'Excuse me,' he turned and fled for his life, and then said it was for his gun. . . .

"There was dirty work at the cross-roads that night.

"The Simple Villagers built a *machan* overlooking the path from Lucy's cave, and, as soon as Lucy was safely off for her night's stroll, the *shikari* took the good M.P. to sit upon it and consort with mosquitoes, while he watched for the horrible Scourge. Nearly all night he sat, and had just gone to sleep when the *shikari*, who was sitting behind him, heard the sounds he had been waiting for. A minute later, he saw what he had been watching for and gently shook his sleeping employer.

"'Look,' he whispered and pointed. The good Traveller rubbed his eyes and looked. There, sure enough, beneath a tree a few yards away, he could just make out, in the dim starlight, a huge striped animal! Raising his Express rifle to his shoulder, he shut both eyes and fired both barrels. There was a terrible roar, or bellow, or bleat, and the sound of an animal falling and struggling on the ground. A moment later, there was a sound of more than one animal struggling on the ground, for the good M.P., in his excitement, had leant too far over the edge of the *machan* and, perhaps helped a little by the wily *shikari*, had come down without using the ladder. Likewise the *shikari*, who with a cry of 'Run, Sahib; run,' landed on the gentleman's stomach in a manner which in no way helped. Knowing the unwisdom of dallying around among wounded tigers (and Heaven alone knew how many there were by now), the Traveller took the tip as quickly as he could, and did his record travel for the *dâk-*bungalow, guided by his faithful follower—who followed in front of course. After a stiff brandy and soda, the good gentleman sat him down to wait for dawn, by which time he had written a full account for the *Crumpington Courier* of his slaughter of the far-famed, terrible man-eater of Soni.

"Meanwhile the Simple Villagers had got busy, and by the time the M.P. cautiously returned to the scene of his prowess, there was nothing to see but gallons of blood upon the trampled grass. But when Lucy came home with a headache after a poor

185

night, she was gratified to find a calf, with two bullet-holes in its tummy, neatly laid beside her cottage door. Equally gratified the next day was the good M.P. to find a fine blood-stained tiger-skin pegged out before *his* cottage door when he returned from a day's tramp with one of the search-parties that had scoured the district in pursuit of the wounded monster.

"Great were the rejoicings and the festivities, and every one was happy. The Traveller, the *shikari*, the villagers, the *bannia's* brother who had sold him the tiger-skin, and Lucy, the beloved Virtuous Tiger of the sweet village of the plains."

"Good Tosh," commented the President. "Let's play Shipwrecked Sailors on a Raft."

BOBBALL AGAIN, AND A STUDY IN CONTRASTS

In this story, the soldier Bobball tells the children a story about the "district-visiting" of a minister's wife to his mother's family in the East End of London. He also tells how his mother was able to "district-visit" the minister's wife in kind. This humorous story can be seen as illustrating some of Wren's feelings about organized religion. See also the sections in Dew and Mildew *(1912) when the local minister and his wife visit the children and their mother, and the late novel* Two Feet from Heaven *(1940), which starts out in the East End and features a minister as the protagonist. "Bobball Again, and a Study in Contrasts" was first published in* The Young Stagers *(1917).*

Hurrah! There was beloved Bobball, sitting pensive on the sand and gazing upon the mighty ocean, his short clay pipe protruding from the red burning bush of his huge moustache. The children ran towards him.

"Gorblessmysoul!" he ejaculated, as his saturnine face lit up with real pleasure, "I was ajust thinkin' abaht you two."

This was untrue. Bobball had been considering the chaplain's phrase, "a waste of waters," as he regarded the separating sea, and thinking of how much he personally would do to remedy the waste, were it only beer.

"That's a nice lill' whip, Missy," he remarked, taking the rhinoceros-hide switch that Boodle had surreptitiously borrowed (in Daddy's absence) the better to correct Jock's besetting sin of laziness. "I usedter used one like that fer to encouridge Bill— that knowin' lill' 'oss I tole you abaht."

"Yes," replied Boodle, "the one that won the great race by a short tongue. . . . This is Daddy's polo whip. He's out visiting the Districts, so he doesn't want it just now."

"Districk-visitin', is he?" said Bobball.

"He's visiting the Districts," admitted Boodle.

"My muvver went Districk-visitin' onct," mused Bobball. "She took me wiv' 'er, she did, too. . . . It *were* a lark."

"Was your mother in India then, Bobball?" inquired the puzzled Boodle.

"No, Missy. She were *not*. She went Districk-visitin' in the East, she did, but it were the East End, an' that ain't no *mofussil* neether. That's in Lunnon, that is."

"I have been to London, Bobball," was the cold reply, "and there are no 'districts' in England. You don't take tents and go out into the 'districts' there, nor go 'up country'; and you don't have 'head-quarter stations' either. . . . Perhaps you are talking Tosh, though. . . .

It was Bobball's turn to be puzzled. He gathered that doubt was being cast upon his statements. He licked a grimy stubby black-nailed finger and held his hand up solemnly before him.

> "See my finger wet!
> See my finger dry!
> Gord cut my froat
> If I tell a lie,"

quoted he.

"It's your fumb," remarked the Vice, observant and accurate. Bobball had used the term finger in a liberal and comprehensive sense.

"Streuth!" murmured the astonished Bobball. "Ain't you pertickler, Mister Sharp-Heyes? Wot I means fer to say *is*, that I'm a speakin' the Troof, an' when I *do* speak the Troof, it 'urts my feelin's, it do, to be doubted. . . . It's caused more'n a lill' onpleasantness between me an' the Colonel, it hev. . . ."

"If you're telling the truth, Bobball, we believe you, *of course*," said Boodle. "We thought perhaps you were talking Tosh, that's all. Now tell us all about it."

"I never talks tosh, Missy," replied the British soldier, in an injured tone.

"It isn't every one who can," agreed Boodle. "Tell us what really happened when your mother took you visiting in the 'districts'."

"Wot I said, Missy, was that my ole muvver took me *Districk-visitin'* onct, an' so she did. Tracks an' all. All proper an' reggler. She Districk-visited the bloomin' clergy an' is 'oly missus—*you* know, sorter civvy's chapling, 'e wos. It were like this 'ere. My farver was a snob. . . ."

"Cocky? Stuck-up?" inquired the puzzled young lady.

"*Naow*, Missy—you know, a *mochi*, a cobbler. That's wot 'e was when 'e was sober, but as 'e was only sober a Sundays, trade weren't brisk so ter speak. . . . Love us! 'E *were* a terror, an' 'e lived 'appy fer years on meffylated sperrits, 'e did—flavioured, when luck was in, by beer, gin, rum an' other sech condimensions. Real sportin' Henglishman 'e were, an' 'ad 'is bob each way on hevery race as was run in the year. . . ."

"This is rather a putrid sort of story, Bobball," yawned the President of the Junior Curlton Club, who had a cultivated taste in such matters. "I wanted to hear about what *you* did visiting the 'districts' in England."

"Well, I was a comin' to that, Missy—but you're so 'asty—like all wimming. . . . Well, ole gaffer, 'e wants me to set-down-to-last wiv' 'im. . . ."

"Didn't he *think* you'd last?" inquired Boodle.

"It's a manner o' speakin' among snobs, Missy," replied Bobball. "'E wanted to set me dahn to the cobbler's last. Sorter happrentice me to 'imself like—an' 'im pinch wot I earnt. But muvver says, 'No.' She calls 'im just abaht wot 'e wos, an' says I gotter stop in our room wiv 'er a makin' matches. . . . When she got too ill to go out a charin', she set all day an' made matches—to fill our 'ungry bellies. ..."

"Matches is *bad* for bellies,' interrupted the Vice.

"Mummy says her mother was a regular match-maker," said Boodle.

Bobball guffawed.

"Quite right, me lord an' me lady," said he, "but she made match-*boxes* I should a said, and she gotter bob a day she did, for the work o' the lot of us—me an' the uvver two kids. . . . An' she wouldn't let farver take me away from it neiver—she knowed wot 'e was—and I was worf a good tuppence 'apenny a day, I was, when I wasn't more'n abaht eight years old. We wos terrors at matches, when it wasn't too cold to feel nothink wiv' yer 'ands. . .
.

"And then the Revering 'Oly 'Ennery 'Opper's bloomin' well Missus from the tin chapel took to Districk-visitin' us, she did. . .

. There we wos, all of us eggsep' the two bibies, workin' away like devils to make seven bob a week for rent, coals, and food—the pore ain't go no right to nothink else—when there comes a knock at our door an' in walks the 'oly female.

"'Don' git up, my good woman,' she says gracious-like.

"'I ain't got time to,' says Muvver, practical-like. '*My* time's took up wiv' *work*—to get food an' fuel, when I paid me rent,' she says.

"'How many hours a day do you work?' says the 'oly lady, a sniffin' the balmy atmosfeer of our little 'ome—(five of us always in the room, there wos, countin' the youngest biby, an' our clo'es an' beddin' wasn't wilets nor yet hotter o' roses, an' that bloomin' biby was *allus* ill, the aggerawatin' brat)—an' lookin' rahnd most disapproval' like.

"'Abaht twenty, as a rule,' says Muvver. "Ow many does your She-reverence do?'

"The kind lidy put this question aside. She was out to hask, an' it shall be answered unto you.

"'What's your husband, my good woman?' was the nex'.

"'A waster. A drunken, idle, wife-beatin', spongin' swine, your She-reverence. Wot's *yours*?' ses Muvver.

"Again the kind lidy took no notice o' the question.

"'This room's very untidy,' says she.

"'I 'ad a hidea it were,' replies Muvver. "I'm afraid all the maids 'ave got their day out, to-day. Would your 'oliness like to tidy it up?'

"'Can you not take a pride in your home?' says the good lidy.

"'No, I can *not*,' says Muvver. 'Will *you* come an' 'ave five kids an' a drunken 'usband 'ere, an' live on seven bob a week, an' show me *'ow* to take a pride in it? Talk sense or go an' 'inder some one else.'

"Then the 'oly an' virtuous female talked to Muvver for the good of 'er soul, she did, an' likewise she lef' a track, a proper 'un—"*Ow will you like 'Ell?*" it were called. . . . Muvver said she'd prob'ly enjoy it fine after wot she'd 'ad in Christian England, she did.

"Goin' dahn-stairs the kind lidy met Ole Muvver Skin-the-Goat. She weren't so perlite as my ole gal.

"'Good afternoon, my good woman,' says the lidy to the

abandoned, slum-dweller, in 'er gracious way. Ole Muvver Skin-the-Goat she eyes 'er, cold an' steady, fer a bit, Then—

"'You be grycious to *me*, an' I'll 'ave yer back 'air dahn in 'arf once,' says she. "Op it, will yer,' an' she p'ints wiv 'er fumb. She *wos* a wulgar ole lot.

"Well, this noble-'earted lady came agin nex' week.

"'This room and these children are no cleaner than they were a week ago,' says she, as though the least she eggspected was that we'd all got noo clo'es an' 'ad the room pipered an' white-woshed.

"'No—there's a week's more dirt on 'em, natrally, yore 'oliness,' says Muvver. 'You yoreself ain't no younger than you wos a week ago—but I got more sense 'n to say so!'

"'That baby's nose is simply filthy,' says the lidy, ap'intin' to pore young 'Meliar alyin' on a sack o' rags, bein' ill as usual.

"'Then fer Gord's sike *blow* it for 'er, Mum.' says Muvver, 'an' do somethink useful terday, if yer niver did before.'

"The kind lidy sniffs as though 'er own nose could do with a treat o' that sort.

"'Cleanliness comes next to Godliness,' ses she.

"'Yus—an' 'ungriness come before eiver of 'em,' says Muvver. 'If you'd bin man enough to 'ave five kids yerself, an' they wos astarvin' before yer bloomin' eyes, would yer bung 'em up wiv Gordliness or cleanliness fust? Or would yer work yer fingers to the bone to git 'em food an' a pinch o' fire an' a roof over their 'eads—their Farver bein' a drunken brute, an' 'im expectin' to be fed an' all?' she says."

Bobball paused to knock the ashes gingerly from his clay, upon his horny palm. Contrary to what one might have expected, the children were now deeply interested. Bobball's earnestness and dramatic manner held them spell-bound as they endeavoured to visualize a new idea, the tragedy of starving children.

"'They ain't any on 'em 'ad nothing more nor a cup o' weak tea since yestiddy,' says she, 'an' they won't neether, till I got these boxes finished an' took to the fact'ry. Would yer run along wiv 'em yerself, while I tidies up?' she says. But the good lidy 'ad nobler work in 'and, o' course.

"Then come the day when Farver done the best night's work 'e ever done in 'is life. 'E got 'ittin' Muvver when 'e was too drunk to look arter 'isself, an' she shoved 'im dahn-stairs proper,

191

an' 'e broke 'is bloomin' neck. Wasn't we all just 'appy neether! An' to fair put the lid on it, Muvver got a fi'-pun-note out of it, some'ow. I dunno' *'ow*—some Serciety or Beryl Club or somethink. Anyways we 'as a blow-out *and* a 'oliday, and she took us Districk-visitin'."

"At latht!" breathed the Vice, who had been waiting for such *dénouement* with patience.

"Yus. We returned the kind call of the good lidy, as was on'y right an' proper manners. The idea come to Muvver while ole Muvver Skin-the-Goat was asettin' congratlatin' 'er on 'er sudden and un'oped-for bereavement.

"'If that stuck-up grycious 'ussy of a Missis 'Enery 'Opper comes insultin' of you agin, you serve 'er the same,' says she.

"'No—I wouldn't like to go fer to sling 'er dahn-stairs. It wouldn' seem 'ospitable like,' says Muvver—a sippin' at the first cup o' gin she'd 'ad fer years. '*I* know what I'll do—I'll spend me 'ollerdy avisitin' of *'er*! I'll leave a bloomin' Track too,' she says.

"Ole Muvver Skin-the-Goat she stares as if she thought the gin 'ad got to Muvver's 'ead a'ready. Then she fair 'owls wiv larfin'.

"'I'll come too,' says she, when she could speak, "swelp me, if I don't! *We'll* be torfs fer a chinge an' go Districk-visitin'—an' see 'ow *they* like it.'

"Also they done it, an' took me an' 'Erry an' 'Erb an' Horgustus an' 'Meliar. When we gits to the 'ouse, ol' Muvver Skin-the-Goat gives a fair rat-tat, while I plays a toon on the bell which was cut short by a femmle a openin' of the door. Like a 'igh class barmaid, she wos, wiv white bonnet-strings 'angin' dahn 'er back.

"'We've come to the Private Bar, Muvver,' says I, an' we all shoves inside, an' through a hopen door we sees 'er 'oliness and a kid 'avin' tea orf a little table, an' in we goes,

"'Don't get hup,' says Muvver, grycious like, in the same sorter way 'er 'oliness did when she Districk-wisited hus. There they sets wiv their mouth open.

"'Ow many howers a day do you heat?' inquires Muvver, a sniffin' the hatmosphere like the good lidy always done in our lil' 'ome, an' lookin' rahn most disapprovin' like. 'This room's 'orrible untidy. Can't yer tike a pride in yer 'ome? Why don't yer put hall these chairs straight—I 'ates ter see chairs hall of a muddle. Why don't yer 'range 'em along. the wall ? '

"'Wot's the meaning of this?' ses the good lidy at last, finding her voice and risin' to her feet.

Then ol' Muvver Skin-the-Goat chips in, 'Wot's yore 'usband, my pore woman,' ses she. 'I 'ope 'e's in reg'lar work, an' brings 'is wages 'ome a Saturday nights? You know, if you wishes ter keep 'im houter the pubs, you must make 'is 'ome hattractive like for 'im, an' I means ter say yer must spruce yerself up a bit like, fer when 'e comes 'ome. 'Ave a bit o' pease-pudden an' a bloater ready for 'im, an' encourage 'im ter wash 'is faice afore 'e eats it. If 'e comes 'ome 'ere an' finds the fire aht, an' you likewise, stands ter reason 'e's agoin' ter foller yer ter the gin-shop and . . .'

"'This is a houtraige,' ses the lidy, an' the kid begins ter snivvle.

"'Some there are as calls it Districk-visitin',' ses Muvver, 'but praps yer right. *You* oughter know, any'ow. . . . That child's nose is simply filthy'—apintin' to the kid as was snivvlin'—'an' wot's it 'owlin' for? Is it 'ungry or wot? Can't yer tike a pride in yer children? Yer know this room an' these children ain't no cleaner than wot they wos a week ago. . . . An' look at that 'ole in 'er stockin'. Shorely you can 'ave self-respeck if you *are* pore. Ain't there sich a thing as a needle an' thread in the 'ol 'ouse? I expecks yer pore 'usbin' 'as to fasten 'is cloves to 'isself wiv nails. . . .'

"'Ereupon the good lidy fair drops the cup o' tea wot she 'ad bin 'oldin' in 'er 'and.

"An' when I sees wot she done I ses 'Gor-blimey, wot *'ave* you done?'

"'Look at that,' ses Muvver. "Ow many times 'ave I told you as woful waste makes wilful want? You pore are the most himprovident class there is. . . . Nor the floor ain't the plaice fer the tea if yer don't want it. 'Ow many times 'aven't I told you as cleanliness comes nex' ter Gawdliness? . . .'

""Ow! look at that,' chimes in ol' Muvver Skin-the-Goat, apintin' to a statoo of a naked femmle in the corner. I don' know wevver it were a 'oly saint or a gordless 'eathen 'ussy—but it was nood ah the same.

"'Disgustin', I calls it. The trash you pore do waste yer money on! 'Ere, 'ang a hantimokasser rahnd the thing an' be decent if

193

you *are* pore.'

"'Go,' screams the lidy, tremblin' an' pintin' ter the door.

"'Wot! Yer don' *like* bein' Districk-wisited?' ses Muvver. 'Well, I *am* serprised. Any'ow you jest read this track, "*'Ow will you like 'Ell?*" an' we'll call agin' nex' week an' 'ope ter find some improvement'—an' hout we all marches lookin' most disapproval'. . . ."

Bobball mused a moment in silence.

"'Ighly irreg'lar it were, an' most unproper conduck on the ol' gal's part—but it done the trick orl right. We never got Districk-wisited no more. . . . Course your Pa's Districk-wisitin' may be different. . . ."

"Good Tosh, Bobball," murmured the President, but the Vice had gone to sleep.

GRAPE-SHOT

In "Grape-shot", the children are rehearsing the story of David and Goliath the day before Boodle's birthday. Wren's daughter, Estelle Lenore, the basis for Boodle, was born on February 14, 1901 in London. She died of pertussis (whooping cough) at the age of nine in 1910 in Nottingham while her parents were still in India. Wren's first stories of Boodle were published as part of the novel Dew and Mildew *in 1912. This story, unfortunately, has some casual anti-Semitic comments in it as Boodle, in the part of Goliath, makes fun of Ficcie, playing the part of David. Grapeshot is a form of artillery shot composed of small balls that scatter when fired from a cannon. "Grape-shot" was first published in* The Young Stagers *(1917).*

It was the President's birthday on the morrow, and, naturally, great preparations had to be made for the suitable celebration of so notable an occasion.

Not only was the Club to be particularly Sporting, Dramatic, and Literary, but it was also to be markedly Social and hold high wassail with cakes and ale—at any rate with cakes; or to be meticulously exact, with a Cake, a Birthday Cake of noble proportions and suitable inscription.

A special feature of the day's festivities was a series of "moving" *tableaux-vivants* to be staged for the delectation of the members, honorary members, and guests bidden to the feast whereof the said Cake was the *pièce de résistance.*

Subjects selected as being suitable to the occasion, to the limited stock of stage "properties," and to the number of actors, were in course of earnest and strenuous rehearsal.

"It's no good," said the President. "Both Daddy and Buster absolutely refuse to play Goliath. I am afraid we shall have to leave it out. I should look such an ass as David if you were Goliath; everybody would laugh at David being bigger than. Goliath. . . . It *does* spoil the idea a bit, doesn't it?"

"What did Daddy and Buthter say?" asked the Vice.

"When I told Daddy he had been chosen by the Committee—

that's you and me—for a part in David and Goliath, he said: 'I'm a proud and happy man this day. I *am* a bit of a David when I get hold of a catapult. It must be a catapult, though. I am a rotten slinger, partly perhaps because I have never slung. Or if you haven't a catapult, I dare say I am still fairly useful at roll; bowl, or pitch. . . . That's it. . . . Give me a good ripe, mango or a custard-apple, say, and I'll get a bull's-eye or an inner every time.' But when I told him that *he* was to be Goliath, he said he felt modest and not equal to the part. He said he'd make a rotten Goliath and the whole subject was a most improper one for tablo-vivong anyway,"

"Doesn't he want us to act it, then?" asked the Vice,

"Not with him as Goliath," was the reply.

"Then I asked Buster," she continued, "and *he* said: 'All I have to do is to stand up and stop a rounded pebble from the brook and from your sling, with my marble brow.'"

"*We* were going to use a marble," murmured the Vice,

"And Buster said, 'No,' it wasn't cricket, and if it was, he wasn't going to bat, nor wicket-keep, nor long-stop."

"I thuppothe *he* wanted to play David too," mused the Vice cynically.

"Yes," was the reply. "And he offered to ask Colonel Jones to come and play Goliath. Said he would add fresh laurels to David's fame, whatever that means."

"What about uth?" commented the Vice.

"You were to be the Philistine army and I was to be David's family," answered the President.

"When I told him he could be Goliath or nothing, he said, Many thanks, he'd have a shot at Nothing as he felt he could do it rather well."

"Funny-Dog," said the Vice.

"Just what I told him," remarked the President, "and he wanted to pretend that he thought it was good Tosh."

"I suppose people *would* laugh if David were bigger than Goliath," she continued.

"I should," said the Vice.

"You *would*," grunted the senior official, perturbed in mind by the inexorable drift of circumstance. She did *not* want to be Goliath.

"I *thaid* I would," countered the other.

"Look here! *I* know," shouted the President, clapping her hands. " I've had such a good think. You shall have a pair of stilts and be Goliath! Splendid!"

The soul of the Vice sank within him. He did not object so much to playing a losing *rôle*, nor a dangerous one, but Goliath was a rooter, a swank-pot, a Bad Man and without one redeeming trait of the Good Egg. Nevertheless, he faced the difficulty like a man, and howled with derisive laughter.

"Oh yeth," he jeered. "Two handths for the stilts, and carry my spear in my mouth, I thuppothe. . . . A spear as big as a beaver's wame—or is it a weaver's beam? . . ."

"I suppose I shall *have* to be Goliath then," growled the President, and added, after a moment's bitter reflection—"Don't see why I shouldn't have a sling too."

"Oh, you'll have a jolly great spear," comforted the Vice.

"Fat lot of good that'll be if I've got to be shot sittin'," was the reply, but even as she spoke, the fertile mind of the President conceived two bright ideas. The projectile should be of the most innocuous description, and she would duck unblushingly when it was projected.

"Come on," she said, "Dress up, and we'll rehearse."

Goliath appeared upon the scene garbed much as had been the Standard-Bearer of the Tenth Legion, save that by way of a spear great as a weaver's beam, he bore with obvious effort a ten-foot mahogany curtain-pole, one end of which terminated in a most realistic spearhead. The one drawback to possession of this truly imposing weapon was the fact that it quite precluded the use of a shield.

David, as became a modest shepherd boy, appeared simply and suitably arrayed in a fur stole clasped about his middle and armed with a modern-looking catapult. Dangling from his neck was what looked uncommonly like a sponge-bag.

"Ready?" he asked.

"What have you got in there?" replied the President, eyeing her colleague's make-up with approval, and pointing to the bag.

"Pebbles from the brook," was the ominously simple answer.

"I thought so. *I'll* choose the pebbles from the brook," and laboriously depositing the mighty spear upon the- ground, the

President quitted the Club premises, rootled in Daddy's office room, and quickly returned with a small soft woollen ball whose proper use was that of a dummy golf-ball by one practising the art of driving. So light and fluffy was it that the most tremendous drive would only send it a few feet,

"There's nothing in the story about Goliar choosing the pebbles," remarked the Vice, as he dropped the ball into his ammunition bag. He too had had a bright idea on the subject of ammunition—and anyhow the President had said that Goliath was going to duck. . . .

The antagonists faced each other.

"Bung off, Lanky," remarked David. "Hop it. Your face will scare my sheep."

"And who might you be, my lad?" inquired' Goliath, adding in sepulchral tones:

> "Fee, Fi, Fo, Fum,
> I smell the blood of
> An Is-rael-um."

"My name and address is David, the son of Jesse," was the simple reply.

"Jessie?" queried Goliath derisively. "What a silly name. I had a doll named Jessie, she *was* an ass. Is your father a woman?"

"My Daddy could do yours any day, ol' Goliar; and you're a *Phyllis* Tine yourself," countered David, and punned in somewhat bad taste.

"Go, Liar! Go, Liar!" he chanted, pointing.

"Nasty little Sheeny," answered the giant, and dropping his spear he crushed his helmet down over his ears until these latter stood out at right angles to his head, raised his hands palm uppermost, and waggled them beside his shoulders, rolled up his eyes, ejaculated "My! vot a pizness," and with an exaggerated lisp burst into derisive song:—

> "Oh, Solomon Levi,
> Levi, Tra la la la,
> Poor Sheeny Levi,

Tra la la la la la la la la la la;
My name is Solomon Levi,
At my Store in Chatham Street,
That's where you buy your coats and vests
And everything that's neat.
Second-handed ulsterettes
And everything that's . . ."

Smack!! and Goliath's song died upon his lips with the suddenness of a cut-off gramophone.

In the utter shock of the suddenness of the surprise, he sat down suddenly and heavily, and with a bound David was upon him and hewing off his head while the Israelitish army in the person of Venus cheered and wagged its tail, what time the Philistine array made known its presence beneath the form of Goliath.

"Golly! What happened?" asked Goliath, scrambling up that Widdy might breathe again. "*That* wasn't the woolly golf-ball."

"No, it was a fat grape," admitted David modestly.

"I *thought* so," said Goliath, licking widely. He pondered awhile, and, in the non-committal voice of one who reserves judgment, added: "We will now do Alfred and the Cakes."

DRUMMERS AND RUMMERS

"Drummers and Rummers" has two contrasting stories about a drummer boy and the "demon rum". The stories are related to the children by Bobball and the nurse, Mrs. Perfect. "Drummers and Rummers" was first published in The Young Stagers *(1917).*

"Do you like Bobball best, or Nurse Perfect?" inquired the Vice.

"Do you like treacle-pudding or sea-bathing best?" was the somewhat scathing reply of the President. "If you are hungry and hollow you'd rather have treacle-pudding, but if you are very hot and sticky and stuffy you'd rather go in the sea."

"No, I wouldn't," answered the Vice. "I'd rather have an ice-cream as big as my head in a pail of lemonade."

The President snorted, but the tenacious mind of the small boy pursued the subject of the comparative merits of Bobball and Mrs. Perfect. Inarticulately he decided that he admired the moral excellences of Mrs. Perfect more than he could do those of Bobball, while he loved the human imperfections of Bobball more than he could love those of Mrs. Perfect. In fact, it rather seemed that Bobball was one large human imperfection—and lovable; while Mrs. Perfect was one small moral excellence—and admirable.

"I wonder if she's called Mrs. Perfect because she *is* perfect, or whether she's perfect-because she's *called* Mrs. Perfect."

"Ask her," grunted the President.

But when they reached the spot on the sands where Mrs. Perfect was presiding over the picnic nominally given by Phyllis and Ethel, her young charges, she was quickly seen to be in one of her frequent moods which were quite unfavourable to the pursuit of investigations of a private and personal character. But faultily faultless, icily regular, and splendidly null, as she seemed to the children before the advent of Bobball, what words shall convey the correctness, propriety, and frozen rectitude of Mrs. Perfect's perfection when that man of war and wrath hove in sight.

"Hallo, Bobball darling!" hailed Boodle. "Come and have some tea and then let's all play pirates-on-a-desert-island, down by the wreck"—and, striking a piratical attitude; she sang in sepulchral voice that well-known old favourite of all the Best Pirates:—

> "Fifteen men on a dead man's chest,
> Yo ho, ho! and a bottle of rum."

"Good a'ternoon, Mrs. Puffick, ma'am. I 'opes I sees you well," greeted Bobball, in propitiatory manner, as he gave his horny hands to the simultaneous embrace of a dozen small ones.

"Afternoon," snapped Mrs. Perfect.

"Ho yus, I could do with a bottle o' rum, Missy," continued the soldier, accepting the united invitation of the children that he would sit him down and be part of the picnic.

"Let's pretend the tea is rum," replied the little girl, "and you can be a dead man and we'll ah sit on your chest."

"That ud be what you might call a rum go, Missy," returned Bobball, with an unexpected flight of wit.

"Rum is a deadly poison," stated Mrs. Perfect.

"Wisht you'd p'ison me wiv' it, Mum, when you've 'ad enough o' my company," replied Bobball.

Ignoring the remark, Mrs. Perfect addressed the children at large.

"I don't think I ever told you the beautiful story of the little blue-eyed drummer-boy and the bottle of rum, did I? she asked.

"No," squealed the children in chorus. "*Do* tell us."

A story was a story even though it were a Perfect one.

"Yes," added the President, "and then Bobball must tell us one too."

Loud cheers.

"Once upon a time," began Mrs. Perfect, eyeing Bobball with extreme disfavour, "there was a regiment of good, self-respecting, total-abstaining men who never drank, nor smoked, nor used langwidge, nor caused their Colonel a moment's anxiety."

A strange sound, as of one who strangled, proceeded from the throat of Bobball, but as the children turned their innocent, all-seeing gaze upon him, he coughed and looked into his helmet as one who suffereth in church.

"Now in this regiment," continued Mrs. Perfect, "there was a little blue-eyed, golden-haired drummer-boy, the sole support, of his widowed mother———"

"Eightpence a day," murmured Bobball.

"———who had brought him up a total abstainer, not to use malt and spiritual liquors or tobacco in any form. Well, one day, as the Colonel came out of the officers' mess, who should he see but this little drummer-boy, whose name was Horace, playing his bugle at the bottom of the steps———"

"They allus plays their little bugles there," murmured Bobball.

"———to give his kind officers pleasure, in his spare time. The Colonel smiled kindly and brightly at him and said, 'Step inside and have some refreshment, my little man.' . . ."

"They allus do—jest like that," whispered Bobball, whose face appeared to grow more and more suffused.

"———and led the way to where the officers sat at their wine—"

"Wot! Wasn't *they* total abstainers too?" inquired Bobball, in pained surprise.

"They were gentlemen," was the cold and crushing answer.

"'And what will you take, Horace?' asked the Colonel.

"'Lemonade, Sir, if you please, and thank you kindly,' replied Horace, who had very nice manners, as all teetotally-abstaining children have. But the Colonel was a gentleman who liked his little joke as the gentry often do.

"'No, Horace,' said he. 'You shall join me in a glass of rum.'

"'Oh, Sir, pray excuse me,' said poor Horace in dismay. 'I have been a total abstainer from birth, belonging to two Band-of-Hopes and a Mutual Improvement Society. My father was a Good Templar, Forester, Ancient Order of Buffaloes, and was buried with banners and a band.'

"'Drink!' said the Colonel, pouring out a tumbler of rum.

"'Oh, Sir, I promised my widowed mother that never would I touch. the accursed poison—no, not to save my life, if it was ever so.'

"'Hear, hear, my little man,' cried the officers who had

gathered round, and prepared to take his part against the Colonel, whose conduct surprised them. But with a wink which reassured them, the Colonel put on a terrible frown and again pointed to the rum.

"'Drink!' said he once more, in a dreadful voice.

"Poor Horace fell upon his knees and raised his clasped hands to Heaven. How awful was his position! Either he must be guilty of an offence against military discipline, or he must break his word to his mother and go against his lifelong convictions.

"'Oh, Sir, I cannot,' he cried.

"'Drink!' roared the Colonel. 'Drink or die!' and he pulled a loaded pistol from his belt——"

"They allus carries loaded pistols in their belts," corroborated Bobball, in a whisper, adding, as an afterthought, "and p'isoned daggers in their braces."

"——and pointed it at Horace's head.

"'You drink that rum, or I blow out your brains,' growled the Colonel, taking out his watch. 'I give you two minutes.'

"'May I spend it in prayer, Sir?' asked the boy, 'for I shall never drink that rum.'

"The Colonel swallowed hard and nodded, and the officers turned away.

"Horace said his prayers, and as he finished up, 'Please bless Colonel Jones, and make him a teetotaller,' the Colonel could bear it no longer. Throwing his arms round Horace, he burst into tears and hurried from the room.

"It was a cruel joke and in a way it brought its punishment, though Horace forgave him. That night the Colonel became a teetotaller and all the officers signed the pledge——"

"Blimey!" whispered Bobball under his breath,

"——Shortly after, the Colonel caught a chill and was taken very ill indeed. The doctor was sent for.

"'What you want is a glass of good hot rum,' said he.

"'No, doctor, I'd sooner die,' replied the Colonel.

"The doctor laughed, and had the hot rum prepared.

"'Drink!' said he.

"'I cannot,' replied the Colonel, 'I promised Horace.'

"'Drink or die,' repeated the doctor, holding out the rum.

"The Colonel feebly shook his head—*and died*——"

"Nat'rally!" commented Bobball. "Serve 'im right."

"Thank you very much, Mrs. Perfect," said the President, and turned with relief and hope to Bobball.

"Now you tell us one, darling Bobball," she besought.

"Well, Missy," replied Bobball, producing a tin tobacco-box and a cutty clay. "I ain't wot you might call a thorough-paced uncorrigible story-teller—like Mrs. Puffick, but has it so 'appens, I also knows a little story about a drummer-boy likewise. But 'is name weren't 'Orrice, an' 'e 'adn't got no blue eyes nor golden 'airs. 'Is name was called Cully 'Ookit an' 'e had black eyes—most days o' the week any'ow—an' black 'air where 'e weren't bald, an' 'e wasn't the support o' no widowed muvver neither. No,—'e'd gorn an' deserted 'er, 'e 'ad, just acause she'd burnt 'is face wiv a fryin'-pan an' bashed 'im a bit wiv a poker, through gettin' delirious trimmings, 'er bein' partial to a drop o' gin——"

"Disgusting," murmured Mrs. Perfect.

". . . an' a bit o' exercise a-Saturday nights. No, 'e weren't no golden-eyed 'Orrice, but the funny thing abaht it is, that when 'e run away an' went fer a sojer, 'e must a 'listed in the Fifes an' Drums o' the werry same Regiment as 'Orrice once adorned, as Mrs. Puffick so truly told yer——"

Mrs. Perfect sniffed.

"There couldn't a bin two sich Regiments, so it *must* a bin the same one—all good, self-respectin', total-habstainin' men as never drank nor smoked nor used langwidge nor caused their Colonel a moment's anxiety. Six 'undred an' fifty of 'em, there was, an' six 'undred an' forty-nine was R.A.T.A., the one an' honly hexception bein' that wicked Cully 'Ookit. Did 'e sit hon the steps o' the Hofficers' Mess a playin' of 'is little bugle in 'is spare time to give 'is kind Orficers pleasure, as 'Orrice 'ad useter do? Not 'alf 'e didn't. Ho no! I *don't* fink. No, all *'is* spare time was a took up in the Canteen where 'e loved ter set an' 'ear the pop o' the ginger-beer an' lemonade bottles a bein' opened for the good, self-respectin', total-habstainin' men as was in the 'abit of rottin' their g— . . ."

Mrs. Perfect coughed loudly.

"—good hinteriors wiv sich gashious swipes. An' one day that abandoned young bloke, Cully 'Ookit, wot did 'e do but walk inter the Canteen, plank down 'alf a rupee, say as 'ow 'e were froze to 'is marrer along o' fallin' in the water when fishin', an' called fer a go o' rum, 'ot, *wiv*. Strike me purple! You should ha' seen the commotion there was in that Regiment o' good, self-respectin', total-habstainin' men! Talk abaht never givin' their Colonel a moment's anxiety! Five 'undred of 'em run straight off to 'is bungalow to tell 'im wot 'ad 'appened, one 'undred ran fer the chaplin', forty sloped fer the doctor, an' the remainin' nine mounted guard over Cully 'Ookit an' the eight pennoth o' 'ot rum as the astounded barman 'ad give 'im before he knowed wot 'e was a doin' of.

"In spite o' the fact that the Regiment 'ad got its route an' was entrainin' fer the Plains in the mornin', the Colonel drops heverything an' hups an' leaves 'is work an' rushes dahn ter the Canteen, follered by all the hofficers. Wot a sight meets 'is 'orrified heye. There, at the bar, stood Cully 'Ookit, an' in 'is 'and a steamin' glass o' the best!

"'*Put it dahn or die*,' roars the Colonel.

"'Ho, Sir, I cannot,' whimpers the little drummer-boy, aturnin' one black heye hup to 'Eavin' while akeepin' the uvver on the Colonel.

"'Put it dahn or. die,' again roars the Colonel, pluckin' a loaded revolver from 'is belt an' lookin' to the primin' thereof, while hall the hofficers turns their 'eads away.

"'Ho, Sir! pray excuse me,' said pore 'Ookit in dismay. '*It's too bloomin' 'ot.*'

"'Fer the last time,' roars the Colonel, presenting the pistol at pore 'Ookit's 'ead—put it dahn hor die. . . .'

"And in three gulps pore 'Ookit puts it dahn, aburnin' 'is little blue-eyed throat most 'orrible in so doin'.

"'Faithful to the last,' he cried. 'I 'ave obeyed your cruel orders though it scald my stummick so to do'—and 'e fell at 'is Colonel's feet dead . . . drunk."

Mrs. Perfect snorted.

"Drunk he were, drunk all night 'e remained, an' so drunk 'e was in the mornin' that 'e couldn't git up—an' the regiment entrained while 'e lay wrop in swinish slumber. So wrop he were that when 'e reached the station the train 'ad gorn, bearin' those six 'undred and forty-nine good, self-respectin', total-habstainin' men to their 'orrible doom. For a havalanche crashed dahn upon that train, leavin' only Cully 'Ookit of ah that battalion to tell the awful tale. . . ."

Bobball sighed, and pressed down the tobacco in his pipe. "The tale's called '*Saved by a Glass o' Rum*,'" added Bobball, as he struck a match and avoided the eye of Mrs. Perfect.

THE RAFTERS

In "The Rafters", the children are pretending that they are shipwrecked sailors on a raft and trying to decide who is going to be sacrificed to provide sustenance for the rest of them. "The Rafters was first published in The Young Stagers *(1917).*

I wonder how you Cast Lots, Bo'sun?" remarked the President, turning to the Vice who was scanning the weary horizon for a sail. (They were shipwrecked mariners on a raft in mid-ocean, and their provisions were reduced to three chocolates in silver paper; a lunch biscuit and a slice of apple rapidly losing its healthy pallor in favour of an unwholesome brownness.)

"I thuppothe you cast lots of things overboard," was the sensible reply. "But there's nothing to cast," he added, in the weak, faint, hopeless voice proper to one who has suffered the last extremes of hunger and thirst for thirty days (including thirty nights).

"Don't be a Fat-head, Bo'sun," said the Captain, with some asperity. "When you Cast Lots, you don't cast lots of something, you just Cast Lots."

"Lots of nothing?" inquired the Bo'sun patiently. "Why?"

"Why, to see who eats the other," was the reply.

"We have only one more meal for you and me and none for the crew, so we must Cast Lots, and the one who wins is eaten by the rest—unless, of course, anybody is decent enough to offer himself."

"A *lot* of himself?" asked the Bo'sun, and added, "Perhaps the Crew would," as he turned and patted the Crew's head.

Venus was the Crew, and was understood to decline to play the *rôle* of Universal Provider in addition. Certainly he shook his head violently when invited to have his throat cut.

"Anyhow," said the Captain, "we can Cast the Lot on him, so he might just as well have been a sport and died to save us, with a smile."

"How could he save us with a smile?" inquired the Bo'sun.

"You've been drinking salt water, my lad," was the unkind reply. " I told you you'd go mad if you did that."

The Crew got up, yawned, shook himself again and took a stroll around the raft—which looked uncommonly like an inverted four-legged table.

"Oh, look at that wretched Crew, he's gone and sat on the food. He did that on purpose so that we should give it him," yelped the anguished Bo'sun, pointing to where Venus was apparently playing at being a hen with chicks.

"That settles it," said the Captain wrathfully.

"The Crew shall be fattened up on the lunch biscuit and the slice of apple, and then the Lot shall be Cast upon him. We can still eat the chocolates as they're wrapped in silver paper."

The Crew, either ignorant of its fate, or truly philosophic, disposed of the offered biscuit in two gulps, but apparently reserved the slice of apple for even more parlous times. And as with fatuous smile and self-satisfied tail waggings the Crew perambulated the raft, the Captain laboriously scrawled with fateful pencil upon an old luggage label the ominous words LOT I. Having done this to his satisfaction, the Captain directed the Bo'sun to seize and secure the Crew preparatory to the ceremony of casting. Nothing loth, the Bo'sun precipitated himself upon the Crew, who in the joy of his heart that such charming activities should break the monotony of the terribly weary life upon the raft, dived between the Bo'sun's legs, upset him and proceeded to roll upon him, with snuffling snorts. And as Crew and Bo'sun grappled in a terrible struggle, the Captain standing aloof, mystic, sibylline, murmured the words, "Behold, I Cast Lots," and flung the fateful document at the Crew. But the Crew was in the very act of leaping back for a fresh rush-and-worry at his prostrate assailant, and the Lot fell on the Bo'sun.'

Petrified with horror, the three froze to a dreadful silence, even the Crew apparently impressed with a sense of the magnitude unmeasured, of some great disaster. The Captain was the first to speak.

"Golly!" he cried. "I'm awfully sorry, Bo'sun, but you're *It*. You're luck's clean out to-day. What rotten Kismet you do have. The Lot fell on you all right, smack in the middle of your chest."

The Bo'sun fetched a deep groan.

"Never mind," quoth he. "If you're going to eat me, I may as well eat the chocolates."

"Not at all," replied the Captain, appalled at such faulty logic. "Is it likely I should want to eat you while I've got chocolate?"

"But if I eat the chocolates and you eat me, you'll get 'em all the same," argued the Bo'sun.

"Don't be a Funny Dog," growled his incensed senior. " And anyhow, I shall want the chocolates to take the taste of you out of my mouth."

"And the slice of apple?" asked the doomed man.

"The Crew 'll want that," was the reply. "Besides, he sat on it."

"Is the Crew going to have some of me too?" asked the Bo'sun, with morbid interest,

"Of course," was the reply,

"Then I don't see why he should have the apple," continued the Bo'sun. "Crews don't mind nasty tastes; they don't care what they eat. Besides, he only sat on one side of it and I can eat down to that."

"Then take your last meal on earth, unhappy man," said the Captain, in voice appropriate.

"On water," corrected the Bo'sun, with irritating precision, as he reached for the apple. "I'm not an unhappy man," he added, munching appreciatively.

"You soon will be," promised the Captain, as he ceased peeling a chocolate, to tap significantly the heavy sheath-knife (or paper knife) at his belt.

No further word broke the brooding silence of the raft until the Captain had finished peeling the chocolates, laid them out before him, a post-prandial *bonne bouche*, produced his pipe, struck a match, affected to light it and cast an experienced eye at the weather.

"Prepare to die, Bo'sun," said he suddenly.

"Haven't finished my apple," replied the Bo'sun. " If you wait a little while I shall taste all the sweeter. Eat a couple of chocolates now and keep one to take my taste away afterwards."

The Captain considered the request, and seemed to be viewing it and the chocolates with favourable eye.

"Which joints of me will you eat, and which will you give the

Crew?" asked the Bo'sun, meditatively eyeing his fat legs and arms.

"Oh, cutlets, steaks, leg of Bo'sun, shoulder of Bo'sun, and that sort of thing for me, you know," replied the Captain. "The crew can have scrag end, head, liver and bacon, devilled kidney. . . . There'll be plenty."

"Wonder if I shall be tough," mused the Bo'sun. "Anyhow, I'll be as tough as I jolly well can," he added.

"*That's* a nice spirit to die in," commented the Captain coldly, selecting his second chocolate. "A real sportsman would trail over the side in the water and soften himself."

"Yes, and get eaten by a shark," sneered the Bo'sun.

An idea struck him even as he spoke, and the somewhat peevish and petulant look (with which he had watched the Captain's sharpening of his sheath-knife and his setting forth of plate, knife and fork) changed to one of bright hope.

"I will do it," he cried, and rolling off the raft clung to the side thereof, while the Captain set about the preparation of a fire.

A blood-curdling shriek and bubbling cry as of some strong swimmer in his agony brought him to the side of the raft as the Bo'sun, like Yser, rolling rapidly, toward the door, howled: A whale! A whale! I am being eaten alive; the beastly thing has bitten me in halves."

"How rotten,' said the Captain, eyeing the rotating Bo'sun dubiously. "I suppose I *must* eat the Crew now," and turned in time to see the last chocolate disappear, enfolded in the long, pink tongue of that treacherous and greedy insubordinate. With a yell of rage the Captain drew his sheath-knife and sprang at the Crew with so flashing an eye and menacing a mien that the Crew leapt overboard and swam in the direction of the body of the Bo'sun, namely, towards the door which—even as the Captain smote his forehead with a cry of "Ruined! Starvation stares me in the stomach"—opened to admit Buster beneath whose arm there shone refulgent a mighty box of butter-scotch.

"Saved!" cried the Captain, raising his hands and upturned beatific face to Heaven.

"Golly! So am I," echoed the Bo'sun, rising like Venus from the waves, or a second Jonah from the temporary accommodation afforded by the whale.

THE VEGETARIAN MUGGER OF SONI

This story is a sequel to the earlier "The Virtuous Tiger". In this story the Member of Parliament is attempting to relieve the villagers of the mugger (crocodile) that lives near their village. "The Vegetarian Mugger of Soni" was first published in The Young Stagers *(1917).*

"Did you ever know any other Virtuous Wild Beasts, besides the Virtuous Tiger of Soni, Buster?" asked the President one day, as they waited for Daddy and Mummy to arrive and make a quorum.

"Lots," was the reply. "The Colour-Sergeant of——"

"No," interrupted the President, "not Tosh now. I want to hear all about the Virtuous Tiger of Soni again—unless you know any others. I love Virtuous Beasts."

"Well—there was the Vegetarian Mugger who, in a way, avenged the intended murder of poor Lucy Gray," was the. reply.

"A vegetarian crocodile! Why, *Buster*, I thought they were the worstest beasts in the world, and *always* ate you up, and then shed crocodile tears about it. *Are* you trying to talk Tosh?"

"No, this is really truly. By a ford of the Soni River dwelt an *ee*normous crocodile. I saw it several times myself. And if not a really strict fruitarian and vegetarian, it, at any rate, *never* took anything stronger than fish. Meat it could not abide."

"If this turns out to be Tosh, I shall be angry with you, Buster," said the President, who was still sceptical. "I want a tale."

"No—this is Honest Injun. Honestest Injun as ever was. There *are* fish-eating crocodiles, you know. Live on fish altogether. Have conscientious objections to taking the life of a dumb animal. . . ."

"Fishes is dumb animals," interjected the Vice. "We kept some once. I heard them be dumb."

"Quite so, Mr. Vice," assented Buster. "But are they exactly *animals*, so to speak?"

"They're not vegetables nor minerables," opined the

President.

"Look here—you little dev—I mean darlings,—are too much for me," said Buster. "This mugger ate fish, the whole fish, and nothing *but* fish, anyhow. He was a strict vegetarian, in the sense that he never ate butcher's meat—so I maintain that he was a Vegetarian Crocodile and, to that extent, a conscientious, and therefore a Virtuous Crocodile. Also he was instrumental in avenging poor Lucy Gray."

"Did he think the Traveller looked fishy and eat him?" asked Boodle.

"No—he did much better than just *eat* him. He made him look an ass!" was the reply.

The children settled down firmly to hear the thrilling true tale of *How the Vegetarian Mugger of Soni made the Travelling M.P. look an Ass.*

"Well, it was like this, dear old Things," began Buster. "The headman of Soni, to whom Lucy Gray was worth such a lot, simply *loathed* the Travelling M.P. He hated him for trying to shoot Virtuous Lucy like you'd hate anybody who came along and shot Venus, and then wagged his tail as though he'd done something you oughter be very pleased about. But of course he dared not show the Traveller that he hated him, and that made him hate him all the more. Then, one day, almost before Lucy's understudy was cold in his grave and the laughter-tears of the Simple Villagers dry upon their cheeks, this Member—or Limb—of Parliament suddenly sent for the headman and told him, through his butler, that he was going to confer *another* blessing upon the village. The poor headman fetched an awful groan at hearing this good news, and said he felt that they ought to name the village after their benefactor.

"'To-day I saw one of those Dread Scourges of your rivers, a terrible reptile that has battened and fattened upon you and your wives, your sons and your daughters, upon your flocks and herds, your men-servants and your maid-servants, your oxes and your asses, for ages. Make arrangements, tie up a calf or a goat by the water-side, and I will also slay *this* monster,' said he. Then he told his 'Travelling-butler' to translate exactly what he had said.

"'The Sahib wants to shoot a mugger. Make *bundobust*,' said the butler.

"'But there is only *one* mugger in these parts,' said the poor headman. 'There *is* only Grandfather, who lives by the ford—and he has been there for a thousand years at least. He is *very* holy. Why murder *him?*'

"'Make *bundobust*,' said the butler. 'Tie up a goat.'

"'But our Grandfather would never touch flesh!' said the headman. 'He is a Brahmin among crocodiles and *very* holy.'

"'What does the worthy fellow say?' asked the Travelling M.P.

"'He is calling blessings upon the head of your Honour, the Protector of the Poor, and says the goat will be ten rupees.'

"'Very well,' said the P.o.P., 'I will shoot the savage saurian before breakfast to-morrow.'

"'What does the Presence say?' asked the headman,

"'He says he will give you one rupee for the goat, and the mugger must be there early in the morning,' said the butler, whose name was Truthful James, he having consorted long with travelling Limbs of Parliament. . . ."

"Don't talk like a Grown-up, Buster," besought the President, "or you'll spoil the story."

"Sorry, Madam. Well—the poor but honest headman, being only a Simple Villager, smiled at the back of his simple mind.

"'It shall be as the Huzoor orders,' said he.

"And he went forth. Then he went fifth—to the *shikari* of the village. Then they went nap—on the Vegetarian Mugger of Soni.

"They made a lovely *machan* place for the Travelling M.P. to sit on—where there was no shade but plenty of nice glare, and then, on a sand-bank, right in the very spot where their vegetarian Grandpa was wont to come daily and bask in the sun, they drove a strong stake. And all the people smiled and said 'Amen.' . . ."

"A strong steak of goat?" inquired the President.

Buster laughed.

"No, a strong stake of wood. The kind you use for burning holy martyrs and things. Then they got a stout cord, and, from a thin iron rod, the village blacksmith made a very big strong hook. Well, next morning, down to the ford marched the Travelling M.P. with his rifle, to rid the village of *this* Frightful Scourge also. Then the headman and the *shikari* showed him how good they'd been, and produced the rope and the big hook and explained, by signs and wonders, that they would tie the rope to the stake and fasten the hook to a pariah-dog. *Then* when the Frightful Scourge rushed out of the water, roaring, with flashing eyes, lashing its tail and flapping its ears, it would see the pi-dog, snap him up in its terrible jaws, and swallow both him *and* the hook.

"*Then* while the fearful reptile was unavoidably detained by the stake, rope, and hook, the intrepid sportsman could take pot-shots at it until he *did* hit it.

"The Travelling M.P. smiled upon them. He beamed hard to show his good-will, approval, and intelligence.

"Then the *shikari*, accompanied by Faithful Fido, the village pi-dog, went and tied the rope to the stake. Then he suddenly grabbed Faithful Fido and drove the hook through the scruff of his neck, and F.F. made himself perfectly miserable about it. He also made the welkin ring. . . ."

"Wat'th a welkin?" inquired the Vice.

"I'll bring one and make it ring for you, one of these days," was the reply. . . .

"'The poor doggie does not seem to like being tied up,' said the Travelling M.P. (Perhaps he thought they had tied a pretty ribbon round Faithful Fido's neck and slipped the hook under it— or bought him a nice collar for the purpose.) Fido's howls were appalling. The more he tugged the more it hurt him.

"'Naughty doggie!' said the Travelling M.P. 'He wants to run about and play.' However, the good gentleman realized that, even as the bleating of the kid excites the tiger, the yowling of the pi-dog must attract the crocodile. He hoped he would be able to shoot it before it got near enough to really frighten poor Fido. He was that sort of kind gentleman, you know. . . . Well, Fido howled and yowled and chy-iked and made a *fearful* row. So much so that he frightened Grandpa nearly out of his twenty-foot crocodile-skin, and caused him to bury himself in the mud at the bottom of his deep hole for a fortnight. He was a very sensitive and retiring old party, like all fish-eating muggers, and he could not *bear* noise and commotion. He didn't really like it even when his old pals, the villagers, used to come and wash their clothes at the ford and beat them on the stones. . . .

"You *should* have heard Fido. *I* heard him miles away. I was staying with the Collector and he was touring in that part of the district.

"'Sounds as though some one has trod on a pi-dog's toe,' said I to him, as we rode toward Soni.

"'Sounds as though they're still standing on it,' said he, as the pleasing sounds continued. Then we saw the sight.

"There was the Travelling M.P. on the *machan* with a look of great determination, a rifle, and a lot of flies, staring hard along his sights at Fido. Under the *machan* sat the headman, thinking of good Lucy Gray, but looking happier than you might have expected. . . .

"'What's up?' said the Collector, as we rode to the spot.

"'I am heah devoting my time to ridding this village of a Scourge,' was the reply. 'This ford is—ah—infested by a huge crocodile. I saw it myself. I understand it has been here for yeahs and yeahs. I consider it *disgraceful*. Think of the toll of human life. . . .'

"Then the headman hopped out salaaming, and unburdened his simple mind, and the Collector grinned.

"'It wouldn't take long to "think of the toll of human life" taken by a *garial*, a fish-eating, bottle-nosed crocodile, would it?' he murmured to me, with a snigger.

"'You are a public benefactor, Sir,' said he to the Political Pimple.

"'Yes—but I maintain that it is *disgraceful* that the public duty should be left to—ah—chance benevolence and the sense of responsibility of the casual wayfarer. What are the officials about? What is the Collector about? . . . If I find that in the stomach of this dreadful reptile there are anklets and bracelets and armlets and——

"'Cutlets,' said the Collector.

"'I shall make the matter public. The Press of the Empire shall ring with it. . . .'

"''Ear! 'Ear!' said I, moved almost to tears by his eloquence, and then the Collector stopped him.

"'Do my eyes deceive me,' said he, 'or is that poor wretched dog *impaled* upon a hook? What ghastly barbarity! What fiendish, awful, unparalleled brutality! . . . I am sorry to take such action against a Public Benefactor—but I am afraid that

215

Section 7486932l½, $\pi\gamma^2$, of the Indian Penal Code leaves me no option. I must order your arrest and——'

"'*What?*' yelped the Travelling M.P., in a voice that much resembled the voice of suffering Fido.

"'That dog is *impaled*, living, upon a barbed hook,' repeated the Collector. '*Barb*arity, as I said before. The Society for the Prevention of Cruelty to Animals would rightly prosecute *me* if I did not prosecute you. The Press of the Empire is going to ring some more. Talk of the Unspeakable Turk and Armenian atrocities,—that dog has as much feeling as an Armenian if you haven't as much mercifulness as a Turk. . . .'

"The kind gentleman was purple and gasping. He fairly threw himself off the *machan* and galloped to where Faithful Fido sat and sang his siren song.

"Sure enough, the hook was through a bit of the scruff of poor Fido's neck.

"'If I were that dog, I'd bite you,' said the Collector, 'even if it made me sick to do it.'

"I don't really suppose that Fido understood English. Not properly. But you'd have thought he did, if you'd seen Fido take the Collector's tip! Directly the Traveller put out his hand to pat the faithful hound, it began to feed. . . ."

"It bit him?" asked the Vice. "*Good* dog!"

"It did so. The kind M.P. wasn't fishing, but he had a bite. 'Twas no mere nibble either.

"'Well—are you going to remove that hook, Sir,' asked the Collector, 'or must I whistle for my mounted-police orderlies and have you arrested at once?'

"The poor Limb almost wept. You see he went through life being a Kind Gentleman to everybody (except over-worked officials, soldiers, and all people of the useful classes), and here he was caught in an act of horrible brutality, and going to be prosecuted.

"'The *shikari* did it,' he bleated, as he dodged Fido's rushes.

"'Yes. I fully expected you'd put the blame on the poor ignorant native and try and get *him* into trouble, to save your own skin—but it won't do, Sir. Let me have your name and address at once. . . .' You should have heard him! Well—at last the Collector softened a little, and then, much against his will, agreed to let the Traveller off—*provided he shot the Dreadful Scourge.* And he was to tie up a calf one day, a goat the next, and a dog the next—and so on to give them off-days and rests. (Fish-eating muggers are equally alarmed by lowings, bleatings, and barkings, you know.)"

"And he never shot the Virtuous Mugger?" asked Boodle.

"He hasn't *yet*," replied Buster. "He's still trying."

"When did he make the bargain with the Collector?" asked the delighted President.

"About seven years ago,' was the truthful or untruthful reply.

THE MODERN DESDEMONA

"The Modern Desdemona" was the last story in the first edition of The
Young Stagers *(1917).   The first part of the story is Boodle asking
Buster for some suggestions as to what drama the children might do.
Another part of the story is concerned with how Ficcie mistakes the
usage of the phrase "on principle."   It is reminiscent of a chapter from*
Dew and Mildew *(1912) where Ficcie starts using the word "bugger"
(a reference to which is found in "The Modern Desdemona").   The last
part is a humorous story of how the children adapted the famous
Shakespeare play of Othello.*

"If you please, Daddy," said Boodle, with that punctilious
politeness which might perhaps cover an error of judgment or
forestall the judgment of error, we borrowed your silk hat this
afternoon, and it got a little egg on it . . ." and the President
wriggled, one bare foot caressing the other.

Daddy rumbled like an earthquake-threatening volcano. "Silk
hat! . . . Egg! . . . Disgustin' conjunction!" Was he going to try
the Discipline of Consequences and make the President wear the
hat she had borrowed—wear it out for the evening walk? She
rather hoped so.

But Daddy's faith in the efficacy of the Discipline of
Consequences had received a rude shock, as has been told
elsewhere.[21]

"And you took my silk hat in defiance of all probabilities of
getting permission!   You took it in anticipation of sanction!
You—"

"No, Daddy—in *The Surrender of Kruger*, and in *William
Tell*. Fic didn't like the apple on his head, but he didn't mind it on
the hat. He said it gave him a thporting chance."

"I say you took it in anticipation of sanction," rumbled Daddy
horrifically, "and that is a very terrible thing!"

"What *is* antiseparation of stankshun?" asked the President,
climbing on to Daddy's knee. "Can we play it? We *really* took it

---

[21] *Dew and Mildew*. John Murray.

in *The Surrender of Kruger*, Daddy, and not in the other thing. You *couldn't* have Kruger without a top-hat, now, *could* you? But what *is* antiseparation of swanktion?"

Buster entered.

"Hullo, dear old Things," said he. "What's the game?"

"You'd better ask Buster to explain 'in anticipation of sanction,' I think," quoth Daddy, departing to see whether the hat in question would stand one more "function" or had better be presented to the Club as a stage-property, "he does a good many things in anticipation of sanction, I believe. And some in anticipation of prohibition," he added, smiling at the blushing Buster as he closed the door. (Buster was alleged to have kissed a Miss Dolores Perdita Eulalie Francesca D'Costa, at a Sergeants' Dance, and to have had his damask cheek smacked in return.)

"Well, what *is* it, Buster? Can we play it?" inquired the President, always in search of a new drama for production.

"It's hard to ex*play*n, President-Sahib," replied Buster, in the distinctly Funny-Dog vein, "though the meaning is easily made clear. Strangely enough, I heard of a good example of 'in anticipation of sanction' when I was dining with the Rutlandshires last night. You *could* act it—but, no, I shouldn't. It borders on the Not Very Nice, I think. No, better not. . . . Anyhow, don't say I'm the Author, if you act it before an audience.

"Tell us it as though it *were* a good play to act," demanded the President, adding, "and I'll see if I like it."

"Very well," proceeded Buster. "*Scene*—the regimental parade-ground of the Rutlandshires. *Time*—Seven a.m., the day before yesterday.

"*Dramatis Personæ*—Private William Jones, Corporal Crook, Sergeant Small, Colour-Sergeant Crocker, The Sergeant-Major, and Second Lieutenant Snooks, Captain Crow, Lieutenant-and-Adjutant Long, Colonel Black, with all the rest of the Rutlands in the background as—*you* know—spectators, chorus, noise without, mob, retainers, family lawyers, and village idiots—regiment on parade in fact. . . .

"*Private William Jones to Corporal Crook*—'I feels very bad inside, I do, Corpril. . . . I'm agoin' to be ill, I am. . . .'

"*Corporal Crook to Sergeant Small*—'Jones feels very bad, 'e do. Wants to be ill, 'e does.'

"*Sergeant Small to Colour-Sergeant Crocker*—'Jones says can 'e be ill.'

"*Colour-Sergeant Crocker to Second Lieutenant Snooks*— 'Pleasir, Privit Jones wishes ter put in a happlication to be took ill.'

"*Second Lieutenant Snooks to Captain Crow*—'Fellah named Jones wants to go sick, Sir.'

"*Captain Crow to Lieutenant-and-Adjutant Long who rides by on his way to the Colonel*—'I say—tell the Colonel there's a bloke in A Company, Privit Jones, wants to fall out. Feels ill.'

"*Lieutenant-and-Adjutant Long to Colonel Black*—'Private Jones, A Company, wants to be sick, Sir. May he?'

"*Colonel*—'No, not now. Certainly not.'

"*Sergeant-Major, approaching and saluting*—'Please, Sir, he *hev*—in hanticipation of senction. . . .'"

*   *   *   *   *   *   *

"I see," said Boodle. "I'll try Fic as Private Jones. . . . Might give him cream for tea. It always . . ."

"No!" shouted Buster. "I'll not be a party to such realism. Talk of the bloke who blacked himself all over to play Othello! No—if you want to play it, *you* be Private Jones and eat the cream."

"Yes," agreed the President. "I love cream."

"What's 'Oh-tell-oh!'" she added. "Could we play that too?"

"Certainly," replied Buster. "Shakespearian revivals are the fashion, just now. I'll show you the pictures and tell you the story—so far as it is fit for the drawing-room. Then you can boom the Bard. The Vice would make a fine Moor—dressed in Nubian blacking and Ethiopian burnt-cork."

And it came to pass that on the following day, Othello was staged in Karabad, though the Sporting and Dramatic Press made no mention of the fact.

*   *   *   *   *   *   *

"Anti-Separation of Swanksion," mused the President aloud.

"On Printhipull," soliloquized the Vice, not to be outdone. For he too had a new expression—and revelled in it, as was his wont.

*   *   *   *   *   *   *

It is strange how a new phrase, a new fact, a new word, will haunt one. You may, for example, live for half a century in blameless ignorance that there is such a disease as Cerebro-Spinal Sclerosis, discover the fact one day, and in the ensuing week you will meet seven different people who have got it. For the first time in your life you encounter the name Pffunfenphluger, and then you encounter it twice more in the next three days. A man informs you at dinner that when he was young, the boys of the village used to play a game called "knurr and spell". You remark that it is a queer and quaint name. Next morning your paper has an article on "Defunct games," and instances that of "knurr and spell." . . .

The Vice stood before the judgment seat and thoughtfully stroked his own. He was "for it" again for making the hens play "Settlers and Indians." In the capacity of Indian he had settled one of the Settlers for good. That particular bird would never settle again in this world. . . .

"I shall have to thrash you every Wednesday and Saturday night on principle, Sir—*on principle*, do you understand," Daddy had finally rumbled as he brandished a hunting-crop with a twelve-foot thong. The Vice did *not* fully understand—but, he thought he did.

So *that* was the correct term, was it—the term applied by adults when alluding to that portion of the human frame?

"On *principle*." He must remember that. It must be a perfectly blameless word, a word of unimpeachable propriety, or Daddy would not use it. *Principle*.

Encountering Venus he remarked :—

"Wenuth. I am going to give you a thmack on principle—*on principle*, do you underthtand," and bestowed a resounding' slap upon what he believed to be the spot indicated. "You may call it that," he added, as he passed on.

The inevitable coincidences followed.

221

When the children went into the drawing-room, to kiss Mummy "good-bye," before setting forth for the evening expedition, there were Callers having tea.

"You'll join the hunt, I suppose, Major, for the short time you're here?" one of the ladies was remarking to a big stout man, a new-comer.

"Oh, yes," was the reply. "I always hunt, on principle— support local industries, y'know."

It struck the Vice as a curious remark to make. Naturally he'd hunt on principle—he wouldn't do it on foot, would he? Evidently quite, a drawing-room word. Not like the dreadful word with which he had shocked and sulked the young ears of Buster, Snooty, Jerks, and Birdie.

Then it was discovered to be a word publicly used by ladies of irreproachable discretion. Nice kind Miss Drake of the Zenana Mission invited the children to come to the annual *tamasha* at her school and see the little Indian orphan-girls enjoy their big treat. After the distribution of sweets and prizes by Lady Morton-Maxwell, Miss Drake made a tiny little speech, in the course of which she said there were several things they did there on principle.

The Vice quite understood that, it *is* tiring to stand too long— especially in the heat of the day. He always lay down, himself. . . . He abandoned other valued *clichés* in favour of this new phrase, and he surprised Mr. Hunter, the new Collector, when that gentleman, seeing him sitting in his rickshaw and contemplating the unbeginning endless sea, remarked, "Do you sit here every evening, little man?" by replying:—

"Yeth thir—on principle."

$$* \quad * \quad * \quad * \quad * \quad * \quad *$$

"Now this is before we're married," said the President to the Vice, "and you've got to tell me wonderful fairy tales, and stories about what you've done, so as to make me fall in love with you. Venus can sit up here and be the Dog of Venice—or is it the Dodge? Anyhow, we'll call him the Dog as he *is* one. He is my father, you know, and you are my suitor."

"Do I have to shoot you, then?" inquired the Vice.

"I didn't say *shooter*," was the reply. "I said *suitor*. . . . If you don't suit me, I say 'Hop it,' and you bung off."

"I'm Oh-tell-oh, aren't I?" asked the Vice. "Is it because I have to tell these tales?"

"'Spec so. You have to tell 'moving tales by flood and field,' I think Buster said. . . . Better begin with one about the Flood. And let it be a good one or you get the push, and the next suitor tries."

The Vice was on his mettle and did his best. Where the genius of Invention failed him he turned to Adaptation's artful aid.

"Oneth upon a time there wath a Flood," he began.

"I know that," said the captious Desdemona.

"But you don't know what I did in it," countered Othello. "You're too clever, Mith Death de Moaner."

"Swam, I 'spec," hazarded Desdemona.

"Wrong again," repeated Othello. "You just listen, or you'll put me out."

"Father will do that," murmured Desdemona, giving the Dog, or Dodge, of Venice a pat on the head.

"It was a *norful* Flood, and rained like anything for days and days. The children couldn't go out to tea-parties and that made it worse."

"I 'spec they paddled though, and that was top-hole," hazarded Desdemona.

"Yeth—until it got too deep. Well, a Sahib named Noah told all the silly natives they'd be drowned if they didn't buck up and build boats to get into. But they said, '*Abhi nakin*'[22] and '*Kal*,'[23] and it rained and rained. And Noah Sahib, he went out in the wet and built a Noah's Ark. Norful big, it was, because he was going to thave Noah Memsahib and the chota[24] Noah Sahibs and choti Noah Miss-sahibs, and the butler and second-boy and cook and hamal and chokra and ayah and syces—I don't know about the sweeper—and all the people in his compound, and two of every kind of animal in the world! . . . He took two in case one got lost

---

[22] Not now.

[23] To-morrow.

[24] Little.

or drowned or anything—and he'd still have one left of that thort.
..."

"He had a long way to go for Polar Bears and Kangaroos, didn't he?" interrupted Desdemona, "*and* I've heard a tale very like this before."

"*I* fetched the Polar Bears and Kangaroos," replied Othello modestly, and all the uvver long-way-off beathts, while Noah Sahib got on with the Noah's Ark."

"I'm very sorry, Othello Sahib," said Desdemona firmly, "but I don't believe a word of it.

"Do *you*, Father?" she added, turning to the Doge, or Dodge, or Dog, of Venice.

Venus certainly shook his head violently—but this *may* have been due to the fact that a large ant was exploring the interior of his right ear.

"No—I thought you didn't," continued Desdemona, on receiving this sign of paternal incredulity. "I don't believe the little liar ever set eyes on Noah in his life."

Turning to her suitor, Desdemona fixed him with a cold and cruel eye.

"Try another," said she. "Better have a go at a 'field' one, if that's the best you can do about the flood."

"I can't think of a field one just for a minute," replied the saddened Othello, "but I wemember the piece of poetry Buthter made up about Mithter Bell of the Rutlands when he was taken ill on the field-*day*. Would that do for a 'field' story?"

"No," replied Desdemona, and, woman-like, at once added, "What was it?"

"Mithter Bell told Daddy at dinner, and I heard him over the banisters, and they all laughed and he had to tell it again. I think it was:—

> "Gregory Greatorex Bell,
>   Sat on the trap-door of—well—
> I know *Satan* came
>   And troubled the wame,
> Of Gregory Greatorex Bell."

"Very interesting," said Desdemona. "We'll be married at

once."

"Shall we, Papa?" she inquired, turning to the Dodge, or Dog, of Venice.

Venus protruded a pink tongue at surprising length, wagged his tail, and nearly yawned his head off.

"Papa smiled with pleasure at the idea of my having a wedding," interpreted Desdemona, "but he's very bored with *you*, Othello. . . . It's a pity, as he is going to live with us after we are married. Still, it can't be wondered at, can it, because after all, you're only a Hubshi, aren't you, really, and most 'strornrally black."

Othello was. From head to foot, he was as black as ink, charcoal, blacking, burnt-cork and water-colour black paint could make him. That his hair was fair almost to whiteness and his eyes very blue, were unalterable facts which militated against the general Moorishness of his get-up.

Although welcoming with ardour the President's fiat that he must be blacked all over for the part, he had flatly and finally refused to wear a turban when his senior had remarked that a *puggri* would hide his hair and a pair of black glare-glasses his eyes. The *puggri* idea having to be abandoned, the President had decided that the black glare-glasses were not a success as part of an Othello make-up, as, if anything, they accentuated the unfortunate fairness of the hair. . . .

As he advanced to make some colourable demonstration of a hymeneal nature, Desdemona waved him off.

"Don't you touch me while we get married," she commanded, "nor yet afterwards. You *come off* against everything. Look at that stool!"

And indeed it was evident that Othello had been sitting on the stool. His only garment must have slipped or something.

"Where's the ring?" asked the bride-elect.

"Othello fumbled in his trunk-hose (recently mere bathing-drawers) and discovered the necessary token. Part of its original cigar adhered to it.

"Now, we're married," said Desdemona, placing the ring upon a finger of her right hand.

"Thanks awfully. Where shall we go for our honeymoon?"

"*I* don't care," said Othello, and that ended Act I, Scene I.

Scene 2.

"You have to strangle me in this scene," announced Desdemona.

The eye of Othello lit up. This was going to be a better "part" than he had anticipated.

"I don't think I shall like it," added the bride.

"Oh, it'll be all right," opined the bridegroom.

"You mustn't strangle me *much*, you know," she directed.

"Only till you're dead, of courthe," he agreed.

"Go and wash your hands while I go to bed," requested Desdemona. "You'll make a norful mess of me and the bed-clothes if you don't. . . . I'll put my nighty on over the wedding-dress."

Othello departed to the bath-room since he might not strangle his bride with unwashen hands.

Desdemona put on her nightdress, and removed her shoes. She then climbed on to her bed, lay down, pulled the sheet over her and gleefully awaited what was in store for her.

Othello entered, his hands looking as though their Moorish owner wore white kid gloves.

"Half a sec," ejaculated Desdemona the Realist, "I forgot my prayers."

Kneeling up, she assumed the conventional attitude of prayer, gabbled "Fwot we are about-receive, Lord, makus trulyfankful-amen," flopped down again, and began to snore.

Othello advanced, glaring horribly, with clutching fingers, and what he conceived to be an evil smile.

He licked his lips with the lick of cruel anticipation. The nearest pigment to his mouth was blacking, and he savoured its rich flavour. Changing his course he steered for the mirror and thrust forth his tongue. It was black. . . . . Was he going to be poisoned? . . . Anyhow, it made him more Othello-like than ever. Probably Buster's friend, who blacked himself all over, quite forgot to black *his* tongue.

Desdemona watched out of one eye.

Othello turned and approached the bed, and then behaved as though playing tigers. With a growling roar he sprang at

Desdemona and seized her by the throat with both white hands,

"Ee-e-e-e-e-e," shrilled Desdemona, as she felt their cold touch, and

"Ka-a-a-a-k! Ka-a-a-a-k," as the touch became a clutch.

She found that she hated being throttled when it came to the point.

"Stop it, you Sneak!" she gasped at her cruel and relentless husband. "Stop it—I didn't *do* it!"

"Didn't do what?" inquired Othello, somewhat relaxing his strangle-hold upon the poor lady's throat.

"Why, what you are strangling me for," replied the gasping Desdemona.

"There you are!" countered her remorseless husband. "You done so many things you don't even know which of them this is to pay you out for."

"Well, which *is* it, then?" squealed the fated bride, as the cruel grip again tightened about her neck, and the incensed Moor protruded a blackened and curling tongue to mark renewed vigour and determination.

"Yah! You don't know yourself," she gurgled, and by way of dying game, used her last breath, in vituperative ejaculations of—

"Black Face! . . . Black Sheep! . . . Black Bird! . . . Nasty Nigger! . . . Old Hubshi! . . . Yah! . . ."

Othello desired to be just though not generous, and relaxed his grip.

"Oh, yes, I do," he said, and pondered a while. "You poked out your tongue behind my back while we were getting married, besides, I'm fierce and jealous; it's in the book—Buster said so."

"Why are you fierce and jealous?" squeaked Desdemona, playing for time.

"Because you ate that last ten pounds of chocolate I left lying on my throne this morning, while I had my porridge," replied the Moor.

"Oh, you *little* liar," shrilled the tearfully indignant Desdemona. "I never, ever."

"*What* did you call me?" inquired Othello, with deadly politeness.

"A kind of storyteller,' snivelled Desdemona. "You know it's a none-truth."

"Then, by my halibut, prepare to die—and less jabber," was the cruel answer.

"Well, I just shan't then," replied the hapless bride, and, moved to righteous indignation, fetched her lord a good useful kick in the stomach.

"'You're a 'palling little liar,' I said, and so you are."

In the fight that followed, Desdemona won, hands down, and by tacit consent the play, "Othello, the Moor of Venice," was removed from the repertoire of the Junior Curlton Club Dramatic Society.

"QUIS SEPARABIT?"

"Quis Separabit?" is another story where Ficcie starts using a word or phrase that sounds good to him, but he uses it in an unfortunate, if humorous, circumstance. "Quis Separabit" was not part of the first edition of The Young Stagers *(1917), but it was chapter fifteen in the first edition of* Dew and Mildew *(1912). This chapter did not appear in subsequent editions of* Dew and Mildew, *but was included in the "new edition" of* The Young Stagers *(Murray and Stokes 1926).*

And it came to pass that the English Mail brought the President of the Junior Curlton Club of Karabad a letter of fourteen words written by her homeward-bound friend, Phyllis, on board the good ship *Asia* of a line well known—too well known—to the Step-children of the grim Mother.

"Daddy," said she at breakfast next morning, "what does 'Quis Spear-a-bit' mean? It says so on the note-paper of the letter Phyllis wrote me from the *Asia*."

"'Quis Spear-a-bit,' my love?" replied Daddy. "Though I am a member of the Bombay Classical Association, I am afraid I don't exactly know. At a guess I should say, 'Who will come pig-sticking,' but as I only spent fifteen years in learning Latin, I am almost totally ignorant of it now. But I'll lay it before the Association."

"He's a wicked Daddy, Darling," interposed Mummy, "and he's pulling your leg again. It's 'Quis Separabit,' and it means 'Who shall separate them,' I believe. Who shall separate the countries the big ships join together?"

"Oh! 'Quis Separabit,'" repeated the President, and again "'Quis Separabit.' I shall remember that because it is Latin."

"So shall I," chimed in the Vice, "'Quis Separate-a-bit,' I know lots of Latin. What *is* Latin?"

Now, as has been said elsewhere, the Vice loved a sonorous word, a sounding expression, and a rounded period, albeit an habitually silent and somewhat phlegmatic person. Particularly he loved it if he had no idea of its meaning.

"Quis Separabit," was oft repeated by him, dwelt in his memory, served as an oath, as a non-committal comment, and as a general observation indicative of surprise, pleasure, grief, pain, acquiescence, dissent, and anything else. He got it very pat.

(And it gave Mr. Theophilus Tipton of the 125th Bendras Cavalry the shock of his life.)

"I am going to ride to the Hill and look for land-crabs, Fic," said the President one evening, as the usual Club cavalcade sauntered beneath the palms of the oasis a mile or so from home. "Shall Abdullah wheel you up too?"

"Land-crabs," observed the Vice, "pop up out of holes and squeege the necks of boys who kick people when soap goes in their eyes. Ayah says so. I kick when soap goes in my eyes. I shall not go."

"Oh, that's all tosh and posh," was the answer. "You could easily do a land-crab if it came for you."

"Not if it was as big as a camel or an emphalant," demurred the Vice.

"But they never aren't as big as a camel nor a nellyphant. Nellyphants are ever so bigger. Land-crabs are—just crabs. Not even lobsters."

"There are debbles that jump on the backs of boys who get out of bed for toys," continued the Vice. "Ayah says so. They choke their heads off and scoop up their hearts and make curried *kybobs* with them. I get out of bed for toys. I shall not go any further than this place."

"Well, you wait here then," decided his sister, "and I shall take Mowlah to hold Jock while I poke about, and Ayah must come, in case there are any scorpulums or scentypedes. Abdullah can stick here and do your *hookums*.[25] Don't be a goat and do any dags, there's a good little pig," and the President departed.

"Wheel me in between those two dear little palms where there is a bank in front what goes downwards," said the Vice to his adoring, faithful slave, the stalwart, bearded Mohammedan peon, who "kept the door," cleaned guns, took messages, dusted the bicycle, and attended dutifully upon the Chota Sahib when he

---

[25] Orders.

took the air abroad.

"This worthless one knows not the language of the Master Folk," was the reply in Hindustani. "The Little Master must give the order in his slave's tongue."

"Go forward and halt between those two small trees," said the Vice in Hindustani. "Stop. It is enough. Go and smoke until I call."

Left to himself—as he thought, though the watchful eye of Abdullah was on him—the Vice sighed heavily and pondered many things in his heart.

Why should dirty little native boys, obviously most impecunious and no-account, ride donkeys and drive herds of other donkeys before them—when he had not a single donkey to his name? . . .

Why should Ayah come into the bungalow after her dinner, dabbing a bleeding cut on the bridge of her nose, and tell Mummy she had stooped suddenly in the dark and hit it on the sharp back of a chair—when he had heard her telling Mowlah that her husband had tried to cut her nose off because he thought she had deceived him? How had she deceived him? Kept back part of her pay and said Mem-Sahib had fined her? Or had she cheated at cards or told him a none-truth? . . .

Why should the mild, peaceful, and *laissez-faire* Daddy have behaved in such a 'normous manner when he found his only son shaving himself with real soap, a real brush, and real razors. It wasn't as though he himself ever *used* that lovely case of seven razors, marked with the names of the days of the week. He used a safety-razor so that he could shave without a glass while he walked about and dressed and ate his *chota hazri*. It wasn't as though the safety-razor had been borrowed—it had been honourably respected and carefully avoided lest Daddy be annoyed. Yet Daddy had turned quite white (with rage?) when he had come into the nursery and seen him scooping the nice woolly soap-stuff off his throat. And Daddy had behaved in a way that seemed almost treacherous; for he had gone out again without a word and then called in a nice seductive voice: "Come and put my spurs on, old chap. Don't bring your razor!" And when he had gone to do it Daddy hadn't even got his riding boots on, and had behaved in a ridiculous manner as if shaving were a

231

crime. If a man ought to shave daily, what was wrong about the Vice-President of the Junior Curlton Club shaving? Especially when he hadn't shaved for months! . . .

Why should Mowlah be in such distress because his widowed sister was going to have a baby? Babies are singularly useless things, but, to give them their due, they *grow*, and become useful for minor parts, and to bowl, after a fashion. Besides, surely Mowlah could tell her not to have one, if he objected so strongly, since he was in authority over her and supported her out of the fullness of his ten rupees a month. . . .

Why did Major Blaste have to undergo an operation? When the Vice had asked Mummy what an "operation" was, she had replied, "An operation is doing something, a work, an action. If I sharpen a pencil, that is an operation." Were they going to sharpen Major Blaste? And if so, at which end? He didn't look as though he needed much sharpening. . . .

It is a puzzling world when one is four, and more puzzling when one is forty, if one acquires the bad habit of thinking.

The Vice closed his eyes.

The shades of night (as happened once before) were falling fast, as through that green oasis passed—Mrs. Willie Baltero and Mr. Theophilus Tipton. I do not know their respective ages, but *he*, when garbed for war, wore one star upon his shoulder strap; *she*, when garbed for war, scarlet lips and a school-girl complexion. It may further be stated that her husband wore a crown and two stars upon the shoulder-strap of the uniform he adorned. From which it may be argued that Mr. Theophilus Tipton was quite young enough to have known better.

Let it be said in his defence that he hastily released the lady's hand as Abdullah suddenly arose and most respectfully salaamed to the Sahib-log.

"What is that blighter squatting in our Paradise for, Dearest?" he grumbled.

"Like the Serpent in Eden," lisped Mrs. Willie (who really said "Therpent"), with ready wit.

"Shall I tell him to *jao*, Dearest?"

"No, Goose-boy. It would look as though we wanted to be alone!" And Mrs. Willie giggled.

"Well, we do!" replied Theophilus, who was a direct person.

"Speak for your naughty self," replied Mrs. Willie, who wasn't.

After a time he looked back longingly at the Eden from which the Therpent had wrought his exclusion, and exclaimed:—

"Look, there he goes! It's all right. Come on, Dearest."

Nothing loath, Mrs. Willie wheeled her horse round and they cantered back to the privacy of the palms.

For the Vice had woke up and said in Hindustani to Abdullah:—

"Go. Bid Ayah and Mowlah return, and ask Boodle Missie Baba to return. I am hungry, and the darkness, in which are devils, cometh. Hasten."

And he had again closed his eyes.

He was a fat and restful person.

At the sound of voices he opened them again.

A Sahib and a Mem-Sahib sat at the bottom of the little bank, their heads not a couple of yards from his feet. He could see them, between the palm leaves.

He had no objection. All Sahibs and Mem-Sahibs were very kind to him.

"Goose-boy," said the Mem-Sahib, "I cannot bear it much longer." She heaved a sigh. "What do you think he did this morning?"

"Don't tell me he *struck* you! If he did, I will strike him, colonel or no colonel, and make him fight me!"

"N-no," admitted Mrs. Willie, with apparent reluctance, "he didn't strike me exactly, but he—oh, he—he came to breakfast in *red velvet slippers with a great yellow sunflower embroidered on each!*"

Emotion choked her.

Mastering it, she continued: "And often he spreads butter on his bread with the butter-knife in the most absent-minded way, and sometimes he whistles between the courses. Isn't it *awful*."

"Awful," agreed Theophilus. "Poor little Lamb."

Theophilus remembered a coarse, spiteful remark, made by a wicked woman, to the effect that Mrs. Willie was "mutton dressed as lamb," and mentally winced at his own use of the pretty, innocent word, after hearing it in such a connexion.

"But the worst, the thing I can *never* forgive or forget, was his conduct at the Great Eastern Hotel when we were at Calbay the other day."

"Unburden your heart to me, Dearest Dear," said Theophilus. "Sympathy eases Sorrow. Was he—er—was he—ah—unfaithful to you in thought or word or deed?"

"Oh, *no*, Goose-boy. He'd never *dream* of being that in *any* way, he loves me too much. No, it was his wicked, criminal carelessness in putting me in an *awful* position."

"Poor little woman! What *did* he do?"

"Why, it was like this. After breakfast he said, 'I must go to my agents and tailors, and one or two other places, and shall only just have time to catch the train for Karabad—so if you'll have lunch and drive down to the station, I'll be waiting there for you. I'll tell them to have a taxi waiting for you at two o'clock and Bagu can go on beforehand with the luggage.' So I said, 'All right,' glad to be rid of him, and off he went. Then I popped across to the Club to see the magazines and a lovely boy I know, and we came back to lunch. And, just as I was thinking what crowds of people there were lunching and how they stared at one—oh, how can I tell it—up to me marched the bedroom-attendant *with Willie's false teeth on a great dish* and bawled out, 'Mem-Sahib leaving toofs in bath!'" . . .

"What *did* you do? How awful! How thoughtless! How careless! How cruel! What *did* you do?"

"Fainted."

"And when you came to?"

"Declared they were not mine—which they weren't—and refused to have anything to do with them. And, would you believe it, instead of grovelling to me in the dust of Calbay Station, my husband was positively huffy about losing his horrid teeth! Said I might have sent the man back to the room with them, and got them myself afterwards! Isn't he a heartless brute?"

"Poor, poor little lady."

The kind, comforting, strong hand of Theophilus took that of the injured woman.

The fluffy, yellow, afflicted head of Mrs. Willie sank upon the shoulder of the sympathetic warrior.

Her bright, large eyes, "wells of dark light," gazed into his.

Face approached face.

Lips assumed a special position, approached still nearer to other lips, and, lingering, loitered with intent.

Nearer and nearer still, prolonging that greatest of joys, the joy of anticipation.

Nearer, slowly but surely, ever nearer.

Then, in a long, rapturous, blissful, beautiful kiss, the souls of these two young things mingled, mingled, mingled—until on their stricken ears fell a deep, sepulchral voice, loudly and distinctly inquiring:—

"*Quis Separabit?*"!

And the Vice proved to be the answer to his own question.

THE ROYAL AND ANCIENT GAME AT KARABAD

The "Royal and Ancient Game" refers to the game of golf, but the game as played in Karabad by the children is quite different from the normal game of golf. In this story, the children have found some pin-fire cartridges and are trying to use them in their version of golf. Buster comes in before they can injure themselves and provides an alternative use for the cartridges. The heart of the story is about the temptation of Ficcie when he has the opportunity to blow up their cat! This story was not included in the first edition of The Young Stagers *(1917), but was in the first edition of* Dew and Mildew *(1912) as chapter nineteen. A reference to this incident is mentioned in an earlier story, "Tosh and Funny-Dog", which indicates that, at least some if not all of, the stories in* The Young Stagers *(first edition) were written after* Dew and Mildew.*

The Junior Curlton had taken up Golf *con amore*. Not the mere ordinary, stereotyped game as played by uninventive and dull Grown-Ups who were daily to be seen solemnly tramping round the Karabad links and behaving as heavily and anxiously as if they were earning their livings. Not at all.

The Junior Curlton game differed more from the ordinary game than, in football, the Rugby game does from the Association. It might even be said without much fear of contradiction that it differed more than the Rugby game does from Croquet.

In the first place, it must be played by three players, and those three players must be the President, the Vice, and Buster the Secretary, and it must be played *in* the Clubhouse. It had a Ritual too.

The President always began by "addressing" the ball severely, and then crying "fore." The Vice then cried "five." The Secretary thereupon asked, "Any advance on five," and replying, "Going, going, *gone*," the President smote with might. It was a tennis-ball, and if it came to rest in the first quarter of the room the President played again, if in the second, the Vice played, and

236

if in the third, the Secretary. But, should it end its frequently very adventurous career in the fourth quarter, all members must first stand on their heads with feet against the wall and afterwards all "address" the ball simultaneously, and smite together. This rule is not likely to be introduced under any circumstances into the ordinary game—but it is undeniable that the standing upon the unusual end of the body introduces real variety, change, and interest.

The Secretary had invented the game, had cut-down "drivers" for the President and Vice, had painted on the Club-room floor the lines that divided the "ground" into four, and had provided the words of the ritual.

It was a thrilling game, and its only drawback was that Buster did not live on the premises. The tee, too, was a sound feature—being indifferently sugar, a biscuit, butterscotch, cake, or sweets, all these being, as the inventor of the game remarked, "good for *tea*." The tee was the property of the person who drove from it, and the duty of the provision of tees was the perquisite of the Secretary. Butterscotch was found to make the best tee.

At first, other members of the Club seemed opposed to the introduction of the game. Venus, for example, had early deemed it his duty to seize and devour the ball as a mark of protest; and Polly Femious always raised great outcry when she saw preparations made for a round. This may, however, be connected with the fact that when deep in thought upon her lofty stand she had once or twice unintentionally hindered the ball's swift career. Nebuchadnezzar the Mongoose, whose name was due to the fact that at times he would go out into the wilderness and eat grass with every appearance of madness, too, had been detected in the act of trying to steal the ball, and was suspected of having bitten it.

An appointment had been made for a game at four o'clock and it was only two. Time did not hang, however, as there was a fine rumble, combined with, a rootle, toward. A rumble was great, but a rumble conjoined with a rootle was greater. There are those, it is believed, who know not the joys of rumbling—nay, do not even know the meaning of the word. Some there may be who have never rootled. They are two glorious pastimes, and the greater of these is rootling.

When you "rumble" you have full and free permission without restriction, let, or hindrance to investigate, overhaul, examine, and entirety disgruntle, the contents of some box, drawer, bureau, cupboard, chest, hamper, work-basket, attic, or lumber-room. Those who have never rumbled in foreign parts—that is in unknown attics—have never really lived. When you "rootle" you keep such of the trophies of your rumbling as take your fancy, keep them for your very own, without any senseless Grown-Up advice, prohibition, praise, or disparagement.

And a big old box of what an age-blunted, world-blasé, perception-dimmed Daddy called "rubbish" was at the disposal of the children as soon as the midday siesta was well and truly accomplished—no shamming and no taking toys or pets to bed. Think of it—*rubbish*—a box of assorted "unconsidered trifles" of the most varied! To prevent misconceptions and misappropriations, when rootling commenced, the President, being a lady, chose first, and then, alternately, these two officials chose.

And this particular rumble long stood out in the very middle of the roadway of that long Avenue of Time—adown which you sometimes cast retrospective gaze ere dropping off to sleep, or while impatiently waiting for an aggravating doll to recover from enteric in time for its evening walk.

It was a most interesting rumble and a highly productive rootle, the choice flower of which fell to the Vice in the shape of a dozen ancient, pin-fire cartridges of assorted numbers, and found, later, some to contain darling tiny, little black balls of lead, others larger ones, and others again some as big as peas, the green ones you get at lunch.

There was an old, bald, brusque, and uncompromising shaving-brush, which would do admirably and equally for the Vice's shaving purposes, for painting the more generous tracts in "The Outline Book for Colouring," for military head-gear of a Hussar-like persuasion, and to lend a Highland atmosphere to the President's skirt-front when playing Rhoderic Dhu.

There were loading instruments used by Daddy in the days when he thought he could make better and cheaper cartridges than he could buy. These would make excellent surgical instruments for the Vice to bring round *qua* doctor, when he paid professional visits to the dolls and the members of the Club. In one of them, too, you could squeege your fingers till you yowled, and it was that which would be awfully handy when playing Frongdyboof and Isaac of York in the torture chamber.

There was an elderly and smelly little pot of ointment of some kind—just the thing to accompany the surgical instruments when the doctor was dealing with an obstinate case of smallpox, headache, or prickly heat among the dolls or pets.

A vulcanite mouthpiece from some pipe, through which Daddy had gnawed his way, appealed to the President as the very "property" to lend a manly and swanksome air to an impersonation of Napoleon Buonaparte or Hubert, what time the Vice was Prince Arthur.

An india-rubber hot-water bottle was full of possibilities—and soon full of water, which it retained but partially and without success. However, no doll could lie upon it without benefit, be she never so afflicted. The Vice, who drew it, traded it to his colleague for an empty cigar-box.

A disabled bath-thermometer joined the surgical instruments and took many air astounding temperature during an epidemic of "harmonia," an obscure disease that smote Margerina and her five sisters mysteriously and suddenly at a levée.

Many and notable were the spoils of the rootle, but the cartridges were *the* prize, both for their own sweet sakes and for the splendid use to which the Vice put them.

For the Vice was delivered of an Idea. As a rule he was a faithful executive and never troubled to plot and to plan, to invent and to create. That was the President's part, and well she played it. But the cartridges and the coming game of golf inspired him, and, after hugging the cartridges to his bosom awhile, he said to the President:—

"I say, Boodle, *I* know. Let's play a cartwidge is golf, and practith driving. I'll try and hit it on the pin, and, if I do, it ought to go *bang* like a firework!"

Glorious idea—a sort of self-registering-the-hit kind of detonating ball! No sooner suggested than put into practice. A cartridge was stood on end with the pin pointing backwards and the Vice addressed it with propriety of attitude and ritual. With driver well swung back to the left shoulder and body poised on right foot and left toe he swiped with all his strength, and smote the pin fairly with the centre of the head of his club. The result was surprising, glorious, thrilling, and infinitely gratifying, There was a sharp bang as the cap exploded, the cartridge soared toward the ceiling and then burst with a terrific roar, filling the room with delightful smoke and a charming smell, and producing a perfect hail of shot. Heaven alone knows why it did not burst when hit, but Time works wonders—especially with explosives, and "there is a Providence." . . .

What a day! What a perfect treasure! Why it was Battle, Murder, and Sudden Death. It was Nelson at Trafalgar, Wellington at Waterloo, Guy Fawkes, and anything else you liked. The next must not be wasted on Golf alone. It must be the *pièce de résistance* of some worthy play. What should it be?

Casabianca was appropriate, but then he was rather a snifter really, fearfully dreary, and not entirely free from suspicion, as it is nowhere recorded that he could swim, and may have made a virtue of mere necessity. Besides, what a silly name for a healthy boy! No, not that 'normous Casabianca, he was quite unworthy the tribute of one of the precious cartridges.

Captain Peel in the trenches at Sebastopol? But that could be played without banging one off. It was, instantly.

The President became Captain Peel by means of donning a "sailor" blouse, Daddy's cross-belt, and a real "sailor" hat. A round tin case made an impressive telescope. To the Vice fell the part of a bravish but ill-intentioned Russian soldier. For this part he blacked his face with a piece of cork burnt with a match, girt his no longer marble brow with a piece of red tape, and stuck between this and his head an assortment of feathers. A dressing-gown and bow and arrows completed the very astonishing likeness to a soldier of the Czar.

This warrior, creeping up to the trenches, two inverted tables of the "occasional" order, while Captain Peel was busy digging with the middle section of the tree from Daddy's riding-boot, laid the deadly shell right beneath the stooping and unconscious officer, struck a match, applied it, and with a yell of "Trait perisher! no, I mean 'Perish traitor!'" fled ere the pistol of Captain Peel could be extricated from his skirt-pocket. Was the bold sailor perturbed? He was not. Snatching up the shell he hastily immersed it in the water-filled tooth-brush goblet which, curiously enough, happened to be standing handy in the trenches.

"Fear not, my brave fellows," cried he to his men, "I have saved all your lives at the risk of my own—but take no notice. 'Tis nothing, I 'sure you." And the play was played—it being doubtful how long the precious shell could stand cold water without suffering serious internal injury. In the next play it should come to no such inglorious end. What should it be? Sir John Moore, and bury him darkly in a flower-pot?

No. It should be the favourite old play of Guido Fawkes with a variation from the original, consisting in the making of that arch conspirator wholly successful. And the doll's house should be the House of Lords, the dolls, Whiskerandos, Bill the Lizard, and as many of Nibble and Twitch as could be got in without undue crowding, being those Lords. The Vice was freely given the part of King James, while the President undertook to render that of the enterprising and wholesalely inclined Guido. The King would, of course, be obliged to sit on the roof—but what is the good of an imagination if you are going to stick at trifles?

The doll's house was larger than a big dog-kennel, had three floors, and would make a most eligible House of Lords. These latter were constrained to be a Two Chamber estate in themselves, as it was found that Nibble, Twitch, Whiskerandos, and Bill fitted not uncomfortably into the top story, while the dolls filled the one below.

It was anticipated that the Lords in the upper of the two Chambers would be merely pleasantly titillated by the explosion, while those in the hall below would require a good deal of First Aid. The King therefore prepared to change rapidly to the rôle of Civil Surgeon after the consummation of the dastardly plot, and laid out the recently acquired instruments and ointment.

"You sit on your legs, My Majesty," said the President. "I'm Lord Mounteagle, you know. There might be an explosion and something might come through one of the windows—so don't dangle them down the front."

The monarch took the tip.

"I think I'll nearly shut the front, and put my hand in and hammer the pin with Daddy's dumb-bell," mused Guy Fawkes. "That ought to do it."

All was ready. The King sat in joyous expectation, the Lords did after their kind, the Conspirator poised the dumb-bell above the cartridge—and Buster entered the Club.

"Hullo, Pups," quoth he, "what's the game to-day? Not playing house on fire again, are you, or *suttee* or anything I'm not old enough for, what?"

"Hullo, darling," replied the President. "You're just in time. I'm Guy Fawkes. . . ."

"Should have thought that was the Guy on top, with the black face," interrupted Buster.

"No! How silly you are, Buster; that's the King."

"Lord! you never know, do you! Is he the King of the Cannibal Islands?"

"No, Buster, *do* be sensible. You're like a Grown-Up. He's King James the First and I'm Guy Fawkes, and I'm just going to blow him up and all the Lords—they're inside. You peep in the window."

"By Jove! You haven't got *gunpowder*, have you? I *thought* there was a rummy smell!"

"We have got some real, live cartridges, and if you hit them they bang like guns and all the bullets come out."

"Good Lord! Here, open that door and let's see what's happening. I can't *get* a Victoria Cross in mufti, and I don't want to earn one."

"It's all right, Buster darling; I'm only just going to hit the pin while I hold the door nearly shut. . . ."

And that game was not played.

"My dear, good little goats, never you play games with live cartridges! Firearms are nasty, dangerous things, and I never touch 'em—but pin-fire cartridges! Where did you get them?"

"We found them in a rootle."

"Well, no matter if you won 'em in a raffle—give 'em all to me. They ought to be in a museum with wheel-locks and other barbarous things."

"But they make lovely pops. You hit them on the pin with the driver and they bang and go up in the air, and then burst termenjously and the bullets fall about."

"My gracious Aunt in Glory!" ejaculated the astonished subaltern, "did you actually *do* it?"

"Yes. It was lovely. You did ought to have been here."

"Did I? Well, let me tell you my life is of great value, young woman."

"*Do* let's do another. I'll drive off."

"If my mother only knew what company I am in! She always bade me beware of dangerous companions who would lead me astray. The senior Subaltern on a Wet Night is nothing to this. D'you know, it's a wonder the thing didn't blow your little fat heads off? Why, you young lunatics, if it had burst when you hit it I expect you'd both be like 'Scots wha hae' by now—gory beds and so forth."

"I thunk of it and I hit it," said the Vice with pride.

"Well, I have a good mind to think of you and then hit you," was the reply. "You might have blown your head off, which would have been no great matter—but you might also have spoilt your clothes with blug, not to mention killing your sister. Don't ever you touch anything that goes *bang* again, when Mummy and Daddy are out; you keep it till I come, and then we can all die together—or live, as the case may be."

"Let's keep one till Mr. Guddle comes again, and offer to let him have a drive," suggested the President, who, like most women, very strongly disapproved of those who disapproved of her.

"The idea does credit to heart and head alike, my dear President; but the Guddle *just* knows what a cartridge is, and I am sure he is in no hurry to test the theories he gives us when we essay salvation once a week at eleven a.m. in our best clothes."

"Then what shall we do with them? They are much too darling to part with now. Will *you* go into the compound and bang them off with a driver, where we can see? Do, Buster, there's a darling!"

"Talk about young barbarians at play—and doing the butchering to make a—er—Club holiday at the same time! No, my babe, I won't. I am too young to die with all my imperfections yet to come. But I'll tell you what I *will* do. I'll do you a fine Guy Fawkes explosion if you'll both promise never to touch cartridges or fireworks or gunpowder or anything that goes bang, when you are by yourselves."

The promise was given, and the addition of the words

"Honour bright" gave it the force and solemnity of an oath, the oath that no member of the Junior Curlton could or would break.

"Then we'll get all the shot out, and the Civil Surgeon can keep them for Black Pills, and then all the powder, and after that I think we *might* use them for golf, and bang them off," said Buster.

An empty tobacco tin made an excellent "thirty-six barrels" of gunpowder, and an erection in the compound, of assorted boxes and toy bricks, a satisfactory Houses of Parliament. Posho was deputed to sustain the royal rôle, while that of Members was entrusted to a corps of lead soldiers who had all seen sorrow before, and could not be induced to stand upon, the field of battle. The part of the Villain fell by lot to the Vice, and, the train being laid over a distance of several yards to connect the House with the Cellars, which bore a strong likeness to the Club veranda, that officer "stood by," with a lighted candle to do the fell deed "weally," before the entry of the myrmidons of the Law.

And upon the Vice fell a terrible temptation.

The President and Secretary had left the Club premises, to burst in as halberdiers, pikemen, and musketeers, too late to save the devoted faithful Commons, noble Lords, and gracious King.

Guy Fawkes was to cry "Ha!" with violence, and, at that moment, was to lay the lighted candle sideways in the little heap of powder that terminated the train, and the halberdiers and company were then to do their burst, it being understood that violent hands were not to be laid upon Guido, until the train was successfully fired and King, Lords and Commons in one red burial blent.

And, as the Vice was about to bawl "Ha!" the inquisitive, officious, and distinctly "nosey" Widdy the Second must descend from a tree, and, with ridiculous affectation of girlishness and frivolity, frisk across the thirsty, struggling lawn, and positively *smell* the "thirty-six barrels" of gunpowder!

Has ever man been tempted more sorely on this earth? Has Wine, or Woman, or Wealth, *ever* sprung more instant and compelling lure on fallen son of Adam? Widdy the smug, the affected, the unctuous, the mincing, the superior, the cocky, the 'normous—smelling a barrel of gunpowder connected by a train with an imminent lighted match, in the hands of a determined desperado! What a shock the 'normous ass would get! She'd know better than to intrude in future. She would, get a lesson like some of those snifters in the Strewelpeter book. It would be mere Justice, Nemesis, Consequence. These fine terms did not adorn the speech of the Vice, but he undoubtedly said quite plainly and distinctly, and in a manner to leave Widdy no shadow of cause for complaint:—

"Well, Widdy, I s'pose *you* know best—but *I* shouldn't go and *thmell* a barrel of gunpowder while it was being blowed up. It doesn't matter to *me*, of course."

Widdy blinked and sat down as close to the "House" as she could squeege, and with her silly nose not an inch from Posho— who was reclining drunkenly against the barrel, which he embraced in a manner suggestive more of its being a butt of Malmsey than a barrel of gunpowder.

She had had fair warning, and had been distinctly told that the barrel contained gunpowder. Moreover, the halberdiers were evidently growing impatient, as witnessed by the President's cry of "Buck up and 'Ha,' Guy Fawkes, and don't you blow it up until we burst in."

Widdy went to sleep, deliberately, ostentatiously, consciously, provocatively. The lips of the Vice parted to utter the fateful "Ha," and his hand moved downwards to the powder. . . .

Would Widdy be blowed up into the sky? Would she be blowed into

There is a Happy Land
Far, far away;
Where little piggies run,
Bright, bright, and gay—
Until the butcher comes
Then how each piggy runs
Three miles away . . .

—as Buster sang? The Vice wished Widdy II no actual harm— only a lesson against vulgar curiosity and inquisitiveness. How she *would* jump! Would her whiskers get burnt? Miss Brown had said that a cat's whiskers are very sensitive, and that by means of them cats find their way about in the dark. It would be interesting to blindfold a whiskerless Widdy and see what happened!

"Yes! all very fine," said Conscience, "but did the chivalrous knights of old go about singeing cats' whiskers and then blindfolding them to see what they did? Would Sir Galahad have done such a thing? Would Sir Geraint or Sir Percival or Sir Bedivere? Would even Sir Lancelot—who was known to have erred and strayed once and done something vague but very wrong, perhaps poked out his tongue rudely at Queen Guinevere when King Arthur's back was turned—have put his hand to such a deed? No. What was the first and foremost duty of a Knight of the latter-day Round Table—which had been revived by Mummy? It was identical with that of a Knight of old, the succouring and protecting of the weak, injured and oppressed.

But Widdy was none of these, so she could claim no exemption under that clause. But surely it was an absolute *sine qua non* and an understood thing that *no* Knight should *ever* go in for injuring and oppressing on his own account! And this was distinct and manifest injuring! Nay, it might be Murder—sheer, wanton, cold-blooded Widdycide, without extenuating circumstances or benefit of clergy. These words, again, did not fall from the mouth of the Vice, but the thoughts they embody flashed through his mind. He withdrew the fatal brand and said aloud: "Widdy, you 'normous creechur, go away. Lucky for you I am a Knight and a Sahib or you'd be blewn to Kingdom Come! Go at once, or I shall get my bow and arrows, and then you'll wish you'd gone before. . . ."

The halberdiers, arquebusiers, pikemen, and musketeers burst in—but not before a small boy had heroically conquered a terrible temptation. On finding the reason of delay, the leader of the halberdiers, *et cetera*, held that Guy Fawkes had done a deed worthy of his knightly rank, and also that he had fully earned the right to take a pot at Widdy II with an arrow, provided she chose to remain and abide the issue, on being clearly shown the fate that awaited her. . . . She did not—and the Vice was rarely successful with a running shot. . . .

It was a *heavenly* explosion and lifted Posho into a rose-bush. And the game of Golf was made beautiful with *bangs*, as the dismantled cartridges, fulfilled the law of such being as was left to them.

AT OXFORD: INNOCENT ERNEST AND ARTFUL EINTZ

This is the first book printing of "At Oxford: Innocent Ernest and Artful Eintz", and the first printing since the story appeared in an obscure fiction magazine, The Blue Magazine *(July 1919). It is the story of five young men at Oxford, one of whom is a German Jew. From a modern viewpoint it is marred by some casual anti-Semitic references which have been previously noticed in some of Wren's writings. Wren himself was a student at Oxford from 1894 to 1898 and was in the Delegacy of Non-Collegiate Students (later St. Catherine's College), a college for underprivileged students. While at Oxford, Wren also attended the Oxford Day Training College. "At Oxford" is the only short story that features students at Oxford, but Wren did include Oxford life in two of his novels:* Dew and Mildew *(1912) and* Soldiers of Misfortune *(1929).*

Mr. Alfred Horridge—who invariably called himself Halfred 'Orridge—had done very well for himself as a scout. Not as a boy scout, *bien entendu,* or one of those hardy and romantic persons who scout upon prairie and veldt, or in front of armed hosts—but as an Oxford scout—which is quite otherwise. "Man and boy," as he said, he had been a servant of St. Aldate's College, for "nigh upon forty year;" and, having retired upon the savings of his wages, tips, perquisites, commissions, pickings, and the other emoluments of a wise and worthy scout, was now the lessee of a fine lodging-house for undergraduates, wherein he preyed upon five young gentlemen.

*   *   *   *   *   *

Four Bloods and a Smug made up Mr. Horridge's *clientèle,* and, of the Bloods, three were Blues and one had a title; while the Smug was a noted scholar, if not a gentleman, from Germany, via America.

Two of the Bloods, the more gory two, Bill Chisholm and Sir Marcus O'Reilly, occupied the ground floor set; the other two,

Fatty Cotman and Pumper Thwaite, the first floor; and the Scholar had a couple of rooms in the second storey. The Scholar was Innocent Ernest according to some people (chiefly ladies), and Artful Eintz according to others—chiefly those who had had financial dealings with him.

At Jena and Heidelberg he had been quite Innocent Ernest among the Gretchens of the *Red Hen* and similar resorts; whereas at Harvard he had been decidedly Artful Eintz when certain wily ones had thought to fleece this simple, sentimental soul, who had strayed from the Fatherland to America.

"My daughter will be awaitin' on you, gennlemen, ter-morrer," announced Mr. Horridge one day, as he cleared away lunch in the sitting-room of Sir Marcus O'Reilly and Mr. William Chisholm.

"Hope she's nothing like you, Horrors," replied Sir Marcus, as he lit his pipe.

"She do favour me a bit, sir, I berleaf," replied the fat, bald, and blue-nosed Mr. Horridge, deftly manipulating the crumb-brush and tray.

"Poor little thing!" sighed Bill Chisholm, the great Rugger Blue, adding: "Didn't know you had a daughter, Horrors. Don't believe it's your daughter at all, you wicked old widower. What an example for us! Shame on your one grey hair!"

"She's my daughter to the best of my berleaf, sir," smiled Mr. Horridge, putting cutlery into one side-pocket of his coat and the cruet into the other, "and a rare good gal to her pore ole father. On the stage she've bin, and tired of it she've got; so she's come 'ome agin, and is goin' to give me a 'and—for a time, any'ow. Thankful I am, too. I ain't the man I was."

"I'm thankful also, Horrors," observed Sir Marcus O'Reilly, better known at St. Aldate's as Marcus Aurelius, or Oreillyus.

"Sir?" murmured Mr. Horridge, folding the table cloth.

"Thankful you aren't the man you were, my lad. *Very!*" was the brusque reply. "Don't forget we want tea for about sixteen this afternoon, at five sharp," and, with his dignified bow and wheezy "Yussir," foxy Mr. Alfred Horridge departed to perform the same office for Messrs. Cotman and Thwaite in the room above.

*　　　*　　　*　　　*　　　*　　　*

"Jolly glad to hear it, Horrors," remarked Fatty Cotman when Mr. Horridge announced that a waitress would appear henceforth in his place, and that she was his daughter. "Better than having *you* breathing about the place like an exgurgitating grampus. What?"

"A man must *breathe*, Mr. Cotman, sir," humbly suggested Mr. Horridge, and, when Pumper Thwaite, the Rowing Blue, had observed, "*Je ne vois pas la neccssité*," the subject was dropped.

When Mr. Horridge carried the tidings to Mr. Ernest Eintz, who was reading a book, that gentleman bade him "wipe off his chin and go gnaw circles in the meadow," which is possibly a Harvard euphemism for "Shut up!"

Miss Horatia Horridge (late Miss Vera de Vere Montressor of the Chorus) duly "waited" next day.

"I shall call her *Horatia Obliqua* when she has learnt to know and love me," observed Sir Marcus, when the girl left the sitting-room after dinner.

"Don't you call her anything at all, Oreillyus," replied Bill Chisholm. "She's going to be my Perox-eyed Daisy, my Lily of the Ballet. I saw her first."

"I saw her put her thumb in your soup, too," said Sir Marcus.

"'In the Soup,'" murmured Bill, reaching for the tobacco-jar. "Ominous words."

"*Dans la consommée*," sighed Sir Marcus. "Yes!"

*　　　*　　　*　　　*　　　*　　　*

"What d'you think of her, Pumper?" asked Fatty Cotman as Horatia closed the door of their room a little later.

"I don't think of her, dear," replied Pumper. "I promised mother never to think of such matters."

"Laddie!" said Fatty Colman. "Child of my Heart! We must remember we are little gentlemen as well as celibate dwellers within a monastic institution. D'you think I'd look better with my hair parted in the middle, or brushed back like a whale? *Really*, though!"

"Certainly," replied Pumper Thwaite promptly.

"Certainly what?"

"*Any* change would certainly be for the better," and, into the ensuing silence, he dropped the pregnant words, "The great love of my life has come to me."

"It did last term, too," said Fatty Cotman unkindly.

"It's come again," replied Pumper, unperturbed.

True it is that "Beauty is in the eye of the beholder!" Where Messrs. O'Reilly, Chisholm, Cotman, and Thwaite saw a rouged, powdered, and dyed chorus girl, red-handed and vulgar, Mr. Ernest Eintz saw a vision, of delight, a blue-eyed, blush-cheeked, golden-haired marvel of loveliness and grace. Where the other four saw a plump and jolly girl, ripe for a lark, a parlourmaid with bar-maidenly and tobacco-shop-girlish manners and standards, Ernest Eintz saw a queen and a divinity. "Though not a classic," he murmured, "*Patuit dea incessu,* or is it *Incessuit dea*—no, *Vera incessuit dea?* Anyhow, 'She walks a Goddess revealed,'" and, as he lay back in his armchair beside the fire, and watched her setting or clearing his table, he thought of the fat-faced, pig-tailed, generous-proportioned *madchens* of the Fatherland, and his soul set her to Wagner music, while tears of sentimentality almost rose to his honest blue eyes. For, kindly and simple and sentimental he undoubtedly was, where women were concerned; and, day by day, he fell more and more deeply in love with Miss Horatia Horridge.

The first time he dared to touch her hand, his heart beat to suffocation, and he trembled at his temerity. And the hand that was touched rose quickly, not to smite him upon the cheek, but rather to chuck him under the chin!

Matters progressed apace, and, by half-term, Miss Horatia began to think long, long thoughts, and to communicate them to her papa in long, long talks. ("That there Mr. Eintz *was* a soppy greenhorn, if ever!")

"Sure you ain't for matterrimony, my dear!" said Mr. Horridge, in the course of one of these communications, only to receive the uncompromising, if cryptic reply:—

"Matrimony me foot! With *him*? The little German Jew!" And, upon another occasion, when papa, slyly smiling, enquired: "And hev the young gentleman knelt down and made a proposal and offered you 'is 'and and 'eart yet, my dear?" the young lady replied:—

"It's the *old* gentleman as is going to sit up and make a proposal before long, I fancy. You're going to offer him *your* hand, old dear—and he's going to put something in it—or he'll hear somethink to his disadvantage! What-ho! and not half!" and the young lady's best chorus laugh tinkled around the old scout's "parlour."

*   *   *   *   *   *

"What sort of a bloke is the learned lad above, Fatty?" enquired Pumper Thwaite one day of his stable-companion. "Ever seen him? Wish he wouldn't wail sentimental German songs in his bath of a morning just when I'm going to bed."

"Most frightful tick," replied Fatty Cotman, pouring himself another tankard of ale. "Extraordinary shocking person. Weird, ghastly tick."

"How d'you know?"

"Wears most awful trousers," was the reply. "Saw him with an umbrella once, too. Plays the piano—and *pays cash* for everything! Horrors says so. Frightful abortion."

"Let's collect Bill Chisholm and Marcus Aurelius and try him for his life," suggested Pumper Thwaite. "You could be Public Prosecutor and accuse him—

"1. Of wearing awful trousers, probably ready made.

"2. Using an umbrella.

"3. Singing love-songs in his beastly bath just as I'm going to bed (on my evidence).

"4. Of paying cash for everything (on old Horridge's evidence).

"5. Of being a frightful tick.

"Then the court could order him to be debagged and driven out into the high, or something jolly like that. We haven't had a rag in Horridge's this term—not since that Rugger match, St. Aldate's v. Magdalen, in the sitter downstairs."

Quite a long speech for Pumper Thwaite.

"There's another charge, too," agreed Fatty. "Worse than any of those! I saw the low townee out with the fair Horatia yesterday. Fact!" And Fatty scowled wrathfully. "On the Upper

251

River in a punt," added he.

Pumper Thwaite laid down his knife and fork and ceased mastication. He looked shocked.

"*What?*" he said.

Fatty Cotman repeated the horrid charge.

"We'll notify Marcus Oreillyus and Chisholm, and fix it for to-night," said Pumper Thwaite. "The merry merchant shall have a fair trial, a fair devil of a slippering, and then be cast forth into the high—without his trousers—hail, snow, rain, or blow. Chasing our Horatia is he? Taking her on the Upper River in a punt is he?" And Pumper swore disgracefully. Fatty echoed him.

"That's just how I feel about it, too," he said. "The little godless tick!"

At the hour of tea they invaded the room of Chisholm and O'Reilly, bearing a large angel-cake and a sad story. Both their hosts were extraordinarily indignant, used the language of strong-silent-men-when-moved-to-wrath-and-speech, and swore horrid vengeance. Each of the four, in fact, seemed to feel that, to him especially and in particular, was the affront offered and the vengeance due.

The hour of the trial was fixed for nine that evening, after coffee in the rooms of Fatty Cotman and Pumper Thwaite.

"Let's have one more whisky and soda, in the best interests of our client," said Fatty, as the hour struck that night; and his proposal was seconded and carried unanimously.

The four then filed from the room and mounted the stairs, and saw that Mr. Horridge was preceding them. Was he also going to the sitting-room of Mr. Eintz?

He was. The four avengers saw him knock and enter even while he knocked, and, at the same moment, their ears were assailed by a piercing shriek—the scream of a female in distress, in danger, in terror (or perchance in the embrace of a young man when her stern father suddenly enters the room).

And then a terrible hullabaloo burst forth, as Horridge stormed, raved, and shouted; Horatia became hysterical, wept, screamed, and called upon the name of her sainted mother; and Eintz expostulated, argued, and besought.

The four, on the landing outside the half-closed door, looked at each other and looked away again. This was past a joke! The voice of Horridge rang above the din.

"'And you shall pay for this, sir! Pay in cash, too. Pay you *shall*—whether in court or out. Which you like—but pay you *shall*. My pore deluded daughter! No, sir! Marry her you shall *not*. I'd sooner see the pore gel dead in her corfin than married to a wiper! Ow!—honly to think that such disgrace should come upon me in my ole age—and me lived respectable all my days!"

"What about your nights, though, old bird?" whispered Fatty to the other three; but there was no answer to his hysterical giggle.

Sir Marcus tip-toed away.

"Ter-morrer you shall pay for this, sir, or I sees a serliciter about persecution fer seduction an' assault," continued the voice of the outraged Mr. Horridge, overwhelming all efforts at reply. "And also I goes to the 'ead of your college and to the Senior Procter, sir. We may be servants, sir, but we 'ave our pride, and we'll 'ave our money, too. My pore innercent, motherless gel! I'd see her righted if you wos the 'ole 'Ouse of Lords, I would. You'll pay for this ter-morrer, an' you'll leave this 'ouse likewise. She confessed all to me this arternoon."

Chisholm faded after his friend.

The voice flowed on. "An' it'd serve you right, sir, if I 'ad your last penny—and then you'd not ha' paid an 'arf o' wot you owe for the 'arm you done this pore, foolish, innercent gel. *'Ow* much?!! Fifty pounds me foot! Why—I see in the papers the other day a case where a gennelman 'ad to pay a thousand pounds and——"

Fatty and Pumper crept downstairs.

Each of the four young gentlemen retired early to his bedroom that night—almost as soon as he had had a drink, in fact; and long, long before the sound of agitated voices had ceased to flow from the room of the deplorable and detestable Eintz.

*   *   *   *   *   *

That individual sat writing at his table the following morning. He looked pale and wan, as well he might, for his sins lay heavy upon him, and, heavier still, their penalty and atonement. *Two*

253

hundred pounds! It was ruin. Two hundred pounds—or disgrace and disaster irremediable. And Horatia! How weakly she had succumbed and acquiesced when her father had sworn she should never marry the man who had sullied the white flower of her blameless life. (Not that he had expressed it precisely like that.) He laid his head upon his arms and groaned aloud. To lose his money and his love! His love and his money! The two best things in life.

He raised his head quickly and cut off a groan in its early youth and promise as a gentle knock heralded the opening of his door.

"I say, you know," said Sir Marcus O'Reilly, entering. "I heard old Horridge last night. Perishing old piffle-merchant. How much has he stuck you for?"

Innocent Ernest blushed; and then Artful Eintz stared hard at the intruder and murmured, "Three hundred pounds."

Sir Marcus gave a long, low whistle.

"I'll get even with him yet," he said, and felt in the breast pocket of his coat. "I'm a bad hat and all that, y'know," he continued, "but I play whatever game I *do* play on the level," and he produced a cheque-book and fountain-pen from the pocket in which he had felt. "Don't know your name, Mr.——"

Artful Eintz told him, and spelt it.

A couple of minutes later Sir Marcus handed him a cheque.

"Halves," said he, "and nothing said. No sense in both of us being in the soup, since you're there already. Is it a bargain?"

"Yes," replied Artful Eintz, and repeating, "Not a word, mind!" Sir Marcus departed, feeling as though he had wallowed in pitch and been decidedly defiled.

In one eye of Innocent Ernest stood a tear of bitter grief as he saw his Horatia in this new light; while in the other eye of Artful Eintz stood a tear of joy, through which he beheld a cheque for £150. He put the pink paper into his pocket-book and threw himself into his armchair.

Oh, Horatia! Horatia! Horatia! And he loved her so! He drew his handkerchief from his pocket, and replaced it as he heard a footstep without. Someone knocked at the door, and in answer to his "Come in," Fatty Cotman materialised.

"Hullo!" said he. "Awful business, this, y'know. Break my

old mother's heart if she got to hear of it. Haven't slept a wink all night. What's that old pillar of the pothouses of Sodom and Gomorrah going to do? Could hear him all over the bloomin' place. What did Horatia say? What's Horridge going to do?"

"Accept three hundred pounds and hold his tongue; and Miss Horridge will hold hers," was the reply. Fatty heaved a huge sigh of relief.

"Get a document from him absolving you from further responsibility—in consideration of the three hundred," he said quickly.

"Trust me," was the equally quick response.

"Only *your* name mentioned, of course?" added Fatty.

"Provided you—er——" replied Artful Eintz.

"Exactly," agreed Fatty. "You'll find a fat envelope, with fifteen tenners in it, before you're a couple of hours older. You'll pick it up and not know who it comes from. Not an idea. You'll find it on this table, I expect. What? But not a word to a soul. What?"

"Your name will not appear in this matter," said Artful Eintz, and Fatty Cotman proceeded to his bank. Not his to leave another feller in the lurch to bear the blame which he equally deserved—not though he were a frightful tick who wore most awful trousers and a nasal, guttural accent.

Both eyes of Innocent Ernest were suffused with genuine tears of real sorrow, horror, grief, and pain as he thought of Horatia's baseness; and the mouth of Artful Eintz smiled widely as he thought of a hundred pounds cash profit. A broken heart is a terrible thing, but so are a broken academic career and a broken bank account. On the other hand, the gain of a hundred golden sovereigns is not. And so Innocent Ernest and Artful Eintz sat and wept and smiled.

In the room below a terrible struggle was going on in the breast of Pumper Thwaite. He had been a little too previous with his allowance that quarter, and he was hoping to buy a hunter for the Christmas vac. But these were small matters beside one's self-respect—and Marcus Oreillyus would lend him a hundred any old time. He despised himself for hesitating so long.

He found Eintz at home.

"Look here," he said, "I can't let you stand the racket alone if old Horridge is making trouble. I'm as much to blame as you. 'Nuff said. If the old scoundrel wants to run you in, I'll come too. But if you can buy him off, I'm with you! I hope to God he'll settle it out of court. He'd take cash for *anything*, I should think."

"Three hundred," said Artful Eintz.

"I'll give you a cheque for a hundred and fifty in two ticks— er—I mean in two shakes of a dead lamb's tail." (Tactless to talk of ticks in front of such an appalling tick as this. Fancy Horatia! Oh, Lor'!) "But mum's the Word, you know."

While he awaited Pumper Thwaite's return, Artful Eintz regretted his folly in not making the three hundred into four hundred. But there was always the chance of one of the guilty payers of three hundred mentioning the matter to the one who had paid four. But supposing they found out that they had all three been paying—even though they had all paid the same amount? Well, *he* hadn't asked them to pay anything, and it was highly improbable that they'd "talk." Each was only too thankful to have got off as lightly as he had.

But oh, Horatia! Horatia! Horatia!

On the other hand, *oh*, two hundred and fifty pounds clear gain and profit! After paying old Horridge the agreed two hundred.

He was hardly surprised when blunt Bill Chisholm paid him a visit.

"I think you're a ghastly tick, Mr. What's-your-name," said he, "and I think I'd be a bigger one if I screened myself behind you. I *am* as big a one really, to come and ask you to bear the brunt of this, and keep my name out of it, but I'm not a bigger one, because I propose to put up whatever money old Horridge is sticking out for. Beastly business to be in, and serve me right. Never again, though. How much have you to fork out?"

Artful Eintz hesitated a moment. Should he risk it? No. "Three hundred pounds," said he.

"You shall have a cheque for that amount to-day," replied Bill. "My guv'nor's a bishop, and this would be a frightful let-down for him. He's a damned good father, too, and I'll raise the three hundred, provided my name doesn't appear."

"It won't," said Artful Eintz,

"I feel an awful cad," continued Bill; "and I *am* surprised at

Miss Horridge."

"So'm I," responded Artful Eintz, and added cryptically, "More than you are."

"Cheque to-day—made out to bearer," said Chisholm, and departed, slamming the door.

A fat envelope was thrown into the room a little later, and Artful Eintz coughed loudly in acknowledgment. Two cheques were brought by taciturn and shame-faced young men in the course of the afternoon.

At tea-time Mr. Horridge received two hundred pounds—*and* notice of their early departure from every single one of the five lodgers !

That night Innocent Ernest kissed the back of his chair (where the head of Horatia had pressed it), broke down utterly, and wept very bitterly; and Artful Eintz went to bed, thinking of his five hundred and fifty pounds, and laughed very happily.

He was a German gentleman, you see.

MAHDEV RAO

"Mahdev Rao" is the story of a Indian Sepoy who was captured by the Germans in the East African campaign of World War I. What makes the story noteworthy is that Wren himself most likely participated in the East African campaign. Wren was appointed a Captain in the Indian Army Reserve of Officers, the 101st Grenadiers of the Indian Infantry, on November 20, 1914 (about three months after the war started), having been part of the "volunteer" Indian Army since 1905. He may have seen action with the 101st Grenadiers at the Battle of Tanga (November 1914) and the Battle of Jassin (January 1915). He was listed as being on sick leave from February 17 to October 18, 1915. More detailed observations about the East African campaign (and the Indian Army) are seen in Wren's 1920 novel, Cupid in Africa. *"Mahdev Rao" was probably published first in one of the fiction magazines of the early twentieth century, but currently (2012) the first known publication of the story was in the "new and enlarged edition" of* Stepsons of France *(1925). It has been reprinted in* Stories of the Foreign Legion *(Vallancey 1945, Murray 1947, Macrae-Smith 1948), and* Tales of the Foreign Legion *(1947).*

The Legion's net is as wide as its meshes are close; and some rare, as well as queer, fish find their way into it.

Possibly the rarest that it ever contained was a Mahratta soldier who, during the Great War, found his way, always toward the rising sun, across a hundred miles of African jungle, until he reached the sea, and there, boarding a *dhow* at night, was carried across hundreds of miles of ocean.

The crew of the *dhow* was an interesting one, among its members being two French gentlemen, one an Intelligence Officer and the other a kindly priest, formerly of Goa—neither of whom was in anywise distinguishable from his sea-faring Arab colleagues.

The *dhow*, of a humble, unobtrusive and diffident disposition, had business at a lone coastal outpost where flies the *Tricouleur*, and where sins and suffers a small garrison, of Colonial Infantry and of the Legion. . . .

258

Here the said priest, whose fairish knowledge of the Marathi tongue had enabled him to understand something of the soldier's story, was glad to assist him to attain his highest ambition—to fight against his personal and national enemies, once more.

As a trained soldier and a stout fellow he found favour in the sight of the Commandant of the post, was duly enrolled as a soldier of France, and eventually found himself precisely where he desired to be. . . .

*   *   *   *   *

Mahdev Rao Ramrao, son of Ramrao Krishnaji, was born in a little mud-walled village that nestles above its rice-fields on the slope of the Western Ghats, in the Deccan of India.

High up above the village, its outline clear-cut against the sky, was the fort, "*Den of the Tiger*," from which Mahdev Rao's forbears, led by Shivaji the Great, had swept down to harry the plains, to plunder towns, and to fight the invading Mussulman. . . .

As he toddled about the crooked streets of tiny mud-built Nagaum, clutching the finger of his grandfather, Krishnaji Arjun, the little fat Mahdev Rao, clad in an embroidered velvet cap and a necklace, learned that he was a Pukka Bahadur, a mighty one, the son, grandson, great-grandson, and general descendant of soldiers, fierce fighting men—from the days of Shivaji the Great three hundred years ago, to the days of Wellesley Sahib (who had fought in those very parts), Nicholson Sahib, Outram Sahib (whose Orderly, grandfather's own father had been), Havelock Sahib, Roberts Sahib, even unto the days of the Great Lat-Sahib Kitchener, the Elephant of War, whose shadow had destroyed the *Hubshis*[26] and their prophet the Mahdi. . . .

And, as he grew up, Mahdev Rao understood that he was a *Kshattria*, of the caste next to the Brahmins themselves; that he was a cradle-ordained soldier, and that he had traditions to reverence and maintain. So he developed into a fine proud youth, self-respecting, ambitious, and religious beyond the conception of the vast majority of Europeans.

---

[26] "Woolly ones" (negroes).

In due course, the day came when, as his father, his grandfather, and his great-grandfather had done, he sallied forth from Nagaum, and tramped to the recruiting-depôt at Belara to take service under the Sahibs as a Sepoy—to serve the King Emperor as his father and grandfather had served the Queen, and his other ancestors had served John Company or their own Rajah in due season. His intention was to be faithful to his salt; his ambition was to rise to be a Havildar, possibly a Jemadar, and conceivably a Subedar; his hope was to return to Nagaum full of honours, with medals and a pension, and to superintend the cultivation of the family plot of land (theirs since the days of Shivaji, the Scourge of the Deccan) and the upbringing of his sons and grandsons. . . . But Fate willed otherwise, and affairs in Nagaum were affected by the fact that an egotistical megalomaniac was making a God in his own image, seven thousand miles away in Berlin. . . .

*   *   *   *   *

As a white-clad recruit at Belara, life went very well for Mahdev Rao the Mahratta, and when he found himself a khaki-clad full private of the Old Hundredth Bombay Rifles, he found himself indeed.

He was that happy man, the man whose day is full of work that is his hobby, work that he loves, work that is his play. The Jemadar of his double-company was an old friend of his father, and his own Havildar was a Nagaum man. Him, Mahdev Rao cultivated with such words and gifts as are fitting—and highly politic. The Captain Sahib of his double-company was a *pukka* Sahib, a great *shikari*, horseman, athlete and soldier. The descendant of Pindaris could understand and admire the descendant of Norman free-booters and Elizabethan gentlemen-adventurers and soldiers of fortune. The Colonel Sahib, with his nine medal-ribbons, white moustache, and burning eye, was Mahdev Rao's idea and ideal of a Man. At an age when Mahdev Rao's people were getting a little senile and more than a little shaky, he seemed as young and active as a Mahdev himself—yea, though as old as Mahdev's grandfather. Sepoys who had seen him at work on the Frontier, when the Ghazis charged home like wounded tigers, spoke of him with bated breath. This was a Bahadur of Bahadurs, a *Man*. Oh, to die in battle under his approving eye! What bliss! . . . The Adjutant Sahib, Mahdev disliked and feared, though he respected him. (It seems the painful duty of a good Adjutant to make himself disliked and feared, as it is his gratifying privilege to be respected.) . . .

And, by the time war broke out, in August, 1914, the Regiment was Mahdev Rao's happy home; the Colonel Sahib was, in his own expressive phrase, "his Father and his Mother," and his Mahratta comrades were his brothers.

Incidentally and severally, his *guru*, his Captain, Lieutenant, Subedar, Jemadar and Havildar were also his Father and his Mother; and the honour of his Regiment was the honour of Mahdev Rao. Even the Punjabi Mahommedans and Pathans of the other double-companies were worthy souls, inasmuch as they were part of the Regiment; and still more so the Sikhs, Rajputs, and Dogras; but, of course, the very salt of the Regiment, which was the salt of the Army, which was the salt of the Earth, was Mahdev Rao's double-company of Deccani Mahrattas.

When it was known, a few months later, that the Regiment was to go on Active Service, Mahdev Rao's cup of happiness was already full, by reason of the fact that he had that very day defeated Pandurang Bagu and became champion wrestler of the Regiment—a distinction which guarantees that its holder would give a little trouble to any wrestler in the world, be his nationality and eminence what it might. . . . Judge of the swamping, seething overflow of the said cup of happiness when the news came, plain and indubitable, through the regimental *babu*, that the Old Hundredth Bombay Rifles were to proceed forthwith to the city of Bombay and embark for East Africa!

Here was news indeed! News of increased saving from pay, decreased expenses, a certain medal, the chances of decoration and promotion; and adventure, experience, change. . . . Of course, to cross the Black Water was to lose caste, but the *guru* and the village priests would soon put that right and provide dispensation at not too exorbitant rates. Marvellous fellows, the Brahmins, at wangling a thing when there was money in it. . . .

*   *   *   *   *

The ten days' journey from Bombay to Mombasa was very wonderful to Mahdev Rao, who had scarcely seen the sea before, and had never set foot on a ship or boat of any description. . . . The problem of how it propelled itself without sails or wheels puzzled him exceedingly, and still more so the problem of how it found its way, day after day, night after night, from one spot on the coast of India to another spot on the coast of Africa. And not just any old spot, mark you, but a definite given place at which it would arrive at a stated time. Certainly the Sahibs up on the bridge could not see across the space of a ten days' journey with the most powerful of field-glasses. . . .

It was a surprise to him to find that the shores of this new and strange continent were remarkably like those of India, and that the coconut groves of the Kilindini inlet, between the island of Mombasa and the mainland, might have come straight from Bombay . . . But then surprises came so thick and fast, that his mind, always more tenacious than acute, became dulled, and he ceased to be surprised at anything—even at the fact that he was expected to fight in jungle so dense that no human being could move through it, save along the foot-wide paths that wound and twisted from village to village or from ford to ford. But *how* was a man to fight in such country, and what was a double-company to do, accustomed as it was to attack in extended order, and taught never to fire a round until there was a visible enemy to fire at? How *could* it fight in single file, with an impenetrable wall of trees, creepers, bush and thorn on either side? . . .

The days between the debarkation at Mombasa and the occupation by his double-company of an advanced outpost (days of weary marching through jungle and swamp) passed like a dream, and Mahdev Rao settled down to the routine of this new strange life in a swamp-jungle, and soon felt as though he had never known any other.

It was not a pleasant life, for it was monotonous, unhealthy, and dull, the heat was terrific, food was not all it might have been, fever and dysentery were rife and, in his own phrase, "air and water were bad."

But Mahdev Rao was too keen a soldier to grumble. One did not expect Active Service to be like a furlough-trip to one's home, nor to have the comforts and luxuries of Nagaum, Belara or Bombay, in this enemy's country—the loathsome swamp where lived the *Hubshis* under the rule of their *Germani* masters (a kind of White Men, he gathered, who were not Sahibs).

So he trudged along cheerily when his half of the little garrison went marching on a reconnaissance into the enemy's country; did his sentry-go smartly; sat watching with keen untiring eyes on the *machan* in the tree-top, when such was his duty; and scouted warily along the jungle tracks when sent out with a comrade to patrol to the next outpost. . . .

"That Mahdev Rao's a good lad," remarked Captain Delamere to Lieutenant Carr as they sat in the grass-hut "Officers' Mess" of the outpost, one evening, and tried to masticate the tinned string and encaustic tiles, served out to them under the name of bully-beef and biscuit.

"Always merry and bright, and chucks a chest when some of the other blokes begin to slouch and lag a bit."

"Yes," agreed Carr; "he'll make a damgood Havildar some day. . . . Might make him a Lance-Naik now. . . . Hardly the brains to go further than Havildar, I am afraid . . . but we c'd do with a few thousand Mahdev Raos out here." . . .

"We'll give him a stripe," said Delamere, as he tried to cut up some black-cake ration-tobacco (horrible cheap poison), with the one and only table-knife.

"Why the devil can't they issue tobacco a man can smoke, if they're going to issue a tobacco-ration at all? . . . " he growled, and added: "Yes—we'll give Mahdev Rao a stripe." . . . But it was some one else, and a very different person, who gave Mahdev Rao his stripes.

For, on the following day, he and Pandurang Bagu, patrolling to meet the patrol from the next outpost, were ambushed.

There was a sudden burst of fire from a tree-top, as well as from the bush before and behind them, and Pandurang Bagu went down with a heavy bullet of soft lead in his shattered hip-joint. Almost simultaneously, Mahdev Rao was felled by the blow of a rifle-butt, as he raised his rifle to fire at big khaki-clad *Hubshis*, in tall khaki grenadier-caps, who rushed at him in front.

"Good!" grunted the Swahili sergeant in charge of the squad. "That one will be able to talk. Kill the other."

Seven bayonets were plunged into Pandurang Bagu as, with trembling hands, he raised his rifle. As one does not get the pleasure of plunging one's bayonet into an enemy every day, the Swahilis and Yaos made the most of their opportunity, and Pandurang Bagu's life ebbed quickly out through dozens of wounds. . . .   The Sergeant was a happy man, and his ebon countenance was wreathed in smiles. He had been sent out, by the *Herr Offizier*, with orders to ambush a patrol and bring in at least one member of it alive—and he had succeeded to perfection.

One night's wait in a most admirable ambush; strict orders *not* to shoot the last man of the patrol—be there a dozen or be there but two—and to spring out at each end of the ambush and capture the survivor alive; five seconds of smart work as per programme, and the job was done.

And done very neatly—for there are few braver or more skilful soldiers in the world than these African Rifles, when fighting in their own unique jungle. . . .

*   *   *   *   *

When Mahdev Rao recovered consciousness (which he did very quickly, thanks to his thick skull and thicker turban) he found himself a prisoner. His hands were bound behind his back, he was stripped almost naked, and his kit and accoutrements were being examined and looted by his captors.

He realized that he was bare-headed and that the long tuft of hair, left among the cropped stubble (that the gods might lift him into heaven, when his time came), was hanging down his back.

He ground his teeth at the shameful outrage these casteless sons of pariah-dogs had put upon him, in knocking his turban off and exposing his bare head. He rose to his knees and staggered to his feet, only to be knocked down again from behind.

"If you strike him senseless, you will have to carry him, Achmet Ali," said the Sergeant. "He has to be in the *boma*[27] by tomorrow morning, alive, and able to answer the questions of the *Bwana Macouba*."[28] . . .

---

[27] Enclosure; jungle fort.

"I am the hero who knocked him down first," said Achmet Ali, and straightway improvised a chant.

> "I am the hero,
> The swift-striking hero,
> I am the hero
> Who knocked him down first."

"Be also the hero that drives him along with a bayonet, then," interrupted the Sergeant, "and you'll be the hero whose head I will blow off if the dog escapes."

And, for the remainder of that day and all that night, the *askaris* drove Mahdev Rao (as the potter and *dhobi* of Nagaum drive their donkeys) with blows and curses.

Once, during one of the brief halts, food was offered him (cold boiled rice and a plantain), and he tried to give these foul Untouchables, these casteless carrion-scavengers, some faint idea of the unutterable pollution of the very thought of taking food from their defiling hands—the filthy *Hubshi* dogs! . . .

"He is too frightened to eat, poor heathen Infidel dog," remarked the Sergeant to Achmet Ali, as he turned towards Mecca and prostrated himself in prayer. . . .

While fording a river, next morning, Mahdev Rao endeavoured to drown himself and the hero, to the boundless amusement of the rest of the squad. The hero revenged himself by making a pattern of cuts upon his captive's back with the point of his bayonet. But they were only about an inch long and quarter of an inch deep, and not likely to affect his value when questioned by the *Bwana Macouba* as to the number and disposition of the British forces.

*   *   *   *   *

The *Germani boma* was very similar to the one from which Mahdev Rao had come, but considerably larger. Dazed and starving as he was, he noted its strength, the height of its palisades, the depth of its trenches, the number of its machine-

---

[28] Great Master.

guns, and the strength of its garrison of native African Rifles (*askaris*) and *Germani* Europeans. He was surprised to see that the majority of the latter wore beards. . . . He had never before seen a European officer or soldier with a beard. . . . Obviously the *askaris* were well drilled and highly disciplined.

Also, everything about the place was well done. The huts were neater and stronger and better thatched than in his own *boma*, paths were more neatly made and kept, the earthworks were bigger and stronger. Evidently the *Germanis* had more coolie-labourers and got more work out of them, or else they gave more attention to these details. Certainly it was a very strong *boma*, and very strongly garrisoned. He had seen twelve machine-guns and two small quick-firers (something like Indian mountain-battery guns) already. He would have a lot to tell the Captain Sahib when he escaped and got back to the outpost. . . . But would they not take very especial care that he did not escape, after he had seen so much? . . . And how was he to find his way back to his Company through that dense blind jungle, if he did escape? . . . It had got to be done, anyhow—and then he could lead the Captain Sahib and the double-company to this place, and they could rush it at dawn, with much slaughter of black untouchable pariahs who kept a high-caste Indian bare-headed, offered him polluted food and water with their defiling hands, struck him, and generally behaved like the savages they were. . . .

Doubtless, however, their *Germani* masters would punish them and do justice. Though not *pukka* Sahibs, they were White Men, and, as such, would have understanding and a sense of decency.

White Men do not offend against the religion of others; they understand caste and respect it; they know that prisoners of war are to be honourably treated. . . . Yes, they understand a high-caste man, and know the difference between a dog of a low-caste negro *askari* of Africa, and a high-caste *Kshattria* Sepoy of India; the difference between one who comes next to the Brahmins themselves and one who is utterly beyond the pale, a walking pollution to earth, air, and water, whose very shadow is a defilement and a desecration to what it falls upon. . . . Yes, it would be all right when he was brought face to face with their officers, even though they were *Germanis*. . . .

He was hustled into a filthy grass hut in which were four negroes—spies, defaulters and guides, the last being kept in bonds with the criminals, by reason of their incurable desire to leave the service of their employers and captors. . . .

Later he was haled forth—still bare-headed, bound, and half-naked—to where, beneath a tree, sat three Europeans, attended by a Sergeant and guard of *askaris*, and one or two nondescript persons, including a half-caste in European clothing, a clerk, and a servant. On a camp-table before the White Men were bottles of beer, glasses, a revolver, a heavy *kiboko*[29] of rhinoceros-hide, a map, and a notebook.

The central figure of the three (one Von Groener), who wore a khaki uniform, blue putties and a white-topped peaked cap, bade the half-caste ask the prisoner the name of his regiment, the number of men in his *boma*, and the number of machine-guns it contained—for a start.

The "half"-caste, a Negroid Goanese-Arab-Indian, put the questions in the barbarous Hindustani of the Goanese quarter of Dar-es-Salaam. Mahdev Rao, a Mahratta, always speaking Marathi in the Regiment, knew little more Hindustani than he did English.

"*Tera pultan ka nam kya hai?*" said the "interpreter." "*Kitni admi tera boma men hain? Kitni tup-tup tup-tup bandook hain?*"[30]

Mahdev Rao had a fair idea as to what the man was driving at, but he looked stupid, and, in Marathi, replied:

"I do not understand."

Mr. Alonzo Gomez had never heard Marathi in his life.

"The man does not understand the language of India, *Herr Kommandant*," he said, in clumsy German, to the officer who sat in the centre.

"But that is absurd," replied that worthy. "If he comes from India he knows the language of India. Tell him I will *kiboko* the flesh from his bones if he tries to fool me."

"*Bwana Sahib tumko kiboko diega,*"[31] answered Gomez to the

---

[29] Whip.

[30] "What is the name of your regiment? How many men are there in your outpost? How many machine-guns?"

[31] "The Master will flog you."

prisoner.

"I will try him in English," said the senior officer to the others. "The English give all drill-orders in English; therefore this animal understands English."

"*Ja! Ja!*" agreed the other two. "*Ganz klein wenig.*"

"Hear, pig-dog," quoth the senior gentleman, "his battalion what his name calls? How large are man-number of it? How large are gun-machine-number of it? Isn't it?"

To Mahdev Rao, at least two of the gutturally pronounced words were familiar. "Sahib," he said in Marathi, "I am a Sepoy and a prisoner of war. I am not a spy. And I am very tired and thirsty." . . .

"The swine is contumacious," said the senior. "He understands both English and Hindustani. He is shamming. We will help him to find his wits—and his tongue," and he gave a curt order to the *askari* Sergeant. (Also to the Swahili servant—concerning the replenishment of the beer supply.) He was a handsome man of about forty, with a small forked beard, a cold blue eye, and a hard domineering expression. Once he had been an ornament of Berlin and Potsdam, an *Ober-Leutnant* of Grenadiers; but debt, drink, cards, and an unfortunate duel, had sent him into exile. In exile he had grown morose, bitter and savage, loathing and blaming everything and every one—except himself.

Of his companions, one was a ne'er-do-well relation of a German General and had been shipped to German East Africa to die of fever, beer, and dissipation; the other was an ex-*Feldwebel* of the Prussian Guard who had made money as an elephant-poacher and then done exceeding well as a trader and planter—well from the financial point of view *bien entendu*; from the moral point of view he had not done very well.

The three were not typical of their class, and were of wholly different fibre from their General (a great soldier and a gentleman).

They were three bad men, bad by the standards of the German colony—and the order that *Ober-Leutnant* von Groener had given, and that his colleagues had applauded, was that Mahdev Rao, prisoner of war, captured in uniform, upon his lawful occasions as a soldier, should be tied to a tree and flogged with the terrible rhinoceros-hide *kiboko* with which the German instils discipline into his native soldiers, servants, coolies, criminals, and lady "housekeepers."

Mahdev Rao was seized by the *askari* guard, and so tied that he was hugging, with arms and legs, the big tree beneath which the "court" was sitting.

In the hands of a huge, brawny, and most willing Sergeant of *askaris*, the five-foot *kiboko*, tapering from the thickness of a man's wrist to that of his little finger, supple as india-rubber, and tougher than anything in the world, is a most terrible instrument of torture and punishment. The "draw" of the scientific pulling-stroke (as of one who cuts through a stick with one slice of a knife) of the *kiboko* lacerates and mangles, blood leaping at every blow. . . .

By the time the three German gentlemen considered that Mahdev Rao was sufficiently exhorted, encouraged, and rebuked (for his contumaciousness), he was also senseless and apparently dead. . . . It was annoying, as the *Herr Ober-Leutnant* had hoped to obtain much interesting and useful information concerning the Indian Expeditionary Force, and to send it to Head-Quarters. . . .

Mahdev Rao recovered consciousness in the same prison-hut. He was alone, and the fact that there was no one present to see such a fall from grace, aided the terrible pangs of thirst in inducing him to drink from the gourd of water that stood in the corner. . . . Later, he ate a couple of plantains. . . . As they were covered by their skins, the interior had not been defiled—or, at any rate, one could take a certain amount of comfort from such a theory and argument.

Later still, he bowed to the inevitable, and ate the cold boiled rice his *askari* gaoler brought him. It was a terrible thing to do—but life was dear—and revenge was dearer. He would live, at any cost, to be revenged upon that—that—swine, and son of swine—that offspring of pariah curs—that carrion-eating lump of defilement and pollution—who had had him, him, Sepoy Mahdev Rao of the Old Hundredth Bombay Rifles, flogged, publicly flogged, by black beasts of *Hubshis*. . . .

Great as were his physical sufferings, his mental sufferings were a thousand times greater. His body felt pain: his mind felt agonizing tortures and excruciating torments unspeakable. . . .

He ground his teeth, clenched his fists, and cried aloud in rage and horror—and then fell silent and still . . . for no—he must not go mad, he must not lose strength, he must not die—until he had had his revenge. . . .

Next day he was questioned again and flogged again.

At the end of a week, the *Ober-Leutnant* decided to send him to Head-Quarters at Mombobora. There was a Missionary Father in the town, who had worked in India and would know the language perfectly. There was also a hospital, where they would patch the dog up, that he might be able to converse with the Father. . . . Anyhow—since the Colonel seemed to think that he, the *Ober-Leutnant*, had shown little skill in his endeavours to get information from this Indian, let him see if he could do any better himself. . . .

At Head-Quarters they learnt nothing from Mahdev Rao, though he learnt much from them concerning the difference between German and British methods of dealing with native prisoners who will not "talk."

He was not flogged, but he was abused, starved, bound, insulted, and finally herded with a chain-gang of negro criminals, and set to such work as road-sweeping and latrine-cleaning.

What this means to a man of caste, no one who has not lived in India can guess, and no one but a high-caste Indian can know. Nothing worse can happen to him.

And, from time to time, he was brought before the Missionary, who talked to him in excellent Marathi, promising him all kinds of rewards if he would describe the composition and disposition of the Expeditionary Force from India. . . . Were there Pathans and Gurkhas in it? . . . Were there field-batteries? . . . Were there Pioneer Corps? . . . Had part of it gone by the Uganda Railway to Nairobi and the Lakes? . . . Were the Sepoys loyal? . . . If he returned to them with much money and more promises, would he be able to induce any of them to desert? . . . What was the state of feeling in India? . . . And much more, until Mahdev Rao, maddened, sullen, brutalized, barely sane, by reason of his wrongs, cruelties, and immeasurable degradations, would lift up his voice and curse the *padre*, the evil white *fakir*, until his guards smote him on the mouth and dragged him away—a naked, filthy wreck of a man. . . .

Constantly he sought an opportunity of escape from the town, but found none.

He must have food, a weapon of some kind, and he must get more strength and recover his health, get rid of this fever, before he could take the opportunity if one offered. But when he was not road-sweeping or road-making with the chain-gang, he was otherwise working, always under the eye of an *askari* guard, who asked nothing better than an excuse to shoot him. . . .

No—he must wait, and it was always possible that the *Germani* officer, who had flogged him, might come to this Head-Quarters, and save Mahdev Rao the journey to that gentleman's *boma*.

For Mahdev Rao's one idea now, his one reason for living, was to avenge himself upon *Ober-Leutnant* von Groener—the man who, instead of treating him as a prisoner of war, had had him publicly flogged, and had then sent him to this place where a high-caste Indian Sepoy was as a cannibal negro criminal, and was herded with them. . . . He did not wish to live. He did not wish to return to India—he was too eternally and utterly defiled, polluted, and out-caste for that. But he did not intend to die until he had met the *Germani* who had had him flogged, the man whom he regarded as the arch-type of his captors, the man who had brought him into this living death of defilement, the man who was the cause of all his woes. . . .

To listen seriously to the Missionary Father's temptations to treachery never occurred to him. He was Sepoy Mahdev Rao of the Old Hundredth Bombay Rifles, a soldier of the King Emperor, and son of a long line of brave and honest fighting men, "true to salt," and loyal as hilt to blade. . . .

*   *   *   *   *

One morning, with the rest of a road-sweeping gang, Mahdev Rao was working at a spot just outside the native "town" of Mombobora, where a little bridge crossed a muddy stream, more mud than stream, that lay between two tracts of cultivation. . . .

A squad of *askaris* tramped past . . . a doctor and two nurses . . . a small herd of cattle . . . a German lady in a kind of rickshaw . . . an officer in a hammock slung from a stout bamboo pole, borne by four Kavarondo natives . . . a file of negresses with water-jars upon their heads . . . and then—did his eyes deceive him?—his Enemy, the man who had had him flogged!

*   *   *   *   *

. . . Strolling along, taking the morning air, came *Ober-Leutnant* Fritz von Groener, who had been summoned to Mombobora by the Colonel, and had arrived on the previous day.

As he reached the little bridge, a crouching man, a filthy, half-naked wretch of the road-gang, suddenly rose and sprang at him, drove him sideways and backwards, before he could raise his heavy whip or draw his automatic—and seized him in a grip, scientific and powerful, the hold of a champion wrestler, in whom was the strength of madness and the lust of revenge.

Before the lounging *askari* guard heard a sound of the struggle, the two, swaying and straining, fell against the low coping of the bridge, toppled over it, and splashed heavily into the liquid mud beneath—the German officer beneath the Indian soldier, whose hands were at his throat, whose knee was on his chest, and who, slowly, strongly, surely, thrust his head beneath the foul slime, and held it there as the writhing bodies sank and splashed in the watery mud. . . .

It is probable that the *Herr Ober-Leutnant* was dead before Askari Mustapha Moussa, in charge of the road-gang, had realized that something was wrong, had reached the bridge-head and had made up what must be called his mind, that it was his duty to risk a shot at the "coolie."

Certainly he was dead enough when the hands of Mahdev Rao were at length torn from his throat, and the two were dragged from the mud into which they were disappearing. . . .

*   *   *   *   *

Rumours of the approach of an enemy force caused much confusion that night, and Sepoy Mahdev Rao, sentenced to be shot at dawn, decided to view the dawn elsewhere than in Mombobora, or to die in an attempt to turn this confusion to good account. . . .

THE MERRY LIARS

"The Merry Liars", the only "Western" that Wren wrote, is a story that the Bucking Bronco tells during a "lying fest." In this tale the Bronco tells how he tried to save his friend with a "piggy-back" ride. "The Merry Liars", like "Mahdev Rao", was not included in the 1917 edition of the Stepsons of France*, but was an add-on to the "new and enlarged edition" of 1925. "The Merry Liars" was reprinted in* Stories of the Foreign Legion *(Murray 1947).*

A competition in lying was proceeding, and entries were good. (One Légionnaire told of his beloved pet rabbit which nibbled lead, ate cordite, swallowed a burning match—and then went out and shot its own, and its master's, supper.)

"Yep," growled the Bucking Bronco, as the little group of Legionaries, from all corners of the earth and all strata of human society, turned toward him, "I allow I can tell as big a lie as Ole Man Dobroffski—even if I *ain't* the Czar of Roosia's gran'pa's little gan'chile, Wilhelmine-Bungorfski-Poporf."

Père Jean Boule, "father" of the Second Battalion, and incidentally an English baronet, moved uneasily. The Bucking Bronco had always disliked the Russian aristocrat, and had never made any secret of the fact. If ever they fought, there would not be two survivors of that fight . . . and the Bucking Bronco was his beloved and loving friend, and a mine of virtues, though a Bad Man—of the best sort. He had been, among other things, a miner, cowboy, tramp, lumberman, professional boxer, U.S.A. trooper, and ornament of a Wild West show, of which he was the trick revolver-shot.

"Ah . . . you allus was a purple liar, Buck," put in 'Erb, the Cockney, as the American produced a deplorable French pipe and some more deplorable French tobacco. (*How* his soul yearned for a corn-cob and some Golden Bar, or "the makings" and a bag of Bull Durham!)

"I give a guy a picky-back once," continued the Bucking Bronco, ignoring 'Erb, whom he usually treated as a mastiff treats a small cur.

"But how interesting!" murmured the ex-Colonel of the Imperial Guard, who called himself "Dobroffski."

"And it killed that guy, and it killed his gal, and it sent me bug-house—*loco*—for Devil-knows-how-long-an'-all," continued the American, ignoring Dobroffski as he had ignored 'Erb.

"What is it that it is, then—this '*bug-'ouse*' and this '*loco*'?" murmured le Légionnaire Alphonse Blanc, whose English included no American.

"Same as what you'd call 'dotty'—or 'off 'is onion'— 'looney'—'balmy on the crumpet'—in yore silly lingo," explained 'Erb helpfully.

"*Fou*," murmured La Cigale, for the benefit of Blanc and Tant-de-Soif, whose knowledge of English was limited also. (La Cigale, the ex-Belgian officer, knew all there was to know about *démence*, poor soul.)

"Wot killed 'em? Was it the sight o' the faices you made— doin' the job o' work?" inquired 'Erb.

The Bucking Bronco leaned back against the wall of rough-hewn, thickly-mortared grey stones, spread his huge legs abroad, and blew a cloud of smoke. He was wearing his *capote* (the long blue great-coat) and red trousers tucked into black leggings, but he shivered as though cold.

"I can see that gal's face now," he said, staring out across the ocean of sand that surrounded the fort; and the enormous powerful man, with his long arms, big hands, leathern face, and heavy drooping moustache, looked ill and fell silent.

"Wish *I* could, Ole Cock," observed 'Erb. "Where's she 'iding?"

"And Bud Conklin's feet, too, a danglin' just above me face. Ole Bud Conklin, what I'd bin a road-kid with, an' took the trail with ever-since-when—ranchin'; gold-prospectin', with a rusty pan and a bag o' flour; ridin' the blind, right across the States; lumberin'; throwin' our feet fer a two-bit poke-out, in the towns; and trampin' through the alkali sage bush, as thirsty as a bitch with nine pups.

"Bud Conklin was a blowed-in-the-glass White Man, an' I was the death of him. Yes, Sir. *And* his gal—a little peach, named Mame Texas. . . . I guess she begun life as 'Mame o'

Texas,' never hevin' hed no parients—nawthen to speak of—'cos Dago Jake had lifted her outer Ole Pete Frisco's ranch when his gang shot th' ol' sinner up, down Texas way (an' *he* never hed no wife—nawthen to speak of) and burnt the place down.

"An' when she filled out and grow'd up a bit, Dago Jake he got that sot on the gal, he allowed as he'd give any man lead-pisenin' as looked at her twice; an' he beat her up every time he got a whisky-jag, so' she shouldn't look twice at nobody else.

"Marry her? No! There wasn't no sky-pilots around Hackberry Crossin' by the Frio River in them prickly-pear flats; an' Dago Jake dassn't show his ugly face near no church-bearin' city—even if he'd held with matterimony as a pastime.

"Nope! Nix on marryin' fer Jake.

"Then me an' Bud eventuates in Hackberry Crossin', travellin' mighty modest and unconspishus, after arguin' with a disbelievin' roller of a Ranger as allowed we'd found our pinto hosses before no one hadn't lost 'em.

"An' it was up to us to lose ourselves an' keep away with both feet after we'd collected that cracker-jack's hoss, an' gun likewise, and the financial events in the pockets of his pants.

"He was a sure annoyed boob when me an' Bud told him good-bye an' set his erring feet for Quatana—having took his belt and pant-suspenders and bootlaces so's he'd hev to hold his pants up with one hand an' his boots on with the other. An' then we burnt the trail for Hackberry Crossin', day an' night, and went to earth at Dago Jake's, sech being Jake's perfession.

"Bud didn' look at Mame twice. Nope, *once* was enuff, but it lasted all the time she was in sight! . . . Bud took it bad. . . . He wrote po'try. An' he made me listen to it while we wolfed our mornin' *frijoles* an' cawfy, or evenin' goat-mutton steaks an' canned termatoes, an' forty-rod whisky. Bud's fav'rite spasm begun:—

> "'*O Mame, which art not in reach,*
> *O Mame, thou art a peach!*
> *I fair must let a screech*
> *Or else my heart it will be too full for speech.*'

An' there was about twenty noo verses each day. He made 'em up outa his silly head while we lay doggo, up in the pear-thicket along the *arroyo* behint Jake's abode.

"An' by the time the Sheriff, an' the Lootenant of Rangers, an' the Town Marshal o' Quatana begun to allow that no such suspicious characters as me an' Bud hadn't ever crossed the Frio at Hackberry Crossin', Bud was nearly as much in love with Mame as Mame was with Bud.

"They *hed* got it bad.

"And soon that low-lifer coyote of a Dago Jake, he begins to smell a rat, and afore long he smells a elephant. Bud wants to shoot him up, but Mame won't stand for it. She don't want Bud to swing fer a goshdinged tough like Jake. '*It would be man-slaughterin' murder,*' says she; '*besides which, Jake kin pull a gun as quick as greased lightnin'. Yew ain't got nawthen on Jake at that game,*' she says, '*wherefore I holds it onlawful and calc'lated to cause a breach of the peace—and o' yew likewise, Bud,*' an' she kisses him like hell, we-all being in the pear-thicket, an' me lookin' the other way like I was searchin' fer me lost youth an' innercence. . . ."

"Wot abaht this 'ere picky-back, Buck?" interrupted 'Erb. "Thought you was agoin' to tell a thunderin' good lie abaht killing yer pal an' 'is donah, through playin' picky-backs with 'em."

Le Légionnaire Reginald Rupert, leaning forward from his place on the bench, smote 'Erb painfully in the ribs: William Jones crushed the little man's *képi* over his face: while La Cigale, in the voice of one who chides a dog, hissed "*Tais-toi, canaille!*" in an unwonted fit of anger at the unmannerly interruption.

"But what is it that it is, this peek-a-back?" whispered Alphonse Blanc to John Bull, as the Bucking Bronco turned his slow contemptuous regard upon 'Erb.

"As to say, *sur-le-dos,*" replied the old Legionary, seizing the Cockney in a grip of iron as he prepared to deal faithfully with Rupert and Jones (who had been Captain Geoffry Brabazon-Howard of the Black Lancers).

*   *   *   *   *

"And the end of it was," continued the American, "that we made our get-away, the three of us, one night; mighty clever, we thought, until we heard Dago Jake laugh—at our very first campin' ground! . . .

"I'd kep' first watch, an' then Bud the next—and Mame, she must sit up and keep watch with him. . . . 'Fore long they was doin' it with their four eyes shut, being as tired as a greaser's mule, and aleanin' agin a tree, wrop in each other's arms. . . .

"I ain't ablamin' 'em any. . . . *They* paid—most, anyhow. . . .

"When I wakes up, hearing Dago Jake's pleasin' smile, he'd got 'em covered with his gun, an' half-a-dozen of his gang (blowed-in-glass-Bad-Men-from-Texas they was, too) had got me covered also likewise.

"*'First on you as moves, and I let some daylight into the dark innards o' that respectable young female as yore acuddlin', Bud Conklin,' says Jake. 'Git up and hands up.'*

"'*Do it smart, Buck,*' ses Bud, and we jumps up and puts our hands up, right there. I guess Bud hoped as how Jake might forgive the gal an' take her back—when he'd done with Bud. . . .

"I'd hev reached for the hip-pocket o' me pants and pulled my gun—for I allow that no moss don't grow on me when I start in to deliver the goods with a gun—for all his bone-head bunch o' shave-tails, but I allowed Jake would shoot the gal up, all right; and that was where the outfit had got the bulge on us. . . . Yep, it was Jake's night to howl. . . .

"And right here's where the picky-back eventuates, Sonny," he added, addressing 'Erb.

"Yep. Mr. Fresh-Tough Coyote Dago Jake had thought out a neat cinch—cool as ice—with his black heart boilin' and bubblin' like pitch. . . . In about half no-time, me an' Bud was roped-up with raw-hide lariats—me like a trussed fowl and Bud with his hands only. They was bound fit to cut 'em off, but his legs was free—and all the time Dago Jake covers the gal, and asks in his dod-gasted greasy voice—like molasses gurglin' outer a bar'l (no, I didn't like Jake's voice)—whether she'd hev her ears shot off or be crippled fer life with a shot in each knee, if she stirred an inch, or me an' Bud tried to move hand or foot. . . . Yes, Sir, Jake fair gave me the fantods that bright an' shinin' morn.

"Then, when they'd done tyin' me an' Bud like parcels, they bound the gal to the tree what we'd been campin' under. They tied her hands behind her; they tied her feet an' knees together;

and they tied her to that tree like windin' string round a bat-handle. . . . And then they puts a halter round Bud's neck an' ties the other end to a branch—*after settin' Bud up on my shoulders, with his legs one each side of my head an' his feet danglin' down on my chest.* . . . Yes, Sir. . . . And I calc'lated that if I *co*-lapsed, Bud's feet would still dangle—about a yard from the ground or a couple o' foot, when the rope stretched and gave a bit, or the bough bent a little. . . . And Mame stood face to face with us six feet away. . . ."

*   *   *   *   *

The Bucking Bronco fell silent—and no member of the little group of Legionaries broke the silence. I could see from their faces that even Tant-de-Soif and Alphonse Blanc grasped the situation—while from La Cigale, Dobroffski, and the Japanese, scarcely a *nuance* of meaning was hid.

It was plain that John Bull, Reginald Rupert, and William Jones visualized the scene more clearly, and felt its poignant horror more fully than did 'Erb, ex-denizen of the foulest slums of London.

"'*Streuth!*'" 'Erb murmured at last, and scratched his head.

"And then, '*I fear I must now leave you for a spell, ladies an' gents,*' es Dago Jake," continued the American, "after he'd smacked his lips some, an' pointed out our cleverness and beauty to the grinnin' outfit—'*but I'll look in a bit later on—say this day week or so, an' pay my respex*'—and the hull outfit rides off, laffin' fit to bust.

"And there was we-all—Bud hevin' as long to live as I could stand up under his weight; an' me an' Mame with as long to live as starvation 'ud let us.

"No, there wasn't no hope of nobody comin' along through them prickly-pear flats. That didn't eventuate to happen once in a month—apart from Dago Jake layin' hisself out to see that it didn't happen till we-all had got what was acomin' to us.

"He c'd fix it to detain anybody what might come to Hackberry Crossin' plannin' to follow the trail we'd took West—which was as onlikely as celluloid apples in Hell—an' nobody never come East along it, 'cos there was a better one.

"Nope—we'd chose that highly onpopulous thoroughfare apurpose, travellin' modest an' onconspishus as before, an' the more so for to avoid unpleasantness for Mame consevent upon pursuit by Dago Jake.

"And there wouldn't be no Ranger patrol along neether. If any come at all, it'd be along the trail we'd reckoned as Jake'd take when he found we'd vamoosed durin' his temp'r'y indisposition of whisky-jag. . . .

"*Gee*-whillikins! what wouldn't I have give fer that same Ranger, that Bud an' I had held up an' dispoiled contumelious, to happen along—even if it meant ten years striped pyjamas in the County Pen or in St. Quentin with hard labour, strait-jacket an' dungeons. I'd ha' fell upon his neck an' kissed him frequent an' free. . . . Yep. . . . And *then* some." . . .

The irrepressible 'Erb improved the occasion, as the big American ceased and seemed to stare into the past.

"Ah!" he moralized, "if you'd bin alivin' of a *h*onest life an' keepin' out o' trouble wi' the p'lice, you'd never 'a come to trouble like *that*. . . . It was all along 'o yore interferin' wi' the copper as wanted to see the receipt for them 'osses, that you come ter grief."

"An' that's where yore wrong *agin*, Sonny," replied the Bucking Bronco with his big-dog-to-little-dog air of forebearance. "Though I allow youse an authority on avoidin' trouble with the perlice"—('Erb's presence in the Legion was consequent upon his hurried leaving of his country for his country's good)—"for it was entirely due to that same Ranger's ferocious pussonal interest in me that I'm alive to-day. He'd allowed he would trail me and Bud if it took the rest of his misspent life—an' arrest us lone-handed. He was that mad! Walkin' on foot without pant-suspenders *is* humiliatin' to a sensitive nature what has jest bin relieved of its gun."

He fell silent again, and nobody spoke or stirred.

"We talked a bit, at first," he continued after a long pause, "an' ole Bud Conklin showed his grit, cheering up Mame, an' sayin' Dago Jake was only playin' a trick on us. But the gal *knew* Dago Jake, an' soon she began to lose holt on herself. . . . I ain't blamin' her any. . . . She loved Bud Conklin, y'see. . . . She cried, and struggled, and screeched, and I wished she'd stop— until she begun to laugh, and then I'd rather she'd cried and screeched.

"And '*Come up, ol' hoss*,' says Bud to me, when fust I staggered a bit—jest quiet like—jest like he'd said a thousand times when a tired pony stumbled under him.

"And by-an'-by he leans down an' whispers, '*I'd kick free of yer, pard, if it wan't for the gal.*'

"An' when I begins to tremble an' sway around, he leans down agin and says very quiet, '*Hold up till the gal faints or sleeps or su'think, Buck,*' he says. '*Hold up, ole pard. . . . She'll go mad for life if I dances an' jerks afore her eyes!*' . . . An' I know he weren't hevin' no daisy of a dandy time up there—and that he'd have kicked clear long ago but for the gal. . . .

"Faint? Sleep? Not she. . . . There she stood, face to face with us—havin' highstericks a spell, then laffin' a spell, then prayin' some. . . . Then croonin' over Bud Conklin like he was her babby. . . . Whiles, she'd praise me fer standin' firm an' savin' her man—an' there was a spell when the pore thing thought I was God.

"One time, 'bout mid-day, Bud Conklin swore an' cursed at Dago Jake till I fair blushed to hear him—an' then I waded in and beat him holler at swearin', an' cursin' the name of Dago Jake. . . . But *that* didn't cut no ice—nor cut our raw-hide lariats neither.

"In all them story-books about Red Injuns an' Deadwood Dicks an' such, the blue-eyed, golden-haired Hero *allus* busts his bonds. He figgers to bust 'em on time; then to find a saddled hoss standin' ready; likewise to pick up a new-loaded gun *and* a square meal by the road-side, before gallopin' a hundred miles to make a fuss o' the Villain and make a date with the Hero*ine*—jest as that husky hoodlum's criminile *ad*vances, drugs, stranglin's and starvin's is gettin' irksome to the young female. . . .

"I guess Dago Jake an' his outfit wasn't the guys as had roped up aforesaid Hero. . . . Nit. . . . But they *was* the guys as had roped up us, an' we didn't bust no bonds. Nary a bust. And once, towards evenin', I began to sway so bad that I half dropped Bud, an' on'y got him straight on my shoulders agin, jest in time . . . (an' I hear the screech that Mame let, *now*, sometimes). '*Air you achokin' any, Bud?*' I ses. '*No, pard,*' ses he, '*I ain't chokin' none, but you couldn't git a cigarette-paper between my neck an' this derned lasso. I allow nex' time will give little Willie a narsty cough an' a crick in the neck.'*

"An' at the same time we notices that Mame was still an' quiet, with her eyes shut. *'Now, Buck,'* ses Bud, *'fall down an' roll clear. . . . Better she sees me dead than watch me dyin'.'*

"'*Fall down, nawthen,'* says I. *'I'm agoin' to stand right here till the Day o' Jedgement; an' then I allow I'll donate Mister Tin-horn Dago Jake a tomato-eye.'* And right then Mame opens her eyes an' smiles sweet, up at Bud.

"'*Hevn't we played this silly game long enuff, Buddy?'* she says. *'I'm so tired. . . . Let's go git married, like we planned'*— an' I heerd Bud cough. She shuts her eyes agin then—an' very slow an' careful I turns right round so's not to see her no more.

*   *   *   *   *

"An' I stood still till it was dark. . . .

"So whether Mame died afore Bud or not—she didn't *see* him die, an' that there fact has kep' me from goin' bug-house like Cigale . . .

"*Her dead face an Bud's boot-soles fer a day or two! . . .*

"Yep. It were that Ranger as arrested us. A dead woman tied to a tree, a dead man danglin' from it, an' a dead man lyin' just below his feet—o'ny he wasn't quite dead.

"He was a White Man, that Ranger. He was hoppin' mad when he figgers out what had happened, an' gives me rye-whisky, an' dopes me to sleep, an' lets me lie there some.

"He was young an' innercent, an' when he'd donated me some grub an' some more whisky, I talked to him eloquential. I *did* wanta tell Dago Jake good-bye, before the Ranger hiked me off to his Lieutenant, an' they rounded Jake an' his gang up. The Ranger allowed it was Bud what had held him up and treated him contumelious that day, an' thet as pore Bud had handed in his checks, an' I'd nearly done likewise, he was agoin' to fergit me. . . . He on'y wanted me as witness agin Dago Jake and Co., for the murder of Mame an' Bud. . . .

"An' as we jogs along I talks to him some more, an' in the end he lets me go to the adobe hut to tell Jake good-bye afore he arrests him.

*　　　*　　　*　　　*　　　*

"'Bout four o'clock a.m. in the early morning it was, and Jake sleepin' off a whisky-jag! . . . But he sobers up right slick when I wakes him and he sees my pretty face. . . . He didn't even reach for his gun—not that it was still there if he had. I allow he thought I'd come from hell for him.

"I *had*.

"Yep. I tells Dago Jake good-bye all-right—all-right. An' without usin' no gun, nor knife, nor no other lethial weepon. I takes my farewell o' that gentle Spani-*ard* with my bare hands, and then I walks outer the shack a-singin'—

> "'Roll your tail an' roll it high,
> Fer you'll be an angel by-an-by,'

an' walkin' with a proud tail accordin'.

"'How *is* Dago Jake?' sęs the Ranger.

"'He *ain't*,' ses I. . . ."

*　　　*　　　*　　　*　　　*

As usual it was 'Erb who spoke first.

"I b'lieve you bin tellin' the *troof*, Buck," said he, "an' that's disqualified in a bloomin' competition for 'oo can tell the biggest lie. My performin' rabbit wins, bless 'is liddle 'eart! Come along to the canteen, and . . ."

"I know a performin' train wot's got yore performin' jack rabbit skinned a mile," interrupted the American.

"Performin' *train*?" inquired 'Erb blankly.

"That's so," was the drawled reply. "You never seen such a slick train in Yurrup nor Africky. . . . I was makin' a quick get-away from that Ranger—an' he gallops on to the platform at the deepôt as this U.P.R. double-express fast train glides outa the station. I leans well over the side of the observation-car and plants a kiss upon his bronzed an' manly cheek. . . . At least, I *begun* the kiss there, but where did that kiss *finish*?

"On the southern end of an ole cow abrowsin' beside the track *thirty-three miles down the line!* Some train, and some travellin' that! . . . You an' yore performin' rabbit! You make me tired."

"'Streuth!" murmured 'Erb again, and scratched his cropped head, as was his custom when endeavouring to grapple with mysteries beyond his ken.

THE DOUBLE SADDLE

"The Double Saddle" is a love triangle and a story of revenge, in which a former officer and a former enlisted man in the French army, reverse their roles in the Foreign Legion. The first appearance of "The Double Saddle" was in the book, My Best Story: An Anthology of Stories Chosen by Their Own Authors, *published by Faber & Faber in 1929 (also published by Bobbs-Merrill in the United States). It is noteworthy that Wren's story is one of five (out of a total of twenty one) stories that does not reference a previous publication. It was reprinted in the Wren collections* Flawed Blades *(1933) and* Dead Men's Boots *(1949), and in* The Avon Book of Modern Short Stories *(1942), a paperback reprinting of* My Best Stories.

Captain Zarles of the Foreign Legion was undeniably a very fine soldier, an admirable regimental officer, and worthy of the great regiment that he adorned. When he sent him to the Military College at St. Maixent to study for his commission, Colonel des Vœux had prophesied that they would undoubtedly make an officer of Sergeant-Major Zarles—but not a gentleman.

However, brave, zealous and experienced officers were of more importance than gentlemen, and the Legion's Mess would soon give him the necessary veneer.

Captain Zarles lived for his work, and nothing else interested him greatly.

Women, a little; wine and absinthe, a little; practical cruelty, a little.

At the moment, the camel question occupied his keen and active mind, almost to the exclusion of his present form of relaxation, the baiting of his wife and of *le légionnaire* the *ci-devant* Vicomte Michel Valmond de la Roche St. Michel.

Something, he felt, could be done to improve the already high efficiency of the various *pelotons* of the Camel Corps, those splendid, hardy *méharistes* who go out on desert-patrol for months on end, preventing or punishing Touareg raids, convoying the big caravans, and generally rendering the Sahara safe for plutocracy, if a duller country for heroes to live in. Also to improve that of the *groupes mobiles* and desert columns on their work of peaceful penetration.

And his great idea, in this connection, was the invention and introduction of a new and improved camel-saddle—a saddle with two seats, in short.

Why, the Zarles saddle would mark an absolutely enormous step in the progress of the equipment of the XIXth Army Corps, the army of Africa.

Where one hundred men arrived to-day, two hundred men would arrive to-morrow—seated on the Zarles saddle—and at no greater cost in camels and the feeding and watering of camels.

That it could be done, Captain Zarles was certain, for he had visited India on his way home from a tour of duty in French Indo-China, and had seen two men riding in comfort on one camel.

He had at once made personal experiment and, in one day, had ridden seventy miles across sand and stone, carrying a gun across his thighs, behind a sturdy camel-man who drove the beast by means of rope-reins fastened to its nostrils. And the camel had also carried the camp-kit of Captain Zarles, and had finished the journey without the slightest signs of fatigue.

The zealous officer had made a careful sketch of the two-seated contraption.

And, this bright and shining morn, Captain Zarles stood eyeing the bony wooden frame of a Touareg saddle with its high-crutched pommel and narrow back-board crupper, comparing it unfavourably with the type represented by the sketch in his notebook. Yes, surely the Arab was wrong and the Baluchi was right.

Both used the same species of camel, the dromedary, and in similar country.

Yet how should the Arab be wrong in the light of five thousand years' experience?

On the other hand, why should the Baluchi be wrong? Presumably the Asiatic had used the single-humped dromedary just as long as the African had, and his practical conclusion—the two-seated saddle—is as much entitled to respect.

Anyhow, Captain Zarles would have a two-seated saddle-frame constructed at once, and he would himself experiment therewith, giving it the fullest trial, and possibly modifying and improving it.

Yes, and this dog Monsieur le Vicomte Michel Valmond de la Roche St. Michel should be his camel-man, his *oontwallah*, as they called the man in the Indian deserts. Quite a promotion for *ce bon sacré chien d'un Vicomte* to be groom to a camel.

And Captain Zarles proceeded to carry out his great idea, of evolving the Regulation Sealed-pattern Zarles' Two-Seated Military Camel Saddle—to his undoing and terrible death.

§2

As some students of history are aware, there was a Valmond de la Roche St. Michel with Roland at Roncesvalles; and there have, of course, been Valmonds de la Roche St. Michel in the *entourages* of most of the kings and queens of France. Their bannerets have been seen in Jerusalem, at Acre, Rhodes, Malta and wherever new pages of French history were written in steel and stone.

The Valmond de la Roche St. Michel of the French Revolution weathered the storm, thanks partly to his courage, ability and stoutness of heart, and partly to his, and his family's, great popularity throughout the countryside.

Paris graciously allowed him to live, and even to retain his château and a small portion of the family lands. The reduced and declining family received further blows during the troublous Napoleonic times—and paid a heavy price for its haughty aristocracy and unbending royalism.

By the time the Michel Valmond de la Roche St. Michel of this story was born, his father was a country gentleman of modest means, with little left to him of his family possessions but its pride, traditions, and dilapidated château, the decaying roof of which he literally kept over him with difficulty.

Thus it was that the latest, and indeed the last, of the Valmonds learned, at an early age, that he must take his profession seriously; though, among the many things that he disliked, work of all kinds was prominent.

What he did like was to lead, as far as possible, the kind of life lived by his ancestors; to hunt, to feast, to carouse, to gamble, to enjoy every *droit de seigneur*, and for a change of dissipation, to visit the gay capital. . . .

Within the shadow of the château, at the foot of the hill that it crowned and adorned, crouched humbly the village of St. Michel; and in the village dwelt Monsieur Farge, butcher, a politically-minded man, gross, violent and of most subversive views.

With him dwelt, more or less in amity, Madame Farge, the female of the species, a scheming and evil woman, more dangerous than her noisier lord.

And beneath their roof, when not elsewhere, sojourned their really beautiful daughter Angelique, in whom mingled and flourished the distinctive virtues of her parents.

At the sign of the *Coque d'Or* she exercised and exploited her charm, and charms; and did that very ancient hostelry much good. Financially speaking, that is to say.

The name and the fame of La Belle Angelique, her reputation—or, as some jealous detractors said, her lack of it—had spread far beyond St. Michel and the parts adjacent.

She was, indeed, what was once termed a 'toast,' a 'reigning belle,' and the *Coque d'Or*, especially on market days, was a place of pilgrimage.

Men fought about her; women talked about her; and Madame Farge, to whose side she, more or less, nightly returned, thought about her—long, long thoughts that somehow ended in a château—in fact, the Château de la Roche St. Michel.

On their way thither, these fond maternal thoughts halted and hovered about the head of one Etienne Zarles and, as they did so, Madame might be heard to curse, and, indeed, seen to spit.

For *ce sale cochon d'un* Etienne Zarles—and might the Devil eviscerate him, impale him on a red-hot stake, and grill him over a slow fire till he looked like a nicely browned *poussin*—dared to raise his sheep's eyes, his pig's eyes, his eyes of a hairless green goat, to La Belle Angelique!

And the hell of it was, Madame freely admitted, that the fool girl was by way of catching the eye that was raised—the bold, buccaneering, come-hither eye of this rollicking rascal, this village *vaurien*.

But there, girls would be girls, and Angelique was a good girl, and would never give her mother a moment's anxiety. Never would she jeopardize her chances of becoming a fine lady, by stooping to folly before she was one. Afterwards was another matter.

The subject being raised in family council, Angelique concurred.

Certainly, *ce bon* Etienne Zarles was a fine figure of a man. But Michel Valmond de la Roche St. Michel was a fine figure of a Bank Balance. And undoubtedly he was aware of Mademoiselle Angelique Farge.

"Nibbling, eh?" grunted the butcher.

"*Il en est bien épris,*" stated Madame Farge.

"With the most dishonourable intentions," blushed Mademoiselle modestly. "Monsieur le Vicomte comes into the *Coque d'Or* almost nightly. . . . Not a reticent or shy young gentleman, that one. . . . He says just what he thinks—just what he likes. . . . Fortunately he does not think much.

"And I am what he likes—for the moment," added Angelique.

"And that penniless *canaille*, Etienne Zarles, is he there also nightly? Does he likewise say what he likes?" inquired Madame.

"Oh! la, la!" blushed Angelique. "*Ce pauvre* Etienne. . . ."

When Lieutenant le Vicomte de la Roche St. Michel, of the 46th Infantry of the Line, came home on furlough and married Angelique Farge, it was a great and terrible surprise to the dwellers on the hill, but to the Dwellers of the Plain it was not unexpected.

It would, they had said all along, take something much more like a man than Monsieur le Vicomte to defeat or evade Monsieur and Madame Farge, when betrayed into their hands by their little daughter Angelique.

Monsieur le Vicomte never forgot his treatment by the butcher Farge on the night when he was trapped by the forceful ruffian and his wife; and, for the rest of his days, he detested his papa-in-law nearly as much as he did the presumptuously insolent young scoundrel, Private Etienne Zarles, of the 46th Infantry of the Line, who had dared to be his rival for the favours of this Angelique, his madly loved and bitterly hated wife, this vixen who could raise him up to Heaven and dash him down to Hell, and who could, and did, make his life a garden of bliss and a desert of jealous torment.

Private Etienne Zarles! That one should learn something.

And to the best of his rather limited ability, Monsieur le Vicomte taught Etienne Zarles something. Self-control, for example, and how to refrain from smashing the sneering, jeering face of the man who put him on the rack of humiliation, jealousy and mental torture.

For Lieutenant le Vicomte Michel Valmond de la Roche St. Michel had the, for him, bright idea of making Etienne Zarles his *ordonnance*, and promoted him to be his soldier-valet, body-servant, butler and general factotum.

It gave the good Vicomte very genuine pleasure to say,

"Fill Madame's glass, Zarles," and to note carefully whether the hand of Private Etienne Zarles trembled as he did so. And to address him as oaf, lout, clod, bumpkin of fish-faced, flat-footed fool.

Or to bid him stand further away from Madame—as, apparently, neither his leisure time was equal to his need for ablutions, nor his income to the purchase of perfume—and to watch the dull flush overspread the sullen countenance of the young man.

The Vicomte exercised much ingenuity in contriving that Etienne Zarles should see a great deal of Madame—in her husband's presence—and that he should appear at the very greatest disadvantage.

And Madame la Vicomtesse? Madame accepted the situation, and everything else that Madame could get, including the whole of her husband's income. . . .

After a brief and passionate honeymoon, trouble had begun quite early, and there was little need of Monsieur le Vicomte's bitter cutting tongue, and Madame's utter incompatibility and hopeless unfitness for her rôle, to widen the inevitable breach. Within a year of the wedding he had observed with some justice,

"Your idea of existence is to spend all day, and to gamble all night."

To which she had replied, with equal truth,

"The shops are shut at night, my cabbage."

An annoying woman. When her infuriated and outraged husband would cry,

"You'll come to a bad end," she, with a feline smile, and

flexing of tense fingers, would coldly reply,

"And you, my cabbage, have come to a bad beginning."

When he would groan, "You have ruined me," she would reply,

"Not yet, quite, my little one. Be patient."

And the kindest thing that Angelique ever did for her husband was to leave him, having faithfully kept her promise that she would never desert him while he had a franc.

Lieutenant le Vicomte Michel Valmond de la Roche St. Michel, instead of returning thanks to Heaven for his good fortune, raved like a maniac, and threatened murder and suicide.

It was Private Etienne Zarles, just returned from furlough at St. Michel, who was to be murdered, and that forthwith, unless he instantly confessed his share in the shameful business of Madame's flight, presumably to St. Michel. And it was Etienne Zarles who neatly recorded the general estimate of Madame's character, by shrugging his shoulders and mentioning, in reply, that his income from all sources amounted to about sixpence a day.

So the murder of Etienne Zarles was postponed, and a violent slap on each cheek substituted.

The suicide of Monsieur le Vicomte was also postponed, and a deeper plunge into even wilder dissipation substituted for that. But dissipation of the kind enjoyed by such gentlemen of rank and fashion is apt to be expensive; and a week of it cost a sum greater than the income of the Vicomte for a year.

After the manner of his kind, the Lieutenant turned first to the gentlemen who lend money; then to the green tables which sometimes return it; then to the horses that run quickly, though sometimes not quickly enough; and finally to various regimental funds that were in his trust.

And, still after the manner of his kind, he came the early and inevitable cropper, and, in ruin and disgrace, fled to escape prosecution.

Private Etienne Zarles, returning to regimental duty from the misery and martyrdom of his experience as a servant in this domestic ménage, quickly found himself. Before long he found himself a Corporal and, again before long, a Sergeant. For he was a born soldier.

As such, he not unnaturally longed to see active service, and, as there was apparently no hope of his doing this as a Sergeant of the 46th Regiment of the Line, he showed the mettle of his pastures by taking the bold and extreme course of throwing away all he had gained by his soldierly virtue, deserting from his regiment, and enlisting, as a Belgian without papers, at a far-distant recruiting depôt of the Foreign Legion.

In the Foreign Legion, Etienne Zarles again found himself, and was justified of his boldness in this apparently over-rash step.

He distinguished himself as a steady, keen and competent soldier, cheerful, willing, zealous and smart—and in addition to these qualities, he had invaluable knowledge of 'the ropes.' None so skilful as he at the legitimate kind of 'creeping,' the propitiation of superiors, and the avoidance of every kind of offence.

Le légionnaire Etienne Zarles became Corporal Zarles in less than due course; Corporal Zarles was promoted to Sergeant for distinguished coolness and courage in action; Sergeant Zarles was promoted to Sergeant-Major for the brave, skilful and tenacious defence of an outpost after the death of his officer; and l'Adjudant Zarles was sent to the Military College of St. Maixent to be trained to fitness for commissioned rank.

It was during a furlough spent at St. Michel, that Captain Etienne Zarles of the Foreign Legion again met Angelique, née Farge.

The Captain, more of a fine figure of a man than ever, took the high hand. He also took, within a week, the hand of Angelique, more than a little weary of life in the minor key, and the village of St. Michel.

Nor had Monsieur and Madame Farge any objection to make to their daughter's alliance *en second noces* with *Monsieur le Capitaine*. Not that it would have interested Captain Etienne Zarles if they had.

"I treat 'em rough," was the Captain's motto and method, whether with reference to women, subordinates, civilians or parents-in-law.

The happy couple spoke quite frequently and freely of the bride's first husband, and when, on one occasion, Madame

Angelique Zarles remarked,

"I suppose that account of his death, in the paper, was true," her Etienne cryptically replied,

"It'll soon be true enough, if it turns out not to be true."

"You mean, my darling," replied Angelique, "that if it ever turned out that he was still alive, you would—er——"

"Precisely, thou crystal dew-drop. I would," her Etienne assured her.

But he did not.

Au contraire, as the French say.

Madame Zarles was far from unpopular with the officers of the Battalion, for she was a beautiful and extremely lively young woman; and beautiful and lively young women are all too rare in those places where units of the Legion are stationed.

It could not be said that she was exactly popular with the wives of the married officers, but then, beautiful and lively young women of the type of Angelique Zarles rarely are.

Nor could it be said that she was a refining and softening influence in their rough and lonely lives; nor that her presence made for that peace, concord and harmony that should distinguish an Officers' Mess.

The Colonel was a great admirer of Madame, and her professed cavalier.

Major Meurice, albeit a married man, made no secret of his conviction that the Colonel would be better employed in looking after the affairs of the regiment; and no less than four Captains, who agreed on no other point, agreed that Major Meurice was an old fool, whose wife should beat him more often than she did.

As for Angelique's lieutenants and *sous*-lieutenants, save for one or two with private means, these were as nothing in her sight, and less than nothing when out of her sight.

It is therefore, perhaps, unnecessary to affirm that life was distinctly thrilling for La Belle Angelique, and that she trod with delight a mazy primrose path of dalliance, a path on which no danger lurked, save that of the wrath of Captain Zarles.

However, that was quite danger enough, for Angelique, by this time, would have been the last to contradict her husband when he remarked that he treated 'em rough.

Should it ever occur—and *le bon Dieu* forbid—that Captain

Zarles came unexpectedly round the corner at one of the sudden turns of the mazy primrose path of dalliance, there would be real trouble. No heroics and highfalutin'; no talk of broken hearts or broken vows; no threats of divorce; nor any of the usual reactions of lesser men.

Not a bit of it.

Just a dog-whip—bless him—and about the biggest thrashing that ever a man bestowed upon a woman. As for the 'shadowy third,' he would be a shadow indeed, by the time her Etienne had done with him—a shadow on the banks of the Styx.

Life was truly thrilling, and there was really no need for the final and crowning thrill which Etienne produced one morning, after inspection of a new draft just arrived from Sidi-bel-Abbès, and posted to his Company.

"I'm making a small domestic change, thou daughter of all delights, and mother of none," he growled, as he flung belts and sword, *képi* and gloves, on to the sofa of their tiny room.

"A new servant, a new male housemaid . . . parlour-maid . . . lady's-maid. . . ."

"How truly interesting!" sneered Madame.

"I positively think you'll find it so, *ma gosse*," grinned her lord malevolently.

Nor did Madame contradict, for a terrible idea stuck her dumb.

Clad in the ill-fitting fatigue-uniform of a private soldier of the Legion, her first, and indeed her only, husband, Monsieur le Vicomte Michel Valmond de la Roche St. Michel, entered the room and, kneeling, removed her husband's dusty boots.

"The new servant, my dear," smiled Captain Zarles. "A clumsy lout, I fear. Something of an oaf, a lump, a clod, a bumpkin. . . . Indeed, as you see, rather what one might call a fish-faced, flat-footed fool—but willing, very willing, and I'm sure he'll do his best to give satisfaction. . . .

"And if he doesn't, we won't return him to store; we'll train him, my dear, *train* him, eh? . . ."

And Etienne Zarles proceeded to train Michel Valmond very much in the way in which Michel Valmond had trained Etienne Zarles.

And he "treated him rough," very much more roughly, if less

skilfully, than he had himself been treated.

It gave the good Captain very genuine pleasure to say, "Fill Madame's glass, Valmond," and to note carefully whether the hand of *le légionnaire* Michel Valmond trembled as he did so; and to address him as "clumsy oaf," "wretched lout," "miserable clod," or indeed as "escaped gaol-bird."

Nor did he forget to bid the *sale cochon* to stand further away from Madame, as he waited at table, inasmuch as that high-bred lady was of delicate olfactory perception.

And sometimes the high-bred lady was not of over-delicate oral performance, when Captain Zarles baited the husband and wife together, as was sometimes his humour; for he was not the man to forgive slights, insults and injuries, nor to forget that Angelique Farge had been content enough with himself, and his genuine, if rough and passionate love, before Monsieur le Vicomte Valmond de la Roche St. Michel came upon the scene.

So life became yet more piquant and thrilling to La Belle Angelique, now that her husband was her domestic servant, and her bigamous spouse their sardonic, watchful tyrant.

Oh! la! la! What with a husband, a proprietor, a brace of lovers and a dozen aspirants, what was a girl to do?

Oh these soldiers, the dear things—senior ranks, professional lovers; juniors, enthusiastic amateurs.

Not being a maiden all unwary—though fresh from a lady's seminary (of a kind)—when she married Captain Zarles, La Belle Angelique contrived to play with fire without getting burnt—or beaten—though the pastime rendered life almost too exciting.

One of the most intriguing aspects of her complicated life was the behaviour of her lawful husband and housemaid, *le légionnaire* Michel Valmond.

She had known him—better, probably, than anybody, including his own mother—as a haughty, arrogant and wilful young man; passionate, dissipated and spoilt; proud, sensitive and weak.

She beheld him now as the model soldier-servant, and also as a human automaton, insensitive, devoid of pride and self-respect, invulnerable to insult, incapable of resenting anything, from a slight to a blow.

And yet, was there something about him of the air of one who waits with inexhaustible patience, one who bides his time with colossal self-control?

La Belle Angelique had naturally never read nor heard of that modest gentleman who proclaimed that his head, though bloody, was unbowed, and that he was captain of his soul.

Had she done so, it is conceivable that her husband, *le légionnaire* Michel Valmond, might have reminded her of this indomitable man.

For it could not be said that, while treating him rough, and indeed, very rough, Captain Zarles got what is colloquially termed 'much change' out of his victim.

His hand did not shake as he poured the wine for Madame. His face did not flush with rage or shame when humiliations were heaped upon him in her presence. The bitterest and most savage insult called forth no answering frown, no sudden gleam or flash of undisciplined eye.

No, it had to be admitted that the man bore the terrible, and indeed unparalleled, situation in which he found himself with astounding stoicism.

"*Mon Dieu!*" decided Madame, "but that one has been through it! . . . Prison, I suppose. . . . Possibly 'the dry guillotine' . . . Poor devil!"

And, with unexpected insight or intuition, she added,

"Too proud to show a sign of pride. . . ."

When, partly in pity, partly in curiosity, and largely because it was her nature *to*, La Belle Angelique laying aside her role of Madame, attempted to adopt that of Mistress, it quickly transpired that the sinner had become a saint, and far more resembled the saint Joseph than the St. Michel she had known.

And to add to the slighted lady's savage wrath, her husband, addressing her as Madame Potiphar, flatly refused to believe the tale she told him.

She was trying to insult *him*, Etienne Zarles, he said; and if she tried again, she would succeed—in getting a sound beating.

Oh, an incomprehensible delightful surprise-packet who could keep a woman guessing, this dear Etienne! Not one of these useful fools a woman could twist round her little finger, bless him!

§3

As a camel-driver and camel-master, *le légionnaire* Michel Valmond gave complete satisfaction to Captain Zarles.

It could not be said that he showed the least intelligent interest in the perfection of the Zarles two-seated military saddle, but he certainly took an interest in the welfare of the splendid *mehara* riding-camel, and in mapping the desert routes, visible and invisible, within a hundred miles radius of Zabat.

When brother officers occasionally asked Captain Zarles why he didn't have an Arab orderly to look after his camel and accompany him on his long rides, Zarles would say that he preferred the companionship of a white man, and that this was a good lad whom he was training, and whom he liked to have about him.

He sometimes mentioned that he knew the fellow's family at home, and had promised to keep an eye on him.

In point of fact, Captain Zarles never more enjoyed this wonderful situation, devised by Fate, than when he sat at his ease in the comfortable rear seat of the saddle, while this anointed dog of an aristocrat crouched in front of him, and drove.

It was Captain Zarles' playful humour to indicate that he would fain go to the right by violently pulling the driver's right ear, and similarly with regard to the left. Should he desire an acceleration of pace, he would administer a painful prod with the muzzle of his automatic; and his favourite way of stopping the camel was to clutch its driver by the scruff of his neck and to squeeze hard with powerful thumb and fingers.

Even Captain Zarles himself sometimes marvelled at what this broken-down gaol-bird would bear without sign of remonstrance or resentment.

One of Captain Zarles' numerous boasts was that he could sleep while he marched.

Many soldiers can do this—if a condition of mental blankness and lethargy, amounting to inability to receive and record sense-impressions, can be called sleep—the eyes of the body open, those of the mind tight shut; a state of somnambulism, in fact.

Undoubtedly he could sleep on horse-back, in brief snatches, actually closing the eyes; and, with feet well thrust home in shortened stirrups, knees wedged beneath holsters, and hands holding the saddle pommel as well as the reins, leave the subconscious mind to maintain the balance of the unconscious body.

As for the comfortable padded seat of his camel-saddle, deep and broad, with its high cushioned back-rest, Captain Zarles could sleep in that as though in his arm-chair at home.

With feet in stirrups, arms folded, and nothing to do but just comfortably sit, and with nothing to look at but the back of *le légionnaire* Michel Valmond, the blue sky and the yellow sand, it was indeed sometimes very difficult to keep awake.

Occasionally Captain Zarles even had a suspicion that the man in front of him was very much more than half asleep, as his body sagged slackly, leaning against the high padded peak of the front seat, swaying gently from side to side with the motion of the camel, as it jogged steadily along at the ambling trot with which it covered eleven kilometres every hour.

On the return journey from a desert expedition, the driver might well have slept without fear of consequences, for the camel would, in any case, go straight as a ruled line to the place where food and rest awaited it beneath the dusty trees of Captain Zarles' compound.

But *le légionnaire* Michel Valmond did not sleep.

Rather, he watched and waited, watched and sought: and one day, seeking with untiring eye, found what he wanted.

His master being apparently asleep, he, greatly daring, turned round and looked at him. His eyes confirming what his ears had heard, he then made a dangerous experiment; and for the first time in months, perhaps in years, he smiled.

Captain Zarles rose to his feet, brushed sand from his riding-breeches, strode forth from the shadow of the palm beneath which he had lunched, and climbed into the rear seat of the saddle of his kneeling camel.

Having adjusted the Captain's stirrups to his boots, *le légionnaire* Michel Valmond saluted, seized nose-rein and stick, sprang into the front seat, brought the camel to its feet, and started it off on its forty-kilometre journey to Zabat.

Before very long, certain rhythmical sounds indicated that

Captain Zarles was exercising his boasted powers of sleeping in the saddle.

Doubtless the outward journey, begun before dawn, the labours of map-making, a long and sporting stalk on foot, gun in hand, a late hilarious party over-night, and a bottle of *pinard* with his *déjeuner* of roll and meat, had combined to give Captain Zarles that after-lunch feeling, to an unwonted degree.

Monsieur le Vicomte Michel Valmond de la Roche St. Michel knew that his hour had come, and he straightened himself on the saddle, squared his shoulders and once again smiled.

Also, he very gently and unobtrusively introduced to the notice of the admirable racing-camel the long thin stick that he carried. Not, of course, by anything so violent and vulgar as a blow, but merely by holding it where the camel could see it, and occasionally swinging it forward as he rode.

The camel, who could take a hint, increased his pace imperceptibly, and did so each time the stick swung forward.

Before long, without jolt or jerk or change of step, the beast was going at top speed, and its driver was gently putting increasing pressure on its left rein. . . .

With a yell of alarm, Captain Zarles was suddenly hurled from his seat, flung from an ugly nightmare of uneasy sleep into a far more terrible nightmare of waking reality.

What in the name of God was this! What had happened? . . . He was on the ground. . . . There was no ground. . . . He was in water. . . . There was no water.

What? . . .

Captain Zarles struggled to rise and found no foothold. His legs, his whole body, his arms, were held as in a giant hand. Rather, a giant mouth was sucking him down and down, swallowing him alive.

Ceasing his wild struggle, he gazed for a moment at a writhing, heaving, seething mass of sand and water where the struggling camel fought against its dreadful death.

Turning his head, the only part of his body that he could now move, he glared wildly round—and encountered the mocking smile of Michel Valmond.

"*Help! Help!*" bawled Captain Zarles.

"There is no help," smiled Michel Valmond.

"*I'm sinking! I'm sinking!*" shrieked Zarles.

"You are, indeed," replied Valmond. "And so am I. . . . We are both sinking. . . . You, being considerably the heavier, will sink first, and I shall have the ineffable pleasure of seeing you do so. . . . Now pull yourself together, my good Zarles, and though you have not lived like a gentleman, try to die like one."

"*Help me!*" screamed Zarles.

"But, my good animal, I brought you here. I, rather neatly, if I may say so, placed you exactly where you are."

Zarles struggled violently and sank the deeper.

"Good," observed Valmond, who, motionless, his arms spread abroad, with palms extended flat, was sinking imperceptibly.

"You will certainly die before I do."

"*Help!*" screamed Zarles again.

"And I thought you were such a very, very brave man, Zarles!" mused Valmond. "Come, come; if you can neither live nor die like a gentleman, die like a man at any rate. Positively the poor camel made a better showing. He didn't cry for help, and I deeply regret that the nobler beast had to be involved in your fate."

Again the agonized man turned his despairing eyes to the unanswering skies and screamed for help.

"Really, Zarles, what an infernal row! You deafen one. But it will not be for long. In a very few minutes there will be complete silence here, and all that will be left of the great and noisy Zarles will be—a bubble.

"Think of it. The last sound, just the quiet bursting of a bubble.

"The great Zarles' suitable epitaph—a bubble upon sand.

"Yes—the bubble 'Zarles' is about to burst.

"And I shall see it, Zarles. It will be the last thing that I shall see, and I can think of no sight more agreeable...

The dying man threw back his head and shrieked again as the wet sand touched his chin.

"*Help! Help!*" he screamed.

"No good, my poor Zarles," observed Valmond. "If a wandering Arab heard you and came, he could do nothing— except sit and gloat. . . . You wouldn't like that, would you?

You, the relentless scourge of the Bad Bedou and the Treacherous Targui, to be seen and heard squealing like a stuck pig? That would never do surely. . . ."

Zarles, his eyes almost starting from his head, glared wildly at his terrible mocker.

"But, I confess," continued the latter, "that I wish La Belle Angelique could be here. Her reaction to the situation would be very interesting. What do you think it would be?"

Again Zarles, with his remaining strength, struggled feebly and bawled for help.

"Personally, I think she would laugh at us both," continued Valmond. "Laugh heartily and say,

"*Oh! la! la! Ce pauvre Etienne et ce pauvre Michel.* In the soup together, this time!' . . . Yes. . . . And if she had a rope and a camel, to which of us would she throw that rope, Zarles? I wonder. To you probably. . . ."

"Yes! Yes!" shouted Zarles, who appeared to be insane with fear. "She will throw it to *me*."

"I think she would," Valmond went on, "because you have a franc where I have a centime.

"But when we all three meet in that happy Hell where there is no money," he added, "I somehow fancy things will be different. . . . For the Devil is a gentleman of ancient family, and will understand a gentleman. And Angelique, another devil, will then prefer me—as she did before, my good Zarles, as she did before. . . ."

Zarles strove to speak, but only 'the bubbling cry of some strong swimmer in his agony' resulted, as sand and water entered his mouth.

"G . . . g . . . r . . . r . . . r . . ." A terrible sound floated for a second above the hideous and sinister quiverings of the quicksand, as the face of Etienne Zarles disappeared beneath its surface.

A bubble formed and broke.

Monsieur le Vicomte Michel Valmond de la Roche St. Michel smiled.

Printed in Great Britain
by Amazon.co.uk, Ltd.,
Marston Gate.